This is the way my story begins. Not with a bang but a whimper. Nothing more than a calm voice, a careful smile, and a pair of spectacles perched on the tip of a thin nose.

But don't let that deter you. You'll be happy to know a bang comes in the end.

Literally.

Along with a kiss, a promise, a death, a broken heart, and an end to life as you and I would have known it.

Because that's the point everything changes. That's the point I mess everything up and send this world spinning down an entirely new path.

MG BUEHRLEN

The 57 Lives of Alex Wayfare

STRANGE CHEMISTRY

An Angry Robot imprint
and a member of the Osprey Group

Lace Market House,   Angry Robot/Osprey Publishing,
54-56 High Pavement,   PO Box 3985,
Nottingham   New York,
NG1 1HW   NY 10185-3985,
UK   USA

www.strangechemistrybooks.com
Strange Chemistry #27

A Strange Chemistry paperback original 2014

Cover art by Rebecca Lown

Distributed in the United States by Random House, Inc., New York.

ISBN: 978 1 90884 493 4
Ebook ISBN: 978 1 90884 494 1

Set in Sabon by Argh! Oxford

Printed in the United States of America

For Joel and Nicholette.
Look. You're holding it in your hands.
At last.

CHAPTER 1

The Disclaimer

This is the way my story begins. Not with a bang but a whimper. Nothing more than a calm voice, a careful smile, and a pair of spectacles perched on the tip of a thin nose.

But don't let that deter you. You'll be happy to know a bang comes in the end.

Literally.

Along with a kiss, a promise, a death, a broken heart, and an end to life as you and I would have known it.

Because that's the point everything changes. That's the point I mess everything up and send this world spinning down an entirely new path. It's the moment I look back and realize all the signs were there, lined up shoulder-to-shoulder from the very beginning, unblinking. It makes me wonder what might've been if I'd sought the truth about my visions earlier. If I hadn't been so afraid of what they meant. If I hadn't let my selfish anger get in the way. Maybe things would be better off now, in that alternate timeline. The one we'll never get a chance to experience. The one I erased.

Porter doesn't think so. At least he says he doesn't, but something's changed in his eyes. He looks at me differently now. He says I did nothing wrong. He says it over and over. That it was "meant to be." I know what he really means is this: what's done is done. You can't change a Variant in time.

Which is true. You can't. Not once you've created one. But Variants can change the future.

And trust me, sometimes that's much worse.

The Inquisition

Dr Farrow sits across from me in a gray business suit. Her posture is impeccable. Her brassy hair is wrapped in a tight bun. A psychiatrist-issue notepad rests on her knees. The sun slants through the blinds of her huge corner office windows and draws lines of gold across the carpet. It traces shadows over my beat-up sneakers.

I expect Dr Farrow thinks I'm like all the other troubled teens who walk through her door. She probably assumes my "acting out" stems from problems at home or school. And if I wanted to, I could tell her what she wanted to hear. Make it easy for her. Blame it all on Mom and Dad, on being unpopular at school, on depression, whatever. Take your pick. But I promised myself I'd tell the truth this time, no matter what. There was a chance, however minuscule, that Dr Farrow could help me. Maybe she'd finally give me the answers I've been looking for. Maybe today, I'd find out what the visions meant.

So when she asks why I played a prank on my history teacher that ended up getting both of us suspended, I tell the truth.

It was supposed to be a joke. Something to embarrass him the way he embarrassed me in class all semester long. A little payback for the F on my recent essay. Only it got way out of hand. Before I knew it I was suspended for a week, Mr Lipscomb decided to take off the rest of the semester (the coward), and my parents made me an appointment with a shrink. And not just any shrink – a psychiatrist straight from one of the best AIDA clinics in Washington DC.

It was all so humiliating.

I tell Dr Farrow that my suspension never really sank in. It still feels like it didn't happen.

She straightens her thin-rimmed spectacles and blots her coral lips together. "How did your teacher's cell phone come into your possession in the first place?" She speaks slowly and calmly with no hint of judgment in her tone.

I shift on the oversized couch. The soft maroon leather squawks beneath my cords. AIDA's founder, Durham Gesh, stares down at me from his portrait on the wall. "I'm the AV assistant at school. Mr Lipscomb scheduled to have a TV and DVD player set up for his next class, so I went to hook it up for him. It was his free period, so he wasn't in the classroom. And his phone was just... sitting on his desk."

"So you used your authority as AV assistant to tamper with a faculty member's personal property?"

Putting it like that makes me feel even worse than I already do. I fight with my body to sit up straight, but all it wants to do is shrink down, turn to liquid, and seep into the couch cushions.

Dr Farrow exhales through her nose with a slight whistle. "Do you mind telling me how you did it?"

I prop my ankle on my knee and finger a loose flap of rubber on the heel of my battered sneaker. "I swapped the phone's vibrator motor with a more powerful one. One that would sting if he had it in his pocket. Then I wired it so once it started vibrating, it wouldn't stop."

"And the explicit rap song ringtone?"

I don't mean to, I truly don't, but the corner of my mouth twitches as I try to suppress a grin. Dr Farrow notices right away.

"Do you still find what you did amusing?"

"No." The urge to grin vanishes. I push my glasses up the bridge of my nose – the black-framed nerdy ones I've worn since I was six. "I just find it ironic. That song was already on his phone. I just set it to the ringtone. I wanted everyone to see the kind of person he really is."

"So that's why you chose to call his phone during an assembly, while he was at the podium addressing the entire school?"

The scene plays out in my head, as fast as a camera flash.

The Prank

I'm in the gym, watching from the top of the bleachers under a string of blue and gold school pennants as Mr Lipscomb steps up to the podium at the center of the basketball court. He's so short he has to stand on a box to reach the microphone. He adjusts his shirt collar – not because it's uneven, but because he always does that when he's about to say something superior – and begins talking about how the mock trial team (his mock trial team) won state last year, and they plan on doing it again this year.

His lips are spread wide. His teeth glisten. His words are coated with supremacy. I crush my cell phone in my hand, remembering how he'd humiliated me the day before.

He'd held up my essay on early American colonies in front of the whole class. The red F in the top corner glared down at me. Several kids laughed. "Been reading too many sparkly vampire novels, Miss Wayfare?"

I honestly had no idea what he meant by that. I never read fiction, and I was too incensed by the F to try to decipher his insult. It was the fourth F he'd given me already that year, and it was only October.

"Watching too many werewolf and zombie movies?" he added.

I shook my head, totally confused.

"No? So you decided to make up something as absurd as cannibalism in Jamestown just to see if I was paying attention?"

Half the class turned in their seats to laugh and stare at me. Tabitha, the girl who's hated me since kindergarten (for reasons unknown, I swear), made a cough into her hand that sounded remarkably like, "Freak."

I don't think I'd ever gone so red in the face. I was livid. "I didn't make it up," I told Mr Lipscomb. "There are eyewitness accounts. I can show you."

He walked down the aisle and dropped my essay on my desk. "Fiction." He said it like it was a dirty word. "Next time, stick to the textbook."

"The textbook is wrong," I mumbled, gripping the edges of my paper in both fists. Just because he'd never heard of the cannibalism cases in Jamestown didn't mean they weren't true.

He made his way back to the front of the class and directed everyone to form groups for midterm projects. Everyone except me. With a smirk he said, "Alex, you can work on your own this time. You can jeopardize your grades all you want, but I won't have you bringing the others down with you. Unlike you, they aspire to graduate."

Yeah. The prick.

So back in the gym, I squeeze my phone in my fist so hard that this time I nearly bruise my palm. I was right about the cannibalism. Not only had I read eyewitness accounts at the library, but I'd actually seen what those people were reduced to during the Starving Time. That's what my visions do – they show me the past in vivid, stomach-wrenching detail. I don't know how it works, or why it happens. All I know is when I was fifteen, I had a vision that made me feel like I was there, like I was one of the starving colonists living in Jamestown. I wandered through the settlement, my stomach yawning with such hunger that even the leather on my shoes looked appetizing. I saw a mother rocking a dead child in her arms. I watched a man climb into a grave he had dug himself, resigning to death. I looked on as another man was hung by his thumbs for carving up his dead wife like a Thanksgiving turkey.

I still feel the sting of that vision. I live with the terrifying bite of it every day. My dreams are plagued by it. Especially after a few days at the library proved all those horrific things I saw actually happened. There really had been a Starving Time, and there really were eyewitness accounts of all I had seen. Somehow that made the nightmares worse. So for Mr Lipscomb to say it never happened, to look me in the eye after class that same day and refuse to let me prove I was right... Well. I just thought I deserved a bit of justice.

So I dial his number.

His phone rings in his pocket. The vibrator motor stings his thigh, and he shrieks into the microphone. He actually shrieks. The ringtone peels through the gym, the rapper rhyming about beating up his cheating girlfriend "because she deserved it" and dropping the F-bomb every other word. The entire student body bursts into howls of laughter. Mr Lipscomb's face is as white as his starched collared shirt, and he swears as he fumbles to rip the phone from his pocket. Not once or twice, but half a dozen times. Each explicit word amplified through the speakers. Then, as if that weren't enough, his foot slips off the back of the box he's standing on. He topples to the floor, still swearing.

By this time, the gym resembles the primate house at the zoo. Whooping, hollering, feet beating on bleachers. Mrs Gafferty, our principal, and three other teachers gather around Mr Lipscomb and escort him out the side doors. Mr Caswell, the boys' gym coach, manages to calm everyone down with his drill sergeant voice and glare. The rest of the assembly is canceled, and soon we're all filing out into the hallway in uniform lines to the tune of muffled laughter and countless retellings of the Mr Lipscomb Incident.

Part of me feels awful for him. My little prank was supposed to make me feel better, but seeing him shriek and swear and fall like that... It didn't bring me any satisfaction.

All it did was make me feel like I couldn't breathe right. Like there was something heavy and cold sitting on my chest.

Not even an hour after the assembly, Mrs Gafferty called me into her office. I guess Mr Lipscomb only has one enemy.

The Whole Truth

After I relay all this to Dr Farrow – all but the part about actually being in Jamestown; I'll save that for later – her expression softens even more. Almost like she sympathizes. "Was this your first time to the principal's office?"

"No."

She makes a motion with her hand, inviting me to elaborate.

I heave a sigh, then hand it all over to her. "There was the time I wired the bell to ring two minutes early for each class. By the end of the day we all got out of school like fifteen minutes before we were supposed to. None of the teachers complained, but Mrs Gafferty knew it was me."

"Why did you do it?"

"Because Mr Lipscomb always holds us after the bell during last period. Half the kids always miss their bus. The parents call and complain, but he keeps doing it. I don't think that's fair."

Dr Farrow lifts her pointed chin. "Anything else?"

I pick at the loose flap of rubber on my sneaker again. "I may have posted a few of Tabitha's personal text messages on the cafeteria's scrolling message board…"

"How did you…?" Dr Farrow holds up her hand and shakes her head. "Never mind. I don't need to know."

I sink lower into the couch cushions.

She hovers her pencil above her notepad. "Tell me what you like to do, Alex. What are your hobbies?"

"I don't know. I guess I like to fix things."

"Yes, I gathered that you're tech savvy. But what else?"

I think about that for a long while. Normal girls would say they liked volleyball or texting or going to the mall. I could lie and say I liked those things too, but I don't. I tell the truth again. "I like to stay in one place."

She stares down her thin nose at me. "What do you mean?"

"I mean…" How can I put it in terms the PhD with dozens of framed degrees and certificates wallpapering her office can understand?

Dr Farrow squints her eyes and sucks in her cheeks. She looks like she's trying to bore a hole in my brain and pluck the answer out herself. I wonder if she learned that technique at Johns Hopkins.

"Do you mean you prefer to stay at home?" She says it like she just uncovered one of my major secrets. By simply staring at me.

I shrug. "I guess that's one way to put it."

She scribbles something onto her notepad. "What do you like to do at home? Watch TV?"

It would have been so simple to say yes. Yes, Dr Farrow, that's why I'm a pariah of my own making. That's why I have no friends and I'm failing eleventh grade. I'm obsessed with television. Totally consumed by it. Is there a cure?

"No," I say. "The only time I watch TV is during movie nights with my family. And even then, I only watch the

same few classics over and over. Arsenic and Old Lace,
Gone with the Wind, Casablanca. Those kinds of things."

"Do you play video games?"

"No."

"Read, then?"

"Never."

She lifts an eyebrow. "Not even for school?"

I tug the sleeves of my navy blue sweater down over my
wrists and clutch them in my palms. "Well, some. Only
when I have to, or if my sisters want me to read to them.
But I never read on my own. And never any fiction."

"What do you do when you have a literature assignment?"

"I find the summaries online. That way it's fact, not
fiction. Gatsby did A, B, and C. That's as far as I go."

"And you find that results in adequate grades on
your assignments?"

I look down at my fingernails. "I get by." I'm not sure why
I lie that time. Dr Farrow knows I'm failing my junior year.

She tilts her head to the side, moving on. "What's wrong
with reading fiction?"

I shift on the couch, and the leather squawks again. "I
don't like being someone else... slipping into someone
else's life. Fiction takes me too far away. To other places.
Other worlds."

I get enough of that already, I want to add.

She nods slowly. "And you like staying at home. I see."
She flips a page on her notepad and scribbles some more.
When she finishes, she looks me in the eye. "It sounds
like you may have a fear of imagination. Of role playing.
That's why you try to stay away from anything fictional.

Television. Video games. Books. You want to stay in the real world. Am I right?"

Not exactly, I want to say. It's not like I fear fictional things. It's that I fear what kind of vision they'll bring on.

When I don't answer, she continues. "And I suppose that's why you're OK with reading history, like you did for Mr Lipscomb's class. History isn't fiction."

A slight smirk hitches on my lips. "I'd hardly call what we learn in history class fact, Dr Farrow." I peel the piece of flappy rubber sole from the bottom of my sneaker and flick it onto her carpet. She follows it with her eyes, frowning.

"OK," she says, drawing out the word. "All history isn't necessarily fact, but you know what I mean. It's not written in the style of fiction. It's written like a summary."

"I still don't read it. Not unless I have a point to prove."

"Why is that?"

I chew the inside of my cheek, once again fighting the urge to lie. Lying was so easy. It hardly fixed anything, but it always stopped people from asking too many questions. Like the ones Dr Farrow asked now. "I don't read history for the same reason I don't touch cats. Or ride Ferris wheels. Or go anywhere near boats or water."

"And why's that?"

I drop my foot to the floor and clasp my hands between my knees. "Because I don't want to have déjà vu."

"And you have déjà vu when you touch a cat?"

"No." I toss my head back with a groan and stare at the white paneled ceiling. There's a yellowed water stain in the corner. "I mean yes. I did have. Once. When I was four."

"Tell me about it."

I close my eyes and tell myself I have nothing to lose. What was the worst Dr Farrow could do to me? Send me to a mental institution? I was pretty sure I'd have déjà vu there too. It wasn't something you could hide from.

I look down at my hands, pressing my slick palms together as tightly as I can. I watch my fingers turn red and my knuckles turn white.

Then I tell her everything.

CHAPTER 2

Vision Number One

It happened at Gran and Pops' old house in Virginia. It was July, and it was hot, and I was outside chasing a little gray bobtail cat around the yard. Pops always told me bobtailed cats weren't as mean as long-tailed cats, which is completely ridiculous, but I was four, so I believed him. And I really wanted to pet the gray one. She was the prettiest. She had blue eyes.

I finally caught her when she ran behind Pops' woodpile. I just reached in and pulled her out. I remember the feeling of my little fists closing around loose skin and fur, pulling on her like she was a rag doll as she dug her claws through the dirt. She cried out but I wasn't about to let go of my prize.

That's when it happened.

I try to explain it the best I can to Dr Farrow. How the shadows at the edge of my vision closed in on me, swallowing me, shutting me out of that July afternoon like a thick, dark curtain. Everything went black, like I'd gone blind. I remember I could still feel the summer heat, my sweaty bangs clinging to my forehead, and that gray cat's body writhing between my hands.

But I couldn't see anything.

Then, as steadily as the darkness came, it receded. Light poured in, followed by new colors and sounds and sensations, all fragmented like I was looking through a kaleidoscope. Eventually everything merged, as though with one twist of the lens the kaleidoscope turned into a telescope, and the world came back into view. Only I wasn't in Pops' yard anymore.

I stood in a perfectly manicured garden behind a little brick house, wearing fancy shoes that pinched my toes and a dress Mom would've never made me wear. My dirty blonde hair, usually cropped short like a boy's, fell in long and loose waves, almost to the middle of my back. I was still me, still four years old, and it was still summer – I could tell by the heat and the smells and the way the sun shone from the same position in the sky – but everything else was different.

I remember feeling dumbstruck. Awestruck. Caught in a moment between complete incoherence and all-encompassing fear. I had no idea where I was. I had no idea how I would get back home. And as the panic set in, I realized I could still feel the cat thrashing in my hands.

Astonished, I looked down at the mass of fur twisting in my fists. It wasn't the gray bobtail. This one had silky black hair, a long tail, and golden eyes. I might have thought it beautiful if it hadn't been hissing and spitting at me, its ears flat against its head. I would have dropped it right away, but I was so scared and disoriented that I just stared at it, stupidly, until it twisted around, lashed out with a guttural wail, and sunk its claws into my chin. I screamed and let go, and it darted into the garden bushes.

As I lifted trembling hands to my trembling chin, wet with blood and tears, the darkness closed in again, and the garden faded to black.

When the light returned this time, it rushed in so full and fast that I heaved a gasp of air, afraid it might drown me. Then, as though no time had passed at all, I was back in Pops' yard, clinging to that gray bobtail.

Which I dropped immediately.

She bounded away with a cry of indignation, but at least she didn't claw me like the long-tail. I remember thinking maybe Pops was right. Maybe long-tails were wilder. And then I remember hearing Pops shout from behind me. The next thing I knew, he was scooping me up in his strong, thick arms, pressing his handkerchief to my chin, and kicking open the front door. "I'm so sorry, Allie Bean," he was saying. "She's never scratched anyone before. I'm sure she was just scared. Try not to squeeze her so tight next time."

I looked up at him like he'd lost his mind. Then I touched my chin.

It was slick with blood.

I remember telling Pops it wasn't the bobtail that scratched me, it was the long-tail, but he just thought I was confused. He gave me a lecture about how bobtails can be mean too, if you're mean to them. I gave up trying to convince him. Something told me it was useless.

That night, when Mom tucked me in bed, I told her what happened. About the shoes that pinched and the dress and the garden. My long hair and the long-tail cat. She told me that it had only been a daydream, that everyone has daydreams, and that they aren't real. It's just our imaginations painting images in our heads. But I was old enough to know what daydreaming was, and that had not been a daydream.

I gave up trying to talk about it, because no one seemed to believe me. I was certain the gray bobtail must have something to do with it, so I left her alone and never dared to touch her again. And since the long-tail had also been involved, I decided to play it safe and consider all felines dangerous territory.

Vision Number Two

The day I discovered my cat theory was wrong, I was seven years old and riding the Ferris wheel at the Town and Country Fair. The back of my bare legs burned on the sun-baked seat. Dad was riding with me and my little sister Audrey, and Mom stood down below, taking photos of us each time we passed by. She wasn't alone that year – my new baby sister, Claire, slept snuggled in a sling at Mom's chest. I remember looking forward to a time when Claire was old enough to ride the Ferris wheel with us, and wondered if she'd like rocking the seat as much as we did.

I leaned out over the protective bar as far as I could, waving at Mom and Claire, and making a silly face for Mom's photo. After she snapped it, Dad gave the seat a good rock, and I squealed, falling back into his arms. He pointed out over the midway as we rose once again to the top and asked if Audrey and I wanted to ride the Tilt-a-whirl next.

Before I could answer, that beautiful August afternoon swept away into darkness – the same darkness that had taken me from Pops' yard when I was four. I cried out and reached for Dad, but there was nothing he could do. He was no longer beside me.

This time, the darkness lasted longer. Long enough to notice there were no sounds. Not one. I should've heard my heart pounding in my ears and my terrified, irregular breath dragging in and out of my throat. I should have been able to feel it. But there was nothing. No feeling. No body, no blood, no breath. Only thought.

One thought.

I'm dead.

I died on the Ferris wheel.

Then light broke out, as if from behind a cloud, slicing through the darkness. It was so bright, and so much like the sun, I half expected to feel its heat. The light swelled and spread, chasing away every shadow until there was nothing but a brilliant white canvas laid out before me. Colors formed and moved within the light, like sunspots dancing before my eyes. Then the colors morphed into shapes, and my senses returned. Sounds and smells gathered and swirled with the colors, and, once everything aligned, I had my body back. And my new vision.

The day was sun-washed and warm, just like the one I'd left behind, and I still felt like I was rising through the air. Slow and steady, just like on the Ferris wheel. My vantage point was the same as well, only instead of looking out over our local fairground, I was standing at a window, looking out over a beautiful old city, my hand pressed to the glass in front of me.

Still rising.

Was I in an elevator?

The city looked like something out of one of my history books. Massive white buildings, ancient and grand, were nestled among ornate gardens, sprawling lawns, soaring fountains, and gleaming sculptures. Curved, elegant boats glided across a central, rectangular, man-made pond. The streets teemed with people, all dressed in suits and gowns, each wearing a hat or carrying a parasol. It was like I'd gone back to another time.

"Isn't it a marvel, Katherine?"

I jumped back, totally unaware there had been a woman in a wide-brimmed hat and lace-trimmed dress kneeling beside me.

"Katherine, be careful," she said.

She reached for me, but I stumbled in the clumsy ankle boots I was wearing and fell down. That's when I realized I was in a small room full of people. Windows surrounded the room on all sides, and all I could see beyond the glass were thick, crisscrossed steel beams, moving slowly above me. Beyond that, blue sky. For some reason, those slow-moving steel beams terrified me.

I tried to scramble to my feet, but someone caught me by the elbow and helped me up. He was a middle-aged man with a kind face, dressed in a deep-blue suit with brass buttons. His hat bore a brass plate that read CONDUCTOR.

"Are we on a train?" I asked, stupidly. Of course it wasn't a train.

He laughed and tapped his hat. "Not that kind of conductor."

The woman who called me Katherine laughed too. "She's thinking of the conductors on the train ride here. They were dressed in similar uniforms."

The conductor nodded, then turned to me. "And which ride do you like best, little lady? The steam train? Or Mr Ferris' grand Wheel?"

One more glance out the windows and I understood what he meant. Why the tiny room felt like it was rising through the sky. I was still riding a Ferris wheel. Possibly the Ferris wheel – the one Pops said he rode as a boy at the St Louis World's Fair.

I reached out to the glass again, to take the scene all in, but my fingertips touched nothing but air. Cotton filled my ears, and darkness came.

"Am I really at the Fair?" My voice sounded so far away.

Lights. Squeals. Laughter. Carnival music.

"Of course you're at the fair, silly." Dad gave me a squeeze and laughed in my ear. Audrey made a face. Mom waved.

I trembled.

Vision Number Three

The Ferris wheel vision tossed my cat theory out the window and replaced it with a new one. Déjà vu. Although I didn't know the term at the time, the concept, however basic, seemed to be the answer. Holding a feral cat produced a vision of holding a feral cat. Riding a Ferris wheel produced a vision of riding a Ferris wheel. But I still didn't know why those experiences should produce a vision at all. What was so special about a cat or a Ferris wheel?

Three more years passed before I could test my new theory. Once again, it was proven wrong.

I was ten, it was summer, and I was in Sunday School. I remember sitting next to Jensen Peters, the most popular boy in fifth grade, and thinking how lucky it was we went to the same church. He usually sat by Billy Piper in the back, but Billy was out sick, and Jensen wasn't the type to sit quietly by himself like I did every Sunday. He needed an audience. And since I was the only other fifth grader in the room, he chose me to applaud for him that day.

He was sharing my art supplies, and I was dreaming of how perfect it would be if our hands touched while reaching for the same colored pencil, when the classroom went dark. This time, though, I felt more annoyed than frightened. It was just my luck that the first chance I got to introduce Jensen to my stunning wit and artistic talent, I got yanked away into oblivion.

My senses left, one by one, until only my thoughts and that deep black remained. I waited, much longer than the second time it seemed, for the light to come and the vision to manifest. The longer I waited, the stronger that same fear I'd entertained before pricked at the back of my mind: Maybe the light wouldn't come. Maybe I really was dead this time.

I died in Sunday School.

But the light did come eventually, and so did the new vision.

At first there was haze. Nothing but thick, gray haze everywhere. Like being trapped in a storm cloud. Then there was rocking. A relentless, random motion, heaving me in every direction. I wrapped my arms around a railing in front of me before I even knew it was there, pressing my cheek to the smooth, slick wood to steady myself. I breathed deeply through my nose, the scent of brine and fish coating the back of my throat.

I was on a boat, out at sea. I couldn't see the water beyond the thick veil of haze, but I could hear it slapping against the hull, the ship surging and groaning in response. Huge white shapes loomed in and out of the fog overhead, which I could only assume were sails, and dark shadows slinked here and there across the deck, perhaps belonging to the crew. None of them seemed to notice me.

I clung to that railing, nestled in my own shroud of fog. Rise and fall. Back and forth. Endlessly tossing. Always that acrid smell of fish – never a fresh, clean breath.

There was no holding it in. I was going to throw up.

The darkness came swiftly, sweeping in and around me like black smoke. I fell into it willingly, dizzy and shaking. The light followed, as intense as ever, pressing all the air from my lungs until I was back in Sunday School, sitting beside Jensen, gasping for breath.

"Oh my gosh, are you OK?" Jensen laid a hand on my shoulder. "Are you having a seizure?"

I remember liking that he was worried about me. I remember liking his hand on my shoulder. I remember how cute he looked with his honey hair swept across his forehead and his hazel eyes wide and full of concern.

I remember throwing up in his lap.

I don't think Jensen ever told anyone about my "accident." No one said anything about it at school. I guess admitting someone threw up on you was just as embarrassing as being the person who did it. Like when a bird drops a bomb on your shoulder. It isn't your fault, but you hope to God no one witnessed it so you can forget it ever happened.

Jensen did, however, tell everyone I had epilepsy. According to the rumor, I could burst into spastic convulsions at any given moment, swallow my own tongue, and ultimately choke to death. Apparently Jensen had performed the Heimlich Maneuver and saved my life that day.

As preposterous as that story was, I had to give Jensen credit. It made us fascinating subjects at school. He was more popular than ever, and, incidentally, so was I. Which is why I had to shut everyone out. I couldn't take one more person asking about my "condition." I hated the way they all looked at me, like I was a grenade about to explode. Mostly because it was true. I did have a condition, and I was about to explode. Each timid glance they tossed my way reminded me of the complete lack of control I had over the visions. And if I had no control – if the visions were random – it meant they could come and go as they pleased, cutting into my life like an unwanted dance partner.

Like my Uncle Lincoln when he's drunk at a wedding reception.

I went over that day hundreds of times in my head, trying to find something that backed my déjà vu theory. The Sunday School lesson hadn't been about Noah's Ark, or Jonah being tossed from a ship and swallowed by a whale, or even Jesus walking on water. It had been about Esau giving up his birthright to Jacob. I read the passage over and over, and nothing linked it to my vision of the ship. Even my art project – a drawing of Jacob's ladder – held no nautical significance.

I had to let my theory go and accept that the visions were indeed random. They came and went, dragging me along like something hooked to its sleeve. It wasn't aware of me, it just swept me along. My wants, desires, and needs never mattered. And soon, that's exactly how I saw my life.

None of it mattered.

Vision Number Four

After a year as a self-made pariah, I had successfully alienated myself from the kids at school. Whether or not I sat alone in the cafeteria was no longer a topic of discussion. No one commented on the fact that I walked home from school by myself. Even the teachers assumed I was just an oddball. One of the shy ones. They never talked to me about my lack of friends or interest in extra-curricular activities. I suppose they didn't want me to feel bad. I had epilepsy, after all.

There wasn't a day that went by I didn't consider telling my parents about the visions or asking them for help. But I didn't want to bother them. They had their hands full already. With Gran and Pops losing their farm and moving to Maryland to live with us.

With my sister, Audrey.

So I lost myself in my fix-it projects. Hunching over a circuit board, stripping wires, making connections – it all provided the clarity and focus I needed to forget about the visions.

When I'd taken apart almost everything in the house and perfected my repair skills, I moved on to custom modifications. I installed a touch screen tablet computer in one of the kitchen cabinet doors so Gran could look up recipes online at eye-level, listen to music, or watch TV while she cooked. I wired all the electronics in the den to a "movie night" setting, so with one press of a button, the projector would turn on, the DVD player would whir to life, the lights would dim, and the window blinds would lower. I even helped Dad get his old Mustang running again, and managed to increase the gas mileage while still maintaining its kick-ass power.

At school I immersed myself in drafting, computer programming, physics, and biology, and kept my pariah status intact by hiding out in the AV room or computer lab during lunch or free periods. My grades were top tier compared to what they are now, and I had a drawer full of brochures for the best engineering schools in the country, courtesy of Dad, who wanted me to become a biomedical engineer like him. The nerdy glasses I wore and my hopeless, shaggy mop of dishwater blonde hair helped round out my geek facade.

In a one-time effort to add an extra-curricular activity to my record, I briefly joined the Robotics Team in my sophomore year at the request of Mrs Latimer, the team leader and head of the AV department, but the Jamestown vision came on full force during our first competition. She found me huddled in a corner in the competing school's vending machine room, all the lights off, rocking back and forth and stuffing myself with Oreos.

I was so hungry.

I was so terrified by what I'd seen.

Now even the smell of Oreos makes me want to puke.

CHAPTER 3

After I dump all of that on Dr Farrow, I totally expect her to look at me like I'm crazy. I expect her to drill me on the visions. Those are why I'm here in the first place, and I'm getting impatient for answers.

But she doesn't go there. Instead, she taps her pencil on her bottom lip and says, "Tell me about Audrey."

For a split second, I think back to a few hours earlier, before I left the house for my appointment with Dr Farrow. Audrey was where she always was, sitting on the daybed on our screened-in porch. She wore fingerless gloves and a black bandana with cartoon pumpkins on it. (Halloween is her favorite holiday.) Her thin, frail legs were curled under her; one of Gran's afghans was draped over her lap. Her homebound algebra homework was spread out on the coffee table before her, but she hadn't touched it yet. Instead, she traced the words of Robert Burns on dog-eared pages with her fingertips. A shiny new bruise graced her collarbone.

I tried not to look at it when I kissed her goodbye.

"I don't want to talk about Audrey," I tell Dr Farrow. I look away and try to swallow the sudden lump in my throat.

She nods and puts pencil to paper. Then, "Tell me how it felt to tell your parents about your suspension."

Oh. That.

Dad

The day of the Mr Lipscomb Incident, Mrs Gafferty called Dad in from work to tell him face-to-face. He sent me out to wait in the car while they talked, and I sank into the cool vinyl in the back of the Mustang. Waiting. Breathing in autumn air.

Even though the backseat was cramped, and I always preferred sitting beside Dad in the front, the back seemed fitting for that day. I was a criminal after all – captured and corralled – headed to the precinct.

There were no words on the way home. Tension weighed heavy on my shoulders in the silence. I pressed my temple to the rear window glass and watched the blur of curb and grass, the swirl of crisp leaves in the breeze, the rise and fall of power lines. They reminded me of the time Audrey and I climbed the old power line poles at the edge of Pops' farm to steal those glass insulators the power companies never use anymore. They were the most exquisite shade of blue-green, like the Chesapeake Bay on a clear day.

Once Audrey caught a glimpse of that color, winking from the top of the power lines, she couldn't rest until we had climbed all the way up and liberated each one. We carried them home, heavy and sagging in our stretched-out T-shirts. I spent a week fastening small lightbulbs inside each one, while Audrey coiled copper wire in intricate and lovely patterns around the outside. It was always that way with us. Whenever we found forgotten or broken objects, I would repair them and bring them back to life, and Audrey would make them beautiful. I was the stoic one with Coke-bottle eyeglasses. Audrey was the beauty, with a laugh that gave color to our world.

Mom called our hobby upcycling, a term that helped us sell several of our hanging lamps at one of the local boutiques in Annapolis' historic district. The rest were strung up in my workshop in the attic, a constant reminder of those blue-green days when Audrey could climb and run and leave beautiful things trailing after her.

We arrived home sooner than I hoped. Dad pulled into our driveway, shaded by century-old sycamore trees ablaze with fire and gold, and cut the engine. Our house, a small brick Colonial, sat back from the road, nestled comfortably in those trees. It beckoned me inside, but I didn't reach for my seatbelt.

Dad pulled his keys from the ignition. He turned around and rested an arm on the back of the passenger seat. His eyes were kind and gray, like always, but his lips were curved in a frown. His dusky blond hair looked like he'd raked his hands through it a dozen times. Probably during his talk with Mrs Gafferty.

"Do you want to tell your mom, or should I?" he said.

My gut tightened. I could already see the disappointment on Mom's face. Hear it in her voice – a shadow behind her ever calm, ever even words.

Dad let go of his frown and a faint sympathetic smile showed itself. He knew all about my struggles with Mr

Lipscomb. And Tabitha, for that matter. He was on my side when it came to both of them, though that didn't mean he was OK with what I did. It just meant he understood. Which, honestly, pretty much made him the best dad in the world.

He was the peace-keeper of our household, always trying to shield Mom from school-related problems and take care of them himself. Not that she wouldn't want to know about them, but Dad figured they would distract her from her work. This time, however, he needed to "inform her of the escalated situation." That faint smile meant he was sorry, but it had to be done.

He dropped his arm and jostled his keys in his palm. "What are we going to do with you, Allie Bean?" He clamped the keys in his fist and heaved open the driver-side door.

Time to face the judge.

Inside, I smelled nutmeg and cinnamon, which meant there was one of Gran's pumpkin pies cooling on the butcher block island in the kitchen. The tinny sound of Pops' radio floated in on a cool breeze from the back porch, and I knew he was out there, sitting in his rocker, listening to his favorite sports program. Any other day I would've gone out to join him. Gran would've brought us hot cider, and we would've nagged her every five minutes, asking when the pie would be ready. Pops might have gotten a swat on the shoulder with a wooden spoon. I would've laughed. And Gran would've broken down and given us a slice. Still warm. With fresh whipped cream melting on top.

Then I would've helped Dad with dinner, helped my youngest sister, Claire, with her homework, then read some of TS Eliot to Audrey until she fell asleep. For the past two months, she'd been falling asleep before dark. Every part of her body was tired. Even her fingernails, she said.

But this time I went straight upstairs to my bedroom to await my trial. I had a good hour before Mom got home to work my stomach into several twisted knots of guilt.

I hated letting her down. Even more than I hated Mr Lipscomb. And I'd been letting her down an awful lot lately.

I hefted myself up each squeaky step to the attic, my feet feeling heavier than usual. The staircase on the second floor led right up into the middle of my room, which spanned the entire top floor of the house. It was more of a workshop than a bedroom really, though I did have a small twin bed in the far corner, a dresser, and a wardrobe. The ceiling was A-framed, sloping down almost to the floor, but each side had a bank of windows extending out from the slanted roof so you didn't have to crouch like you did in other attics. The ceiling and walls were covered in old architectural drawings and machining schematics, as well as a few watercolors Audrey painted for me, and a poster of a 1963 Corvette Sting Ray.

Silver, with a red v-stripe on the hood.

I totally planned to own one someday.

Three drafting tables Dad salvaged from an old factory stood strategically placed around the room, each covered in a heap of random parts, wire spools, and trays of tools. If I had it my way, my room would be in a constant state of organized chaos, but Gran insisted on tidying while I was at school. I could tell she'd been there that day because a path was paved through my boxes of spare electronics, and the faint scent of her lemon verbena perfume still hung in the air. Dancing with dust motes.

I dropped my backpack on my oval rope rug and crossed the room to my workbench. I flipped the switch to one of Audrey's glass insulator lamps and stared at a project I'd been working on for Craig, a kid in my Biology class. For a hundred bucks, I was supposed to modify his DVD player into a smartphone dock and wire it to stream internet movies to his TV.

I didn't ask which kinds of movies he'd be streaming. A hundred bucks was a hundred bucks.

I cranked open the casement window next to my bench and got to work. The scent of burning leaves curled in and wrapped around my shoulders. The whir of distant leaf blowers and the rhythmic whoosh of cars passing by lulled me into a sort of hazy stupor while I worked. Every now and then leaves scuttled across the pavement in a gust of wind.

I heard the front door open and close when Mom got home, but I kept my nose down. I didn't even stop when the smell of lasagna baking in the oven made my stomach tumble and growl.

I simply worked.

And waited for the gavel.

Mom

It was dark outside and the crickets were chirruping by the time Mom climbed the steps to the attic. She carried a plate of lasagna and salad with both hands. Her long, pencil-straight chestnut hair was tied back at the base of her neck, but a few sleek strands had fallen out. They brushed her cheeks. Her glasses hung from a chain around her neck. The great shadow of disappointment stood behind her, hands in his pockets, head hung low, a little to the right.

She slid the dinner plate in front of me, sort of like a peace offering, then sat on my bed and folded her bare feet under her long legs. The mattress coils squeaked. She frowned down at the quilt Gran made for me and traced the stitching with her slender fingers. The shadow traced it too.

We sat in silence for a long while, the light from Audrey's lamp casting a blue prism across Mom's hair. We sat until steam no longer rose from my dinner.

Finally Mom spoke. Her voice was thin. Tired. "I can't help but wonder if you're trying to punish me, Bean."

Her words were so unlike anything I expected that I swiveled around to face her full on. "What do you mean? Why would I want to punish you?" I sounded more like a child than I meant to.

Her eyes remained fixed on the quilt. "For working so much. For not being here." She swallowed. "For not finding a cure." Her voice cracked on the last word, and in an instant I was at her side. I folded her in my arms. Her shoulders shuddered. I felt her warm tears slip down my neck.

Is that what she thought? That I got in trouble to get her attention? That I resented her for slaving away day and night, searching for Audrey's cure? How could she think I was that selfish? If I was the best cancer researcher at the AIDA Institute, I'd slave away too. Gran said it was Mom's destiny, and I believed it. If anyone could find a cure for Audrey, it was Mom. And I would support her every step of the way. Even if that meant giving her up to her research.

I thought she knew that.

She pulled away to wipe her nose with the back of her hand. The blue prism swam in her eyes. "It's just, you've been acting out so much lately. And getting suspended? That goes on your record." She shook her head and sniffed. "It makes me wonder if I had been here for you – if you could've talked to me – you wouldn't have taken your frustration out on your teacher."

I looked down at my feet. They were so heavy the floorboards groaned beneath them.

It killed me that she thought it was her fault.

The thing was, I had wanted to tell her about my visions for years, tell her they weren't just daydreams, but I didn't want her to think I was crazy.

I didn't want her to feel she had to find a cure for me too.

The Diagnosis

After I've told Dr Farrow everything, after I've drained myself until I'm nothing but a collapsed vessel on her couch, she removes her glasses. She sets her notepad and pencil aside.

"So. Alex. Here's what I see." She leans forward with folded hands. Her nails are glossy and cream-colored. They match her pumps. "I don't believe your visions are a product of an attention seeking disorder, like I originally thought when I looked at your file. Your ongoing attempts to isolate yourself from social situations rule that out. A social phobia of some sort crossed my mind, because those can trigger psychotic episodes in extreme cases. But you're perfectly capable of going out in public, going to school, talking to strangers like me without a drop of sweat or anxiety. The only time you demonstrated anxiety during this session was right before you told me about your visions. Your palms became sweaty. You were fidgety. You held your breath. But that's a typical reaction when one is about to divulge a secret they've been holding onto for so long."

She sits up and straightens her back. I wait for answers. She remains silent, watching me.

"So?" I say. "What's wrong with me?" I push my glasses up my nose with my knuckle. AIDA's founder continues to stare down at me from his portrait, a condescending look in his two-dimensional eyes. Something about his expression makes me feel uneasy, crazy even, and I look away from him, pulling my sleeves down over my wrists tighter than before.

Dr Farrow's coral lips form a straight line. Her brow creases. She opens her mouth to reply, but closes it again.

Heat spreads across my skin. "You think I have schizophrenia, don't you?"

She lifts her hands. "I didn't say that."

"Good, because I don't. I read all about it. Not all the symptoms match. I'm not emotionally distant. I joke. I laugh. I can express ideas in a coherent, organized manner. I don't think the government is out to kill me."

"That's true. And yet you're experiencing extremely vivid hallucinations. You are unable to differentiate whether they are real or unreal."

I start to shake. I fist my hands at my sides. There is a film of sickly, sweaty heat coating me beneath my sweater and cords. It clings to me like plastic wrap. Epilepsy was bad enough. I can't have the kids at school thinking I have schizophrenia. Not to mention Mom.

I cock the pistol and fire all my burning questions at Dr Farrow. "If they aren't real, then why do I have a scar on my chin? Why did I get seasick just by sitting in a Sunday School classroom? Why did I feel like I was starving after Jamestown? How can my visions show me things that really happened in history, before I even learn about them?"

She shrugs one bony shoulder. "You probably retained the knowledge subconsciously. You saw an advertisement, heard a song, saw a heading in a newspaper. Things like that can stick in our subconscious minds without us being aware of it. Seems like I remember something about the Starving Time in Jamestown, though I can't place where I heard about it. So even though I never officially learned about it, it's there, in my subconscious." She leans forward again, her elbows on her knees. "Alex, I'm not saying you have schizophrenia. I'm not saying you have anything. All I'm saying is that I'd like to continue meeting with you. I want to know more about your visions. I'd like to dig deeper. And then, later, if I think it necessary, I might run a few tests."

"What kinds of tests?"

"Mental acuity. Possibly a few brain scans."

I shake my head. How long will all that take? "Isn't there some kind of pill you can give me? Something that will stop the visions? Just so I can get through a normal day at school?"

The possibility of never having another vision, of being normal, tugs at my sleeve. It taps on the window. I look out through the glass and see myself sitting in the school cafeteria, talking casually to Jensen Peters, flipping my hair over my shoulder and flirting with him like I actually know what I'm doing. I see myself standing in front of Mom's full length mirror, wearing a dress for the first time in my life, ready to go on my first date. I'm hanging out with Claire, laughing and talking about her latest Hollywood crush, whom I've never heard of, and I don't feel the urge to make fun of her mercilessly. I'm reading one of the countless novels Audrey has recommended to me. I'm strolling through a college campus, I'm tall and grown up, and I haven't had a sleepless night in years.

I look happy.

A pill could do that for me, couldn't it?

"Why don't we meet a few more times," Dr Farrow says, "before we talk about medication?"

All my hopes deflate and fizzle. They drop to the floor at my feet with a thud, one by one, like dead birds.

I knew it wouldn't be that easy.

Normal is never easy.

Movie Night

It's an hour's car ride back to Annapolis from DC, and I'm silent the whole way home. I feel empty and hollow, like Dr Farrow sucked everything out of me, leaving behind a cold, hardened-steel shell. My eyes glaze over as I stare out the window in the back of Mom's Civic. The sun set long ago. Glittering lights fade to black as we leave the city, and then, one by one, they multiply again as we near the Bay. It's the same route Mom takes every day to and from work. She knows it like she knows the freckles on my shoulders. If she's tired of the same old boring drive, she's never said. I know she'd drive all day, every day, if it brought her one step closer to Audrey's cure. Still, I feel bad she has to make the extra trip just for me.

For me and my issues.

It isn't until I'm back home in the kitchen and smell Gran's lemon poppyseed muffins that I finally let my guard down. The hardened-steel shell begins to melt. I'm exhausted, like I ran an emotional marathon. All I want to do is trudge up the stairs and collapse face-first into my pillow, but a hug from Gran and a mouthful of muffin soon sets me to rights.

Thankfully, tonight is our family movie night – a time-honored tradition in the Wayfare house – which means homemade pizza, soda, popcorn, and no chance for serious discussion over the dinner table. I have no desire to fill the whole family in on my talk with Dr Farrow.

While Dad and Gran put the finishing touches on the pizzas, Mom enlists Claire and I for Mega Couch duty in the den. Ever since I can remember, we've always pushed our two couches and three ottomans together to make one massive lounging zone. Dad calls Mega Couch "the ultimate movie viewing experience," and I totally agree. I can't wait to sink down into the cushions, get lost in a film I know is "safe," and worry about everything else in the morning.

"So what's on the playbill tonight?" Mom asks me as she nudges the last ottoman into place with her knee.

I pull one of my favorite films out of the DVD cabinet: Charade, with Audrey Hepburn and Cary Grant. It's a delicious murder mystery, full of the best kinds of twists and turns. No one is who they say they are, and it keeps you guessing all the way until the end. I hold it up and Mom grins. It's one of her favorites too.

She showed it to me for the first time when I was nine and laid up with chicken pox. It was the only thing that kept me captivated long enough to keep my mind off all the itching. I remember lying stretched out on Mega Couch, oven mitts on my hands, sipping chocolate milk through a purple curly straw. I remember falling in love with Cary Grant. I remember hating him when I thought he might not be a good guy after all. And most importantly, I remember not having déjà vu. No bad dreams. No visions. No escape from the chicken pox, not even for one second.

"We're watching that one again?" Claire says, tossing a throw pillow onto Mega Couch from the other side of the room. "We've seen it a hundred tiiiiimes." She bends down to swipe another pillow off the floor. Her chestnut hair spills in front of her face.

I've always been jealous of how much she looks like Mom – perfect apple cheeks, dark eyes, willowy frame, that satin hair – while Audrey and I look just like Dad. Dusky blond hair, pale gray eyes, button noses. But one thing Claire didn't inherit from Mom is her penchant for drama. She doesn't have one ounce of Mom's calm manner and even temper.

"It's Alex's turn to pick," Mom says. "What she says goes."

"But it's so unfair." Claire flings the other pillow across the room. "We never watch anything new. I can't talk to my friends about these old movies. They haven't heard of any of them."

"So?" I say, kneeling down on the floor and sticking Charade in the DVD player.

"So you don't have any friends. You don't know what it's like."

Mom unfolds one of Gran's afghans and drapes it over the back of the couch. "That's not true. Alex has friends."

Claire fists her hands on her hips. "Name one."

Mom's face goes a little blank as she thinks about it. Then she says, "Paisley," and smiles at me. "She sits next to you in Sunday School."

I turn my head to the side so she can't see me grimace. Paisley isn't exactly my friend. She does sit next to me in Sunday School, but we never speak. She's weird, even for my standards. For one, she always wears flannel pajamas and hiking boots. To church and to school. And two? She always has a handful of mayonnaise packets in her backpack.

Which she snacks on.

During class.

I shudder just thinking about the sound she makes sucking on those packets.

"And what about Jensen?" Mom says. "He's been your friend since you two were in the church nursery together."

I roll my eyes. "Mom, just because Paisley and Jensen are in my general vicinity at church and school doesn't mean they're my friends."

"See?" Claire says. "Jensen isn't her friend. She just has that huge crush on him still."

I don't even attempt to dispute it like I normally would. Claire's like a pit bull when it comes to arguing. Once she sinks her teeth in, she doesn't let go. And I don't have the energy to spar with her tonight. Besides, it's not like my crush on Jensen was ever a secret in this family. Even Pops knows about it. He used to pinch me right above my knee where it tickles, and if I laughed, it meant I was "boy crazy." Boy crazy for Jensen Peters.

I laughed every time, dammit.

"Can't you just try a new movie?" Claire asks, sticking a brightly colored DVD case under my nose. It looks like some sort of tween musical. I resist the urge to gag. "I saw it at Madeline's and it's so awesome. I know you'd like it if you just gave it a tryyy." Her whining is truly an art form. She's as incessant and irritating as the seagulls down at the docks in the summer.

Again, I'm too tired to argue. I pull the DVD case from her fingers and pop it open. "Fine. You guys watch this, and I'll eat in my room. Happy?" I flip Charade out of the disc drive, and I shove Claire's movie into the player a little too hard.

Mom notices. "No," she says, kneeling beside me. She switches out the DVDs and hands Claire's movie back to her. "We're watching Charade."

"This is so stupid!" In a fit of pent up frustration, Claire slams a foot against Mega Couch.

"Hey." Mom pushes herself to her feet. Her fierce expression dares Claire to continue with her tantrum. But Claire never stops once she gets going. Punishment be damned.

"Do you know how embarrassing it is being her sister?" Claire says, flicking her wrist at me. "Everyone makes fun of her. I mean, she's scared of movies. We live on the coast and she freaks out if she gets too close to a boat. We can't have a cat, even though Audrey really wants one, because it'll 'upset Alex.' Everything 'upsets' Alex. Why can't she just be normal?" She storms out of the room just as Dad and Gran come in bearing trays of pizza. Mom darts after her to lay down the law. I sit on the floor, poking at a seam in the carpet, reminded yet again of the huge wake my visions leave behind.

If only Claire knew how much we both want the same thing.

If only Dr Farrow had listened to me and given me some sort of medication. I'd be well on my way to becoming the person my family needs me to be. All their attention could go back to Audrey, where it belongs. But I guess since I've gone seventeen years without any medication, Dr Farrow thinks a little while longer won't do any harm.

She couldn't be more wrong.

CHAPTER 4

In Which "A Little While" Amounts to
Exactly One Day

The next day at school goes by just like any other. Classes are slow, teachers lecture in sensible shoes, and the cafeteria pizza is so greasy I have to blot it with a stack of napkins before it's remotely edible. In Driver's Ed, I fail the parallel parking test. Again. Madame Cavanaugh keeps me after French to let me know my grade is slipping. Again.

Same old, same old.

In English, Mr Draper taps and screeches his way across the chalkboard, filling its surface with definitions of words like denouement and omniscient. He loves deconstructing classic literature and pointing out symbolism his students would never discover on their own. For him, that's what makes the text come alive. For me, it's what helps keep my grade above a D.

Turning fiction into mechanical puzzle pieces – like something you could manufacture in an assembly line – was the only way I could pass his literature assignments. Plug protagonist into slot A. Attach conflict and dramatic

47

irony, using two minor characters and one antagonist. Rotate ninety degrees and locate symbolism. Slide climax into place, and fasten with resolution. Use the provided bonding compound if structure seems unstable.

No problem.

We're right in the middle of discussing hidden meanings in The Great Gatsby when the classroom sounds fade away, leaving only a faint resonance like the school bell after it rings. Mr Draper is still talking and gesturing. I can see his lips moving, but I can't hear his words. Papers shuffling, books opening and closing, pages turning, sneakers scuffing the tile floor – it all disappears.

I grip the sides of my desk as the darkness slinks in and around Mr Draper and my classmates like satin cloth, swallowing them whole. I curse the fact that Dr Farrow refused to write me a prescription, but there's nothing I can do about it now. I just have to let this new vision run its course. It'll all be over in a few minutes.

They never last longer than that.

Vision Hallucination Number Five

When the darkness receded and the light poured in, I found myself standing smack in the middle of a busy city street. Cars puttered past on either side of me. They were classics – old Fords, Cadillacs, Oldsmobiles – but they looked brand new, all shiny and black with tall, whitewall tires. I gaped at them as they passed by, their engines sounding like ratchets. The drivers gaped back, some even shouting at me to get out of the road. One of them honked a horn behind me, and its throaty ah-ooga! almost made me jump out of my skin.

That's when I realized I had a body, and if I didn't want it flattened, I better get moving.

I scurried through a break in the traffic to the sidewalk in what felt like stiff ankle boots. My hands were shoved in the pockets of a long wool coat. A row of brick mid-rise buildings stood before me, and I stopped short when I caught my reflection in a bakery store window.

I'd never seen my reflection in a vision before.

I stood and stared, running my fingers down my mess of long, dark, wavy hair. It was pulled back in a loose ribbon at the back of my neck. Soft, wavy tendrils framed my face, gently brushing my red cheeks in the crisp autumn air. I leaned in closer to the glass and touched my cheekbone. Deep brown eyes, the color of coffee, stared back at me. I wasn't wearing contacts, but I could see everything clearly. (I guess one doesn't necessarily need glasses during a hallucination.)

With the dark hair and dark eyes, I half expected to have a completely different face, but everything else was the same – my nose, my lips, my chin – only I looked thinner, possibly two sizes smaller beneath that long wool coat. A plain black skirt peeked out from under the hem, falling just past my knees, and thick thigh-high black socks drew my eyes down to my battered, black boots.

When I traced my eyebrows, my nose, my lips, the sensation beneath my fingertips felt the same, but I couldn't get over how different I looked. Like I dyed my hair, lost fifteen pounds, and bought colored contacts. Dad would've killed me. He was so proud that I shared his gray-blue eyes and dusky blond hair.

A knock on the window in front of my face made me jump. I peered through the glass past my reflection and saw a hefty man in a white apron shooing me from his display window. I guessed I must have looked like a lunatic to his customers inside. I waved at him, mouthed I'm sorry, and started down the sidewalk with no idea where it might lead.

It was a brisk autumn day, the pale blue sky streaked with half-hearted wisps of clouds. A biting breeze cut across the street every now and then, and I was thankful for the warmth of my coat and thick socks. Tall brick shops and apartment buildings stretched on down the road as far as I could see, and the sidewalks were filled with people, some in a hurry, others milling about and chatting with neighbors. The clothing styles made me think my vision was set in the Twenties. Prohibition. The Great Depression. But there was only one way to find out.

I heard the newspaper boy's voice before I saw him, shouting the latest headlines over the putter of the traffic, the clopping of horses' hooves pulling wagons, and the murmuring pedestrians. Men in suits and long coats stopped briefly at the boy's stand to swipe a paper from one of the stacks and push a few coins in his gloved palm. The fluid motion of it all meant it was a daily ritual for them. The newspaper. I wondered what they'd think of its modern day death or the dawn of the Internet.

A thought tugged at the back of my mind, tiny at first. If Dr Farrow was right, and this was all a hallucination, what was stopping me from having a little fun? I decided to do a bit of self-diagnosis.

I leaned over the nearest stack of newspapers, The Daily Herald, and caught the date at the top. Friday, October 21, 1927.

The date was off. It was October, yes, but it wasn't the twenty-first nor a Friday. And it definitely wasn't 1927.

If my vision was right, and the twenty-first landed on a Friday in 1927, how would Dr Farrow explain that? I really didn't think I could retain those kinds of details in my subconscious mind. I couldn't even remember all the dates I'd spent so much time memorizing for history last year.

The newspaper boy caught me staring and approached, his hand held out. He was tall and thin, with a youngish face, sunken eyes, and a cap set askew on top of greasy hair. I patted my coat pockets for change, but they were empty. Did teenagers really wander the streets without any money in 1927? I didn't think I'd ever left the house with less than a five dollar bill.

The boy shooed me away the moment he saw I was broke.

But this was my vision. My hallucination. It wasn't real. It was all in my head. So who said I had to pay for anything?

I slid a newspaper from the top of the stack and started off, tucking it under my arm.

That's when things got ugly.

"Stop! Thief!" The boy leaped over his newspaper stacks like a pole vaulter. His long, gangly legs landed him at my side in an instant. He seized the paper with both hands, but I mustered my best vise grip. (Having two younger sisters who were always getting into your stuff helped perfect the art.)

"I don't have to pay," I said through gritted teeth, my arms tangled in his as we wrestled. He smelled like sauerkraut and woodsmoke.

"Everyone has to pay. It's two cents or nothing." His boot came down on mine in an effort to shake me loose.

You wouldn't think a smashed toe would hurt in a hallucination, but the white-hot, blazing pain was the first clue on my way to learning the inevitable: Dr Farrow was a complete and utter idiot. There's no way I could've dreamed up the detailed agony that was my throbbing toe.

I wasn't that creative.

The boy yanked the newspaper from under my arm, and I let him do it. I couldn't care less about the paper now. All I could think about was my toe – my poor, mangled (the nail probably split in two) toe – and the fact that these visions were definitely not hallucinations.

"Is there a problem here?"

I hadn't realized another boy had approached, or that a crowd had gathered around us for that matter, until he spoke. He looked to be the same age as Newspaper Boy and me, but the serious expression he wore was mature beyond his years. His voice was calm and purposeful. His eyes were a striking blue-green, like the color of Audrey's glass insulators, his dark hair was cropped short with faint sideburns, and he wore an oversized wool coat with black leather gloves. He was handsome, like those resolute soldiers in old tintype photographs. So handsome, in fact, just looking at him made my ears warm.

I took a step back, feeling stupid for making a scene. Newspaper Boy swept his cap from the ground, which had fallen during our struggle. He ran his fingers through his greasy hair and situated the cap back in place. Then he pointed a bony finger in my direction. "She tried to steal from me. Said she didn't have to pay."

The blue-eyed boy turned his attention to me. He scanned me from head to toe, making me feel exposed.

"Want to explain that?"

I tugged at my coat, wrapping it tighter around me. "What do you mean?"

He gestured at the crowd, which had begun to move on. "Everyone else has to pay. Why not you?"

I hated where this was going. Not only did I get in trouble in real life, but my visions had to follow suit as well. Why didn't I ever have visions of sunbathing on the coast of Fiji? Or hiking across the Isle of Skye? Or winning the Nobel Peace Prize?

I had to get out of there. The black needed to come now.

I shrugged both of them off with a wave of my hand and walked away. Maybe if I went back to that spot in the street, the black would close in around me and I'd be back in Mr Draper's class. I had never moved from the same spot in my previous visions. Maybe walking down the street made the vision last longer this time. Either way, I didn't want to experiment with the visions anymore. When I got home, I would tell Mom all about them. I'd tell her that she wouldn't have to worry, though, because once Dr Farrow finished her tests, she'd write me a prescription. Everything would be fine. I'd be normal. Claire wouldn't have a laughing stock as a sister anymore.

I made it back to the bakery and glanced at my reflection one last time. Some of my hair had fallen from my ribbon during that ridiculous struggle with Newspaper Boy. For the first time in my life, with my hair darker and my face thinner, I actually resembled Mom a little bit.

So different, yet still so very the same.

A strange nostalgic feeling tapped at my shoulder and called my name, but I shrugged it off and turned to step out into the street. Tires squealed and a woman's scream pierced the air.

Up the road to my right, a black roadster had swerved into oncoming traffic, and it was heading my way. While the other cars in the street careened out of its path, heaving to the side and almost tipping over on their tall, thin wheels, I stood rooted to the sidewalk, unable to move. I couldn't tear my eyes, or my feet, away.

As the roadster sped closer, two men hefted guns out the side windows and aimed the barrels right at me.

Only one thought crossed my mind.

Now would be a damn good time for this vision to end.

CHAPTER 5

Blue

Before I had a chance to scream or run, the blue-eyed boy slammed into me, tackling me flat on my back. Wind burst from my lungs and the back of my head smacked the concrete. A blaze of white light flashed behind my closed eyelids, but the sharp, blinding pain was the least of my worries.

A barrage of gunfire rang out, and I stiffened beneath the boy, expecting the bullets to slash through his body and pierce mine. Instead, the windows of the bakery shattered, and a thousand razor-sharp diamonds showered down on top of us. I buried my face in the boy's neck, and a scream ripped from my throat as shards of glass and brick struck the top of my head and lodged in my tangled hair.

I'd seen enough gangster movies to know what a Tommy gun sounded like, but to hear one in person, to be so close you could feel the percussion of the bullets battering inside your ribcage...

That was something else entirely.

A dozen thoughts flashed through my mind as I clung to that boy, my muscles tense and cramping. The baker

who shooed me from his window – was he dead? Were
his customers bullet-riddled, their bodies slumped on the
floor? What if the boy hadn't knocked me down? Would
I have been shot? If I died in one of my visions, did I die
in real life? Would Dr Farrow have a "perfectly logical"
explanation for that too?

It felt like ages before the gunfire stopped and the
roadster sped away, but as soon as it did, Blue Eyes pulled
me to my feet.

"Run," he shouted.

I ran.

I wasn't sure what we could possibly be running from
now that the shooting was over, but it didn't take long to
find out. The bakery exploded and I felt the pressure of the
blast on my back as it shoved me to the ground. I hit the
concrete, shielding my head with my hands.

Blue Eyes reached for me, finding my sleeve and fisting
the material in his hand. More glass and brick plummeted
down on us like thick, random raindrops. Only everything
was hot. Scorched. My skin, my clothes, the sidewalk, the air.

My ears felt thick and full, like I was wearing those
smooshy, expandable earplugs. My mouth was dry and
gritty, and I tasted the salty tang of blood on my teeth.
Every bone and muscle in my body felt cracked in half,
and I wanted nothing more than for the vision to end. I
wanted to see Mr Draper sneeze into the old handkerchief
he carried in his back pocket and ask us what the billboard
in The Great Gatsby symbolized. I tried desperately to
summon the black by squeezing my eyes shut as tightly
as I could, but my senses never left. I still felt the concrete

biting into my palms and cheek, and how difficult it was to get one good, decent deep breath.

As the thickness in my ears faded, I could make out a dog barking nearby, men arguing, a siren off in the distance, a child crying. I slowly lifted my head, the pain of hitting it on the sidewalk sending a rush of dizziness through me. I tried to look around, but everything looked tilted.

Two strong hands took hold of my arms and hauled me to my feet, holding me steady as the world shifted, then came back into focus.

"Aw, geez. You're covered in blood." Blue Eyes took my face in his leather-gloved hands, swept my hair from my eyes, and tilted my head in every direction, assessing the damage. "Can you hear what I'm saying?"

I nodded.

"What's your name?"

"Alex." My tongue was a blob of wet sand.

"That's a boy's name."

I rubbed my jaw. "Yeah. It's also a nickname."

"Short for something?"

"Duh."

"'Duh?'" He scrunched his nose. "What day is it?"

"October twenty-third. Tuesday."

He frowned. "You hit your head harder than I thought. Come on, I'll take you to Doc Stein."

Blue took two long strides, pulling me along, but I stopped and wriggled my arm free. "No, it's all right, my head's fine. I don't have a concussion."

He wrinkled his brow. "A what?"

"I'm fine. I just need to sit down." And wait for the black.

He hesitated, searching my eyes. Then he reached out and pulled a piece of glittering glass from my hair. "All right, but you tell me if you feel faint or you need to throw up."

I nodded again. He took my arm, gently this time, and led me around the corner, down a back alley to a stack of wooden crates. He pulled one down and helped me sit on it, then leaned beside me against the wall of the building. He crossed one ankle over the other.

We stayed like that for a long while, me taking in slow, shuddering breaths and staring at my boots, him rolling that piece of glass between his gloved fingers.

I just couldn't get over what happened. I'd never witnessed such public violence in my life. Back home, they said we were desensitized to violence, us modern American teenagers with our graphic movies and video games. But now I knew that wasn't exactly true, at least for me. I was so far removed from violence in my cushy home, in my cushy city where police patrolled day and night, in my cushy world where lawmakers did their best to keep criminals off the street. No amount of blood and gore on screen could've prepared me for the true horror I'd just experienced.

While I felt paralyzed with shock and fear, the boy who saved my life appeared unshaken. Maybe violence was like germs or allergies. If you exposed yourself to real violence, did you build up a tolerance against it? Were these drive-by shootings normal for him, living in a time when gangsters ruled the streets and cops craned their necks the other way?

I stole a glance at Blue. He was watching me. When my eyes met his, a memory, faint and sort of sweet, tickled the outer reaches of my mind, and I felt the unmistakable sensation of déjà vu. It made my stomach dip. I was just about to ask if I knew him from somewhere, but he spoke first. The memory fluttered away on a breeze.

"I'm sorry you had to see that," he said.

I swallowed, trying to get rid of the wet sand feeling. "Does that – this sort of thing – happen often?"

He tossed the piece of glass in the air, and we watched it hit the ground and roll away. "Not often, but it's getting worse."

"Were those men gangsters?"

He slid his back down the wall and sat on the ground, his arms propped on his knees. "They work for the Cafferelli Brothers. The Cafferellis think they own the whole damn neighborhood."

I'd never heard of the Cafferelli Brothers before. Al Capone and Bugsy Malone, sure. But Cafferelli? "Why would they attack a bakery?"

"Sloan's isn't exactly a real bakery."

"You mean it's a front? For liquor or something?"

He nodded. "Sloan tried to do business on his own, but when the Cafferellis found out, they wanted a cut. They've been at odds for months. Which is why I'm curious..." Blue lifted his handsome face up at me. A swipe of dark stubble lined his jaw. "Everyone around here knows to stay away from Sloan's. Why didn't you?"

I kept my head down and stared at my boots. Keeping my eyes focused on one spot seemed to help with the dizziness and the shock. My throbbing toe didn't matter much anymore compared to my throbbing head. "I'm not... from around here."

"Where are you from?"

"Annapolis."

"Maryland? Really? What are you doing in Chicago?"

Chicago. Was that where I was? I knew the accents sounded a little off from what I was used to on the East Coast, but I wouldn't have been able to peg it on my own. I'd never been to Chicago.

"Just visiting," I said. I pulled a few more pieces of glass from my hair. They were tinted pink with blood. I looked Blue in the eye. "Are they – those people I saw in the bakery – are they dead?"

He glanced away, which was answer enough. I played the scene back over in my mind, and there was no other way to reconcile it. If it hadn't been for Blue, I'd be dead along with them.

"You saved my life."

He gave a half-hearted shrug and said nothing. I could tell he didn't want me to make a big deal out of it. So I just sat there, pulling glass and brick from my hair, wondering how sick my subconscious must be to come up with such a horrifying vision. And what did it mean to have this hot guy come to my rescue? I bet Freud would have something to say about that one.

After a long while, Blue asked, "Feeling any better?"

The wet sand feeling seemed to have moved to my ankles and feet, making my legs heavy and somewhat still immobilized from shock, but I thought I might be able to stand. I nodded and he pushed himself to his feet. "Where are you staying? I'll walk you."

I took his outstretched hands and stood up. My muscles

shuddered and felt like oatmeal. "Shouldn't you talk to the police before we leave? Give them your statement?" I asked.

His eyebrows shot up his forehead. "Are you nuts?"

"I thought you of all people would want to. You were all Defender of Justice at the newspaper stand." I wobbled, and he gripped my elbow to steady me.

"That was different."

"Yeah, that was a newspaper and these are human lives."

"You really aren't from around here, are you? I can't go to the cops. They know me. They'll rat me out."

"So you're just going to walk away?"

"Yep. You point the way."

I stood there, staring at him, trying to think of what to do next. I guess I didn't necessarily have to talk to the police. If Dr Farrow was correct and this was just a hallucination, then I didn't have to do anything. And if I was correct and my visions showed me things that really happened in the past, then how would my witness statement make a difference? The explosion had already happened. Those people were long dead.

I didn't know what to make of it all. I just wanted to forget about it and find a way out of the vision. "I think I can manage on my own from here," I told Blue, "but thank you. For everything." I paused so he knew I was sincere, then willed my oatmeal feet to move down the alley.

Within seconds, I heard his footfalls behind me. "Wait," he said, catching up. "I'd really feel better if you let me walk you home."

What was he, a compulsive gentleman? "Really, I'll be fine."

He hurried in front of me, his hands out, making me stop. "Look, Cafferellis' thugs? They saw you. With me.

That means you're in trouble. And it won't matter to them that you're a girl."

Maybe not, but it wouldn't matter at all once the vision was over. I stepped around him. "Don't worry," I said. "The Cafferellis won't lay a finger on me."

I rounded the corner, Blue trailing my heels, but we stopped short the moment we saw the bakery scene in full. Glass covered the sidewalk in a lace veil of winking ice. Spots of blood mingled with the glass, and I remembered what Blue said. Aw, geez. You're covered in blood.

Was that my blood on the concrete?

I reached up and my fingers skimmed over a knot forming at the back of my head. Even that slight touch was enough to make me wince. Then there came a sharp ache, spreading from the knot to my temples. The kind of headache that causes you to shut out the world and lie still and silent until the sun goes down.

I tried not to think about it.

Instead, I patted my hair gently, assessing the damage. There were more glass bits, and the hair around the knot was coated in thick, sticky blood. At least that meant the wound was clotting. I could live with clotting. Healing. Even if it did feel like an ice pick stuck in my skull.

I remembered the blood I tasted in my mouth and ran my tongue over my teeth. There it was again, that salty tang. I found the source – a slice inside my lower lip. I wouldn't be able to leave that alone for a while.

As beaten up as I felt, I was glad to be alive. Especially when I saw a pair of paramedics pushing a stretcher out of Sloan's Bakery – a large body draped in a white sheet.

Another crowd had gathered, all looking on but giving the scene a wide berth. Eyes were wide. Whispers swirled behind cupped hands. A handful of policemen stepped in and out of the bakery, some asking questions, some canvassing the scene, and one standing off to the side, smoking a cigarette. He didn't wear a cap like the others. His hair was jet black and combed to the side, and he had a scar on his lip that made him look like he was mid-snarl.

My eyes lingered on him for a moment too long. He must have felt my gaze because his eyes snapped to mine. He took one last puff of smoke, flicked his cigarette over his shoulder, then started toward us.

Blue gripped my wrist. "We gotta move."

I didn't resist this time. We hurried down the sidewalk, turning left down a side street after the newspaper stand. Newspaper Boy scowled at me as we passed. Another turn down a street on our right and Blue broke into a run.

I couldn't bear the thought of running while I was so sluggish and bruised, but to my surprise, running wasn't as difficult as I thought it would be. I kept pace with Blue, even though I could tell he was sprinting at full tilt. He still had hold of my wrist, but he didn't need to pull me along. Perhaps it was adrenaline – fear that the snarl-lipped cop would catch up with us – but it didn't feel like it. It felt like something different.

It felt like running was something I did every day. And not the track and field type running, but real run-for-your-life running. I'd never run this fast or this hard in my life. Mostly because I could barely make it around the track at school without keeling over from an asthma attack. But in this body, my lungs were clear. My leg muscles were rock solid. They burned to go faster, to run harder, regardless of how battered I felt.

I felt Blue tug at my wrist, guiding me off the sidewalk and down a dusty path behind a row of tiny brick houses. When we were halfway down, he slowed to a stop, and we both bent over, our chests stretched full. We gulped and gasped until the blood in our ears stopped pounding, and we could once again hear ourselves think.

I stared down the path, my hands on my knees. "Do you think he followed us?"

"No." Blue spat on the ground. "He doesn't have to. He knows where I live."

"So why did we run?"

Blue continued on down the path, his boots scuffing at the dirt and gravel. I followed.

"Because I needed to get away. I need to think."

"About what?"

"About what all this means. About what he's going to tell the Cafferellis." Blue looked shaken. His calm exterior had given way to panting breath and darting eyes.

"So, back there," I said, pausing to gulp a breath, "when we almost got shot and blasted to bits, that didn't unnerve you one bit. But now that that cop saw you, you're white as a ghost?" I rested a hand on his forearm. He stopped walking and looked at me, but his eyes wouldn't focus. They were hazy with worry. "Tell me what you're up against here."

"What we're up against."

I nodded, letting him know I was on his side. Then his eyes found mine, and they suddenly snapped into focus.

"What did you mean when you said the Cafferellis wouldn't lay a finger on you?"

I dropped my hand from his arm. "What?"

"Are you working for them? Are you in the Family?"

"What? No. I've never heard of the Cafferellis before today."

"Then why did you say it?"

How could I explain that I would've said whatever I could to get rid of him? That I thought this whole thing would be over, that he'd disappear, if he'd just let me walk out into the street?

"I don't know." I took a step back, scrambling for something to say. At a complete loss, I tried the only thing I could think of. "I'm sorry. I don't even remember saying it." I touched my head lightly as I spoke, using my most convincing where-am-I? look.

Blue lifted an eyebrow.

"I can't really remember much of anything," I said. "Honest."

Thankfully, he bought it. His suspicion lifted, and he sighed. He pushed his gloved hands into his coat pockets. "Well, you did hit your head pretty hard back there. Bound to be a bit screwy for a while after something like that."

"Yeah, I guess." I gave a half-hearted smile.

"Come on. Let's get you cleaned up."

We walked past brick house after brick house, each with their own tiny backyard and shade trees. Wet clothes hung heavy on clotheslines, taking longer to dry in the cool fall air. Leaves shuffled and scraped against each other, and one fell to the ground every now and then as we passed, too weak to hang on.

Everything seemed gray – the sky, the buildings, the leaves, the grass – everything except Blue's red nose and cheeks. I wondered why he didn't wear a cap. His dark hair was trimmed so neatly around his ears, his eyes so chilled and blue. Wasn't he cold?

He veered off the road and into one of the backyards, and I followed after him. He stopped at a clothesline in the back and unpinned a damp rag.

"Is this your house?" I asked.

"Nah." He reached out and dabbed at a scrape on my cheek. "It's Mrs Dudek's. But she won't mind if I borrow this. I'll let her know what happened when I see her at church."

Since I didn't have a mirror, I lifted my chin and let him clean my wounds, trying not to wince. I watched cold, gray clouds slide across the sky as he wiped the blood from my skin. My eyebrows. My lips.

I'd never had a stranger be this kind to me before. This caring. Standing this close and intimate. I felt awkward, but he seemed in his element helping me. Like it was the most natural thing in the world for him.

My gaze fell from the sky to his face, and his eyes met mine for a split second. Again, my stomach dipped. I recognized him. Knew him from somewhere. Especially those blue-green eyes. Had I seen his picture in a history book? Was his face archived somewhere in my subconscious, like Dr Farrow had explained?

"I'm sorry I'm so jumpy and accusing," he said with an apologetic half-smile. He dragged the cool cloth across my neck, then dabbed at a scrape along my jaw. "It's my brother, Frank. He's got me so suspicious. He's been mixed up with the wrong guys since we were kids. For a while he was in good with the Cafferellis, then he started rubbing elbows with their rivals, the Fifth Street Gang. He'd lost a lot of money gambling, so he did a side job for them. The Cafferellis found out, and he's been their target ever since. Of course, Fifth Street took him in with open arms. Claimed they'd protect him if he joined their gang. Anything to hack off the Cafferellis. Seemed to only get Frank in more trouble. Now he owes more money than ever."

He took my wrists and turned them palm up, then dabbed the blood from my hands where I'd scraped them on the sidewalk.

"How much money does he owe?" I winced at the sting of the cloth.

He shook his head in that life's a bitch sort of way. "More than we can afford, that's for sure. I've been working two jobs. So has Ma. Just to pay his debts. And what does Frank do? He hides away with the Fifth Street boys, drinking, gambling, losing more money he doesn't have, leaving Ma and me stuck with the bill."

I frowned down at my clean, pink hands. "That's awful."

He stepped behind me and pulled the ribbon from my hair, letting it fall around my shoulders. "Yep. And now, thanks to Frank, you're tangled up in this mess too. He doesn't care who he leaves hurting in his wake. He never did."

But Blue did care. He cared enough to take the time to wipe the blood from a stranger's face and hands. There weren't too many people like him back in the real world. Maybe that was proof enough that he was a figment of my imagination.

He parted my hair carefully around the knot at the back of my head and dabbed it with the cloth. I squeezed my eyes shut, trying not to make a sound. I bit my lip. I played with the cut inside my mouth.

"It's not as bad as I thought," Blue said, stuffing the rag in his coat pocket. "You don't need stitches." He pulled a comb from his trouser pocket and combed the blood and glass and brick from my hair. He was overly gentle, like he'd never combed a girl's hair before. Despite the pain from my tender scalp, I couldn't help but smile to myself at the sweetness of it all.

Blue was as nice as they came.

When he was done, he tied my hair back into a loose tail with the ribbon, then turned me around and surveyed his work. "Much better. A few aspirin and you'll be right as rain." He tucked his comb back into his pocket with a smile.

"Thanks," I said, returning the smile. "So now what?"

"Now I've got to get home. I've got some cash saved. It might be enough to pay off Hansen."

"Hansen?"

"The cop."

"You have to bribe him?"

"Yep. Once the Cafferellis hear I was at Sloan's, I'm dead meat. They'll think Fifth Street planted me there as a lookout. See?"

I shook my head. "Not really."

"Doesn't matter. I just need to get you home. You don't need to be dragged into this any further." He looked at me expectantly. "So? Where are we headed?"

I'd been so wrapped up in Blue's life – Sloan's, the Cafferellis, Fifth Street – that I hadn't realized he'd expect me to have a life of my own. I ran through several fake stories in my head, but I wasn't sure any sounded plausible. All I really wanted was to get back to the bakery. So I played dumb again.

"I don't remember."

This time he looked genuinely concerned. "Do you remember anything at all?"

"Some things. My name. I know I'm here visiting... my aunt." Good Lord, I was bad at lying. "But I can't remember where she lives. Maybe if we go back to the bakery, it'll help me remember."

"Can't go back. At least, not while the cops are still there." He looked apologetic, but firm.

"Then what should I do?"

"You'll stick with me. We'll lay low for the rest of the day. Then I'll take you back tonight after the coast is clear."

I wanted to object, to take my chances and head back myself. But then again, what exactly did I have to hurry back home for? We seemed to be out of danger for the moment, and the idea of spending the rest of the day in Twenties Chicago was too appealing to pass up. Even if it was just a dream, it was one I didn't need to wake from just yet. The black would pull me out eventually, wouldn't it? And it would be like no time had passed at all, just like all the other visions.

We wound through the quiet neighborhood, keeping to the deserted pathways behind the homes. I had no idea which direction we were headed, but I was content to fall in stride beside Blue and listen to the cadence and velvet tone of his voice as he told me about his town. It was a

Polish neighborhood – his father, Benedykt, came over from Poland and settled there when he was a teenager. That's where he met Blue's mom, Helena, and raised Blue and Frank until a few years ago, when he died from the Spanish Influenza. I told Blue I was sorry, that I couldn't imagine losing a parent. He frowned and shrugged and said he was just happy his father never saw the kind of a man Frank had become. Then he cleared his throat and moved on to a different subject.

Even though Blue was American born with a slight Chicago accent, he could speak Polish fluently. He spoke a bit to me, but I couldn't decipher any of it, even if I tried. And when I attempted to pronounce a few of the words myself, I just ended up laughing. They sounded so strange on my tongue. Even Blue's real name, which I found out was Micolaj Piasecki, was hard to get right. He told me Micolaj was just the Polish form of Nicholas, and with a wink and a smile he said I could call him Nick.

Nick.

So now he had a name. But I still preferred the nickname I'd given him. I'd have to warm up to Nick.

His family was Catholic, and he showed me the cathedral where they attended mass. It was a beautiful building, the kind I'd only seen in movies or history books. There was a gothic look to it, stalwart and strong, like nothing could sway the faith held inside. He told me we'd come back for a look inside later, after we stopped by his house for some aspirin for my head.

I was actually excited to see Blue's house. (I mean Nick's house. Nick's. That would take some getting used to.) I wanted to see what it was like in a normal Twenties home.

And I couldn't wait to meet his mom, whom he talked about like she was his hero. I wanted to see where he grew up, where he went to school, and I wanted to meet Old Man Nowicki, who ran the deli where he worked as a delivery boy.

But I didn't make it that far.

We came to another busy street, just like the one near the bakery. Blue said his apartment was only three blocks away. The buildings were taller in this part of the neighborhood, some squat, some so narrow they looked like they might topple over. Every shop had an awning, and they stretched down the street as far as the eye could see, one of every color. Old Fords and Oldsmobiles puttered past while other cars sat parked this way and that along the sidewalk. (I guessed there weren't many parking laws back then.) Women ushered their children along, pulling them from the front window of a candy store. A group of boys ran past, a dog at their heels along for the fun.

It all seemed so idyllic. So peaceful and slow-paced. But I was learning fairly quickly that those idyllic moments could be swept away in a flash, like a wink of sun slicing off the side of a Model T.

"Shit."

Out of nowhere, Blue seized my elbow, his thumb digging in, and steered me down an alley on our right. When he saw the alley was closed off by a fence halfway down, chained and padlocked shut, he added, "Shit, shit, shit."

"What is it?" I whipped my head around, but didn't see anything out of the ordinary.

He kept pushing me toward the fence at the end of the alley, his expression grim. "Hide," he said, giving me a push in the direction of a rusted-out dumpster.

"Behind it?" "No, inside. Quick."

He wore the same look he had when we ran from Hansen, so I obeyed. I pulled myself up and threw a leg over the edge. I only had time to glance at the mound of garbage I was about to fall onto before Blue took the liberty to flip me over the rest of the way. I landed hard on an uneven surface of broken crates, empty milk bottles, and something gooey that smelled like rotten bananas and diapers.

"Not a word," he whispered. I heard his boots scuff the brick stones as he stepped away from the dumpster. I could tell he had his back to me. "Don't show yourself. Don't even move. No matter what happens to me, no matter what you hear, don't move. Promise me."

"I promise," I said, so soft I almost didn't hear it myself.

A thick lump of fear lodged in my throat. I couldn't swallow. I couldn't breathe. I simply huddled on that mound of garbage, so rigid my muscles trembled, staring out a small hole in the corner of the dumpster, eaten away by rust. I saw brick stones, but I couldn't see Blue.

Then I heard them.

More footsteps, slow and purposeful, making their way down the alley toward us. My heart seized, but the blood still thumped through my head like a bass drum.

"Well, lookie here, fellas," came a man's voice. "It's Nicky boy. Just the fellah we wanted to see."

I cringed at the bright joy in the man's tone. I cringed at the laughter of his cohorts that followed. There had to be half a dozen of them.

They had to be the Cafferelli thugs.

I shifted silently in my hideaway and peered out the hole at a different angle. I saw him – the leader of the pack. Twice the size of Blue, tall, broad-shouldered, black hair, dark circles under his dark eyes, and a nose that looked like it had been broken one too many times. He wore trousers with suspenders, a white undershirt, and an unbuttoned wool coat. The others were dressed in similar clothes. They didn't look as menacing as modern street thugs, but something about the hungry, sadistic looks on their faces told me they were just as dangerous.

I still couldn't see Blue, but I heard him reply. "Loogie."

I guessed that was the leader's name.

"Hansen said he saw you at Sloan's today," said Loogie. "What were you doing up there, Nicky boy? Long way from home."

"Just making a delivery for Old Man Nowicki."

"Is that so?" Loogie took a few steps forward. His lips stretched wide across crooked teeth. "Wrong place, wrong time?"

"That's right."

He took another step closer. He rubbed his knuckles with his other hand, warming up his fist. "So you weren't keeping an eye out for Sloan? He didn't pay you to keep watch?"

Blue was silent. I shifted again, trying to get a look at his face. He wouldn't have taken a job for Sloan or any other gangster, no matter how much money his brother owed. Blue was too good. I knew it in my gut.

So why was he so quiet?

Loogie stepped all the way up to Blue, out of my eyesight. The others moved in closer. I chewed on my lip.

"You didn't do a very good job, Nicky boy," Loogie said. "Sloan pays you to watch his back, and what do you do in return? You let him bleed to death." He chuckled, his laughter light as foam. "One would think you were on our side."

"If it were up to me," Blue said, teeth clenched, "I'd let the whole lot of you bleed to death."

I heard one of the guys spit. Maybe it was Loogie. Maybe that's how he got his nickname.

"Boys," said Loogie, "I think we have ourselves a threat."

They all moved out of my eyesight, closing in around Blue like a pack of wolves. Then I heard the first blow, sounding like a low thump right in the gut. Blue groaned. I craned my neck to see better through the rusted hole, and I watched as the barrage came. A few loud thwacks to the jaw. Several more fists to the gut. Blue's face turned reddish-purple. Spittle hung from his bottom lip.

If Blue had been hired to keep watch for Sloan, he'd given it all up to save my life instead. He'd traded Sloan's life for mine. I couldn't watch him get beaten to a pulp after he'd risked his life for me. I had to stop it.

My body snapped into action, quick, like it had been itching for it the whole time. I reached down and curled my fingers around a broken milk bottle. I pushed myself up, the garbage beneath me shifting with a great deal of noise. I leaned over the edge of the dumpster and hauled myself over the side, landing somewhat clumsily on the balls of my feet. All six of Cafferellis' thugs jolted around, one freezing mid-kick. Blue was on the ground, clutching at his ribs. Blood trailed from his nose. It dripped on the brick stones.

"What have we here?" Loogie said, his startled expression morphing into a grin. He rose up from kneeling beside Blue and ran a hand through his glossy black hair. His eyes slid over me. His lips stretched thin, almost white.

Back home, I would've run for my life if I'd come face-to-face with a guy like him in an alley. But in this body, I wasn't scared.

Why the hell wasn't I scared?

"Attack dogs are all well and good, Nicky boy," said Loogie, "but you should ask for your money back. This one's a poodle." The others laughed as they slinked toward me.

Six to one. I didn't know a damn thing about fighting, but I knew those weren't good odds. For a split second I remembered the pepper spray Dad always tried to get me to take to school. The pepper spray I kept in my work bench drawer at home because I thought it was stupid.

Yeah. Not anymore.

Blue shot me the fiercest look. I knew he wanted me to run – and if I had, I could've probably outrun them in this body – but my feet were planted. And my fists craved contact.

It was a wild feeling, oddly overpowering, like before when I discovered I could run like an Olympic athlete. It was like this body had fought its way through scrapes like this many times over. Like it had trained for this very moment. I was hungry for a fight, and somehow I knew I could hold my own.

I lunged forward to meet them. I sliced the broken glass bottle across the chest of the guy closest to me, the short one with his front teeth missing, then swept his feet out from under him. He clawed at me to keep his balance, but I shouldered him off. Down he went, eyes wide. He clutched at the smear of blood on his shirtfront.

Thick fingers grabbed hold of me – they were everywhere, grappling, pinching, squeezing. I kicked and swung the bottle, slicing flesh every chance I could, but there were too many of them. I was tangled and twisted, caught in a net of groping hands. They swore at me. Called me a bearcat and other names I won't dare repeat.

By that time Blue was at my side, swinging punches, hacking through the net to free me. But even though I felt trapped, I never felt defeated. I kept going, lashing out like a cornered badger. I buried the bottle in one guy's stomach, then crushed his nose with the back of my elbow. I landed a fist in another guy's eye.

I was feral. I was strong. I couldn't be stopped.

Until I heard the cock of a pistol.

That unmistakable click.

I froze. So did Blue. The mouth of the gun kissed the stubble on Blue's jaw, right below his ear. I dropped the milk bottle and raised my hands in surrender, and Loogie nodded at his boys to grab me.

They were bruised and bleeding, but they seized my arms anyway and pulled me back. My eyes never left Blue's. A stream of blood traced a red line down the side of his face from a gash above his temple. His bottom lip was swollen and purple. He still clutched at his ribs. A violent shudder tore through him, like it was the dead of winter.

For me, fire blazed through my body. The need for revenge coursed through my veins. Blue had saved my life and here I was, unable to save his. A million attack plans rushed through my head, but none were a match for a bullet.

Loogie scrubbed a hand over his face, wiping blood and sweat from his eyes. He breathed in and out of his nose like a bull. "I was going to let you off with a few bruises, Nicky boy. Maybe a few broken ribs. But I think this calls for something more permanent."

He jerked his head at the toothless guy, who let go of my arm and loped over to Blue. He pulled a knife from his boot, then he and Loogie pushed Blue down to his knees.

"Giuseppe said to make sure you don't squeal about what you saw at Sloan's." Loogie grabbed Blue's hair and yanked his head back. He moved the gun to Blue's chest. "I think that can be arranged. Open his mouth, Teeth."

The guy called Teeth pulled on Blue's jaw, and Blue struggled to keep his lips shut.

"No use fighting it," said Loogie. "He'll cut your mouth open if he has to."

Teeth dug his fingernails into Blue's mouth, prying until his jaw started to open.

"No," I screamed. I wrestled against the arms that held me back. They were like iron shackles, unyielding. "No. Please."

Teeth angled the knife into Blue's mouth, and Blue sucked in a ragged breath around the blade. My heart collided against my ribs.

I couldn't let this happen.

I swung my head to the side with all my might, smacking one of the guys in the nose. He let out a yell, and the moment he dropped my arm to cover his face with his hands, I took my chance. With two less guys holding me back, I had enough momentum to twist my way free.

I flung myself at Teeth, aiming at his waist, and tackled him to the ground. The knife clattered on the brick stones and spun out of reach. I drew back my fist, ready to pummel Teeth's face into the pavement, when I heard it.

The gun shot.

Then everything went black.

CHAPTER 6

The Most Unkindest Cut of All

Within seconds, light and sound rushes in around me, and I'm back in Mr Draper's class, sitting at my desk. All that emotion, all that adrenaline still flows through me.

I can't help it. I swear. Out loud.

And it isn't pretty.

Mr Draper stops lecturing and stares at me, his arms still in the air like he's conducting a symphony. All eyes in the class turn to me. Tabitha's giggle comes from the back of the room, accompanied by her trademark, "Freak." Someone else, I think it was Robbie Duncan, calls me Wayspaz. I hear Jensen tell them both to shut up.

I barely take time to notice.

With one sweep of my arm, my books topple into my backpack, and I'm out the door before Mr Draper can find the words to object. I sprint down the hall and burst out the double doors to the parking lot, stopping only when I realize I have no transportation home.

But home isn't where I need to be. I need to be back in Chicago. Now.

I hurry from the school grounds before a teacher tries to wrangle me back inside. I have to find a place to be alone – a place to hide where no one can bother me. I can't be distracted – I have to find my way back to Blue. Even if it is just a stupid hallucination, there's no way I can just let it go now. Just forget everything that happened. I have to know if he got shot.

If I caused him to get shot.

Halfway back to my house I remember there's an abandoned auto garage a few blocks ahead. The kind that looks like an old gas station, with rusted out pumps in front and weeds reaching up through cracks in the pavement. I pass it every day on the way to school, and every day there seems to be more amateur graffiti painted on the building's faded bricks or another window broken out.

Broken windows mean I can get inside.

Four more blocks and I'm there, jogging right up to the overhead garage doors. Several glass panes at the bottom are busted out. I toss my backpack inside and crawl in, taking care not to snag my clothes on the jagged frame.

Inside, shafts of light spill across an empty concrete floor, stained almost black from years of oil and grease and grime. A rodent scurries behind a stack of spiderweb-covered boxes in the corner, swollen from water damage. Two pigeons flutter and coo at me from a nest in the rafters. More graffiti covers the walls like wallpaper, each angsty statement vying for center position. I smile when I see For a good time call scrawled above Tabitha's name and number.

I drop my backpack against the wall under Tabitha's number, and it echoes throughout the vacant room. I sit beside it, resting my back against the cool concrete block wall.

It's so quiet. I only hear the whoosh of the occasional passing car, the rustling of the pigeons above me, and the random squeak of the old JOHNSON'S AUTO sign outside.

I close my eyes and tip my head back against the wall, only to feel a sharp pain when I do. My hand flies to the back of my head, right to that blasted bruised knot beneath my ponytail. It's smaller than in my vision, but it's there. A little bit of dried blood is tangled in my hair. I feel my ribs for more bruises and every last one is accounted for. The slice inside my lip still gives off that salty tang. Even my right fist aches. Not broken – I can flex it – but the longer I focus on it, the more it hurts. Luckily I didn't take a fist or elbow to the face. I can't imagine having to explain that to Mom and Dad. A few bruises I can hide. A busted jaw? Not so much.

I slam the fist that doesn't hurt onto the floor. It all felt so real. It had to be real. It couldn't be a hallucination. It was like I traveled back in time, set foot in a different decade, breathed 1927 air, then brought all the evidence back with me.

I close my eyes and try to find my way back to Blue.
Nick.

I picture the alley, Loogie's thin, stretched lips, Nick's blue-green eyes, the feel of the broken milk bottle in my hand. I summon all the sights, smells, and sensations and try to bring on déjà vu, but it doesn't work. I'm still sitting in the garage beneath Tabitha's number.

I stand and go through the motions of the fight. I can feel the grubby hands of the thugs on me. I kick and spin and slice and punch until I'm sweaty, not even caring if I bring on an asthma attack. But when I open my eyes, I'm still in the garage. The pigeons are staring at me. And I feel like a complete idiot.

My knees meet the floor. I pull my sleeves over my palms and swipe at the beginnings of tears. I close my eyes and hide in the darkness of my sleeves, sniffling. There's only ever been one thing I've seriously prayed for on my own, and the weaker Audrey gets, the more I wonder if God even gives a damn about my prayers. But praying is my last resort. I don't know what else to do.

Please send me back. I have to know what happened to Blue. I have to know if he's all right. If it was real, if there was any truth to my vision at all, send me back. Please.

I lower my forehead to the cool concrete. It smells like motor oil. I squeeze my eyelids tight until spots dance before me, almost as if that will make my prayer more powerful. I remain there, bowed down, tears welling, until my aching body demands relief.

At last I sit up and open my eyes to garage and graffiti. More tears blur my vision. Vibrant colors and jagged shapes swim together.

"I'm not going back," I whisper to the pigeons.

I heave my backpack over my shoulder and trudge toward the garage door. Once home, I'll search for Nick's name online. I'll find out if October 21, 1927 really was a Friday. I'll look up the Cafferelli Brothers. I won't stop looking for answers.

A breeze kicks up outside and swirls in through the broken windows smelling of fish and chips from the restaurant across the street. An old, weathered yellow flyer taped to the graffitied wall across from me lifts and rattles in the gust then settles again. I glance at the two bold words printed across the top.

I gasp.

RISTORANTE CAFFERELLI

I rip the flyer from the wall. It's an advertisement for an Italian place in the historic district. But it's not just the name that takes me by surprise. It's what's written in black Sharpie underneath.

Alex,

If you're looking for answers, I've got a few. Come have a chat with me. I'll be the old codger in the Orioles cap, eating a cannoli. (They have really good cannoli here.)

    Porter

In Which I Meet Someone Even More Crazy Than Me

I step off the city bus downtown and hitch my backpack higher on my shoulder. I haven't been to the historic district in a while, and I realize how much I miss the cute folksy shops all decked out for Halloween. The smell of cinnamon and cloves from a candle shop mingles with the briny sea air. A dozen seagulls squawk at me and half hop, half fly out of my way as I cut across a drugstore parking lot.

I'm not sure what I'm doing, following a cryptic flyer to meet some old guy I don't know. I know a hundred different ways this meeting could take a turn for the worse, but then again, I don't think anything could be as scary or dangerous as what I've just gone through in my vision. And putting myself in that situation was involuntary.

Still, I wish I had Dad's pepper spray.

Ristorante Cafferelli is quaint and bright, with a wall of windows overlooking the Bay. Murals of grape-studded vineyards cover stuccoed walls, and red and white checkered tablecloths drape over small square tables. The scent of fresh baked bread and sautéed garlic wafts out from the kitchen.

I spot the worn, orange Orioles cap right away. The man called Porter sits over by the windows, blowing steam from a wide mug of coffee he holds in both hands. He looks to be in his sixties – late sixties? – but fit for his age with only a few wrinkles. He wears jeans, a faded black polo, and slip-on boat shoes. White stubble dots his cheeks and chin, and a bit of short white hair peeks out from underneath his cap around his ears. He's the only customer in the place.

I walk right up to him despite every instinct telling me not to. I guess my need for answers, whatever they may be, outweighs all the lectures Dad gave me as a child.

"Are you Porter?"

He looks up, a little startled at first. Then he clears his throat and sets his mug down. "I am."

"I'm Alex."

He leans back in his chair and folds his hands on the table. "Of course you are." He pauses, staring at me. "How did you know how to find me?"

I drop the flyer in front of him and point at it. "Didn't you write that?"

He leans forward to look, then a small, knowing smile breaks across his lips. "Not yet. But I guess I will. Soon."

Not yet? My brow crinkles. "How did you know I'd be at Johnson's Auto Garage? Do I know you?"

"Mmm," he says with a slight nod, looking down at his mug. He turns it slowly around in his hands. "But it's been a very long time since we last spoke."

He looks up at me then, and I feel that same nostalgia tugging at me like needle and thread. The same feeling I got when Blue looked me in the eye. There's something about this man I recognize. Something in the way his laugh lines surround his sad, watery eyes, or the way he looks so very tired and yet so very alive. But the memory is too transparent to grasp in full.

It hurts my head too much to think about it.

He gestures to the seat across from him. "Why don't you sit down? I suppose you came for answers, like the flyer reads, and that's what I'll give you. If you want them."

I sit only because I feel like I know him from somewhere, even if the memory is a wisp of candle smoke. It's not like I'm not scared, because I am. Mostly because I can't remember if the memories I have of him are good or bad. All I know is they're there, somewhere. Eluding me. Just like everything else having to do with the visions.

Porter watches me with kind eyes and a smile that almost seems paternal. It's the same look I've seen on Pops' face when I catch him watching me from across the dinner table. The silent pride of a grandfather.

"You look good," Porter says. "All grown up." He adds that part like it's some kind of inside joke.

I don't get it.

"Let me buy you a drink," he says. He flags down a dark-haired waitress. "Is Chianti still your favorite?"

I wrinkle my nose. "I'm seventeen."

He laughs. "True. And you may not like it in this body anyway. The taste buds are always different."

The waitress approaches, and Porter orders me a cappuccino. I don't object, even though I don't like coffee. I'm too curious about what he means by *in this body*.

"What would you like to know first?" He speaks and moves like a gentleman straight out of the classic films I watch with Mom and Gran, very formal and proper, although he doesn't exactly look like one in his jeans and ball cap. His clothes look out of place, almost like he's wearing a disguise.

I think about his question for a moment, pulling the sleeves of my army-green parka over my wrists and gripping them under the table. I have no idea where to begin, and I'm cautious about saying too much at first. I'm still not convinced the flyer was meant for me.

The waitress sets the cappuccino in front of me. The foam is swirled into a peace symbol on top.

Porter slides his half-eaten cannoli toward me. "They really do have the best cannoli in town." He nods at it, insisting I finish it. But I'm too nervous to think about food.

"Why don't I talk and you eat?" he says, nudging the cannoli again. "Perhaps I'll start with the visions. I assume they are why you're here, yes?"

I sit up at attention. "How do you know about the visions?"

"You've always had them. And the dried blood in your hair was a tip off. You've just come back from one, haven't you?"

My hand flies to the knot on the back of my head, the surprise clear on my face.

"I'm sorry you got hurt," he says. "It can be such a dangerous journey, no matter how old you are or how much experience you have."

I don't even try to figure out what that means. "What are they?" I say. "The visions?" The words tumble out, my voice sounding like gravel.

"They're a side effect. Of your ability. No other Descender has them, though. Only you."

"Descender?"

"A Descender is someone who descends to the past. That is your ability."

"You mean, by imagining it? Someone who can visualize the past in their mind?"

"No. I mean someone who can travel to the past by means of their soul."

I let out a puff of air. "What, like time travel?"

"You say it like it's science fiction, and yet you've known they weren't just visions for years now, haven't you?" He leans forward, his pale eyes locked on mine. "You've known on some level ever since Jamestown."

My mouth drops. "How did you know about Jamestown?" I place my fists on the checkered tablecloth. "Have you been talking to Dr Farrow? Is this one of her tests?"

"Doctor who?"

"The idiotic psychiatrist from AIDA who thinks I have schizophrenia."

"Ah, yes. The one you spilled all your secrets to." He cocks a white eyebrow at me. "You were supposed to come to me when you were ready for answers, you know, not some doctor. And by all means not someone who works for AIDA."

"How was I supposed to know that? I don't even know you."

Porter waves a hand like it's no big deal. "Doesn't matter now. I've taken care of it. No harm done. I just wish you would've paid attention to the signs. I thought you'd be smarter than that."

"What signs?"

His brow knits together again, and he gives me the same look most people give Audrey when they find out she has cancer.

Pity.

"I suppose you didn't know what they were," he says. "Your memory issues must still persist, despite your IQ. I guess I underestimated your defect. It really is quite severe, as far as Descenders go."

I heave a sigh. I'm getting tired of his riddles and nonsense. "I didn't come here to be reminded of how much of a freak I am. I get enough of that at school. So if you don't have any answers for me..." I grab my backpack to leave.

"Oh, no, Alex, I'm sorry." He stretches a hand toward me, and I pause when I hear the sincerity in his voice. "I didn't mean to offend you. I'm going too fast, and I realize I'm not making much sense. I don't blame you for wanting to leave." He lowers his hand and his voice softens. "I must have practiced what I'd say to you a thousand times, and here I am getting it all wrong. I apologize, truly. What do you say I start over? From the beginning?"

I frown and drop my backpack at my feet. Waiting.

It's not like I would've left anyway. I don't know if I could walk away from this guy now, even if he is frustrating. He's the first person to give me answers that line up with what I already believe – that my visions aren't hallucinations. He's the first person to give me validation, no matter how confusing he's been so far. And if he knows about the visions, then he might know how I can get back to Blue.

"What do you know about the AIDA Institute?" he asks.

I sigh through my nose. It's the same sassy sigh Mom grounds me for when I use it on her. "What everyone knows. They're the biggest cancer research institute in the world."

"Right. But cancer research isn't all they do."

"I know. They have tons of different divisions. They're like an organization of superheroes – the best doctors, researchers, scientists, archeologists – all working to find cures, end world hunger, create a better environment. They're 'saving the world, one person at a time.'" I add that last part, recalling AIDA's popular slogan I've heard hundreds of times, but I say it with a bit of a bite to it. "I should know. My parents are two of those heroes. They joined the AIDA Corps when they were in college. They've been working for AIDA ever since."

"I know. That's why I chose them." When I look at Porter like he's crazy for what feels like the millionth time, he says, "Give me ten minutes. If I haven't answered all your questions by then, you can go. And you'll never see me again in this lifetime. I promise."

CHAPTER 7

Answers. Sort Of.

Porter folds and unfolds his hands on the table. His forearms are covered in freckles and thick white hair. He rubs the pinky knuckle of one hand with the thumb of his other.

I take a sip of my cappuccino, but it's gone cold.

It tastes just as disgusting as I remember.

Porter takes a deep breath, then begins. "AIDA was founded in the Sixties. Do you know who the founders were?"

I think back to my recent meeting with Dr Farrow, to the portrait of Durham Gesh hanging on her office wall, with those eyes, condescending and cold. I pull my sleeves down over my wrists again. "I thought there was only one founder. Durham Gesh. His portrait's everywhere at AIDA Headquarters. I've seen it a hundred times. He's famous. Everyone loves him. They talk about him like he's a saint. Supposedly he saved thousands of lives or something back in the day."

"That's right," Porter says. "Durham Gesh was one of the founders. Some would say he is the only founder. He was the face of the Institute. He did all the socializing and networking and schmoozing. But there were two founders of AIDA. Two very brilliant, very ambitious scientists. One was Gesh, the other was Iver Flemming."

"Never heard of him."

"That's not surprising. He was a quiet man who kept to himself, content to work in the background and stay out of the spotlight. Very few people know of his involvement with AIDA. He was always like that, even when Gesh met him at a private primary school in Denmark. Gesh was the charismatic, outgoing one, while Flemming was the studious one holed up in his dormitory with his nose in a book. But they had similar interests, similar IQs, so they became friends and remained friends all throughout medical school. Shortly after they graduated, they founded an organization devoted to the cure of cancer and other terminal illnesses. They were visionaries. Luminaries. Throughout the next twenty years, they cured countless diseases, even a few cancers, which attracted the attention of the media and philanthropists. People came from all around to be treated at AIDA. Everyone believed they were geniuses. There was no other explanation for their success rate. And they were geniuses. But there was more to it than that. They had an upper hand. A secret weapon no one else knew about. They could travel back in time."

"You mean they had visions? Like me?" I push my glasses up my nose and lean forward. I rest my elbows on the table.

"No, no visions. Only you have those. But they could descend to any time period they wished, just like you can.

They used their ability to their ultimate advantage. They could go back and save invaluable research that had been lost or destroyed. They could talk to other scientists and medicine men and gain their ancient knowledge. They could move floppy disks, documents, even ancient scrolls to secret locations, then come back to retrieve them when they returned to the present time. Sort of like a time capsule. They gained knowledge no other scientist or doctor had access to, and they healed thousands by forging new roads in medicine. Can you see how that ability could be used to save the world?"

Theoretically, yes, I can see it. The idea of traveling back in time to recover knowledge that had been lost sends shivers through me. All the information lost during the Dark Ages could be restored. All the mysteries throughout history could be explained. Ancient treasures uncovered. The reason for the disappearance of certain civilizations revealed.

Maybe even the information Mom needs to perfect Audrey's cure could be handed to her on a silver platter.

But the logic is still fuzzy. "How did they travel?"

"By accessing Limbo."

"Limbo? Like Dante's Limbo?"

Porter's eyes light up like he's impressed. "Exactly, yes. The Isle of the Blessed. Elysium. Abraham's Bosom. Barzakh. They're all referring to the same place. Everyone passes through Limbo on their way to Afterlife when they die, but only a few can access Limbo while still alive. Gesh discovered how to do it as a child. He later taught Flemming." He levels his eyes at me. "And then he taught you."

A chill washes over me. Goosebumps rise and salute on the back of my arms. "How could he have taught me? I've never met him before in my life."

"You have. You just don't remember."

I narrow my eyes at Porter. "Right. Like I don't remember meeting you?"

"Yes. Exactly."

I stare at him for a moment longer, but he doesn't elaborate. I want to know what he means, but there's something else I want to know about even more. "Is Limbo the 'black'?" I ask, recalling the deep darkness that envelopes me before my visions.

"Yes, the black is part of it. But there is so much more to it than that." He tilts his head to the side. "Have you figured out how to access Limbo on your own yet?"

I frown down at my cold cappuccino. "No. I just get yanked into the black randomly, whether I want to or not."

"So you haven't figured out what triggers the pull?"

I look up at him. Was there a trigger? "I used to think it was déjà vu, but I disproved that theory a long time ago."

Porter cracks the smallest grin at the corner of his mouth. He reaches into his jeans pocket, pulls something out, and sets it on the table between us. It's a pure white stone the size of a quarter, smooth and round, shaped like an M&M. "Do you know what this is?"

"It's a game piece," I blurt out without thinking. Then, once I realize what I said, I cover my mouth with my hands. It wasn't a guess. I know it's a game piece, but I've never seen one like it in my life. Not even in my visions.

Porter says, "Do you remember what the game is called?"

"Polygon," I whisper through my fingers.

Porter's grin widens, and he nods. "Exactly right."

How do I know the name of a game I've never played?

He slides the game piece closer to me, and I reach out to touch it. Someone carved thin letters on both sides of its smooth surface. LVI on one side, IV on the other. As I rub my fingers across the engraved letters, trying to figure out what they mean – are they Roman numerals? – my mind is suddenly flooded with memories. The sights and sounds of the restaurant fade away as thousands of images shuffle before me. Hundreds of faces I've never seen before, places I've never been, sounds I've never heard; they all flurry around me, each image as brief as a camera flash, gone before I can fully examine it.

Then one single image, clearer than the others, comes into focus: I'm a little girl with long blonde braids, sitting at a little white table in a little white room. I'm playing Polygon with a little blond boy with dark brown eyes behind wire-rimmed glasses. I place a white stone on the game board, then he places a black stone next to mine. He bursts out laughing because it's the first time he's ever beaten me at this game. He pumps a fist into the air and shouts in a language I've never heard before, "Til sidst, vinder jeg!" But I understand his words perfectly. Finally, I win.

I can't explain how I know this little boy, why my memory of him is so strong, how I can understand his language, or why I have that niggling feeling like I've known Porter my entire life. All I know is that I've never felt such strong déjà vu before. The letters carved on the game piece, the way the light winks off the little boy's wire-rimmed glasses, the way Porter rubs his pinky knuckle with this thumb – it all combines and swells and swirls until the black swallows me like a tidal wave, and I am plunged into the dark.

Limbo

This time, the light doesn't rush in and flood my senses. I remain in the black. As silent as death.

No breath, no sound, no taste, no touch.

Just black.

Lonely, lonely black.

It feels like hours, days, even weeks pass, staring into that yawning black, feeling nothing but nothing itself, before I finally see something in the far distance. A blue-white flicker of light, like the guttering flame from a match. Hauntingly faint. So faint I can't tell if I'm really seeing it at all. Perhaps it's just wishful thinking.

Then, a voice.

"I'll just let you settle in, shall I?"

Porter stands next to me in the dark. I can make out his polo, jeans, and ball cap, but only just, as though he's illuminated by the faintest glow of a crescent moon. Has he been there the whole time?

"It's a bit disorienting at first," he says. "But you'll get used to it."

I look down and realize I have a body too, faintly lit. I'm still wearing my nerd glasses, my army-green parka, jeans, and Gran's old flowery scarf from the Seventies, but my body doesn't work quite right. I feel sluggish and willowy, and, at the same time, like I'm not there at all. "Why are you still wearing your cap?" I say, gesturing to it. "Have our bodies left the restaurant?"

"No, only our souls have left." He taps his cap with his finger. "My cap isn't really here. You're seeing my soul through a perception filter. My body. Your body. You see what you think our souls should look like. You hear my voice as you recall it in the restaurant."

I gape back at him in awe. The thought is too profound to grasp. "What's happening to our bodies right now? Are we slumped over at the table?"

"No," he says with a chuckle. "Time does not pass in Base Life while our souls are in Limbo. Our time spent here will be but a fraction of a second there."

"So I'll return to the same time I left? Just like every other time I have a vision?"

He nods, and I turn my gaze back to the faint flicker of light in the distance. "And the light? Is that just my perception too?"

"No, the light is real. That's where we're headed. That region of Limbo is called Polestar. That's where every soul passes through on its way to Afterlife."

I expect to get a chill when he says that, an overpowering sensation of wonder, but my body remains somewhat unresponsive. I look down at my hands, turning them front to back, back to front, slowly. They look translucent. I lift a foot, then I lift the other. It feels like I'm pulling my shoes from mud. I expect to hear the slurp of suction, but there's no sound.

"Like I said, you'll get used to it," he says. "It takes a lot of practice, but soon you'll be bounding around this place like a young colt. Just like you used to."

I frown because he keeps saying confusing things like that. "What do you mean, 'just like I used to'?"

He opens his mouth to reply, but hesitates. He rubs his pinky knuckle. "I'll... get to that part soon enough. For now, you need to know where we are." He stretches his arms out wide. "This region of Limbo is called Eremus. It means wasteland or wilderness. It surrounds Polestar on all sides. It's very easy to get lost out here, so be careful. When in doubt, just look for Polestar and head in that direction."

"How did I get here? I mean, how did I stop here, in Limbo?"

"You stepped through."

"Stepped through what?"

He stands up straighter, like Mr Draper when he's about to lecture. "We are every one of us connected to Limbo at all times. Just as we are connected to Life, we are connected to Death. That connection is Limbo. Most souls have such faint connections to Limbo that they don't even recognize it's there. When their bodies die, they hardly see Limbo as their souls pass through. It is but a blink on their journey to Afterlife. But there are a rare few who have powerful, intense connections to Limbo. When they pass through, they see it in its entirety. The full spectrum, from one end to the other. You and I, we are in the latter group. Our connections to Limbo are so powerful, so constant, we can simply step into it and walk around, as easy as stepping through a door."

"But how do you find the door?"

"The door is déjà vu, just as you suspected. Everyone experiences it, but it's stronger for people like you and I. It's that otherworldly pull toward Limbo, tugging at your edges. When you experience déjà vu, you let go of Earth, of gravity, of all worldly things. You let the current pull you, like you're caught in a net. That's how you step through."

I know exactly what he means. It's the pull into the black, that involuntary tug I've felt during my visions. When I saw the Polygon game piece and all those memories came swirling in around me, I felt it full force. I've tried fighting it before, especially the time I was in Sunday School with Jensen, but it was no use. The pull was too strong. Too enticing, even.

"So that's why you gave me the game piece," I say. "To trigger my déjà vu."

He nods. "The game piece is yours. I gave it to you a long time ago, when I taught you how to play Polygon. You've used it as a sort of talisman ever since, a sort of key to access Limbo."

"But why would I want to access Limbo at all?"

"Because this is only the beginning. You are merely standing on the porch steps. From here, you can go anywhere."

Anywhere.

I held the word in my hands like treasure. Anywhere meant Chicago. It meant finding a way back to Blue.

Porter takes my hand, which feels like light pressure at first, nothing more. Then the pressure builds, steadier and steadier, weighing heavy on my chest. It feels like a wide elastic band has wrapped around me, tightening until I can't move. I can't breathe.

It feels like my soul is having an asthma attack.

I gulp and gasp but nothing fills my lungs. I try to squeeze Porter's hand, to let him know I'm drowning where I stand, when I hear his voice in my ear again.

"You don't have to breathe, Alex. Stop fighting. Let go."

But I can't. I don't know how. The elastic band pulls tighter and tighter. My ribs collapse inward. My lungs can't expand.

"You don't have lungs," Porter says. "You don't need air."

The band stretches and pulls and presses, so tight it finally snaps.

A flood of sensation rushes over me like I'm caught in a wind tunnel. My skin, or what I perceive as my skin, feels like it's being suctioned from my body. Pulled in every direction. My hair whips out of my ponytail and tangles around my face. My scarf tugs at my neck, threatening to strangle me.

Then, suddenly, everything stops.

The Forest of Lights

I'm standing beside Porter in the black as though nothing happened, but we've moved. We're no longer in the empty stretches of Eremus. He lifts a hand to the view stretched out before us and says, "Welcome to Polestar."

For the first time in Limbo, I can see the shapes and shadows of an organic landscape. It reminds me of standing in one of Pops' farm fields in the middle of the night with only a full moon to light the way. There are jagged mountain peaks in the distance. Directly ahead, the faint silhouette of a ruined castle rests on a hill, surrounded by rolling plains.

Then, all around us, is the forest of lights.

Trees tower over us, the tallest I've ever seen, stretching on into the distance. And in between them, everywhere I look, there are shafts of faint, blue-white light, stretching from ground to sky, filling the valleys and plains. Some are as thin as wisps of smoke, others are as thick as the tree trunks. They move and sway as though rustled by a breeze. As though alive. They fade in and out, the light stronger one moment, then softer the next, rippling and winking amid the black and the trees. They are the color of white-hot fire. Of lightning. Above us, the sky is dotted with flickering blue-white stars. At our feet, tiny wisps of light curl around each blade of grass.

"What are they?" I hear myself say.

I find it impossible to look away from the forest of lights. It's the most beautiful, ethereal, and compelling sight I have ever beheld. Tears well in my eyes, but I dare not even move to blink or wipe them away.

"They're called soulmarks," Porter says. "They are the marks left by souls as they pass through Limbo. Every soul who ever was has left a single mark here, its journey forever etched into the black."

He takes my hand again, and we walk forward down a sloping path through the trees. I hear the sound of water before I see it. The trees open up at the bottom of the hill, and we come out beneath the silent, haunting silhouette of the ruined castle. It looms overhead, its walls crumbling from age. A river winds around the foot of the hill like a moat, cutting us off from the castle. When we reach the river, we step onto a bridge, crystal clear as though made of glass. I can see the water coursing beneath my feet, like I'm hovering over it. The river is lit from within – thousands of soulmarks swirl and swim gracefully through the current.

I kneel on the bridge and reach down to let the water flow between my fingers. It doesn't feel like water. It feels ancient. Magical. Like the memory of water.

The soulmarks glide up to my skin and sweep past it, glittering as they pass by. Their reflections dance upon my face.

"There are soulmarks everywhere in Limbo," Porter says. "Cleave a mountain rock in two and there will be soulmarks inside, twinkling like diamonds. Take a spade to the soil and you'll find soulmarks reaching far into the depths like roots. They even inhabit the sky like stars. They are the lifeblood of Limbo. Without them, there would be only black."

"Do I have a soulmark?"

Porter nods. "I was hoping you would ask me that."

He takes my hand again and the pressure builds once more. This time I let myself give in to it, just like how I fell into the refuge of the black when I was seasick on the ship. The forest of lights, the river, the castle, the mountains – they all disappear. I feel the suction pulling at my skin, my hair, my scarf, but the sensations pass sooner than last time.

When it's all over, we're standing in a new region of Limbo. There are no stars; the sky is black. No valleys or grass or rolling hills. Just an endless expanse of night like Eremus. The only difference is the cluster of dazzling white soulmarks standing upright before us. They are spaced evenly apart, like rows of perfectly manicured fruit trees in a garden.

"Where are we now?" I ask. I step forward and move between the rows, letting myself get lost in the garden of lights. They surround me on all sides. The lights bewitch my senses.

"We've stepped below to a different level," Porter says, following me. "There are millions of levels in Limbo.

Billions, trillions. An infinite number, perhaps. And you can step between them if you know how."

"Which level is this?"

I look over my shoulder at him and see a flicker of pride pass over his face. "This is your level. I made it just for you."

"My level?" The soulmarks sway gently, silently, glinting white like a stand of silver birches in sunlight. "Why would I need my own level?"

The pride on Porter's face fades, and for the first time he looks somber and a bit too serious. It makes me nervous.

"Because your soulmarks are in danger. I had to move them here to keep them safe."

A chill sweeps up my spine like a cold, wet feather. Not because of the danger, but because he said soulmarks.

Plural.

I look around at the lights again, as though I should recognize them. "You said every soul who ever was has left a mark in Limbo. A mark. A single mark."

Porter lets his gaze drop to his feet. He rubs circles around his pinky knuckle with his thumb again. When he finally speaks, his words come gradually. A slow drip. "Every soul passes through Limbo to Afterlife once, leaving one mark. That is the natural order of things. When I die, I will leave one mark. But you... You've already passed through. More than once."

"More than once?" I say, the words catching on my throat. "There must be at least a hundred here."

Porter swallows, looking sheepish. "There are fifty-six, to be exact."

I look out at the soulmarks, a feeling of dread settling in the pit of my stomach. "You mean I've been to Limbo fifty-six times?"

"No, you've been to Limbo hundreds of times. You've passed through fifty-six times."

"What do you mean 'passed through'? I've passed through Limbo to Afterlife?"

Wouldn't I have remembered that?

He really digs his thumb into his pinky knuckle now. "No, not exactly. 'Passing through' can refer to passing through to Afterlife, but it can also mean passing through to Newlife."

The perception of my pulse starts to race. My translucent palms are slicked with sweat. I force myself to ask, "What's Newlife?" even though I'm pretty sure I already know the answer.

"Newlife is the answer to all your questions," Porter says, stepping toward me. "Newlife is why you and I are standing here. It is the reason you have memories you can't place. It is the reason you descend into the past involuntarily. It is the reason you exist. It's what I've been trying to explain to you all along. If you have fifty-six soulmarks in Limbo, it means you've lived fifty-six past lives."

I stare at Porter like he just slapped me in the face. I feel stunned and sick and like I need to wake up from this very long, very surreal dream. All those visions – the ship, the Ferris wheel, the cat, Jamestown, Chicago – were glimpses of my past lives? I had traveled back in time to my own pasts?

"You're the only one of your kind," Porter says, making it sound like an honor. "The only reincarnated Descender.

A Transcender. When your very first life ended, Flemming intercepted your soulmark as it was being written in Polestar. He sent your soul back to Earth, and when your second life was over, he sent you back for a third. Like a needle and thread, he worked your soulmarks in and out of the black. He wove your lives throughout history."

When I don't say or do anything but gape back at him, Porter continues, the words spilling out of him like he can't say them fast enough. "You have Level Five clearance, just like Flemming and Gesh. Lower level Descenders aren't allowed to descend without permission, and it takes years and meticulous research to find a soulmark that matches the exact time period they need for their missions. Once a Descender uses a soulmark to descend, that soulmark burns up. It can never be used again. But you're free to access Limbo and descend as much as you wish. Your soulmarks never burn up. And you have every time period laid out for you here. Each one organized, right at your fingertips." He glances around at my soulmarks. That same flicker of pride is back in his eyes. The blue-white light shimmers against his age-spotted skin. "You can travel all the way back to the fifth millennium BC."

I don't know what that means, but it sounds really far back in time. I open my mouth to respond, but nothing comes out. All coherent thought has left, and I feel dizzy. My knees lock, then give out. Porter catches me up in his arms, then lowers me to the black ground. He holds me steady until I can sit up on my own. The stubble on his chin snags my hair like Velcro when he pulls away. I swear he smells like pipe tobacco.

Or is it the perception of pipe tobacco?

"I'm sorry, Alex. I went too fast again. I meant to take it slow. Once I realized you didn't remember anything about Limbo at all, anything about me, about your past, I knew I had to go slow. I got ahead of myself. I wanted to show you your level, to show you that your soulmarks were safe, but you don't even remember why they need saving."

"It's OK," I say, not really listening. I'm too overwhelmed to make sense of anything he's saying. And I'm too distracted by the grove of soulmarks. My soulmarks. Beauty and elegance softly swaying all around us. Alluring. Radiant. Each one representing a life.

A whole life lived.

And forgotten.

Were they beautiful lives? Was I alluring and radiant? Or was I a freak in each one just like I am now?

The soulmark next to Porter catches my eye. Which life did that one represent? Had I been rich? Poor? Had I lived in the rain forests of Brazil? In a medieval city in Morocco? On the streets of Brooklyn?

I try to look away from that particular soulmark, but I can't. The way it sways is hypnotic. It bends in the middle like it has hips. I become lost in its dance, its captivating pull.

I reach out to touch it.

"No, don't!" Porter shouts.

Like a child about to touch a hot stove, I try to yank my hand away, but it's too late. The soulmark pulls my fingers in like a magnet. My hand fuses to the shaft of light. The soulmark swells and expands, then swallows me in brilliant white.

CHAPTER 8

Biceps, Pickled Cucumber Soup, and John Philip Sousa
It was a long time before I opened my eyes, fighting against the heavy resistance of deep sleep. Gravity felt so much stronger after being without it for so long in Limbo. It pinned me to a stiff, spring-coil mattress, my ear pressed to a firm pillow. A scratchy woolen blanket was draped over the top of me. Even that felt like it weighed fifty pounds. I winced when I tried to lift my head – that blasted knot had returned, only it was bigger now. My body ached like it had been pummeled in a boxing ring.

I knew right away I'd descended into one of my past lives, but which one, I didn't know. I felt so far removed from Porter and Limbo, like it had been weeks since he showed me the forest of lights.

It took a while for my eyes to focus on my surroundings, but soon everything became clear, even though I wasn't wearing my glasses. A dark-wood dresser stood across from me against a yellow floral wall. Midday sunlight glinted off its brass pull handles. An oval mirror hung above it, and a lace runner spanned the top with a dozen picture frames arranged purposefully upon it. Black and white faces stared out at me from within the various frames.

One face looked like Blue's.

I peeled the blanket off me, padded across a bare wood floor to the dresser, and picked up the frame. It was Blue. He was leaning against a brick wall, wearing a white undershirt, his bare arms folded across his chest. He was smiling and looking at the camera. I couldn't help but notice how the black and white photograph didn't do his blue eyes justice.

There was a man leaning against the wall beside Blue, same build, same dark hair, similar smile. He had his head tossed back in mid-laugh. I guessed it was Blue's older brother, Frank. As I scanned the rest of the photographs, catching Blue in various poses at different ages – as a boy riding a bike; opening presents on Christmas morning in pajamas; hugging a beautiful, smiling woman I could only guess was his mother – I realized something rather euphoric. My heart began to race.

I didn't know how I had gotten there, but I was in Blue's house.

I was back in Chicago.

Is that why I was drawn so strongly to that particular soulmark in my garden? Because that was the one that would lead me back to Blue? Had it known I wanted to get back to him more than anything? Or had it been just a coincidence? Was Porter still standing beside that soulmark waiting for me? Would he be furious with me when I got back?

I shoved all those thoughts aside. After all the stress and shock Porter had put me through, the least he could do was let me have a few hours to myself to process things. I needed time to digest everything he told me. I needed to slow down so I could grasp the concepts of time travel and reincarnation. It's not like time would pass while I was gone anyway. And I needed to know what happened after I heard the gunshot. I had to know how I ended up at Blue's house in my past life and if he was all right.

I set the picture frame down and caught a glimpse of myself in the oval mirror. A stiff, cream-colored nightgown hung from my bony shoulders. My long dark hair was rolled into rag curlers all over my head, some white, some red, some blue, like the colors of the American flag.

I made my way over to the bedroom door and eased it open. There was a small landing and a staircase leading down. I took the stairs gently, but they still managed to squeak and announce my presence. At the bottom, Blue peeked around the doorframe of a sunlit room. "You're up," he said, flashing me a grin.

He was alive.

I couldn't help it. I threw my arms around his neck. He laughed in my ear, his breath a puff in my hair.

"What was that for?" He leaned back to see my face. His smile was like sunshine. Infectious. The only sign of the fight in the alley was a shiny silver bruise – a swipe of charcoal below his left eye – and a cut above his right temple. His bottom lip was pale purple, only a little swollen.

"The last I heard was the gunshot," I said. "I thought you were dead. I thought it was all my fault. I've been so worried, you can't even imagine. How long was I away?"

"Away?" He cocked his head to the side. "You mean asleep? You blacked out after you tackled Teeth. You've been out like a light ever since. I bet you're starving. Come in and have a seat. I'm making soup."

He motioned for me to follow him into the sunlit room. It was a small kitchen awash with soft yellow light reaching lazily through white lace curtains. A large soup pot sat on top of an ornate green and white gas stove that stood on spindly legs. It was just like the one Gran and Pops had at their old farm. A porcelain-topped table stood in the center, surrounded by four white chairs. Blue pulled one out for me, and I sat down, tugging the hem of my night gown out from under my foot. It was too long for me. I guessed it was Blue's mother's. She must be tall, like my mom.

"Hey, I got you a present," he said, reaching for something off the counter and tossing it onto the table.

A newspaper. All shiny and new and ready to turn my fingertips black.

I grinned. "Did you pay for it?"

"Naturally," he said with a bow of his head.

I shook my head, smiling. As I watched him tend his soup at the stove, I got lost in the sight of him. I'd forgotten how handsome he was. He wore dark slacks, the kind men wore every day back then. His feet were bare, like mine. A soft, white undershirt and dark suspenders stretched across his muscular shoulders. I imagined this was the sort of thing Pops wore when he was a teenager. If so, I could see why Gran fell for him. There was something about a young man in that classic, old fashioned style that made a girl's heart flutter. For one, the shirt sleeves were shorter, showing off a lot more bicep than modern T-shirts. I thought about how Jensen's short sleeves came almost all the way down to his elbows.

Not that Jensen had much to show off in the bicep category.

But Blue...

The fingers of a blush stroked the back of my neck. Before it spread to my ears and cheeks, and before Blue turned around to see it, I snapped my attention to my hands.

Hands were so much more interesting than biceps, right?

That's when I noticed my fingernails were filthy. Outlined in grime like I just came in from gardening with Gran. Only I never bloodied my knuckles planting hostas.

I scrubbed my nails clean at the sink with a nail brush. The soap was harsh and made my skin squeak, but it did the trick.

"So what happened last night?" I asked, joining him at the stove. "After I blacked out? I heard the gun go off. That's the last thing I remember."

With a large knife, Blue scraped a mound of freshly chopped dill from a cutting board into the steaming pot. "After you tackled Teeth, I knocked the gun out of Loogie's hand. It went off when it hit the ground. No one got hurt, if that's what you were thinking."

"What happened then? How did we get here?"

"Mr Clemens – he owns the hardware store on the corner – he heard you shouting, so he knew something was going on. Came out with his shotgun." Blue smiled at the memory and gave his soup a good stir. "Cafferellis' guys hit the bricks, and Mr Clemens helped me carry you home. We'll be safe here; this is Fifth Street territory." He rapped his long wooden spoon on the side of the pot and set it down. "Ma patched you up the best she could and got you dressed and in bed. I told her not to bother curling your hair, but she did it anyway. Made it easier for her to look at that knot at the back of your head." He reached up and flipped one of my striped cotton curlers with his fingers. "Looks cute, though. Very John Philip Sousa."

At first I thought he meant I looked like the heavily bearded composer on the cover of one of Pops' old records, the guy who wrote all those patriotic marches the marching bands play during parades, but I shot him a playful glare when I got the reference. The red, white, and blue rag curlers. "Oh yes, I know, very Stars and Stripes Forever."

We laughed as he ladled soup into two bowls. "Hungry?"

We sat down, and I leaned over my soup. The hearty smell filled my nose. My stomach growled.

Blue's soup was an old Polish recipe called Zupa Ogórkowa, which I tried to pronounce and failed. He said it meant pickled cucumber soup, which didn't sound appetizing in the least. Who was the genius who thought putting pickles in soup was a good idea? I prepared myself for something truly disgusting, but it so wasn't. It was steaming hot chicken broth seasoned with dill, with sour cream stirred in to make it creamy and silky smooth. The few slices of pickles floating beside tender potatoes and carrots made it a bit salty and sour, tart on my tongue. I supposed it was the same idea as Gran adding lemon juice to her chicken noodle soup. Either way, it was glorious, and I loved every bite of it. I devoured two bowls and half of a third before my stomach felt content.

Blue pushed his bowl aside and folded his arms on the table. "There's something I've been dying to ask you." Suspicion sat on his right shoulder. Intrigue sat on his left.

I raised my eyebrows as an invitation for him to ask away. I didn't want to stop slurping down my soup just to say shoot.

"When Ma gathered your clothes up... She took them to the laundry, by the way. She wanted to get the blood out and mend a few tears for you." He shook his head and waved that trail of thought away. "Anyway, she found something in your coat. In the hidden pocket on the inside."

Hidden pocket? Intrigue sat up straighter. So did I. "What was it?"

He hesitated, looking a bit surprised that I didn't know what was in my own pocket.

"You still don't remember anything, do you?" he asked.

I shook my head and touched the bruised knot for good measure. It wasn't exactly a lie when I truly didn't remember who I was in that past life, was it?

"I'm sorry," he said. "That must be awful. Your aunt must be worried sick about you."

It took me a moment to remember the story I'd made up about visiting my aunt. I supposed it was awful, in a way. I probably did have an aunt back in 1927, one I'd never get to know because I couldn't remember anything from my past fifty-six lives.

"I guess you won't know what all the money's for then, huh?" Blue said.

"What money?"

His cute lips curved into a grin. "The fat roll of twenties you had stashed in your coat pocket."

Dirty Cabbage

Back in Blue's mom's room, the one I spent the night in, he and I sat cross-legged on her bed and counted the money. There were five hundred dollars in all, the twenty-dollar notes laid out evenly on the blanket between our knees like floor tiles. There was a hunger in Blue's eyes. He couldn't look away.

The old bills were larger than the ones I was used to, and instead of a portrait of Andrew Jackson, Grover Cleveland was on the front. A steam train and a steam ship faced each other on the back. I wondered what each bill would be worth today if I took them back home, but how would I travel with them? It seemed all I knew how to transport through time were injuries.

"What could I buy with this much money?" I asked.

Blue whistled and scratched the shadow of stubble on his cheek. "That's half my year's wages."

"Could I buy a Model T?"

He nodded, the green ink from the bills reflected in his eyes. I stared down at the money. I so wanted to buy a Model T. But I thought of a better use for it.

"How much does Frank owe for all his debts?"

Blue tore his eyes from the cash. "Don't even think about it."

"Why not?"

He shook his head and climbed off the bed. "You're not giving it to Frank."

"But it would solve everything. It would get the Cafferellis off your backs."

He paced the room, still shaking his head. "No way. I got a bad feeling about that money. It's meant for something. No one carries around that kind of cabbage unless it's dirty. I mean, you don't even remember who you are. You could be some gangster's squeeze for all we know. With my luck, the moment you hand it over, you'll remember what it's for and want it back. Besides, I won't take money from a girl."

"Now hold on right there," I said, standing up. I could always argue better on my feet. "I bet you take money from your mom."

"That's different."

"How so?"

"She's my mom."

"She's still a girl."

Blue groaned up at the ceiling and clasped his hands behind his head.

"And what about Sloan?" I said. "You won't take money from a girl, but from a bootlegger, sure, why not?"

He froze for a moment, then slowly turned around to face me. "How did you figure out I was working for Sloan?"

"When Loogie asked why you were hanging around the bakery, you said you were making a delivery." I frowned. Blue hadn't been wearing a uniform. He didn't have a delivery truck. "You weren't, were you?"

He looked down at his feet. He shoved his hands in his pockets. "No."

The front door opened and closed, and a friendly voice called hello up the stairs. Blue and I looked at each other.

Helena was home.

A Seamstress' Treasure Trove

Blue's mom was a gust of summer wind. A smile in heels and flesh-colored stockings. She made a fuss over you and hugged you like you were a toddler with a skinned knee. She was tall and fashionable, looking like the quintessential Twenties woman with a dark bob and cloche hat. Her cheerful presence in the apartment sent shadows scurrying in every direction. They hid under doors and behind curtains. It was as if the sun only shined on Helena Piasecki. It went with her everywhere, tucked in her pocketbook.

She had already worked a full day at a shop down the street, taking in the neighborhood wash and repairing garments. She took my clothes in with her that morning, and since they wouldn't be cleaned and mended for a few more days, she brought back a few things for me to wear – items women had dropped off at the shop but for some reason or another never came back to pick up.

"Unclaimed garments," she said, laying them out on the bed. Her Polish accent was faint, like Blue's. "A seamstress' treasure trove."

The first item was a grass-green trench coat, soft to the touch with a tweed lining. Lighter than the heavy woolen thing I wore the day before, but the lining was thick enough to keep out cool breezes.

"I'll trust you not to scuffle in back alleys while wearing this coat, missy," Helena said when I tried it on. She poked me in the ribs with a wink.

No, this was not the sort of coat I would "scuffle" in. It was the sort of coat I'd wear downtown, to the theater or a soda shoppe.

Just thinking about going to a soda shoppe made me giggle to myself.

"Watch out, Sousa. She's trying to turn you into a lady," Blue said, leaning against the doorframe and watching my reflection in the oval mirror.

"Pfft," said Helena. "She doesn't have to be a lady. She can be whatever she wants." She tapped me gently on the cheek. "So long as it doesn't get her killed."

The second thing she brought from the laundry was a pair of gleaming white gloves. She stroked them with her fingertips, admiring them. "These belonged to a French woman who didn't speak a bit of English. She wore white from head to toe, from the tall white feather on her hat all the way down to her pointed white heels. She even kept a tiny white mouse in her breast pocket for company."

Blue and I exchanged a glance and laughed.

The final item Helena brought for me was a dress, but she wouldn't let me see it until after my bath.

"Then Nicky will take you downtown for the evening," she said. She sat on the edge of the claw foot bathtub, still in her stockings and heels, running the water. There was something lovely about the sound her heels made on the pale green tile floor. "I want you both to stay as far away from Cafferelli territory as possible. At least until your memory comes back, or all this business with the bakery blows over."

An entire evening with Blue in 1927 Chicago?

Yes, please.

Snapping the Net

While I soaked my aching body in the bath, looking forward to my night out with Blue, I felt a pang of guilt for leaving Porter behind. It all happened so fast. Once the soulmark yanked me in, there was no way I could have pulled away. It would've been like trying to swim up a waterfall. All I remembered was Porter shouting for me to stop, then waking up in Helena's bed. I hoped he wasn't angry with me. I hadn't meant to touch it. Then again, if he was angry, did I really care? Chicago was where I wanted to be. Not Limbo. Not Ristorante Cafferelli. Not Mr Draper's class. Chicago, where no one knew about my "seizures" and no one called me Freak or Wayspaz. It was a clean slate. A chance to be normal.

I sank lower in the steaming water and let it slip over my shoulders. I closed my eyes and tried to let my muscles fully relax.

Alex.

Porter's voice was so loud in my ear, it was like he was right beside me. I jumped, and my bottom slipped on the porcelain, plunging me all the way under the water. I grappled for the sides of the tub and pulled myself up, gasping for breath and swiping water from my eyes.

I looked left and right, my heart in my throat, but Porter wasn't there.

You need to come back now.

His words resonated inside my skull like the gong of a bell. His voice filled every inch of it and set my teeth on edge, making me wince. I pressed the heels of my palms to my temples and told him to get out of my head. The intrusion, the overwhelming pressure, was unbearable.

I didn't tell you the rules. You have to come back before you–

I dug my palms into my temples. I felt my grip on the past slipping away from me. Limbo tugged. Beckoned. Was Porter pulling me out of the past? Could he even do that? I struggled to resist the pull, but it was like being underwater and trying to keep my body from floating to the surface. I fought with everything I had, desperate to stay submerged in the past. I clung to 1927. I tried to ignore the tugging at my edges, the net pulling my soul skyward, and simply focused on Blue. I wouldn't leave just yet. I refused.

Alex.

I fought harder.

I struggled longer.

Until finally the net snapped.

The pressure lifted.

I sat in the tub, breathing hard, heart pounding, water dripping from my ruined curls.

Porter was gone. Equal parts relief and guilt twisted inside me.

I would do as Porter said and return to Limbo, but I'd go when my evening was over. I wasn't ready to say goodbye. I wasn't ready to return to the land of Wayspaz the Fix-it Freak.

The Eel's Hips

Back in her bedroom, Helena combed out the curls she'd kindly tied for me the night before. She giggled when I told her I slipped in the tub.

"That's all right, kitten," she said as she fastened my wet hair in a flat bun at the nape of my neck. "You'll wear a hat and no one'll be the wiser."

Apparently, all the women wore their long hair in a bun in those days if they didn't feel convinced to cut it. I didn't know why my past self still had long hair, especially since cutting it meant so much to the women of the age. Short hair meant freedom. Independence. Equality. All things I believed in. So why hadn't I chopped mine off? Was I too conservative? That didn't seem to fit. What proper conservative lady knew how to fight like a wildcat? And wore beat-up ankle boots? Helena said I probably kept my hair long out of respect for my parents. Blue on the other hand, still believing I was some gangster's squeeze, suggested I had a backward thinking husband at home, waiting for me to cook his supper.

I elbowed him in the ribs for that one, and prayed to God it wasn't true. Girls didn't get married at seventeen back then, did they? The thought made me feel sorta queasy.

When Helena finished my makeup, I looked in her mirror and turned my chin to the left and right. A movie starlet stared back at me. Helena showed me how to blot my red lips on a tissue. Then she showed me the dress. Brand new in her eyes, mint vintage in mine. It was a navy blue slip-on dress with a low waist and tiny white polkadots. The hemline hit just above my knees. Long, flowing sleeves gathered daintily at my wrists. Tan stockings and white heels made me look twice my age. It was like I'd rummaged through Gran's closet for a costume party. Not quite flapper, but definitely chic. Claire would be so jealous. She was the fashion guru of the household.

Helena let me borrow a silk scarf to go with the green trench and white gloves. When she secured a navy blue cloche hat over my hair, I almost didn't recognize myself. I felt very much the part, standing next to Blue in his white collar shirt, green sweater vest and tie, caramel-colored suit, and brown flat cap tilted to the side. Helena whistled and said he was the eel's hips, whatever that meant. When I told him he looked smokin' hot, he just shook his head and said, "Nah, I'm not hot at all. This suit breathes really well."

I won't lie. In that moment, my heart melted a little for Nicholas Piasecki.

"Now, Nicky," Helena said, shooing us down the front steps of their apartment to the sidewalk. "Show her a good time, will you? Poor girl's lost her memory. The least you can do is make it a night she'll never forget."

CHAPTER 9

Burgers, Fries, and Piano Wire

Chicago was alive and bustling. The sky was bright and blue. Possibility nipped my nose, riding on the back of a crisp breeze. I couldn't believe I'd been let loose in a big city with a boy. I'd never gone anywhere alone with a boy, unless I counted Dad or my six year-old cousin, Harrison.

Which I didn't.

No boy had ever looked twice at me back home. I was the Fix-it Freak in nerd glasses with epilepsy, for goodness sake. A far cry from suitable dating material. At the rate I was going, I'd have a master's degree before I had my first kiss.

Not that I was one of those girls who spent their time agonizing over things like kissing and dating. I had better things to do.

But that didn't mean I didn't want them.

Being out with Blue made me feel normal. I never felt so comfortable and relaxed with anyone outside my family before. It didn't feel like I'd just met him. It felt like I'd known him my whole life, like I was remembering him rather than getting to know him, just like I felt about Porter. Blue treated me like an equal. He didn't laugh or call me freak.

Never mind kissing and dating – Blue showed me what it was like to have a friend.

We boarded a streetcar and headed downtown. Buildings grew taller and wider as we moved east. The traffic got thicker, and police officers manned hand-operated stop lights in booths perched above the cars. The city was exuberant and full of life, but I could sense tension rolling through the streets. It was like a thick fog, slinking in and around everyone, everything. Like pressure pressing up against glass, just enough to make it moan and creak. Enough to make you feel suffocated. Caged.

Eventually, as I learned long ago in history class, the glass would give. The Roaring Twenties would shatter into a million pieces like Sloan's bakery windows. Two more years of pressure, of expansion. Then...

Crack.

We hopped off the streetcar and ducked into a diner that was one of Blue's favorite places to eat. It was a tiny hole-in-the-wall joint with really bad lighting. We wove our way through the tables and chairs and slipped into one of the back booths. A layer of grease and smoke coated your skin the moment you walked in, and the smell alone could clog an artery. Cooks in white paper caps and grease-stained aprons flipped burgers and grilled buns, and waitresses bobbed from table to table. At the counter, men sat shoulder-to-shoulder in trousers, caps, and coats, hunched over from a hard day's work.

They laughed. They smoked. They argued over how the Chicago Bears were doing.

I loved every minute of it.

No movie I'd seen had ever come close to replicating what it really felt like to be in the Twenties. They all seemed so clichéd now. I wished I had my cell phone so I could take a photo or video. I wanted to remember this experience forever.

And yet, even amid the hustle and bustle of the after-work dinner crowd, that looming pressure continued to build. Like a storm brewing in the distance.

I had to warn Blue.

"I've been thinking about the money," I said, my voice low. Not that anyone could have heard me over the lively debate going on at the counter and the sizzle of the grill.

Blue leaned closer, his hands clasped between his knees under the table. The cap he wore cast a shadow over his face. "You and me both."

"Do you have any money saved up?"

He sputtered a laugh. "What for? Frankie'd just find a way to spend it."

I pulled my gloves off and crossed my arms on the table. "I wish I could give your brother a good punch in the nose. I can't believe he parties and gambles and makes you and Helena foot the bill."

Blue shrugged. "He doesn't care."

"Well, maybe you should cut him off. You're just enabling him, you know."

"It's better than finding him in a gutter somewhere with a bullet in his head."

We sat back when a frazzled waitress in a blue and white gingham uniform approached our table. Since Blue knew what was good, he ordered for both of us, then she hurried to the next booth. We leaned back in and continued.

"You're right," I said. "But I hate that he uses you like this. Puts you in the middle. Makes you take a job for Sl–"

Blue put a finger to his lips, and Sloan's name fell dead on my tongue.

"I told you, he doesn't care," Blue said. "But that doesn't matter. I care about him. That's the only thing that counts."

I frowned, pursing my lips. I knew then that Blue would've never embarrassed Mr Lipscomb in front of the whole school. He would've never put Tabitha's texts on the cafeteria message board. He wanted justice, like me, but not at the expense of someone else.

"Why do you have to be so good?" I asked.

He gave me an adorable half-smile. "Good is relative, Sousa. Especially in this town. Don't you forget it."

I returned the smile and let him win the argument, but we both knew the truth. Nick Piasecki was good. Through and through. Relative or not.

I didn't know what I'd do if my sisters treated me the way Frank treated Blue. Or if they treated our mother the way he treated Helena. I didn't think I could be so forgiving. Especially if they were burning through my money like an expensive date when the Depression was right around the corner.

I leaned in closer and lowered my voice even more. "Will you do something for me?"

He leaned in too, until he was just a breath away. I could smell his aftershave. His eyes rested on my lips. "What's that?"

"Save up. As much as you can in the next year. Hide it from Frank. Don't let him know about it."

Blue's mouth broke into an easy smile once again. He leaned back and rested an arm on the back of the booth. "And here I thought you were going to ask me to kiss you."

My ears burned when he said that, and I was thankful my hat covered them. I tried to act like his remark hadn't completely knocked me off my axis. "Will you do that for me? Will you promise?"

He nodded. "Yes, ma'am. I promise."

Only then could I fully relax for the evening. Knowing Blue and Helena would be all right when the Depression came made it easier to leave them behind at the end of the night.

When I went back to Limbo.

The waitress appeared again, balancing burgers, fries, and two ice cream sodas in her arms. The burgers were the size of our heads, and when Blue took a bite, juice streamed over his fingers and down his chin. He used about a dozen napkins to sop it all up.

I popped a fry into my mouth, and my eyes flew wide open. "Oh my gosh, these are incredible. They taste like real potatoes."

Blue snorted a laugh. "As opposed to what?"

I laughed too. "I don't know. But they don't taste like potatoes back home in Annapolis. They just taste like... grease and salt and preservatives."

Blue perked up. "Hey, are your memories coming back?"

Whoops.

"Huh. I guess a little bit." I sipped my ice cream soda like the return of my memory was no big deal. The bubbles tingled my tongue.

He quirked an eyebrow. "Remember where your aunt lives?"

I shook my head, still sipping.

He hefted his burger back to his mouth and smiled. "Good."

I smiled too. Because we both knew that once I "remembered," it would be time for me to leave.

I guess he wanted me to stay as much as I did.

He wiped his mouth and hands after another sloppy bite. "OK, I got it. You're on the run, see? Your husband, he told you he was a piano salesman, and he always traveled to New York to make deliveries to the big theaters and speakeasies and such. Only he was really a big-time gangster. You'd been suspicious for a while, but you figured it out when he kept coming home flush with cash. Your daddy had been a piano salesman too, and you knew they didn't make that much money. So you did a bit of digging. You found out the filthy liar had this whole other life. A secret life. Maybe even a secret gal or two. So you raided his stash – he always kept a wad of bills sewn in the hems of the drapes – and you hopped on the first train to Chicago. Maybe you even changed your name. Maybe it isn't even Alex. Any of this ring a bell?"

"Um, no." I stole a fry from his plate because all mine had disappeared. Somehow.

He didn't notice. He was too impressed with his own version of my backstory. "Oooooo. And his gangster name? Steinway."

"Because he pretends he's a piano salesman?"

"Because he strangles his enemies with piano wire." Blue grinned wide. He was so proud of himself.

I stole another fry. "Real original, Piasecki." I'd almost called him Blue out loud, but caught myself.

"Hey, I just tell it like it is," he said with a shrug. "Personally, I don't know what you ever saw in the guy. I always thought you could do better."

"It was the piano," I said wistfully. "Never could resist a man who played the keys."

Fast Memories and Marquee Lights

After dinner – in which I tried my best not to get burger juice all over my dress – Blue said he had a surprise for me. "Bet your mobster husband never took you to see one of these," he said.

We stood outside the Chicago Theater, waiting in line under a huge, glittering marquee that read The Jazz Singer. My jaw dropped when I first saw it.

"We're going to see The Jazz Singer?" I couldn't help it. I squealed. I clung to his arm and may have bounced a bit. (I wasn't usually the squealing or bouncing type.)

"You've heard of it?"

I nodded, biting my lip to suppress any more squeals. Not only had I heard of it – it just happened to be the first talking movie ever – but I'd seen it dozens of times with Gran and Pops during our movie nights. Audrey,

Claire, and I had all the songs memorized. I even went through a phase where I refused to call Mom anything but Mammy.

She hated it.

"It just came out last week," Blue said, beaming up at the marquee, "but Mom and I, we've already seen it twice. You just wait. It's like nothing you've ever seen before." He laid a hand on both of my white gloves still clinging to his elbow. To anyone looking on, we probably looked like a proper Twenties couple.

Something about that thought sent a flutter through my stomach.

God it felt good to be on a date with a boy, if that's what we were on. If not, it was the closest I'd ever come to a real date, so I'd take it. I never thought any other boy could make my stomach flutter the way Jensen did. I never thought Jensen would become a fast memory. But in that moment, standing beneath the marquee lights, sharing a smile with Blue, my whole life back in Annapolis slipped away. Like the sun burning away morning mist.

And I wanted nothing more than to bask in Blue's rays for a little while longer.

The Jazz Singer was incredible. My cheeks hurt from grinning so much. It took everything within me to keep from belting out the songs with Al Jolson. I had to pretend like it was the first time I'd ever seen a talking picture, because Blue kept stealing glances at me, wanting to see my reaction. The moment Al spoke his first words on screen, loud and clear, in perfect unison with his lips, people all throughout the theater gasped and looked around.

"They're looking for Al," Blue whispered. "They think he's gotta be here somewhere, talking into a microphone."

Good Lord, it was glorious. To see The Jazz Singer when it was first released? To walk the streets of 1927? To breathe the air, wear the clothes, see it all from a modern perspective? Descending to the past was like a drug. I knew from that moment on I'd never get enough.

What else would I get to see? Martin Luther King's famous speech? The Boston Tea Party? Could I walk the Trail of Tears? The Underground Railroad?

Whatever it was, I was ready. I wanted to see it all.

After the movie, Blue wanted to show me the lake. We walked to the shore, the setting sun at our backs. We stood shoulder–to-shoulder on the edge of a little concrete pier and looked out across the water. The breeze ruffled my skirt. Seagulls squawked overhead.

I never knew Lake Michigan was so vast and beautiful and alive with waves. I thought it would be boring, like any old lake, but I was wrong. It was just like the ocean back home. A view at the end of the world.

The wind kicked up and made me shiver. Blue wrapped a strong arm around my arms and pulled me close. I leaned into him, my cheek against his chest. Why couldn't I meet a guy like him in Base Life?

Alex.

My fist flew to my temple, and I swore under my breath. Porter's voice elbowed its way inside my head, just as startling and unsettling as the first time.

"You OK?" Blue asked. "Is your head still hurting you?"

You can't fall in love. It's against the rules.

Love? Dammit, Porter, who said anything about love? Why did he keep forgetting that I was only seventeen? I fought against him again, like pushing my way out of a bramble bush, and Limbo's hooks popped loose, one by one. I managed to shut Porter out faster than before. I refused to let him take this night away from me.

The best night.

Couldn't he just wait a few more hours?

"Just a little twinge," I told Blue, settling back into his arms.

We turned around so we could see the skyline bathed in sunset oranges and pinks. Glittering lights switched on here and there as the city came to life. There was an energy, a charge, streaking and zigzagging through the air, making the hair on the back of my neck prickle.

I could feel my time running out. I only had a few more hours in 1927, at best. Then the black would take me. I needed to make those last hours count.

I told Blue I needed to roar.

He took my hand. "I know just the place."

CHAPTER 10

Star Gazing

"You coming, Sousa?"

I looked up at Blue, hanging by one arm from a fire escape ladder. His suit jacket flapped in the wind. We were in a dark alley, behind what appeared to be an abandoned shoe factory. It didn't look very roar-worthy to me. "That's just to throw off the coppers," Blue had told me.

"I don't know about this..." I rubbed my arms. The night had gotten progressively cooler, and I'd never been too fond of heights.

"Climb on up here," he said, smiling down at me. "I'll warm you up."

I tried to give him a disapproving look, but I'm pretty sure I failed. "I don't think that's what your mom meant when she said 'Show her a good time.'"

He laughed, a deep belly laugh that echoed down the alley. "Too bad. She should've been more specific."

I hesitated, still rubbing my arms. Blue climbed up a dozen more rungs. The farther he climbed, the more alone I felt in the alley. And the last time I found myself in a Chicago back alley? Things didn't go so well.

I stepped up to the ladder and closed my fingers around one of the rungs. A layer of rust coated my white gloves. When I tried to dust it off on my coat, it only made the stain worse.

On the one hand, if I climbed all the way up, the gloves Helena gave me would surely be ruined. On the other, my first kiss might be waiting for me on the roof.

My heart thudded at the thought.

I took a deep breath.

I pulled myself up.

"Attagirl," Blue called down.

I laughed and shook my head as I made my way to the top. When had I become this person? Chasing a kiss to the top of the sky?

He helped me onto the roof, and we gazed out at the city, breathing in the night and listening to the distant street sounds. The stars seemed close enough to fog with your breath.

We owned the city. We owned the stars. It was all ours for the night. And I would've stolen my first kiss right then and there, but Blue had other plans.

He led me to a trap door at the center of the roof. It swung open with a rusty squawk, and we both kneeled down and looked inside. A ladder affixed to the side led down into a dark room. Amber light from the buildings across the street tried in vain to shine through grime-coated windows. It was a storage room of sorts, stacked to the ceiling with odds and ends, but I couldn't make out anything in particular in the shadows.

"I'll go first," Blue said, swinging his leg over the edge and stepping down. "There are a few rungs, then you have to drop the rest of the way. Not too far, though."

He got to the last rung and dropped down. I heard his feet hit the ground, followed by a stumble and a thud, and then he swore. Only he didn't say any of the words I was acquainted with. I distinctly heard him say, "Applesauce."

"Applesauce?" I threw my head back and laughed. I'd never heard anything so adorable in all my life.

"Stop laughing at me and get yourself down here," he called back.

But I couldn't stop. I laughed all the way down the ladder and kept laughing as I dropped to the floor. It was farther than I thought it would be, and I lost my balance like Blue and fell right on my butt. I laughed even more until tears stung my eyes and my ribs hurt.

"Oh, come on," he said, hauling me to my feet. "It's not like you've never heard that one before." I could hear the red coloring his cheeks. He was embarrassed, which made it even more adorable, but he wasn't the type to stay embarrassed for long.

He pulled me over to a thick, heavy metal door and said, "Ready to roar, Sousa?" He shouldered it open with a creak and a groan, like it hadn't been opened in years.

All at once, the squawk of trumpets, the growl of saxophones, and the happy gallop of piano keys rushed out to meet us. A puff of smoke-filled air ruffled our clothes. We stepped out onto a darkened storage balcony, following a sultry woman's voice below us. She stood on a stage before a full orchestra, caught in the net of a blue spotlight. Her sequined dress hugged her every curve. It winked up at us as she whipped her hips to the side, like it knew we were spying. She threw her arms in the air and sang about naughty eyes and a new kind of lovin'.

I was utterly transfixed.

Blue pulled two chairs to the edge of the balcony. I sat beside him, his knee resting against mine, my arms folded on the railing in front of us. Two birds alone in the rafters. Two shadows. The crowd below, laughing and dancing and swirling their drinks, never knew we were there.

We were star gazers.

"Is this a speakeasy?" I whispered, unable to tear my eyes away. The amber glint of liquor flashed in the hand of every guest.

Blue rested his chin on his forearms beside me. "Yup. It's called Peg Leg. Fifth Street runs it. But Frankie and the guys are never up here dancing. They stay downstairs. And you don't want to know what they do down there."

I didn't even begin to let my mind wonder about that. Instead I drank in the light, the jazz, the beaded fringe, the striped jackets and dandy shoes. I wanted to remember every detail. "How did you know how to get in?"

"Frankie showed me a year ago. There's a piano in the storage room back there. He knew I liked to play. I come here every now and then to practice. No one can hear me while all this is going on."

I cocked my head to the side. "You play the keys?"

He grinned. "Yup."

"Hmmm." I looked away like I wasn't interested. A man in a fedora flipped a woman over his shoulder. She flashed everyone a glimpse of her garter belt.

"I hear some women can't resist a guy who plays piano," Blue said.

I shrugged. "Some women may have weaknesses like that. Not me."

He laughed and nudged my elbow with his.

The band transitioned to a slower tune, and a trombone and clarinet pursued each other through the twists and turns of a mournful duet. Couples swayed and glided across the dance floor.

I turned my face to Blue, my cheek resting on the back of my wrist. There was something magnetic about him that I couldn't explain. No matter what glorious sights 1927 Chicago had for me, my gaze never failed to find its way back to him.

"What do you want to do?" I asked him. "You know, when you grow up?"

He furrowed his brow. "When I 'grow up'?"

"Yeah. When you're out of school."

"Been out of school for a while now. Had to start working because of Frank."

"Oh, right. Good ole Frank," I muttered.

"Yup. Good ole Frank." He propped his chin on his fists. "I don't know. I'll probably just keep working at the deli."

"But if you could do anything you wanted, what would you do?"

He squinted out over the crowd, thinking. "Maybe become a pilot. Or play in a jazz band. Or join the Police Academy."

"Hm," I said. "That last one wouldn't make you very popular around here."

"Good thing I don't care about being popular," he said with that easy grin of his. "What about you, Sousa? Got any plans of grandeur?"

"I really don't know." A week ago I was content to follow in Dad's biomedical engineering footsteps. Now I wasn't so sure. "Maybe I'll join the Academy with you. Put some of my back alley fighting skills to good use."

"Don't you think that might upset your gangster husband?"

I groaned. "I don't have a gangster husband, Blue."

"Blue?" he said, raising an eyebrow.

I laughed, feeling stupid. I knew I'd slip up eventually. "It's your nickname. The one I gave you before I knew your name. It's just something stupid I do in my head. I do it for everyone I meet." I tried to shrug it off, my silly little quirk, but he grinned.

"Not stupid. I like it." He looked out across the crowd. "Blue and Sousa. Has a nice ring to it."

"Speaking of rings," I said, waggling my bare ring finger at him. "See? No husband."

"Pfft. That doesn't mean anything. You could've hocked that old handcuff when you got into town."

I laughed at his choice of words. "Well, even if my life was like that, even if I was on the run from some gangster, I'd never go back to that life now."

"Why not?"

"Because this life is better."

"How do you know this one's better if you don't remember the old one?"

"Because I didn't know you then. Now I do. That makes this one better."

His mouth hitched up on one side. "Aw, you can't say things like that to me."

"I can't?"

His hand found mine. "Not without expecting me to ask you to dance."

He pulled me to my feet, and then it was my turn to be embarrassed. "I'm not very good at this sort of thing," I said, looking down at my feet.

Believe it or not, I had danced with a boy before. Once. It was Jamal Webber, and it was during rehearsal for our fifth grade play. Everyone had a dance partner because it was set at a sock hop. I tried really hard to learn the moves, but I was hopeless. I stepped on Jamal's brand new sneakers at least a dozen times. By the end of rehearsal, Jamal had another partner, and I was given backstage duty.

I started to second guess stealing a kiss from Blue. I was probably even worse at kissing.

"Just follow my lead," he said. "We don't have to get fancy."

His hand slid around to my back and pulled me close. We swayed with the mournful trombone and clarinet. I felt the warmth of his hand on my back and his chest against mine. He danced better than Dad. Better than Pops.

I rested my head against his lapel. I swayed. I committed it all to memory.

The singer's words hung in the air around us like mist. She sang of loving her sweetheart night and day, of him leaving her all alone, of her tears. She told him he'd regret it, that his heart would break one day. He'd miss the dearest pal he ever had. Someday. After he was gone.

The words caught me up and wouldn't let go. Every minute I spent with Blue brought me closer to the moment I had to leave. I could feel it all fading away – that yawning, empty feeling that comes with the ending of things.

Something told me this was the last time I'd ever see Nicholas Piasecki.

I squeezed my eyes shut and pushed the thought from my mind. It was just as unwelcome as Porter.

"You know," I said, smiling up at Blue and trying to ignore the heaviness in my heart. "The boys back home in Annapolis don't like to dance."

"What?" He was incredulous. "Why not?"

"They think it's stupid. They'd rather play video games."

He tilted his ear closer to my mouth. "Video what?"

"Sports, I mean."

"Sports?" he scoffed. "What a load a'hooey. Don't they like girls?"

I laughed. "Yeah, they like girls."

He shook his head. "If you're stuck on a girl, dancing is the fastest way to get your hands on her. What kind of goof wouldn't want that?"

"I guess no one's ever been stuck on me enough to ask."

He lifted my chin with his knuckle. His mouth hitched up on the side again. "Been hanging out with a bunch of blind guys, Sousa?"

I laughed and buried my face in his jacket. He wrapped both arms around me and rested his cheek on the top of my head.

Your heart will break like mine, and you'll want me only. After you've gone, the sequined jazz singer sang. After you've gone away.

CHAPTER 11

Play It, Sam

When the song was over, the band leapt back into a lively swing, but I didn't feel like being upbeat just then. Instead, I led Blue back toward the storage room and pushed him through the doorway.

"Want me all to yourself?" he said with a laugh, clapping a hand on his cap so it wouldn't fall off. "All you had to do was ask."

I gave him one more playful push, then heaved the door shut, leaving the sounds, the laughter, the lights, and the smoke behind us. "I want you to play for me." I spoke the words into the dark. Blue was a silhouette against the dim amber lights outside. I wanted him to play for me the way Sam played for Ilsa in Casablanca.

"OK."

I followed him to an old grand piano standing by a wall of grimy windows. Stacks of boxes and crates were mounded all around it, but the top was propped open. He dusted off the bench and we sat side-by-side. He lifted the fallboard, flexed his fingers, then played a sweet and lilting melody, his hands moving like shadows across the faint ivory keys.

He played effortlessly. Happily. Passionately. He played so that I envied him and wished I had a speck of discernible musical talent within me.

When he hit the last note, he lifted his hands with a flourish, and we laughed. He wrapped an arm around me and gave my shoulders a squeeze. "How was that?"

"Perfect." I pressed one of the black keys. Then one of the white. "Did you write it?"

He laughed at me. "Yup. Just call me Hoagy Carmichael."

"Who?"

He squeezed my shoulders again. "Never mind. You just remember it's called Stardust. It'll be our song."

I tucked our song into my pocket. I buttoned it closed. There was no way I'd ever forget it.

"Ready to go?" he said after we sat there for a while. "There's one last place I want to show you."

I nodded, even though I didn't like the word last.

Two Wishes and a Taxi Cab

We walked hand-in-hand toward the lake shore once more. Neither of us said a word. Silence always seemed to make time tick a little slower.

Across Michigan Avenue, we strolled through Grant Park to a wide-open plaza at the edge of the lake. In the center of the plaza, a huge fountain sent a single shaft of brilliant white water soaring into the air. Three massive round tiers, illuminated by dozens of dazzling lights from within, made it look like a wedding cake. A giant shallow pool, reflecting all the light like smooth onyx, was its pedestal. I'd seen some beautiful fountains in Washington DC before, but this was by far my favorite.

"It's brand new," Blue said, as we approached. Our shoes crunched on the gravel. "The Clarence Buckingham Memorial Fountain. One of the biggest fountains in the world. Mom and I were here when they dedicated it. John Philip Sousa was here too," he added with a grin.

"Well, it wouldn't be an event without Sousa, would it?"

We stepped up as close as we could, but it was blocked off by a low railing. "Damn," I said. "I wanted to make a wish."

"What's stopping you?"

"I'd have to cross the railing."

He shrugged. "So cross the railing." He jumped over it in one smooth motion and walked right up to the edge of the fountain. I hesitated, half-tempted to follow.

"Come on," he taunted. "You need to make that wish of yours. It feels important."

He was right. It was important.

I looked all around, but we seemed to be the only ones there. The diamond lights of Chicago glittered behind us. The fountain lights played across Blue's caramel-colored suit.

I climbed over the railing.

He pulled two pennies from his pocket and handed one to me. He pressed his lips to his own, then flipped it into the water. I closed my eyes and clutched my penny to my chest. I wished long, and I wished hard.

I wished that I would see him again.

Somehow.

Then my wish became a flash of copper, sinking to the bottom of the onyx pool.

"What did you wish for?" Blue asked.

I smiled at the fountain. "Can't tell you."

"No?" He stepped closer to me, his teasing, easy smile making me feel shy all over. His hands closed around mine. "But you told Clarence Buckingham."

"Only because he can keep a secret."

"Ah. I guess you're right. I don't think he's let one slip yet." He pulled my white gloves off one-by-one and tucked them in his pockets. Our fingers entwined for the first time, skin to skin. "I've been wanting to do that all night," he said, smiling down at our hands. His were smooth and cold. His fingernails were wide and squared off at the tips.

It was the first time I'd ever held a boy's hand. I started to shiver and hoped Blue wouldn't be able to tell. I prayed my palms wouldn't get sweaty.

"What did you wish for?" I asked him. It came out like a whisper compared to the rush of the fountain. The roof of my mouth had gone dry.

He looked up, glancing at my lips before his eyes met mine. "You really want to know?"

I held my breath and nodded. My heart was in my throat.

His gaze fell to my lips again. He leaned in ever so slightly. "Are you sure you want to know?"

I nodded, unable to speak.

He leaned in a bit more, his nose brushing against mine. I closed my eyes and stood up on my toes to meet him the rest of the way. My mouth parted.

The warmth of his lips grazed mine, then he paused and whispered, "But what if it doesn't come true?"

"Blue." I opened my eyes and gave him a shove.

He caught my face in his hands and pressed his lips to mine.

I froze at first from the shock of it, but I thawed out soon enough. I hooked my arms around his neck and melted into him. I didn't know kissing would come so easily until I kissed Blue, especially since he seemed to know what he was doing. I simply followed his lead. I kissed him like I would never see him again. Like it was my one and only chance. He kissed me the same way – like he sensed the cold and lonely shadow of finality closing in around us.

We kissed so at least one of our wishes came true.

Alex.

This time Porter shoved his way into my head without mercy, the pressure between my ears unbearable. I gasped and nearly jumped out of my skin. I stumbled backward toward the edge of the fountain, and Blue grabbed me before I tumbled into the water. I couldn't see straight. The pressure behind my eyes was blinding.

"Come on," Blue said. "Kissing me wasn't that bad, was it?"

I barely took notice of his joke. I sat on the fountain's edge, my palms pressed to my temples. Go away, I shouted at Porter.

Your time's almost up. You have to leave your host body where you first found it.

How am I supposed to do that? I yelled back at him. I'm all the way across town.

I waited for his answer, but none came. I didn't even know if he could hear me shouting at him in my head. I felt his presence lift, then disappear, leaving me alone with Blue. I stared down at my shoes, breathing hard. Everything was tinted red.

Limbo tugged at me, tilting the Chicago skyline and making me feel nauseous like after a carnival ride. The more I fought against it, the more I couldn't tell the difference between the past and the present. It felt like I was straddling a fence, being stretched from both sides. My body belonged in the past, yearned to stay in the past, but my soul belonged in the future.

And it was heading back to Limbo whether I liked it or not.

Blue sat next to me and rubbed circles on my back. "Sousa? You OK?"

What was I supposed to do? Ask Blue to take me back to the bakery? Back into Cafferelli territory? All I wanted to do was kiss him until the black came to take me away. I wanted to breathe him in until there was no more breath. I wanted his scent and his face and his warmth to be the last few memories I took with me to Limbo.

But if I stayed with Blue until my time was up – if I was sent back to Limbo while still sitting here beside him – the old me, the 1927 me, wouldn't know who he was. She'd find herself in the arms of a stranger. Dressed in strange clothes. Far from her home.

What would she do? Hit him? Run from him? Tell him to never lay a hand on her again?

I couldn't do that to Blue. I couldn't do that to her. Going back to the bakery was the only way to leave her with some semblance of normalcy. She'd still be freaked out – she'd have lost two days of her life, with no memory of either. Two days I stole from her.

From myself.

But at least she'd know how to get home. I owed her that much.

I jumped to my feet and started back toward Michigan Avenue. I'd hail a cab and get as far away from Blue as possible before I ascended. Far enough away so he couldn't follow. I fisted my hands at my sides, fighting off tears.

"Alex," he called out, running after me.

I walked faster. I didn't want to run, but I would if I had to. Luckily, though, I came to a smaller street before Michigan Avenue and spotted the bright yellow of a taxi a block away. I lifted my arm and flagged it down. Even if I ascended to Limbo on the way to the bakery, my past self would still be able to find her way home. All she'd have to do is tell the cab driver where to go.

Blue caught up to me just as the gleaming yellow Checkerboard Taxi pulled up to the curb. He caught my hand. His eyes pleaded. "Did I do something wrong?"

I shook my head, staring at his shoes. The reflection from the fountain sent orange light dancing across the leather.

"Did you remember where your aunt lives?" His voice was soft. Heartbroken.

I nodded.

He shifted his weight from his left foot to his right. I could feel his pulse throbbing in his hand. His skin felt like fire. He started to say something several times, but couldn't seem to find the right words.

"I left the money in Helena's bedside drawer," I said. "I want you to have it."

He furrowed his brow. "What? No, Alex–"

"I want you to pay off Frank's debts. Then I want you and Helena to start fresh. Save up all the money you make and keep it hidden." He kept trying to interrupt me, but I refused to let him. "I've already made up my mind. And I don't care what you believe about taking money from a girl. You'll take it, and you'll do as I say. It's my money, I can do whatever I want with it. Now promise me. Promise you'll pay off his debts and you'll never work for Fifth Street again."

For a long time, he was speechless. Finally he cleared his throat and nodded. "I'll pay you back." His voice was thin.

"No, you won't. Then you'll just be trying to pay off another Frank. I won't allow it."

He let a ghost of a smile appear at the corners of his mouth. He brushed a strand of hair from my face. "You get a little bossy when you're tired, you know."

I tried to smile, but it came off as more of a wince than anything. I looked down so he wouldn't see it. "This was the best night of my life. I want you to know that." I spoke the words into his breast pocket. Then I tore my hand from his and climbed into the cab. I slid onto the bench seat in the back, and Blue latched the door behind me. He reached in through the window and found my hand again.

"You don't have to go just yet," he said. "You could stay one more night." His voice wavered. He refused to look me in the eye.

I couldn't look at him either. I couldn't bring myself to say goodbye.

The taxi pulled away from the curb, and Blue's hand slipped from mine. I turned around and looked out the back window. He stood there, a hunched shadow, a bent frame, watching me go. His hands were in his pockets.

"Where to, miss?" the cab driver asked.

Through blurred tears, I handed him a five dollar bill. "As far as this will take me."

CHAPTER 12

Impact

When I return to my garden in Limbo, Porter is there waiting for me. He's still wearing his black polo and orange ball cap, but the laugh lines around his watery eyes are long gone.

"What the hell do you think you're doing?" he says, storming up to me and grabbing me by my coat collar. "Do you think this is some sort of game?"

"I didn't do it on purpose, I swear," I say, cowering. "I didn't know I wasn't supposed to touch the soulmarks."

"I'm not talking about touching soulmarks. I'm talking about ignoring me when I told you to leave. I'm talking about staying as long as you could in that body with no regard for the rules. I'm talking about making an impact." He pushes me away like he can't stand the sight of me, and I stumble backwards. He turns his back to me, pacing. Steam rises from his shoulders.

"I thought we were supposed to use time travel to help people," I say. "I thought that's what I did."

He wheels around and aims a finger at me. "That's not

149

what you did. You played dress-up while you chased after some ridiculous teenage fantasy. You can't make that much of an impact on the past. You can't fall in love."

"I didn't."

He gives me this cynical look that makes me think twice about my answer. I hadn't fallen in love, had I? It was one day. One date.

"What about him, then?" Porter says. "You don't think he fell in love?"

I don't know how to respond. I'm too shocked to form a coherent sentence. Surely Blue hadn't fallen in love with me. We shared a kiss. A single kiss. We held hands. It didn't mean he was in love.

Porter squeezes the bridge of his nose like he has a migraine. "Our impact on the world as a whole, as humans, is microscopic compared to the ebb and flow of the universe. We think we're so important that if we go back in time and move a pebble in the street in 1943, we'll send the world toppling off its axis. It's simply not true. What can change the course of the world, however, is the impact we make on individual lives. This is why we never stay longer than a few hours, and we never manipulate historical events. We never interfere in the lives of historical figures. We are spectators only. We are listeners. Gatherers of knowledge. Now and again we move something – an artifact, a document – to a secret location so we can recover it in Base Life, but we do so after years of meticulous research. We only take things that are deemed lost or destroyed in the present time. We change things that no one will notice. We don't make an impact. But you?" His short laugh is dry and hollow. "You broke just about every rule we have – short of killing someone – on your first run. I think that must be some kind of record."

I sink down to the black and hug my knees to my chest. I feel like throwing up.

I hate screwing things up. I don't take things apart and leave the pieces scattered across the floor. I finish what I start, and I make it work better than it did before.

Porter heaves a sigh. The steam rising from his shoulders starts to fade. "We all remember our first loves, Alex. Second and third loves come and go, but first loves..." He pauses as though recalling his own. "They change our lives. They make an impact. That boy is going to make decisions now that he wouldn't have made if he hadn't met you. Those decisions will change the course of his existence. They'll make a ripple effect. It will change things on Earth. If you go back to your Base Life now, there's no telling what could be different. He may decide to take a different path in life because you left him that money. And worse yet, he may miss out on another love because he was looking for you or waiting for you to return. In that case, a child who was meant to live may never be born. Generations would disappear overnight. Do you understand what I'm saying to you?"

My tongue is thick and stuck to the roof of my mouth. Of all the things I could possibly screw up, I had to go and delete entire generations from existence. With my first kiss.

"Is there a way to fix it?" My throat is so dry, I can hardly hear my own words.

"You think I would've let you go if there wasn't?"

I scramble to my feet. "What is it then? I'll do anything."

Porter hesitates. He looks like he doesn't trust me. "You'll have to go back to 1927."

"OK. Then what do I do? Tell him he can't keep the money? Tell him I really am married to a mob boss?"

"No. This time you won't be speaking to the boy at all. You'll go back to when you first landed, when you woke up in his apartment that morning. You will dress yourself in whatever suitable clothes you can find, and you will sneak out without speaking to the boy or his mother. No sleeping in until lunchtime. No pickled cucumber soup. No date. No kissing. And you'll take the money in the bedside table with you." I open my mouth to interject, but he continues. "You'll take a taxi back to the bakery, leave your host body there, and report back here. Understand?"

I stare at him like there are marbles spilling from his ears. "You can't be serious. Everything I went through, everything that happened... You want me to erase it?"

He lifts his chin, daring me to defy him. "Yes."

"But..." I grasp at straws, trying to delay the inevitable. "I didn't sleep in until lunchtime. I landed at lunchtime."

"You landed in a sleeping body. You slept for hours before you woke up. This time you're going to wake up before morning. You'll sneak out without a sound. That way all he'll remember of this whole fiasco is that he saved a girl's life in front of the bakery, and she saved his in the alley. He brought her home, nursed her wounds, and she was gone the next morning. It'll be a story he can tell his grandchildren, a mystery he'll wonder about from time to time, but it won't make a life-changing impact."

"How do you know about all that, anyway? The bakery? The alley? The pickled cucumber soup? I didn't tell you about any of it."

"I saw it when I tapped into your soulmark."

"You mean, when you were inside my head, you were spying on me?"

"No. When you tap into a soulmark, if you have the strength to touch it and not be pulled into the past, you can see fragments of that soul's entire timeline. I saw bits and pieces of what you saw. Peg Leg. Buckingham Fountain. The soup."

I look out at all fifty-six of my soulmarks. "So your past is written on your soulmark like a record? If I tap in, I can see what my other lives were like without traveling into those bodies?"

"Theoretically." The word is short and clipped. "But you don't have the strength. And you're not allowed to touch a soulmark again without my express consent and supervision."

"So you know what I was like in 1927, don't you? You know what the money was for. Why I could fight and run so well."

He purses his lips. "Yes, but I'm not going to tell you. Maybe never knowing the truth about that life will be sufficient punishment for what you've done. And after you return, I'm going to remove that soulmark so you'll never find it again."

I must have a pitiful look on my face because Porter softens. "You can't get attached to your past lives, Alex. You can't get attached to the people you meet there. Trust me when I say they are but strangers on a train. Unfamiliar faces in a stack of photographs. If you try to find them in your Base Life, they'll all be dead and gone. Long since buried." He steps up to me and places his hands on my shoulders. "You, Alex Wayfare, won't truly know any of them. And they won't truly know you."

I know he's right – if Blue, Nick, happened to run into my 1927 self later on, she wouldn't remember him at all. She wouldn't know him, and he wouldn't know her.

But I know Nick Piasecki, the deli delivery boy from 1927. That fact wouldn't change. I would never unlearn him, never forget his face. I'd know him for the rest of my life. And he would know me.

At least, some form of me.

I drop my shoulders under the weight of his hands. They feel so heavy all of a sudden. "When do you want me to go back?"

"Right now." He gestures to the soulmark closest to us. "Take hold of it. It'll do the rest."

I ease up to it, apprehensive about the magnetic pull. The soulmark sways slowly before me, taunting me. Almost like it knew what it was doing when it pulled me in the last time. I look back at Porter over my shoulder. "I have no other choice?"

The look he gives me is enough.

I reach out.

It sucks me in.

Return to Sender

This time I felt myself land. The black released its hold like a glove slipped from a hand. Porter was right, I did land in a sleeping body. It was difficult to shove off the heaviness of sleep, but I managed to do it far quicker than last time. I awoke to Helena's darkened bedroom awash with moonlight.

I rolled out of her bed without a sound. My bare feet met the wood floor. In the oval mirror above the dresser, my 1927 self stared back at me. Cream-colored nightgown. Bony shoulders. Dark hair rolled in Sousa curlers.

Sad eyes.

I picked up the photograph of Blue, the one of him leaning against the brick wall beside Frank. My fingertips traced the outline of his face. I swallowed at a knot in my throat that wouldn't go away. A few hours ago, I thought I'd never see him again. Now I was back under his roof, just a few steps from his bedroom door.

I guess both of our wishes came true after all.

It didn't seem fair, erasing the best day of my life from history. Erasing my first kiss. Just when I finally began to feel normal, the universe had to call a do-over.

Maybe I wasn't meant to be happy. Maybe I'd been happy enough for one soul over the course of fifty-six lives. Maybe this was the universe's way of balancing things out. I took something, and now it was time to give it back.

On a chair in the corner, I found my original clothes. The black skirt, the brown coat, the worn black boots. I guess I woke up before Helena could take them with her to work. I was glad I didn't have to steal anything of Helena's, and glad I wouldn't end up ruining the French woman's white gloves after all.

When I was dressed, I pulled the Sousa ribbons from my hair. Dark ringlets fell all around my face. I held the ribbons in my open hands, wishing I could take them with me. I could see it now – I'd be the only person in history to choke up every time she heard Stars and Stripes Forever.

I kept one of the ribbons to pull my hair back in a tail, just like it was the day I first saw my reflection. I slid Helena's bedside drawer open, and my hand closed around the roll of twenty-dollar bills. I was tempted to leave just one twenty in the drawer, but I didn't want Porter to send me back again.

Once was all I could take.

I inched open the bedroom door and peeked out into the hall. The house was still. A grandfather clock ticked below in the foyer. A slice of moonlight shone from beneath Blue's bedroom door.

I wanted to open it. Tiptoe to his bed and kiss him goodbye on the cheek. I wanted him to wake up, grab my wrist, and tell me not to go. To pull me under his blankets and make me forget all about Mr Lipscomb and Dr Farrow and Tabitha and suspension and schizophrenia. Hulking shadows of disappointment. Claire's embarrassment. Audrey's pale, shorn head under her bandana. Something told me Blue was more than capable of making me forget it all. When I was with him, everything else seemed hazy.

Alex.

I closed my eyes and sighed. I know, Porter. I'm going.

I made my way down the stairs, biting my lip and treading lightly on the outside of each step so they wouldn't squeak. Even though I was careful, several of them still sounded their protest against my weight.

I eased open the front door and stepped outside. The chill of black sky morning filled my lungs, making me shiver. The streets were deserted and cold. I looked back over my shoulder to take in the Piasecki apartment one last time.

Then a light flicked on upstairs. A shadow moved down the hall.

"Alex?" I heard Blue whisper.

I jerked the door closed behind me.

And I ran.

Porter's Reasons

This time when I return to Limbo I don't remain standing for long. I crumple to the black and start to cry like an idiot.

The funny thing about Limbo is, the perception of crying is just as powerful as the real thing. I even go through my normal routine: start crying because I'm overwhelmed, I've screwed something up, and can't fight the tears any longer; feel like a baby for crying and try battling the tears again; tell myself I can cry if I want to and let another wave of shudders crash over me; feel self-conscious because by now someone else knows I'm crying and they're standing there awkwardly, not knowing how to react; dry my tears, insist I'm all right, and begin to mend.

The awkward person in this case is Porter. His hands are in his pockets. The bill of his cap hides his face.

I'm actually glad he feels awkward.

"I'm sorry you had to do that," he says.

"No you're not." I swipe at my eyes with my sleeve. "You called my day with him a ridiculous teenage fantasy."

He heaves a regretful sigh, like he's ashamed of himself. "I'm sorry. Sometimes it's hard for me to remember you're only seventeen. You were very different in your last life. Very wise, very steady, very mature. I was angry and frustrated with you…" He shakes his head. "It doesn't matter what I was. I should have prepared you better." He offers a hand to me to help me up, but I don't take it. He frowns and replaces it in his pocket. "I had to know I could trust you, Alex. I had to know that bringing you here wasn't a mistake. If I can't trust you, then everything I've worked toward for the past seventeen years will be in vain."

"And what is it you're working toward exactly?" I say through the perception of a clogged nose. "Why are we here, Porter?"

"Because I need your help."

"With what?"

He opens his mouth, then closes it. "It's complicated."

Of course it is.

I groan and fist my hands. My nails bite into my palms. I'm too exhausted and upset to sit through more of his riddles and nonsense. I need to get away, to go somewhere where I'm allowed to cry and smash things.

I push myself to my feet and lift my chin. "I want to go home."

The lines around his eyes sag. His shoulders slump under the weight of my glare. "Certainly."

Within seconds, light rushes in all around me, and my soul slips free from the black like a suction cup. We're both back at Ristorante Cafferelli. The Polygon stone is still in my hand.

No time has passed at all.

I shove the stone into my backpack, and push my chair from the table.

"I'm sorry," Porter says again. He pulls a small white card from his pocket and hands it to me. "When you're ready to talk again – if you're ready to talk again – call this number." The card is blank except for a small phone number embossed in black.

I take it and stuff it in my backpack. I glance down at the bright yellow flyer on the table. "What are you going to do about that?"

It takes a moment before Porter realizes what I'm talking about. I can tell he still feels awful for making me go back and erase everything – it's pressing on him, making it hard for him to concentrate.

"I'll take care of that later."

I still don't know what he means by that – does he have to go back in time and leave it at the garage? – but I realize I don't care anymore. I heft my backpack over my shoulder and storm toward the door.

I don't look back.

CHAPTER 13

The Aftershock

When I get home, I drop my backpack by the back door and collapse onto a stool at the kitchen island. I peel off my parka and scarf, pull my glasses off, and bury my face in my hands. My body feels like it hiked the length of the Blue Ridge Mountains. I guess traveling back in time almost a hundred years can do that to a person.

The house is quiet and still. Gran must be out shopping. Pops and Audrey are probably napping. Claire is still at school, and Mom and Dad are at work. The silence gives me a little time to think of an excuse for bolting out of Mr Draper's class a few hours earlier. I figure playing the sick card is the best way to go.

I slide my glasses back on and trudge into the bathroom to give myself a once over. I brush out all the blood from my hair and comb it over the knot on the back of my head. I still have the bruises on my ribs, and a few on my arms, but my sweater covers them up. The only sign of my injuries are a few tiny scratches on my knuckles. I don't think anyone will even notice.

I head to the family room and slump down at the computer. My arms feel like sodden logs. My fingers pause, resting on the keyboard, wondering if I should go through with what I'm about to do. An Internet search on Nick could bring up a whole host of crap I'm not sure I'm ready to deal with. But I have to know. Did I ruin his life? Did I change it somehow, the path he was meant to take, all because I barreled into his world, selfishly wanting to prove Dr Farrow wrong about the visions? Or did I fix everything by erasing our night together?

I had to know how his life turned out. Did he live a good life? Did he join the Police Academy? Did he fall in love? Get married? Have kids? Are his grandchildren and great grandchildren living somewhere in Chicago? Did Frank ever turn his life around? Did Helena live to a lovely old age, rocking her grandchildren to sleep?

If it was a good life, I think I could forgive myself for being such a selfish ass. For playing with something that shouldn't be played with. Granted, I didn't know I was altering time and history when I traveled to Chicago the first time, but the second time...

God, I just didn't care, did I? I was too caught up in all of it. Too wrapped up in what it felt like to be normal, hanging out with friends, getting into trouble, kissing beside fountains, not worrying every minute of every day about grades and bullies and a sister who has trouble keeping her dinner down. It was an escape. The most selfish of all selfish escapes.

I type in his name. At first, there are no results for Nicholas or Micolaj Piasecki. Mostly because it takes several tries before I spell the name correctly. Finally, though, I spot one result.

An obituary.

Nick's name is written in bold capital letters across the top. There are no sentimental words, only facts. He was survived by his mother, Helena, and brother, Frank. The funeral was held at the St Stanislaus Kostka Parish.

Nick died on Christmas Eve, 1927, from six gunshot wounds to the chest. It was believed to be the work of the Cafferellis, due to Nick's involvement with the Fifth Street Gang. He was found in the back of the deli delivery truck he drove for Old Man Nowicki.

Two months after I walked out of his life.

I cover my mouth with my hands. A sharp breath rakes through me. I knew he would be dead and gone, but I didn't expect it to happen like that. Not to someone so young.

Someone so good.

I grip the keyboard with both hands, wanting to break it in half. I could've changed things, but Porter wouldn't let me. If Porter hadn't made me go back and erase my night with Blue, my impact could've changed the course of his life. I could've saved him. Given him more time. He wouldn't have continued to work for Fifth Street. He'd made a promise to me, but I erased that promise.

He wouldn't have gotten murdered on Christmas Eve.

I march back to the kitchen and yank my cell phone from my backpack. I fish around for Porter's business card, then punch in his number.

He picks up after one ring. "Alex?"

"You knew, didn't you? You knew Nick would die if I went back to erase everything."

"Slow down–"

"How could you let me find out this way? Why couldn't you at least let me warn him?"

"I don't know what you're–"

I hang up on him, too disgusted to hear his voice or his excuses. I turn off my phone in case he tries to call back.

I wind aimlessly through the house, anger and grief twisting inside me, until I find Audrey asleep in Gran and Pops' bed. Her thin body is curled onto her side under a threadbare quilt, a pale blue stocking cap pulled low over her ears and forehead. Pops snores away in the wingback armchair in the corner, his head lolled back, his chin twitching under his short, scraggly gray beard. I pull my glasses off again and drop them on the bedside table. Under the quilt, I slide in beside Audrey and hide my face against her warm, bare arm. The tender darkness tries to coax tears out of me, but I'm too furious to give in.

I thought I'd be happy, thankful even, to know the true reason behind my visions. Now I wish I'd never sought the answer. Never gone to see Dr Farrow. Never met Porter at the cafe.

Audrey stirs when she notices I'm beside her. She stretches her arms above her head and rolls over to face me. "You're home early." Her keen gray eyes notice something's wrong right away. "What is it?"

I shake my head and press my face into the pillow. It smells like Gran's lemon verbena and Pops' pipe smoke.

"Did you have another bad dream?"

Audrey's the only person I ever told about the visions. I told her they were dreams so I could go into all the details without sounding like a complete psycho. She always liked hearing about them, but I don't want to talk about this one. If I could have it my way, I'd forget it ever happened.

"No," I mumble. "Felt sick so I came home."

She smooths my hair from my face. "Did you call Daddy and let him know?"

My reply is a groan in the pillow.

"OK, OK," she says. "I'll let you be." She's quiet for a minute or two, then says, "Except…"

I lift my head. "What?"

"Weren't you supposed to walk Claire home from school today?"

Applesauce.

Big Sister Time

I make it to Claire's school only a few minutes late. She's at the playground hunched over on a swing, twisting around in circles, then spinning free. All the other kids are filing onto school buses or into their parents' minivans.

I stick my fingers in my mouth and whistle for her, and her head pops up. She scoops up her pink backpack and races toward me. Her super straight chestnut hair swings behind her.

"You're late," she says.

"I know." I start back home the moment she catches up. "I got sick. I left school early."

"Did you call Daddy?"

I groan again, this time out loud. At least I have two annoying sisters to help keep my mind off Blue and Porter.

"When are you going to get your license?" Claire asks, half-jogging to keep up with me. "You need a car. Madeline's sister has a car. She picks her up every day."

Madeline's sister is none other than my bestest friend in the world, Tabitha. "Well, Madeline's sister doesn't have to pay for her car. So that makes it easy."

"It's a convertible."

"How nice."

"It's black."

"Ah, the same as her heart."

We turn a corner and continue down a tree-lined sidewalk. Blazing yellows, oranges, and reds pave the path under our feet.

"You could fix up an old car like you did for Daddy."

Even though I appreciate Claire's confidence in my fix-it skills, I still reply with, "I don't think so."

"Why not?"

I push my glasses up. "Because I'm not going to waste money on something I'd hardly ever use. I like walking."

Claire kicks at the leaves in front of her. "I hate walking."

"Then you buy a car."

"Hey, look," Claire stops and waves at a car headed our way. "That's Madeline's sister."

I pull her arm down, but her other one shoots straight up.

Tabitha pulls up beside us in her black BMW convertible, one wrist resting on the steering wheel. Her blonde curls lift in the wind, then settle around the shoulders of her too-tight cashmere sweater.

Jensen Peters sits in the passenger seat.

"Hey, Wayfare," he says with a half-smile. I expect the sound of his voice and his attention to make my stomach flip like it usually does, but it doesn't affect me at all. If anything, it makes the sting of what happened with Blue hurt even more. "What happened back there in Mr Draper's class? You OK? Do you need a ride?"

Tabitha slides her diva sunglasses down to the tip of her nose. "Yeah, Wayspaz, need a ride?"

Claire leaps up to the side of the car. "Yes! Can we ride home with you and Madeline?"

Tabitha shrugs like it's OK with her, but I pull Claire back. "Absolutely not," I say. "You don't get into cars with strangers."

"They're not strangers," Claire says. "They go to our church and your school."

"That hurts, Wayfare," Jensen says with a pretend pout. "I thought we were friends."

Friends. Right. Didn't he know it was his rumor that started me on this all-expenses-paid Freak Ride at school?

"She wishes," Tabitha says with a laugh.

I give her a sarcastic smile, thinking of all the ways I can turn her BMW into a heap of scrap metal. If only I had a socket wrench...

"Oh, come on," she says, draping her arm across Jensen's shoulders. Her manicured fingernails play with the honey blond hair at the back of his neck. "I'll give you a ride. No skin off my nose."

Claire jumps for the car again, but I snag her by her backpack. "No, thanks." I pull her away and start for home.

"Have it your way, Freak." Tabitha peels away from the curb, but her trademark insults don't bother me as much anymore. Once you've been in a gang fight, been shot at with Tommy guns, traveled to Limbo and back, had your first kiss erased from existence, and let a friend die because you couldn't save him, a few stupid names are a drop in the bucket.

Just a few blocks from home, Claire says, "Madeline said you can't drive because you have seizures."

"Oh, give me a break. Not you, too."

"She also said if you had a car, you'd want to ride on Jensen's lap in the back seat."

"What?" I stop short and stare at her.

She shrugs her shoulders up to her ears. "I don't know. That's just what she said."

"You better not repeat that to Mom and Dad."

"Why not? Is it bad?"

I push her out in front of me so I can walk by myself. Big sister time is so over.

Porter, the Hacker

By the time we get home, I'm so confused and frustrated and annoyed that I don't notice Mom's car in the driveway. Claire runs inside to catch her stupid after-school TV shows, and I almost smack right into Mom when I walk through the kitchen door.

"What's wrong?" I blurt out, knowing something's up right away. She never comes home early. And it couldn't be because I cut class. Dad never calls in reinforcements for things like that. So it must be about Audrey.

I bristle at the thought. Audrey looked fine when I left to pick up Claire, but what if I was too busy thinking about Blue and hating on Porter that I didn't notice something was wrong? "What happened?"

"Nothing happened," Mom says, palms out to calm me. She must know what I'm thinking because of the panic written on my face. "We just had a security breach at work, that's all."

My entire body sags in relief, and I slump against the kitchen island. She wraps her arms around me, and I lean into her, feeling exhausted all over again.

"Audrey says you got sick at school today." She smooths my hair from my forehead. "You feel warm and clammy."

"I feel horrible," I say, which is the complete truth.

"Why don't you go rest until dinner? I'll call you when it's ready."

I nod and trudge toward the doorway, but I don't leave the kitchen just yet. I lean against the doorframe and watch her grab a box of taco shells from the pantry and a package of ground beef from the fridge. I love seeing her like this. Making dinner. Doing something a normal mom would do. Something mundane. "What was the security breach?" I ask. "Everyone OK?"

"Everyone's fine," she says, peeling the plastic wrap off the beef. "I don't know all the details, but apparently someone hacked into the medical database last night."

I can't help but drop my jaw. "Someone hacked into AIDA?"

Mom nods.

"But that's impossible," I say. "You guys have incredible security. It would take a genius to break in. I should know, I've tried to–"

Mom looks at me, an eyebrow quirked.

I stop short, realizing what I was about to say, then quickly rephrase. "I mean, I've tried to think of a company with better security. There isn't one. AIDA's is foolproof. Even better than the CIA."

Mom smiles to herself as she slides the beef into a skillet on the stove. "Well, better than the CIA or not, someone broke in and deleted a bunch of files from several departments, including Dr Farrow's office. They won't be taking any more appointments until the new year while they sort it all out, so I guess we'll have to find someone else for you to talk to."

I grip the doorframe to keep my legs from giving out on me again. Someone broke in and deleted a bunch of files. The very files that probably held all Dr Farrow's notes about my visions. Three guesses who that someone was. Now I know what Porter meant when he said he'd taken care of it.

Mom turns to look at me. "You need to go lie down, Bean. You look worse than when you came in." She shoos me out the door with a wooden spoon.

I find my way to Gran and Pops' bedroom and crawl back into bed beside Audrey. I fall asleep right away, but rest is futile. I can't stop dreaming about Blue lying there left for dead, blood leaking from his chest, the light in his blue-green eyes going dark.

Jensen, Jensen, Jensen

At dinner, I chase diced tomatoes around my taco salad with my fork. Grief coils around my ankle like a ball and chain. Mom and Dad give me space, thinking I still feel sick. Pops and Claire are oblivious. But Gran and Audrey watch me like a pair of hawks.

After dinner, they clutch my arms, one on either side, and drag me into Gran's bedroom. Audrey sits beside me on the bed, and Gran closes the door.

"All right, Bean. Spill." Gran crosses her arms over her favorite oatmeal-colored cardigan. There are fall leaves stitched on the pockets. She stares me down with the same look she uses on the neighborhood boys who steal our newspaper. "You're not sick, are you? This is about a boy. Your mom used to sulk around the same way when she was your age."

"Is it Jensen?" Audrey asks in her soft, careful way.

I toss my hands up. "It's not Jensen. Would everyone stop talking about Jensen? I don't like him like that anymore. And heaven forbid I have anything else to sulk about other than a boy."

Gran sits on the other side of me. The mattress sinks on her side, raising Audrey up six inches on the other. "You two lovebirds have a fight?" Gran says.

I groan and fall back on the bed. Gran and Audrey lie on their sides on either side of me. I'm barricaded in by concerned faces.

Two very cute concerned faces, at least.

"Look," I say. "I don't like Jensen. He doesn't like me. We're not lovebirds. That's not why I'm upset. End of story."

Gran shoots Audrey a look. "OK, Pea Pod, I played bad cop. Now it's your turn." She climbs off the end of the bed and leaves us to ourselves.

I narrow my eyes at Audrey and clasp my hands behind my head. "OK, Pea Pod. What ya got?"

"Come on," she says, giving me a shove. "I'm starving for drama. You still get to go to school. I have to spend my freshman year at home with Gran and Pops, remember?"

"Believe me, going to school is worse. I wish I could stay home with Gran and Pops."

"What happened with Jensen?"

"Oh, for the love of Pete." I sit up and look her in the eye. "I swear to you, it has nothing to do with Jensen. Now will you please stop saying his name?"

"Is it about your appointment with the psychiatrist you saw yesterday?"

I flop back down on my back. Grief tightens around my ankle even more, cutting off circulation. "No. I just had another bad dream, all right? A very, very bad dream."

"What was it about?" Her voice is pink silk, soft and warm. It usually comforts me, calms my nerves, but this time the wound is too deep to soothe.

I chew the inside of my lip, trying not to picture Blue's face when the taxicab pulled away, or his teasing grin right before he caught my face in his hands and kissed me. I try not to remember the look he gave me when I jumped out of the dumpster in the alley. Or the first time he called me Sousa. And I try desperately not to think about him dying, all alone, in the back of his delivery truck.

God, he didn't deserve that.

I should've been there.

I should've prevented it.

My throat tightens and it's hard to speak. I stare up at the lace valance across the top of Gran and Pops' bay window. There's a cobweb in the corner, and it could use a dusting. I think about climbing up there and taking care of that for them right now.

"Allie?"

I can't tell Audrey about Blue dying, even if I tell her it was all just a dream. I've never been able to talk to her about death. Not when my biggest fear is coming home to Mom standing in the kitchen, eyes rimmed red, holding one of Audrey's bandanas in her hands. If it hurts this much to lose someone from a past life, how much will it hurt to lose my sister?

I sniff and wipe my nose with the back of my hand. I can't let her see me fall apart. I have to be strong for her. Always strong. So I pat her hand and just say, "I'll be OK."

CHAPTER 14

Neighbors

When I wake up the following morning, it's half past eleven. A note on my bedside table from Mom and Dad says they called in to school for me, they hope I feel better, and they love me. The smell of Gran's homemade cinnamon rolls lingers in the air from breakfast. I make my way downstairs, hoping to find a few left.

The house is empty. I find two cinnamon rolls on a plate under a dishtowel on the kitchen island. A note from Gran says she and Pops took Audrey to one of her appointments.

It's been a long time since I've had the house to myself. Part of me wants to stay and take advantage of the peace and quiet, maybe work on some of my projects, but I know I wouldn't be able to concentrate. There are too many questions left unanswered.

I power on my cell phone while I take a bite of cinnamon roll, expecting to see a dozen calls from Porter, but there isn't even one.

I redial his number.

"Hello?" he says in his distinctive, gentlemanly voice.

"Where are you? I need to talk to you. Do you live somewhere downtown?"

"Alex?"

I lick the glaze from my fingers and rummage in a drawer for pencil and paper. "Give me your address. I can take the bus."

"I didn't think I'd hear from you so soon."

"Address," I say, pencil poised.

He's quiet for a moment, then says, "142 Elmwood."

I start to write it down, then drop the pencil. "142 Elmwood is just down the street."

"Well, you needed protection. Someone had to keep an eye on you–"

I hang up on him and grab the last cinnamon roll and my army-green parka on the way out the door.

142 Elmwood is a cute two-story Victorian with yellow siding, white trim, and two bright red Japanese Maples in the front yard. Porter sits on the front porch in a rocking chair when I arrive, smoke curling from a cigar in his hand. He's wearing jeans again and another black polo. No cap today, just very, very, short white hair.

"This is Mrs Yoder's place," I say, crossing the leaf-covered yard to the porch. Sunlight warms the top of my head.

Porter nods and rocks back and forth. "She rents the top floor to me."

I stand at the base of the porch steps, my hands in my coat pockets. "How long have you been here?"

"Renting from Mrs Yoder? About three years. Before that I lived in that apartment complex on Baybury. Before that I rented a house on Maple."

I narrow my eyes at him. "You've been spying on me my whole life?" The thought gives me the creeps. What had he seen?

He points his cigar at me. "I've been protecting you. There's a difference."

"How do I know you're not just a filthy old man who has a thing for nerd girls?"

He frowns at me. "Do you think I look like a filthy old man?"

I shrug. "How would I know? I don't exactly keep a checklist for profiling pedophiles."

He makes a face, the kind I make when I try a sip of coffee. "That might be the most disrespectful thing I've ever heard you say. Do you speak like that to all your elders?"

Elders. That makes me snort. "Sadly, I haven't met too many elders worthy of respect outside my family. Adults seem pissed off because of their life choices and take it out on us kids because, unlike them, we still have time; or they're blind and forgot what it was like to be a kid so they try to put us in a glass box; or they're jackasses just for the fun of it; or they're blissfully ignorant of, like, everything. Which one are you?"

He levels his eyes at me. "I'm not a liar." He flicks his cigar and flecks of ash sprinkle to the porch floor.

I level my eyes back at him, my chin lifted. "All adults are liars. They lie under the guise of protection, but it's still lying."

"Protection can be a good thing," he says. "It can give a child freedom to grow, to live their life without shadows of despair lurking beyond every turn. It gives a child boundaries, a sanctuary within the cruel world. Protection builds walls. Keeps a child safe, just like I've kept you safe all this time." He leans forward in his rocking chair. "Tell me, are you happier now that you know the truth? Or have you been wishing you'd never met me at Ristorante Cafferelli?"

I scowl at him. I'm not sure why. Maybe it's because he knows too damn much, or because he makes too much damn sense. "So what exactly have you been protecting me from?"

He sucks on his cigar, then puffs out a cloud of smoke that veils his face for a moment. "From Durham Gesh."

A cold breeze rustles the leaves and bites through my parka, making me shiver in the sunlight. I pull my sleeves down over my wrists. "What does the founder of AIDA want with me?"

Porter raises an eyebrow. "If I tell you more of the truth, the truth you say you want to hear, do you promise not to storm off again?"

I roll my eyes and flop down on the porch steps. "Come on. I stormed off because you made me erase everything, and I was trying to wrap my head around all this time travel and reincarnation stuff, and I was frustrated, and you were super confusing and annoying."

I catch the smallest grin behind his cigar. "Fair enough," he says. "Shall I try to be less confusing and annoying today?"

I push my glasses up. "That would help. Seriously."

"How about you ask the questions this time?" he says. "I'll answer as simply as I can."

I lean my back against one of the porch pillars, hoping Porter's serious about keeping things simple. "OK. Start with Durham Gesh. Why do I need protection from him?"

He breathes in another mouthful of smoke, then drops his cigar and flattens it with his heel. "Because at the end of your last life, you and Gesh had a falling out. You didn't agree with his methods anymore, so you left AIDA. Escaped is a better word for it. He's been looking for you ever since. It's my job to make sure he never finds you."

The way Porter says that makes me feel like a rabbit out in the open with wolves on the prowl. "What happens if he finds me?"

"He'll force you to work for him again."

"And what if I refuse?"

"You won't."

"How do you know?"

Porter glances down the street in the direction of my house. "There are exactly six reasons why you won't, and four of them share your last name."

My family.

"He'd threaten my family?"

His rocking chair creaks. "He'd do much worse than threaten."

My hands are fists on my knees. My heart is in my ears. "That doesn't make any sense. I've never done anything to him."

"Not in this life, no. But he knows you were reincarnated again. He knows I'm hiding you. For him, that's enough."

I shake my head. "Then I'll work for him. I don't care. I worked for him before, right? If it keeps my family safe, I'll do anything."

Porter stops rocking. "You can't work for Gesh."

"Why not? All of this," I say, waving my hands, "my ability, the visions, being a Descender, it's caused enough trouble for my family already. It needs to stop. If I can stop it by working for Gesh again, then I will."

Porter scrubs a frustrated hand over his face. "He can't find you, Alex. If he finds you, it'll ruin everything."

"Why?"

"Because you're a Transcender." Porter says it like I'm stupid. Like that should mean something to me. "You're more powerful than all of us, all of the Descenders combined, which makes you dangerous. You're the only one who can bring Gesh down, and he knows it. So he wants you contained. If he finds you, he'll break you. Make it so you can't fight back, can't do anything except follow his orders. He did it to you once before. He'll do it again. It's his specialty."

A memory flashes before me. I'm that little girl with braids again, the same little girl playing Polygon, but this time I'm strapped to a chair in the middle of a sterile medical room. The lights above are harsh and bright. The boy with the wire-rimmed glasses watches me from the doorway. He looks worried for me, his dark eyes round and wide. A tall man in a white lab coat shines a blinding light in my right eye. It's Gesh, I know it is, I remember it being him, but I can't see his face past the light.

"Kan du huske hvem du er?" he says. Do you remember who you are?

I shake my head no.

He slaps me, hard. So hard I almost pass out.

"Husker du nu?" he says. Do you remember now?

Tears spill down my cheeks and lips. My whole body trembles. I rub my bare forearms and wrists, my palms sliding over rashes and scars and burns and bruises.

I cower as he raises his hand to strike me again.

That's all I can remember. The memory is gone. Out of reach. But I can still feel the sting of his hand on my cheek. I can still feel the painful scars on my wrists.

I let go of my sleeves, which I'd been gripping this whole time. I push them up to expose the bare skin underneath. I run my fingers over my wrists. They're pink and perfect. No scars. But I remember them now. Burning cigarettes pressed into my flesh. Ropes tied tight, rubbing my skin raw. Serrated knives slicing patterns in blood.

My nails bite into the palms of my fists. I squeeze my eyes shut. That memory of Gesh awakens a mixture of fear and hatred I hadn't known was inside me. I don't remember anything else about him, or my last life, but I have a feeling Porter was right to keep me hidden.

My teeth chatter, and I start to shiver, suddenly feeling cold and bitter. Porter notices my discomfort and motions for me to follow him inside. We climb painted stairs to the top floor. Porter's apartment is sparse, to say the least. A tiny kitchenette in the corner looks out over the street, and a futon and over-stuffed armchair take up all the space in the living room. It smells like burnt toast, coffee, and cigar smoke. It's hard to believe Porter has lived like this, without anything to his name, for so many years.

All because of me.

Porter fills an electric teapot with water from the tap. I fall onto the cushions of the armchair, feeling bad for treating him the way I have. He'd only been doing what was best for me. This whole time. "I remember him," I say. "I remember Gesh."

Porter turns off the tap and looks at me.

I rub a hand over one of my forearms. "He tortured me, didn't he?"

Porter's eyes close for a moment, like my words pain him. Then he plugs the teapot in and flips the switch. "Gesh is a very troubled man."

"That's why I didn't agree with his methods at AIDA." I swallow a knot in my throat and hug my arms across my chest. "He hurt me. Hurt others too, I guess."

Porter gives me this grave, solemn look. "I won't let him hurt you ever again. Or your family. I'll do whatever it takes to keep you safe."

Somehow I know he's telling the truth. "Is that why you hacked in and deleted Dr Farrow's files? So there'd be no trace of my abilities?"

Porter pulls two mugs out of a cabinet and sets them on the counter. "I have to erase any trail that might lead Gesh to you. He has spies everywhere, especially at AIDA. Imagine one of them stumbling across Dr Farrow's files –

all her notes about a seventeen year-old girl plagued with realistic visions of the past. That would've led him straight to your doorstep."

I bury my face in the crook of my arm, feeling like such an idiot. If Porter hadn't been there to cover my tracks...

"Incidentally," he says, "I heard Dr Farrow accepted a very lucrative job offer in San Diego. She boarded a plane this morning. We won't be seeing her again anytime soon."

I peek up at Porter from behind my arm. "You made that happen?"

He drops a teabag into each mug. "Couldn't risk her being interrogated too heavily about the security breach."

I watch him pour hot water over the teabags, the steam curling past his face and up to the ceiling. "You must be a pretty good hacker to break into AIDA's database."

"I should be." He hands me a mug and sits down on the futon with his own. "I designed the system."

Answers... For Real This Time

I sip my tea slowly, so it doesn't burn my tongue, and Porter tells me all about Gesh.

"In the beginning, Gesh and Flemming lived by a strict code of ethics. Descending would be used for the good of humanity, nothing more. But Gesh lost sight of the code somewhere along the way. Once AIDA became large enough, and Gesh had trained enough recruits to do his cancer research for him, he took a step back to explore his own passions and greed. Descending was no longer a means to saving the world. It became a vehicle for conquering the world." Porter leans against the back of the futon and props an ankle on his knee. "Imagine if I wasn't there to chaperone your descent to Chicago. Imagine if you could get away with anything. What would you have done?"

I know exactly what I would've done. It involves Blue's bedroom, his biceps, and a lot more kissing. But I don't dare say that to Porter.

"You see," Porter says, dunking his teabag up and down, "you were upset that I made you erase your first kiss. But you only erased it in that boy's past. In your past life's past. Not in your present. That kiss will still be your first, forever and always. You feel sick about it because the boy you shared it with won't remember. That your night together may have prevented his unfortunate fate. But what if you didn't care about that? What if you only cared about your own experience and nothing more?

"When Gesh discovered he could experience all the pleasures of the world – all the pleasures of a lifetime – in no more than a blink of an eye, he was hooked. He descended into bodies and used them however he saw fit. Gambling, drugs, sex, murder. He could live as wretchedly as he wanted – he could push life to the limit in those other bodies – and never sully his present day reputation as the revered founder of AIDA. The saint who dedicated his life to saving the world, one person at a time." Porter makes a sound in his throat like he's disgusted.

"For a while, when he was younger, sex was his main conquest. He took what he couldn't have in Base Life. An enemy's wife. A rabbi's daughter. An actor or actress he fancied. It was all a game to him, seeing how far he could go. He could make all the impact he wanted, and all he had to do was go back and erase it, like you did your first kiss. Poof. It never happened. He did the same with drugs. With gambling. He pushed everything to the limit, even going so far as assassinating half a dozen US presidents, simply because he could get away with it. He used the past as his own personal playground. He stopped searching for cures long ago. Now the only things he searches for are lost treasures and unclaimed inheritances, just to line his own pockets."

Porter places his soggy teabag on a saucer on his lap. "Remember I mentioned moving documents and other things to hidden locations to recover in Base Life? Like a time capsule? It's just as easily done with treasure. And a lot more profitable. Within a few years, Gesh was the richest man on earth. Only no one knew it. They still don't know it. He started companies and organizations all over the world to cover his tracks and launder the money he makes from his discoveries. Under the banner of AIDA, he bought out museums, universities, gave grants to private archeological teams – all so he could keep his personal name in the clear. He wanted AIDA to be recognized for every major historical breakthrough, not himself. Did you hear about that recent lost artifacts discovery in Scotland?"

I nod, remembering how it was all over the news. The largest and most priceless archeological find in history. Gold, silver, rubies, coins, armor, weapons – all sleeping peacefully in the highlands since the Dark Ages. My eighth grade history teacher made us write a report on it. "A team from a Scotland museum dug it all up. It was worth millions."

"That's the one. It took Gesh years to discover it. He sent dozens of Descenders back to the Dark Ages and the time of the Crusades, sending them into bodies of soldiers, of civilians. Each time he gathered more clues about the location of the lost hoard, until finally, he got the tip he was looking for. He bought the land using a phony identity that couldn't be traced back to AIDA. Then when the time was right, he sent anonymous tips to the museum. His museum, mind you. When his team dug it up, the news spread fast. The museum took in donations from philanthropists to purchase the hoard from the landowner, which was Gesh. No one knew the massive amount of money they donated to Gesh went straight into Gesh's pockets. Gesh walked away with millions and got to keep the treasure. It belongs to the museum now, which belongs to AIDA, which belongs to him. He's playing God with the world, and no one's the wiser."

"What a brilliant, sick, twisted bastard," I say, shaking my head.

Porter nods. "I thought the novelty of it – if you can forgive me for using such an innocent term – would eventually wear off, but it hasn't. He won't stop until he has everything. Until the world is his."

I grip my mug so hard it's in danger of cracking in two. Of course he won't stop. Not the kind of man who'd smack and cut and burn a little girl who didn't perform the way he wanted. The feeling of fear and hatred inside me that awoke when I remembered my past life with Gesh is now a solid knot of disgust lodged in my chest. I know what it's like to feel that lure of addiction. The feeling of Base Life slipping away. The thrill of attaching myself to another existence, one where I'm not the Fix-it Freak. Wrapping my arm around Blue's. Looking up into his blue-green eyes. Letting it all go for the chance to be someone else just a little while longer.

It was so easily done. I can see why he was hooked.

But I'd never let myself go as far as Gesh. That was his weakness.

Not mine.

"At least some good comes out of all this," I say. "AIDA truly is saving the world. They've saved countless people. Audrey's still alive because of AIDA. They've paid for all of her treatments. And Mom and Dad have always had all the money they need for their research."

"No thanks to Gesh," Porter says. "AIDA's a non-profit. It's one of his most brilliant schemes. All that funding your parents get? It comes from donations, not from Gesh. But you're right. There are plenty of people who work for AIDA who still care. Your parents are a perfect example. Most of the employees have no idea what goes on at the top of the corporate ladder. In the smoke-filled back rooms."

Porter was right. Mom and Dad had no idea who they truly worked for.

"It's unethical for Gesh to use other people's bodies for his own gain," Porter says. "Especially when they can't remember what he makes them do or how he uses them.

That's partly why Flemming started doing research on reincarnating souls. A reincarnated soul descending over and over via its own soulmarks wouldn't have to violate a stranger's body. And Gesh was on board with the idea at first. Not because he cared about ethics, but because your soulmarks would be reusable. No more burning up soulmarks never to be used again. And he hoped you'd be able to remember your past lives. That way, when you descended, you'd fit into those lives seamlessly. You'd remember your mission and have all the memories of your host body. You could go back to any time period and find any lost document or artifact with ease. No years of research required. You'd know right where to look. But it didn't turn out the way he hoped. You didn't remember your past lives. You remembered the mission and your Base Life, but nothing else. Just like when you were in 1927 – you didn't know who you were, who your family was, or what the money in your pocket was for. Gesh considered it a defect in your memory. You had other defects too, ones neither Gesh nor Flemming anticipated. Gesh thought a reincarnated Descender would make things easier, but your defects only presented more obstacles for him and the Descension Project. That's why Gesh experimented on you. He tortured you for years, using all sorts of indecent methods, trying to get you to remember your past lives, fix your defects, turn you into the ultimate Descender. The ultimate Transcender. But something backfired. I don't know what happened exactly, but you turned on him. Became his enemy."

"And then I escaped?"

Porter nods. "I'm not sure how. I remember hearing gunshots, and then the facility alarms went off. You disappeared and went into hiding. I tracked you down a few months later, but you were dying. You made me promise to reincarnate you. To help you continue AIDA's original mission and stop Gesh. I hid your soulmarks so Gesh couldn't find them. I made sure you were reincarnated into a good family. I chose your mom and dad, even though they work at AIDA, because I figured Gesh would assume I'd take you as far away from him as possible. He'd never suspect I'd hide you right under his nose. Then I changed my name and went underground until you were grown and ready to travel again."

I stare at my hands like they aren't really my own. Like I don't recognize them anymore. "You did all of that for me? Because I asked you to?"

Porter sips his tea, and a small smile reaches his eyes. "I would've done it for you anyway."

Sabotage

"So how do we stop Gesh?" I ask. "Can't we go to the police?"

Porter chuckles. "And tell them what?" He carries his empty mug and saucer to the kitchen and sets it in the sink.

"That he's laundering all that money," I say. "That it's all tied to AIDA. It's fraud, isn't it?"

"We don't have proof. And even if we did, he'd never be convicted. Not someone who's had every president in his pocket since Nixon."

I sit up and almost spill my tea in my lap. "He has the government on his side?"

Porter lifts an eyebrow. "Where do you think the United States gets most of its funds? Taxes?"

Something inside me stirs as I sink back in the armchair cushions. I can't tell if it's shock and disbelief that our country is basically run by Gesh, or if it's knowing the most powerful man in the world thinks I'm a threat. "There's nothing we can do?"

"Not in Base Life. But in Limbo," Porter wags a finger at me, "on our turf, we have a few advantages."

"Like what?"

Porter scrubs his mug with a soapy dishrag. "Before I left, I stole a copy of Gesh's itinerary." He smiles across the counter at me. "I know when he's going to send Descenders, where he'll send them, and what treasure he's sending them to look for. My plan is to send you back in time to derail his plans."

"How?"

"If Gesh is looking for a certain treasure, you'll find it first. If he sends a Descender to find the whereabouts of a lost relic, you'll get to it before he does."

"You want me to sabotage his treasure hunts?"

"Precisely. He's obsessed with them. That obsession is his one true weakness."

"But why do you need me for that? Why can't you do it? You're a Descender, too, aren't you?"

"Yes, but your past lives were reincarnated with all of Gesh's treasure hunts in mind. The years in which you were born were never coincidences. Each time and place, and each family you were born into, had a specific purpose."

I wrinkle my nose, not really getting it, but he shakes his head. "Don't worry. You'll see what I mean when you go on your first mission."

"But isn't sabotage too convoluted? Couldn't we just go for the more straightforward, obvious solution?"

"What's that?"

I fist my hand into the shape of a gun. "Take him out."

The edge of Porter's mouth tugs into a smile. "Tell you what, if you can find him, I'll let you have the first shot."

"He's in hiding, too?"

"The day you left, he packed up everything. Lit a torch to the research facilities and disappeared. Remember, he has unlimited resources. We'll never find him in Base Life."

I frown down into my mug. "So this is the only way to beat him? By slashing his tires? It seems juvenile."

"It is juvenile. All weaknesses are. But it's the only thing that will work, the only thing that will smoke him out of his hole. You have to understand how Gesh works. I've known him long enough to know that nothing comes between him and the hunt. And you and I are about to do just that. Every time he shoots, he's going to miss. It'll make him crazy. He'll start getting sloppy. Making mistakes. If all goes to plan, he may crash and burn all on his own, and we'll never have to lay a finger on him. Never even see him face-to-face. He'll never find out who you are, and your family will remain safe, free to devote all their time to finding a cure for Audrey, just like they are now. Things can remain the same on the surface, and no one will know we're involved."

I raise my brow at him. "That's a pretty good plan, Porter."

He bowed his head. "Thank you. I've had a few years to perfect it."

A pang of guilt for setting Porter on this course pricks me in the gut. That coupled with the hatred I remember feeling for Gesh, and the fierce, instinctive need to protect my family from him at all costs, tingles and sparks beneath my skin. I down the rest of my tea, join Porter at the counter, and hand him my empty mug.

"When do we start?"

The Raphael

Porter orders pizza, and we spread Gesh's itinerary and research papers out on the floor like a carpet. We eat from paper plates on our laps while Porter tries to explain Gesh's theories to me. I thought I was smart, but it's like the papers are written in an alien language. Most of what Porter says about the space-time continuum, dimensions, manifolds, and longitude and latitude soars right over my head.

Until he narrows the focus to my first mission.

"Portrait of a Young Man by Raphael," Porter says. "The most famous missing painting of all time." He tosses a photo of it in front of me. I wipe my hands on a napkin while I look at it.

The subject in the painting looks out at me from the corner of his eye. He wears a black beret and something that looks like a thick fur stole over one shoulder. But there's something about his feminine features and the way his long hair curls like silk at his chest that throws me off.

"Looks to me like it should be Portrait of a Young Woman," I say, wiping pizza sauce from my mouth.

Porter pages through more of Gesh's papers. "There are some who would agree with you. Others say it's a self-portrait of Raphael himself. Either way, it's been missing since the Nazis stole it in 1939. Last seen in 1945 in the possession of Hans Frank, one of Hitler's governors. Gesh sent a Descender back to infiltrate Hans' home in Neuhaus." Porter holds up one page in particular and squints as he scans it. "Apparently, Hans ordered one of his men to transfer the painting to his summer home in France before he was arrested by the Americans. But the painting never arrived. Hans' man went into hiding with it. Gesh sent Descenders back dozens of times to track the man down." Porter places the page he was reading in front of me and taps it. "The man's name was Schneider. On his deathbed, he told the Descender that he hid the painting inside the backing of another. A large landscape of the Rhine River Castle that had been in his family for years. The last Descender Gesh sent in search of the Rhine River painting learned that it was last seen in 1961, at the estate home of Charles Mitchell, outside Cincinnati. Now, in order for Gesh to find out if that's true, he needs to find the soulmark of someone close to the Mitchell family somewhere in Polestar. Once he does, he can send a Descender back into that body and retrieve the Raphael, if it's there. Obviously he hasn't found a suitable soulmark yet, or else we would have heard of the Raphael's discovery. But lucky for us, I have." Porter's eyes meet mine. "I'd like to send you back there now."

"Like right now?"

"Well, within a week, preferably. You'd have some studying to do."

"On paintings?"

"On the Sixties."

Rules of Thumb

In one week, I manage to secretly learn everything I can about 1961, as well as fail two pop quizzes at school. (If they had been about John F. Kennedy and nuclear threats from the Russians, I would've aced them.)

After school on Halloween, I wave to Dad and Gran as they head off to take Claire trick-or-treating. She's dressed as Dorothy from The Wizard of Oz, and she convinced Dad to go as the Scarecrow. Gran refused to dress up, but promised that if anyone asked, she'll say she's Auntie Em.

Audrey is dressed in her usual costume, a black cat suit Gran made her when she was Claire's age. It's actually kind of upsetting that the black leotard and tights still fit her like a glove, but it's her favorite, so none of us discourage her. I sit by the fire in the family room with Pops, ready to take over candy duty if Audrey gets too tired. But there's a twinkle in her eye and a spark of energy about her – I can tell she's going to try her hardest to stay awake. Just seeing how much she treasures the little things, like passing out candy to trick-or-treaters or reading Robert Burns before she falls asleep, makes me want to show her the whole world before it's too late.

If only I could take her to Limbo with me. She could spend a lifetime there, traveling to the past, slipping into healthy bodies, never hurting again, while no time passed in Base Life at all. She could see everything.

I scrub tears from my eyes before she sees them, and decide that if Porter wants me to go on this mission for him, he'll have to give me something in return. A payment for my services.

That night, after dinner, I steal away to the front porch by myself. I curl up on our porch swing and finish off a mug of Gran's cider. Candlelight from Claire's jack-o'-lanterns flickers in the dark on the porch steps. I'm shrouded in a pocket of shadow, ready to meet Porter in Limbo.

Ready to experience the Sixties.

I pull the Polygon stone out of my pocket and run my fingers over the carved letters. LVI. IV. I see the little boy with the wire-rimmed glasses. Then the black takes me.

When I find my way to my garden of soulmarks, Porter is already there waiting for me.

"Ready for your first mission?" he says, his chin set proudly.

I square my shoulders. "Ready."

"Remember, you're just a spectator. Do not make an impact. An easy rule of thumb is this: No Acts of God. No floods. No forest fires. Don't destroy anything. Do not take a life, do not make a life."

"Make a life?"

"There will be no sexual intercourse during your travels. I know sex isn't a big deal to you kids nowadays, but it's one of the most dangerous things you can do as a Descender. Your host body could conceive. That child would change history."

"Couldn't I just go back and erase the sex?"

Porter glares at me.

I raise my hands in surrender. "I'm joking. Yeesh. You're like an insurance agent and a parent wrapped up in one."

He's still glaring at me.

"Porter, I'm serious. Consider me traditional in that sense, OK? You have nothing to worry about. I'm not like Gesh."

He makes a gruff noise in his throat, then moves on. "Remember the drill? Everything I told you? The addresses? The names? The safe deposit box number?"

"Yup."

"Make sure you write it all down first thing when you land."

"I got it, Porter."

He nods, then claps me on the shoulder. "Get yourself back here safe and sound."

CHAPTER 15

Mission Number One

The moment I landed, I knew something had gone terribly wrong.

First of all, I was naked.

In a river.

At night.

With four other kids my age.

And it was freezing.

I was so going to kill Porter when I got back to Limbo.

My arms suction-cupped over my chest under the water, but it was hard to cover up everything because, unlike in Base Life, my 1961 body actually had a chest.

Four blazing car headlights from the shore flooded the whole area with light. It reflected off the top of the water. It lit up the forest on the other side. The sharp, driving beat of Runaround Sue tumbled and rolled down the river. The singer crooned in his funky, raspy way, growling about Sue loving him then putting him down and going out with every guy in town. While the other four kids in the water, two girls and two guys, splashed and roared with laughter,

I scanned the shore for clothes. I spotted a few garments hanging from tree limbs near the cars.

Which meant running for it.

The moment I decided to go for the bank, all or nothing, two bare arms wrapped around my waist from behind. Some guy's lips grazed my neck. His teeth closed around my earlobe and tugged.

I responded as naturally as I could.

By screaming and slamming the back of my fist in his face.

"Holy Hell, Susie," he said, his voice muffled by cuppedhands.

But I didn't look back to see if he was OK. I splashed toward the shore and snagged the closest dress and pair of flats, and disappeared into the trees.

"Jim, are you all right?"

"What's gotten into her?"

"Hey, Susie! That's my dress!"

The dress was tight, and it kept getting snagged on a sticker bush, but I managed to squeeze it over my curvy, hourglass hips. The red wool was thick enough to warm my frigid bones, which were chattering just as much as my teeth.

"Susie!" A short girl with a cherub face, blonde and thin, pushed her way through the bushes to find me, clutching a towel around her. "Here's your dress. Mine's too small for you."

"It's fine," I said, giving up on the zipper in the back. "I'll just leave it unzipped. I'll get it back to you, don't worry."

She frowned down at the green drapey thing in her hand that must have been my dress. "What's wrong with you? Why did you hit Jim?"

I steadied myself against a tree trunk with one hand and pulled the flats on with the other, rivulets of water streaming from my hair down my bare back. I tried to remember what Porter told me about conversation. Be evasive. Don't pretend you have amnesia like you did in Chicago, just try to end the conversation every chance you get.

"I don't want to talk about it," I told the blonde, hoping she would drop it. All Porter told me about my life as Susan Summers was that I had two older brothers, Daniel and Bruce; a mom and a dad, Deborah and John; and I came from old money, raised in an affluent circle made up of politicians and land owners. I knew Charles Mitchell's address, I knew the painting I was looking for, and I knew the address of the bank in Cincinnati where Porter wanted me to secure the Raphael if I found it.

But I knew nothing about my skinny-dipping companions.

"Can you take me home?" I asked the blonde.

"You mean back to Jim's?" Her brown eyes were wide and round and innocent.

"No, I mean my home. Where I live. With Deborah and John."

She sputtered a laugh. "But you've been planning this night for weeks."

I struggled with the skirt of my dress, still tangled in a sticker bush. "We'll do it another time, OK?"

"But this is the only night we have Jim's place all to ourselves," she whined, flopping her arms at her side. "His parents get back tomorrow afternoon."

I stopped cold and stared at her. "We're staying the night at his house? All by ourselves?"

I peeked through the trees and watched the earlobe nibbler climb out of the water. He was tall and muscular, with broad shoulders and the kind of abs they put on the cover of magazines. His white blond hair was slicked back and dripping wet. His lips were full, his eyes dark and broody. The cocky scowl on his face looked well worn in, like it was his favorite expression. He pressed a collar shirt to his bloody nose, more worried about that than getting dressed it seemed.

Not that I was looking.

Magazine abs or not, he was so not my type.

"I can't go to his house," I hissed, ripping the skirt from the persistent sticker bush with one good yank. Ear Nibbler Guy had to be at least nineteen or twenty. There was no way I was going home with him. My dad would kill me. Not that he'd ever find out, but still.

"Since when did you become such a party pooper?"

"Just drive me home, OK?"

"Drive yourself," she said, heading back to the water. "I'm staying."

"Wait," I said, following after her. "You have to drive me. I don't know how." I stumbled over roots and rocks, every bush wanting a piece of my skirt.

She wheeled around, her nose wrinkled. "You got smog in the noggin or something? That's your car."

She pointed to the one thing that could make my mortifying night bearable – a 1960 Corvette convertible. Bright turquoise. It wasn't quite a '63 Sting Ray, but it was close enough to make my heart flutter. My fingers slid across the glossy chrome as I made my way to the driver's door. A tiny, hopeful spark ignited within me. If my past self knew how to drive, did that mean I did, too?

I threw open the door and slid across the smooth leather, envisioning myself cruising off into the night and leaving my skinny-dipping friends behind. I ran my hands over the steering wheel, which was just as bright turquoise as the rest of the interior. My fingers found the keys and turned the engine over, then I gave it a good rev to see what she had.

Oh, it was glorious. Pure, throaty thunder.

I didn't even think about it – I just pressed the clutch and threw her in reverse. I eased it back like a pro, as though I drove a manual every day. I was so impressed with myself that I didn't notice Ear Nibbler trying to flag me down.

"Susie! Baby! Wait up! My wallet's in there!"

For a second, I thought about taking off and letting my past self deal with the Ear Nibbler situation after I was long gone, back in Base Life, but I worried about the whole impact thing. Porter wanted me to behave as normal as possible, and tearing off like that would probably cause a fair amount of suspicion.

I hit the brakes and snatched Ear Nibbler's wallet from the passenger seat. It flopped open, and I scanned the contents as he ran to catch up to me, trying to pull his pants on at the same time. I kept my nose down when he reached my door and zipped his fly right next to my ear.

"What's got your cage rattled?" he said. "It was your idea to come down here in the first place."

But I wasn't listening. I was staring at the name on his driver's license: James Charles Mitchell.

Porter, you freaking genius. He had said none of my past lives had been coincidences, and I guessed he was right.

"Get in," I told Ear Nibbler, plowing the car into first. "You and I are going for a drive."

Runaround Sue

It was like I knew the roads by heart. The Corvette felt like an extension of me, fluid and sublime. We flew across the southern Ohio hills through a flurry of autumn leaves, the wind in our hair. Ear Nibbler had since pulled on a preppy, baby blue sweater and buckled his seat belt, still checking the side mirror every two seconds to see if his beautiful nose was intact.

"Oh, please," I said. "I didn't hit you that hard."

"You clocked me like a prize fighter. Where'd you learn to hit like that?"

1927, I thought to myself. "You scared me. You shouldn't sneak up on me like that."

He propped an elbow on the passenger door and rubbed his forehead. "I don't get you, Susan. You wanted to go steady a year ago, but I wasn't ready. Now that I am, you get cold feet?"

"They're cold because that water was eighteen below."

He sniffed and shook his head. "Real swell. Why don't you give me my pin back if you're so indifferent?"

Crap. Wasn't giving a girl your pin really serious back then? I bit my lip to stop talking before I screwed something up.

Magazine abs or not, Jim Mitchell was way too high maintenance for my taste. What had my past self seen in him? And what kind of girl had I been? Skinny-dipping in October? Sneaking around and spending the night at an older boy's house? Going steady with a preppy rich boy who whined when I didn't let him snuggle up to my birthday suit?

I glanced in the rearview mirror at myself for the first time that night. Again, my reflection took me by surprise. It was still me, still my face, but I was a few sizes larger, with all the extra curves. My lips were stained red, and my eyebrows were angled and sharp. My hair was still damp, but I could tell it was chin-length and wavy. And blonde.

Really blonde.

I looked like Tabitha when she played Marilyn Monroe in the spring musical last year.

So far, the only things I liked about the 1961 me were my groovy driving skills.

Wait. Groovy was a term from the Seventies not the Sixties. Wasn't it?

Letting my muscle memory guide me, I turned down a long, white gravel driveway bordered by a row of manicured trees on either side. I hoped it led to the Mitchell estate. When Jim didn't object (and continued to sulk at himself in the side mirror), I kept going. The driveway opened into a wide circle laid out before an enormous brick mansion – the historic home of one of the first Ohio governors. The colonial facade and meticulous landscaping were lit up by spotlights, but it didn't look like anyone was home. I slowed to a stop in front, gaping up at all the windows.

A fountain gurgled somewhere off to the side.

The Raphael was in there. I could feel it.

"If this is about Cindy," Jim said with a frustrated sigh, turning in his seat to face me, "it was only that one time. I told you before, I only have eyes for you." He moved in to kiss me, but the more he leaned forward, the more I leaned back.

What was with this guy? He seriously thought I'd kiss him after he just admitted to cheating on me? I wished I could warn my past self about going out with such a loser. I sincerely hoped I didn't end up married to him.

I fumbled for the door handle behind me. "Why don't we go inside and have some time to ourselves before the others get back?"

He gave me a knowing look and grinned. "Just what I was thinking."

Yeah, I bet it was.

The moment he closed the huge, ornate front door behind us, he pushed me up against the wall of the foyer and crushed his chest against mine. His hands groped at my butt. His mouth slobbered all over my neck. He smelled sour, like booze and cigarettes. He went for my ear again, but froze when I yelled, "Stop." I shoved him back and pointed a well-aimed finger in his face. I didn't want to hit him, but if he laid another hand on me, I'd finish the job on his nose.

He looked so confused, like a spoiled dog used to getting his way.

My mind raced, scrambling to think of a way out of this ridiculous – and possibly very dangerous – situation I'd gotten myself into. I shouldn't have gone back to the house with him alone. I should've waited until Cherub Face and the others were heading back too.

"I need to freshen up," I said.

He groaned and dropped his arms. "Aw, come on. Not this again."

"We've got plenty of time," I said, inching away from him. "Count to a thousand then come and find me." I darted out of the foyer and into a dark parlor before he could say no. I paused, hidden in the shadows, holding my breath, until I heard him counting.

"One, two, three…"

I let out a puff of air. Thank God.

I padded barefoot, carrying my flats, through more than a dozen rooms before I spotted the Rhine River Castle painting. It was hanging in a boy's bedroom on the second floor above a neatly made bed. In the dim light from a bedside lamp, I hefted the painting off the wall and onto the bed. It was wide and heavy and covered in several layers of dust.

Jim's voice echoed up the foyer stairs. "Four hundred twenty-three…"

I snagged an antique-looking pocket knife from a bookshelf in the corner and started to pry off the backing with shaking hands. It looked like it had never been done before, which gave me hope.

When Jim reached seven hundred and eighty-two, the back popped off with ease. I shifted a little to my right to let the lamplight spill over my shoulder. My stomach did a back flip.

The Portrait of a Young Man peeked out at me with his impish half-smile.

"Why hello there, gorgeous," I whispered. "I've come to rescue you from your tower."

I pulled it out and held it up in the full light. Knowing I was the first person to see it in over sixty years warmed me with a sort of awe. It was worth over a hundred million dollars in Base Life. And I was holding it in my hands.

I laid it carefully on the bed, then opened the closet and rummaged for a backpack or tote bag, anything I could carry it away in. It wasn't very large, but it was painted on a thin piece of wood panel, and I was scared to death of scratching or cracking it. The best thing I found was a shallow, rectangular garment box. I dumped out its contents – a few photo albums – and placed the painting inside, wrapped safely in two thick sweaters. I returned the Rhine River Castle painting to its spot on the wall, stuck the photo albums back in the closet, and dusted the bed off as best I could. The pocket knife went back on the shelf, and the closet door was shut.

"Nine hundred eighty-five…"

I bolted for the hallway. I couldn't take the stairs down to the foyer without running into Ear Nibbler, so I raced to the far side of the second floor, hoping to find a second staircase.

There wasn't one.

Or at least, not on that side of the house.

"One thousand. Ready or not, here I come."

Footsteps climbed the stairs.

I ducked into another bedroom at the end of the hall, this one large and shadowy, with a faint shaft of moonlight stretching across a center rug and four-poster bed. I rushed to the closet and closed the door behind me, then squeezed through a wall of clothes to the back. The corners of the garment box dug into my palms. My heart pounded in my ears.

"Come out, come out, where ever you are." Footsteps entered the bedroom. "I know you're in here." He went to the window and whisked the drapes to the side. "You've always had your eye on my parents' room, you naughty thing."

Ugh, how gross was that? I heard him kneel down and look under the bed. Then I heard him cross the room to the closet. My palms went slick and I almost dropped the garment box.

If he found me, I made up my mind to ascend back to Limbo. I'd lose the Raphael, change history, and have to go back and do it all over again. But I was OK with that. Anything was better than trying to wriggle out of his grabby hands again.

His feet stopped just outside the closet door. I drew in a deep breath and pressed myself against the wall, but something hard dug into my back. I reached behind and felt for it. My fingers closed around a tiny metal latch.

A door.

With one fluid motion, I flipped the latch, pushed the door open, and slipped through. I closed it behind me just as Jim opened the closet.

Barefooted, I ran down a narrow stone staircase, getting a face-full of cobwebs, and stumbled out into a dark, musty room in the basement. I fumbled for a light switch and finally, after stubbing my toe twice, found a pull string at the center of the room. A bare bulb flicked on above me.

It was a servant's bedroom – the bed and washing bowl were still in the corner – but it had since been turned into a storage room. Mold grew on the damp stone walls. The need for a staircase leading between the master bedroom and the servants' quarters wasn't lost on me, but I didn't stop to ponder how many mistresses the old Ohio governor had employed. I found the exit and shouldered it open.

A stack of wooden stairs brought me back up to the first floor in the kitchen. I bolted out the back door and ran around the house. There wasn't enough time to put on my flats. I crashed across the gravel drive, rocks digging into my bare feet, racing toward the Corvette.

"Susie!" Jim shouted, tearing out around the back of the house after me. I hadn't realized he was so close.

I slid on the gravel, slamming into the passenger side door. I pushed the garment box down into the foot well, then climbed over the gearshift and into the driver's seat.

"What the hell are you doing?"

"I forgot something at the river," I yelled with a wave of my hand. "Be back in a jiff." The engine roared to life, and the tires spit gravel as I tore down the drive.

Poor Jim. I couldn't help but feel a teensy bit sorry for him. After all, his baby ran off with another man. A young man to be exact.

I guess he should've kept away from Runaround Sue.

CHAPTER 16

Saying Goodbye

After half an hour without headlights behind me, I pulled off to the side of the road to look for a map. The bad thing about the 1960 Corvette? No glove box. And of course no GPS.

In the trunk, I found a towel, a black purse, two empty bottles of Tequila, and an overnight bag. The purse contained a pearly pink wallet with a ten dollar bill and Susan Summers' driver's license, a half-empty pack of cigarettes, and a tube of lipstick so red it was almost orange. At least the overnight bag proved helpful with extra clothes – a pencil skirt and sweater – but how was I supposed to find my way to Porter's bank without a map?

I shimmied into the spare clothes, then started off again, hoping my instincts would guide me to Cincinnati.

At around one in the morning, after over a dozen U-turns, I spotted the city lights in the distance. I pulled into a breakfast diner parking lot and wrangled the convertible top into place. Then I slept, rather uncomfortably with the garment box under my feet, until dawn.

A knock on the driver's side window jerked me awake. "Hungry, sweetie?"

I opened my eyes to the oval, cheery face of an older woman with pointed glasses. Her silver hair was teased in a beehive, and she wore an apricot-colored waitress dress. The name tag at her breast said LAMERLE.

"Come on in, sugar," she said, waving me toward the door of the diner. "I've got grits. I've got hash. I've got flapjacks." She kept listing foods as she walked, but I couldn't hear her anymore.

After I checked to make sure the Portrait of a Young Man was safe and secure, I opened the passenger door and almost fell out onto the pavement. Every muscle was stiff, and my stomach growled, demanding a living sacrifice. LaMerle unlocked the diner and held the door open for me. I fell into a blue vinyl booth by the front windows so I could keep an eye on my hundred-million-dollar Corvette. A drumline marched and pounded inside my head.

"You look like you could use some coffee," LaMerle said. She shuffled behind the counter. The coffee maker was filled, then set to percolate. "You like ice in yours? Folks say I'm crazy, but I like mine with ice. You let me know if you want ice."

I sat there, forehead and nose pressed to the laminate tabletop, wondering if I was experiencing a hangover. My mouth certainly felt rank enough, but maybe I was just tired. I didn't feel drunk last night, but then again, I wasn't sure if I would've noticed anyway. The only time I ever had alcohol was when Uncle Lincoln handed me a frozen peach schnapps at Christmas and told me it was a slushy. I spit it out on his salmon corduroy pants.

I downed LaMerle's coffee, without the ice cubes, even though I hated the stuff in Base Life. In this body, though? Coffee was a sweet, dawn-kissed beauty. It was a pure need, like warm blood and fresh air. Like life couldn't start without it. It was strong and helped shovel the heaviness of sleep off my back.

LaMerle whipped up some fried eggs and a strange kind of sausage made with pork and oats she called goetta, and I devoured those as well. When the breakfast crowd picked up, I left her a nice tip for letting me sleep in her parking lot and giving me directions to the bank.

The Cincinnati Mutual Bank and Trust was a two story brick building at the center of town. Porter had descended back to 1953 a long time ago and opened an account there, which he still had today. He chose that particular bank because it was one of the only ones still intact, having never moved their safe deposit boxes or gone through the renovation after a fire or flood. I was to leave the painting in his box, where it would remain hidden until he collected it in Base Life, over fifty years later.

Which, you had to admit, was pretty freaking genius.

But first, I had to find the key.

There was a post office across the street from the bank where Porter kept his safe deposit box key hidden on the roof. That was so he could retrieve it throughout time. I thought that was pretty ingenious too. I found a fire escape ladder at the rear of the building and climbed. I was still afraid of heights, but since I'd climbed a much taller building with Blue, this three story number wasn't such a big deal. At the top, I found the air vent on the north side Porter told me about. My hair whipped and swirled as I searched for a loose brick in the low wall surrounding the roof. When I found it, the cement around its edges brittle and flaking away into dust, I pried it out of its pocket with my fingernails.

A flutter of triumph. The tiny brass key winked at me from inside.

I retrieved the garment box from the car and entered the bank. It smelled like new carpet and cigarette smoke. I lifted my chin high. I told the portly, mustached teller exactly what Porter said – that my name was Casey O'Neil and I wanted to open my family's box, number fourteen.

I expected some resistance, but the teller just nodded and brought me back to a vaulted room with hundreds of narrow brass doors. He stuck his own key into one of the doors and unlocked half the lock. I unlocked the other half with my key. Then he slid the safe deposit box out of its cubby. It was a larger box than all the others – nearly three times the size. He set it on a metal shelf, then left the room to give me privacy. I lifted the long, wide lid.

Inside, there were treasures. A drawstring pouch full of pearls. Several stacks of cash, all in different currencies. An etched, wooden box with gold coins. Dozens of passports, driver's licenses, and birth certificates. It was Porter's secret stash – one he could access across time. I ran my fingers over the pearls, the cash, the coins, just to feel the thrill of all that wealth kiss my skin. Then I placed the painting in the box, still wrapped in a sweater.

It was hard to say goodbye, to leave the Raphael behind in that cold, sterile bank vault. But I'd trusted Porter this far, Lord knows why, and I hadn't caught him in a lie yet. I just hoped we were doing the right thing. That I was on the right side. (And that stealing the Raphael from Gesh would feel like a good kick in his balls.)

Driving 101

After I replaced the safe deposit box key in its hiding place, I stopped at a small hot dog joint for lunch. Two construction workers across the street whistled at me when I climbed out of the 'Vette, which had certainly never happened to me before and took me by surprise. I considered flipping them the bird, the sexist jackasses, but wasn't sure about the kind of impact that would make. It couldn't have made much of a difference, right? But I was too scared to chance it. So I flipped them the bird in my mind.

I stopped short before I entered the restaurant, confused by a sign on the window and the two separate entrances. In large painted letters, one side of the sign read: WHITES with an arrow pointing to a door on the left. The other side had an arrow pointing to the right and read: COLOREDS.

The hell?

Of course I'd learned all about segregation in school, and read about it last week when I did my last minute research on the Sixties, but seeing it in action was enough to turn my stomach. I didn't want to eat on the WHITES side. I'd much rather sit on the COLOREDS side, but if flipping the bird at those construction workers might've caused a stir, then making a radical statement like that certainly would.

I turned back to my car. I wasn't hungry anymore.

What good was traveling back in time if you couldn't change things? If you couldn't make a difference? Tell people of their ignorance? Warn them of the outcomes?

I rested against the fender of the Corvette, my arms crossed over my chest, and watched all the boat-like, flashy cars cruise by. I marveled at the hairstyles.

On the thinly veiled surface, the Sixties didn't seem too different from Base Life. There was an obvious absence of personal electronics and digital technology, but I liked the mechanical knobs on the 'Vette, the real handed clock towers across town, and the way music sounded floating through tinny speakers. I was fascinated by the bits of conversation I overheard as people walked by, of bomb shelters and the Russians, and how JFK was the hippest Catholic ever. It all seemed so quaint and innocent, but it was a lie. Scratch an inch beneath the surface and you'd find the ugly things they swept under the rug. The segregation, the riots, the hate. All that hate covered up by fluffy hairdos and modest hemlines and bright orange lipstick.

It made me sick. And I wanted to go home.

I let myself enjoy one last cruise in the Corvette, winding through the country hills back toward Jim's house. I sang along to When the Lion Sleeps Tonight and Only the Lonely and Will You Love Me Tomorrow. I couldn't remember the last time I'd listened to the radio – I streamed all my music from the Internet back in Base Life. The jokes the Sixties DJs inserted between each song were so silly they were hilarious and made me miss commercial breaks. A little. And it made me want to take Claire's advice and fix up an old car of my own.

Now that I knew how to drive.

A few miles away from the Mitchell estate, my hair-swept cruise through rolling farm fields came to an unexpected end. I pulled off onto the gravel shoulder as the 'Vette sputtered and rolled to a stop. Glancing at the gas gauge, I saw the needle was well past E. If it had been any other issue, I probably could have gotten the car rolling again, but the thought of fueling up hadn't even crossed my mind.

Talk about failing Driving 101.

Without a cell phone to call for help, I lay on the hood listening to the radio for almost an hour – shielding my eyes from the sun and letting it warm my skin – before I heard the distant rumble of a single vehicle. It was a dirty, rusty, mint-green Chevy truck with a huge chrome grill on the front. I hopped down when it slowed and pulled to the side of the road in front of me. It sputtered and wheezed, then sighed and settled on its tires.

The driver's door squawked open, and a young guy with dark hair in nice-fitting jeans and a white T-shirt – sleeves rolled up like James Dean – climbed out. "Need some help?" He flashed me a charming grin as he approached, wiping his hands on an oil-stained rag he pulled from his back pocket.

I nearly collapsed where I stood.

It was Blue.

CHAPTER 17

A *Ghost*

"What are you doing here?" The words tumbled out of my mouth, raspy and dry.

Blue stood before me, as sure and as bright as the sun. As real as the wind. As alive as my swift pulse. But it didn't make sense. How could he be here? In 1961?

He nodded at the Corvette, still wiping his hands on the rag and answered my question literally. "You broke down. Thought I'd stop to lend a hand."

He looked almost exactly the same, except he was a few inches taller, and the bridge of his nose was wider. His skin was tinged red from the sun. His hair was a bit longer, a bit shaggier, with the top sticking off to the right like he always ran his fingers through it that way. His eyes were just as shocking blue-green as before. The laugh lines around his eyes were mischievous. Teasing. His voice, kind and smooth, sent a shiver through me. I stepped toward him and lifted a hand to touch his face. "I thought I'd never see you again."

He frowned and leaned away from my hand. "Do we know each other?"

I lowered my hand.

He didn't recognize me. I looked completely different than I did in Chicago.

"It's me, Sousa."

He stuffed the rag in his back pocket with a slight shrug. "Doesn't ring a bell, sorry."

I couldn't speak. My heart had seized. It was hooked on my ribs.

Maybe it wasn't him. I mean, it couldn't be, could it? He was just a lookalike. It had to be my guilty conscience playing cruel tricks. "Sorry. It's just... You look like someone I used to know."

"I do?" He popped the hood on the Corvette and leaned in to have a look. "What was his name?"

"Nick Piasecki." I expected his head to pop up, for him to react to the name somehow.

He didn't.

"Don't know anyone by that name. Is it your carburetor, do you think? The carburetors on these new 'Vettes can be testy."

It took a moment before I processed his question. I was too caught up in the way his white T-shirt stretched over his shoulders. The way it had in his kitchen in Chicago. The shape of his back, his waist, his hips, even his butt – they were all the same. "Uh, no," I said, swallowing. "Just ran out of gas." The words fell like dust to the ground. They kicked up in the breeze and swirled away into the fields.

"Oh, well that's no problem. I always keep a spare tank on my truck."

I leaned against the 'Vette, my arms crossed, watching him. How could this guy look so much like Blue? Maybe Nick was a distant relative, but this guy said the name didn't ring a bell.

He came back to the 'Vette, carrying a red metal gas tank with a nozzle. He stuck out his hand. "Jack Baker. It's a pleasure."

His hand even felt like Blue's. It was rougher, but the shape, the size, everything matched. "God, even your fingernails are shaped the same," I said, turning his hand over.

"As that guy you knew?"

I nodded.

"What happened to him?"

I slid my hand from his and re-crossed my arms. "He died."

He pressed his lips together in a sincere frown. "I'm real sorry to hear that."

I swallowed again and nodded. This guy wasn't Blue. He was just his ghost, sent to haunt me the day after Halloween.

The ghost filled my tank, replaced the gas cap, then patted the trunk. "You're all set."

I finally managed a weak smile. "Thanks. Who knows how long I'd be here if you hadn't come along?"

He hoisted the gas tank over his tailgate and set it in the bed of his truck. "You headed to the Mitchell place?"

I nodded. "Jim and I are going out. I mean, going steady." I didn't know why I told him that, I guess I just wanted to see how the words sounded on my tongue. I still couldn't get over the fact that I would have chosen someone like Jim as my boyfriend. And maybe I wanted to see a reaction. Something to tell me Blue was in there somewhere. Inside that Jack Baker shell.

Jack's chin tipped up. "Ah. Jim." It was a loaded ah.

"You know him?"

"Eeyup."

"He's a piece of work, isn't he?"

Jack laughed. "I wasn't going to say anything."

I shook my head, looking down at my shoes. "I don't know what I see in him."

"No? Well, I can come up with about a million guesses. Just off the top of my head." He grinned, teasing me. Did he mean I was with Jim because he was rich? If that was true, it made me dislike my 1961 self even more.

Jack clapped a hand on his driver's door handle. "I best be off. Maybe I'll see you around, Sousa."

My heart jumped when he said that. He sounded just like Blue. He gave me a smile – Blue's smile, a stolen smile – then climbed into his truck.

The thief.

I watched him drive off, my heart a tangle of confusion, until he was a speck of mint-green rust on the horizon. My skin felt cold and foreign. My limbs were hollow. My chest was thick. Knotted.

I had to get out of this body.

I drove to Jim's driveway and parked right after I pulled off the road. I didn't care that I wasn't leaving my host body where I landed. She'd just have to get by from here. Hopefully she'd chalk her memory loss up to all the Tequila she drank. Hopefully Jim would too.

There was no way I was coming back to this life again

for a do-over.

Me and the Sixties? We were over.

The Grilling

Now it's my turn to be furious. When I ascend to my garden, I march right up to Porter and punch a finger in his chest. "What the hell aren't you telling me?"

His welcome-back smile fades. My outburst takes him completely by surprise. "What do you mean?"

"I saw Nick."

"What?"

"I saw him. I broke down on the side of the road, and he stopped to help me. Nick, the boy from 1927, was there in 1961."

"Alex–"

"Are you behind this? Are you messing with my head?"

Porter lifts his weathered and age-spotted hands. He looks utterly confused. "I didn't do anything. I stayed away from your soulmark this time. I let you do it all by yourself."

"Then how could he be there? He died."

"Alex," he says again in his calm, paternal voice. "Sometimes grief can make us see things that aren't really there. Things we long for. Things we've lost."

I glare at him. The last person who said I was seeing things couldn't have been more wrong.

"It's my fault," he says. "I shouldn't have sent you on a mission so soon. I should have given you time to grieve."

I rub my forehead and shake my head. "He looked just like him. He was the same age. His voice, his ears, his hands." My voice reduces to a pained whisper. I didn't realize how much I missed Blue until I saw him again. I'd felt guilty for what happened to him, yes, but I meant it when I made my wish at the fountain. I'd wanted to see him again, even though I knew it was impossible. Just a stupid wish made in the flurry of the moment.

Now? I'm not sure how I feel. All I know is Porter isn't telling me the whole truth. And he'd said he wasn't a liar.

Porter rubs his pinky knuckle. "I'm sorry you had to go through that."

"Are you saying it's impossible? There's no way it could've been the same Nick?"

"How could it have been? You said he was the same age. How could he be the same age in 1961 as he was in 1927?"

I throw my hands in the air. "I don't know! I thought maybe it could be some sort of paradox thing. I mean, I did mess with his past."

"If you caused a shift in his history, you did it without my knowledge. There's no precedent we can use to compare. But I can look into it for you if you like."

I stand there, frowning at him. Adults are always taking time to "look into things." In my opinion, it's just another trick to keep teenagers in the dark. They probably hope we'll just forget about whatever the "thing" is and let them off the hook. But what else can I do? If Porter doesn't have any immediate answers, all I can do is wait. Finally I nod, and Porter smiles like he's fixed everything.

"Good. Now tell me." He clasps his hands together. "How did your first mission go?"

"You mean besides seeing Nick and landing naked in a freezing river with a bunch of other naked people? Just swell."

"Did you find the painting?"

"Yeah, yeah," I say, waving an annoyed hand at him. "It was right where you said it would be."

"Alex! This is excellent news. Is it in the vault?"

"Yes."

"I knew you could do it. My little ace in the hole." He claps me on the back. "I better be off, but we'll celebrate when I get back, all right?"

I feel his soul begin to depart, to dissolve into the black, but I reach out a hand and say, "Wait. Why are you in such a hurry?"

His soul comes back into view. "There isn't time to waste. These are critical hours."

"Tell me why."

"Because we have the Raphael in our possession. I have to fly to Cincinnati and collect it, then make sure it's discovered by the right people right away. The news has to spread; there has to be a media frenzy. Everyone has to know it's been found, otherwise Gesh can go back and erase everything you did. He could send a Descender back a day before you and steal the painting for himself. No one would be the wiser."

"Who's going to discover it? Who are the 'right people'?"

Porter pauses, then smiles. "Well, that's up to us, I suppose. Who do you think should get the glory?"

I feel the weight of one hundred million dollars in my hands. That kind of money could change the world.

Well, a good chunk of it at least. "Could we make it so a philanthropist finds it and gives some of the money to Audrey's foundation? She's been reading a lot of Robert Burns lately, and…" I pause, thinking of her favorite poem, Sweet Afton. "I'd love for her to go to Scotland. I want her to see the River Afton before she dies."

I look up at Porter, hoping to see agreement on his face, but he's giving me the same sympathetic look Jack Baker did. "I'm sorry, Alex, but that's too risky. Too close to home. Gesh will try to track the money down, no matter what we do with it. He'll find it went to your sister. Your mom. It'll lead him right to you. I can't risk that."

I turn away from him, unable to bear the disappointment. I stroll between my soulmarks, hanging my head. "I just thought…" I squeeze my eyes shut. It doesn't matter. Porter is right. We can't chance leaving a trail.

He's silent for a while. I feel his presence fade into the black, and I think he's leaving. Just like that. But then his soul reappears right in front of me.

"I'll see what I can do. There might be a way to cover the money trail." He takes me by the arms. He smiles at me with pride. "Be happy, Alex. You did well. This is what our powers were meant for. We don't change the past, we change the future." He gives my arms a reassuring squeeze. "Go home. Get some rest. I'll be in touch soon."

And then he's gone.

CHAPTER 18

Afton

The jack-o'-lanterns are still flickering when I return home to the porch swing. I'm still holding the Polygon stone. The front door opens, and Audrey pads out in her bare feet to share the swing with me. She has no idea I've been gone for almost an entire day. For her, only mere seconds have passed.

"You're up late," I say, tucking the stone in my pocket and wrapping my arms around her. She pulls her knees to her chest. I push the thought of her never getting to see the River Afton out of my mind.

"I've been saving up energy," she says.

"You have?"

She snuggles into me and shivers. "For a non-rainy day."

My cheek rests against her black wig and felt cat ears. Her skin smells like cloves and Smarties candy. Her wig smells like must. I rock the swing with my toes.

After a few minutes, her head snaps up. "Look. A kitten."

The gleaming eyes of a small, black cat blink at us from the front yard. Audrey unfolds herself from the swing and creeps down the porch steps, her hand held out. The cat is shy at first, but eventually makes his way into her arms. He rubs his head against her chin with sweet determination. I can hear him purring from where I sit. Audrey brings him up the porch steps and into the light. Two black cats stare back at me. Both delicate. Both wide-eyed, innocent, trusting. Beautiful.

"No collar," Audrey says, setting him on the swing between us. "And he's so thin. Do you think he has cancer? I heard cats can get leukemia too."

I frown at the little thing, his skin stretched over his ribs. He does look frail, but he has an energy about him just like Audrey. He climbs over our laps, back and forth, unable to decide on which to settle.

Audrey scratches him under his chin. His purr is so loud, you can hardly believe it could come from such a tiny package. "Can we keep him?" she asks. "Just until he's stronger? He could keep me company while you guys are gone during the day."

I bite my lip, watching the cat turn circles on Audrey's lap. "I don't know…"

"Are you still afraid?"

"No," I say. "Not anymore." And it's the truth. Now that I know what my visions are, there's no reason to be scared of déjà vu.

"Can you ask Daddy, then? If he thinks you're OK with it, then he might say yes."

I reach across and scratch the cat's ear. He licks my thumb. "I suppose. But what are we going to call him? Nothing spooky just because it's Halloween. And nothing stupid like Blacky or Binky."

Audrey snuggles him to her chest. "Of course not. We'll name him Afton."

For me, that seals the deal.

Keeping Afton doesn't take much persuasion. The whole family is thrilled when they meet him. Dad gives me a nudge and says he's glad I finally "came around." Pops winks at me and tells me to watch out – long-tails can be "tricksy." Gran sets to work making a temporary litter box, and says she'll pick up all the necessities tomorrow at the store.

They're all so genuinely happy about it. It makes me feel good to mark one thing off my Normality Check List. I leave them alone to cuddle Afton and head to bed.

Before I turn out the lights, I do an Internet search for Jack Baker on my laptop. I get a list of over a hundred Jack Bakers currently residing in Ohio. There's a chance one of them is the guy from 1961. He could still be alive. But what good would it do to track him down?

Whoever he was, he wasn't Blue.

And I've seen enough ghosts to last me until next Halloween.

Driving Super Powers

The next day after school, I ask Dad if I can practice parallel parking the Mustang. He gives me a look that says, "Remember last time?" But I tell him I've gotten better and promise not to peel the rubber off the sides of his tires again.

He must feel sorry for me because he agrees. Being the only junior in my Driver's Ed class and not having my license yet does wonders for my pariah street cred. Like Claire said, most people think I'm not allowed to drive because of my seizures. But the truth is worse. I was a hopeless driver.

Key word being was.

The Mustang is a 1969 Mach 1 coupe, black with a red stripe down the side. She's a beauty. Always has been, even when she was rusting on a pedestal of cement blocks in Dad's parents' garage. She was Dad's first car. He bailed hay and shingled roofs for two summers to afford her. Then, after only one month of four-speed bliss, some drunk guy plowed into the front end while she was parked at a bowling alley. Dad was crushed. By that time school had started again, and his dad, Grandpa Wayfare, was strict about not letting his kids work during the school year.

Then came graduation, then college, and the old Mustang sat in the garage, rusting away, but not forgotten. Dad always planned to get her running again. Maybe he daydreamed about working on it with a future son, but if so he never said. He seemed just as happy to work on it with me.

We spent three summers rebuilding the engine and transmission, traveling around to junkyards to hunt for fenders and bumpers, and researching new performance parts that would make it safer to drive and pass inspections. He wasn't worried about restoring it to perfection. He just wanted to drive it. To feel it grip the pavement and roar into the corners.

Those three summers were some of the best of my life. I had an endless supply of oil and grime beneath my fingernails, a perpetual sunburn on the back of my neck, and skinned knuckles that turned to tiny, spiderweb scars, but I wouldn't have traded it for anything. Especially when Audrey helped out. She would skip around the car and play hopscotch, ready at a moment's notice to hand us whatever tool we needed. She sang us all the songs she learned in Sunday School and music class, and practiced her ballet routines.

She used to be an amazing dancer.

Unlike me. I can balance circuits and tires, but that's about it.

All those memories flutter before me like a flip book when I nestle into the Mustang and breathe in the vinyl. Dad slides in beside me, a bit timidly. The car rumbles to life, and just as he opens his mouth to give me the usual pointers, I slam it into gear. We're out of the driveway and tearing down the street before he knows what hit him. I move through the gears as smooth as butter. I take the corners on rails.

After the initial shock wears off, Dad loosens up. He grins from ear to ear. I drive just like he does when he's behind the wheel, after he winks at me across the dinner table and says, "What do you say, Bean? Wanna go for a spin?" He keeps a low profile driving to work or school, but lets it all out when we go for our After Dinner Spins. He says it's good for the car. "She's all muscle," he says. "You gotta use it or lose it."

When we get back home – after I successfully parallel park three times – Dad says, "Did they teach you to drive like that in Driver's Ed?"

I laugh and toss him the keys. "Nope. You did."

He shakes his head as we walk to the screened-in porch. "I have to admit, you've made astonishing progress. What changed?"

I hold the screen door open for him. "I've had it in me the whole time. I just had to let loose. Then it was like second nature."

He grins at me and ruffles my hair as he passes by. "Well aren't you full of surprises?"

If only he knew.

Making Amends

A week goes by, and I still haven't heard one word from Porter. Half of me is rattled with nerves, waiting to hear what happened with the Raphael. My fingernails are bitten to nubs. I can't wait to see the world's reaction when it's discovered. But the other half of me wonders if I'll ever see Porter again. I called his number a few times but there was no answer. No return call.

What if something happened to him? What if Gesh found him?

What if he's a supernatural con man? It would be the best heist in history. He gets me to deliver the most sought-after painting in all the world, then disappears into the night. Maybe he doesn't care about helping me at all. Maybe he just wants the treasure for himself.

Maybe he's a supernatural liar.

But on an unusually warm November morning, I wake up before dawn to an alert on my cell phone. I set the alert to crawl the Internet for any new articles about the Portrait of a Young Man. Seems The New York Times was the first American paper to get the news.

While there are no specific details, the article states the painting has been found and is currently located in a bank vault in an undisclosed location. The Czartoryski Museum in Poland is excited to have the painting returned to them, and they plan to give a substantial reward to the unnamed person who found it, whoever that is.

I smile to myself. Porter really is a genius. An honest, supernatural genius.

Two hours later, I get a text from him, asking to meet in my garden.

"Anything new happen while I was away?" he says, walking beside me through my soulmarks, his hands folded behind his back.

"Well, we got a cat. Audrey named him Afton. I earned major points with Claire for that one. She doesn't think I'm a total loser anymore. Just half a loser. Oh, and I took my driving test."

His brow lifts. "And?"

I can't help but grin. "I passed."

"Congratulations." He squeezes my shoulder. "That's a significant rite of passage, Alex. You're well on your way to becoming an adult." Then he adds, "Yet again."

"Hey, I figured if I'm going to be traveling all across time, it should at least be legal."

His belly laugh echoes throughout the garden.

"I also aced an algebra quiz," I say, "got called out for daydreaming like a hundred times because I couldn't stop thinking about the Raphael, and I ran an eight-minute mile. Eight-minutes! My best time ever and no asthma attack. Do you think I can run better now because I could run so well in 1927?"

"It's definitely possible. You can retain certain abilities after you descend, just like you retain some of your injuries. They're called residuals. They're not constant, and they're never certain, but it's one of the perks of being a Descender."

"How is a bloody knot on the back of my head a perk?"

"Well, not the injuries, obviously. That's one of your defects. No other Descender retains injuries like you do. But residuals can come in handy. They can also be addicting. Gesh has collected hundreds of different residuals from his host bodies. He knows how to fly planes, navigate oceans, perform brain surgery, take a sniper shot, play the most manipulative mind games…"

"So, residuals are like super powers."

Porter nods and rubs his pinky knuckle. "Which is why Gesh is untouchable in Base Life. He's too powerful. Too knowledgeable. That's why we have to hit him where it hurts: his treasure hunts. His ego."

"Why do I retain my injuries and other Descenders don't?"

"I suspect it has something to do with the link you share with your past bodies. It must be powerfully strong."

We stroll, and I think about this for a while. What other abilities did my past bodies have? Within the blink of an eye, could I know how to perform brain surgery? Or fly a plane? Could I ace all my classes, graduate early, and head off to Harvard by the end of the semester?

We stop at the edge of my grove of soulmarks. Where there was nothing but black before now stands a tall, narrow stone fountain and two ornate stone benches on either side. The ground is bricked with round, flat stones. Tall, squared hedges form a backdrop behind the fountain. It's a garden lit by moonlight. By soulmark light.

"I thought you deserved a proper garden," Porter says. "It's a work in progress, but I'll keep adding to it whenever I have the strength. It's the least I could do to repay you for all your hard work with the Raphael."

I step up to the fountain and dip my hand in the gurgling water. It's warm, just like it would be at the end of summer. "Thank you, Porter."

"I know it's not Buckingham Fountain, but it's all I could muster for now. I thought perhaps it could be a memorial to Nick. To help you grieve."

I nod at him, a small knot forming in my throat. I can't believe I ever thought he was a con man.

"How did it go in Cincinnati?" I ask to change the subject, clearing the knot from my throat and sitting beside him on one of the stone benches.

"As smooth as I could have hoped. I retrieved the Raphael – gorgeous, isn't it? – and moved it to another vault. I won't go into all the details, it's best for you not to know, but I managed to ensure a tidy, untraceable donation makes its way to your sister's foundation."

I sit up, a weight lifting from my shoulders. "Are you sure the money's safe?"

"I wouldn't have done it if it wasn't foolproof."

The warmth of pride and accomplishment unfurls inside me. I finally did something with my ability. I did my part for Audrey. Letting her keep the kitty version of Afton was one thing, but making it so she could see the real Afton... That makes me feel like I've truly done something with my life.

"I hope you didn't go to much trouble," I say.

"No trouble. You deserve part of the reward. You're the one who found the painting. And at such a humiliating price."

I assume he's referring to Ear Nibbler and the River of Nakedness. "Yeah, how did you do that, anyway? How'd you know I'd be Jim Mitchell's girlfriend in a past life?"

"Honestly, I didn't. I knew you'd be close to the Mitchell family, but I didn't know in which capacity. Gesh did his research on the Rhine River Castle painting. He knew it was last seen with the Mitchells. So he had Flemming start that particular Newlife of yours in Ohio. Flemming made sure you were born into one of the area's affluent families so you'd grow up in the same circles as the Mitchells. That way, come the early Sixties, you'd be able to visit the estate one way or another without suspicion. The girlfriend part was an added bonus. Made it easier for you, didn't it?"

I roll my eyes. I suppose that's one way of looking at it. "He did that for all my lives? Made them best suited for his treasure hunts?"

"Almost all of them, yes."

"What about my 1927 life? What was my purpose then?"

Porter narrows his eyes at me knowingly. "You don't get to know about that life, remember? That's your penance."

Drat. He remembered. "How about Jamestown?"

"Isn't that one obvious? He wanted access to the early colonies."

"And the time I was on the ship in the ocean?"

Porter scratches at the stubble on his chin. "Sailing from England to Roanoke, I believe."

"Get out," I say, punching his bicep. "I was a member of the lost colony?"

"Yes," he says, rubbing his arm. "But trust me, you don't want to go back there."

My head is foggy with possibility. "Heck yes, I do. I could be the person who discovers how they disappeared. Mr Lipscomb would flip."

"Hm," he says, nodding. "I know all about your Mr Lipscomb. But the discoveries can't ever be credited to you personally, remember? And we don't use our travels to get back at people."

"But isn't that what we just did with the painting? Getting back at Gesh?"

"No." Porter looks out at the fountain, his watery eyes reflective. "That's simply making amends."

CHAPTER 19

Rumors

That Friday after school, I head to the library to do all the research I can on the year 1876. Porter filled me in on my next mission: to find a hoard of gold coins stolen in a train robbery in Missouri by the Carter Gang.

The Carters weren't quite the James Brothers, but they managed to make a name for themselves. Mostly by being bumbling idiots. Within three months of embarking on their new train-robbing venture, they were all either imprisoned or killed. All their loot had been found and accounted for, except one chest of gold worth millions today.

The leader of the gang, Cask Carter, always buried his loot near the sites of the robberies to collect later, but he died four months after this particular robbery, and the location of the coins died with him.

It's my job to make sure that doesn't happen.

It's also my job to cram as much as I can before Sunday, because that's the day Porter wants me to descend.

Since it's Friday, I have the library mostly to myself. The only sounds are the heater kicking on and off, and the librarian, Mrs Hazelwood, sucking on her iced coffee through a straw at the front desk. There are a few people hunched over at the computers and a handful of kids in the children's section, but the rest of the place is empty. Which is why it surprises me when I turn a corner, leaving the nonfiction section, and almost bump right into Jensen.

"Hey, Wayfare," he says, looking at my stack of thick, hardback books. "Doing a little light reading?"

"Heh. Yeah." I veer past him and head for a table in the back, hoping he doesn't follow.

He does.

Great.

The books topple from my arms and onto the table. A couple tumble to the floor. Jensen retrieves them for me and looks at the titles.

"Famous Train Robberies of the 1800s," he says. "Rare and Priceless United States Coins." He quirks a brow at me. "Going treasure hunting?"

I actually let myself smile. "Yep. I'm traveling back in time to thwart a heist. Want to come along?"

"Sure. Is your time machine a two-seater?"

"No, but it's got a trunk."

He lets out a laugh and flops down onto one of the orange plastic chairs at the table. He rolls the sleeves of his light blue collar shirt up to his elbows and kicks his long legs out, making himself comfortable. His sneakers are gleaming white. His shaggy honey blond hair hides his eyes.

I bite my lip, wondering if this is a good idea. Usually when Jensen is around, so are all the other popular kids. I never knew him to be the loner library type. It's not that I mind talking to him – in fact, I often daydreamed about meeting him this way a few times before, having him all to myself for a while – but I don't feel like getting harassed by Tabitha and her flock of phonies. If that's the price I have to pay for a moment alone with Jensen, I'd rather keep my money.

And my dignity.

I take a seat and glance at the paperback in his hand. "Jane Austen?"

He jumps when I say it and nearly falls over in his chair trying to shove the little paperback book in his back pocket. His ears are so red, they could match my 1961 lipstick. "For my sister," he says.

"Riiiight."

He looks like he's been caught with his hand in the cookie jar, but after a moment he lifts his chin, like he's summoned the courage to own up to the truth. "I read my sister's copy of Sense and Sensibility and liked it. I thought I'd give Pride and Prejudice a shot."

I give him a look that says, "Good for you," and open one of the books in front of me, Train Robberies of the Midwest.

He drapes his arms on the table and looks at me from under his floppy hair. "This is the part where you say guys who read Austen are super sexy."

"I wouldn't know." I flip through the pages. "I haven't read anything of hers."

"What?" He sits up. "I thought all girls read Austen."

"Jensen, that's sexist."

"You know what I mean. You should give her a try. You'd like her."

I shrug. "I don't really read much."

He eyes my massive mound of books with a look.

"OK," I say, pushing up my glasses. "I don't read much fiction."

"Fair enough." He drums his fingers on one of the tomes. "Oh, I hear congratulations are in order."

"Why? Am I pregnant?"

"No," he laughs. "For getting your license."

I scan through the index of Train Robberies of the Midwest looking for the Carter Gang. "Oh, yeah. About time, right?"

"Yeah. It's cool. I always thought you couldn't drive because of your seizures."

A strand of ice slithers down my back and I freeze. My eyes snap to his, and I lose my place in the book. Did he seriously just say that with a straight face? "Oh, come on, Jensen. You know as well as I do that's not true."

"It's not?"

"Of course not. You started that rumor after that day in Sunday School, remember?"

"When you threw up on me?"

"Yes."

"I never told anyone about that."

"No, but you told them I had a seizure instead, and that you saved my life with the Heimlich Maneuver."

His nose wrinkles. "No, I didn't."

I just stare back at him, not getting the joke. I can't decide if he's playing with me or if he's serious. "If you didn't start the rumor, then who did?"

"I don't know, Wayfare," he says, his hazel eyes tight around the edges. "Maybe one of the other dozen kids in the class?" He pushes off from the table and stalks away, not carrying himself as tall as usual. The Victorian lady on the cover of the Austen novel in his back pocket peeks out at me. Even she looks disappointed.

My forehead smacks down onto Train Robberies of the Midwest.

It must be some sort of record. In less than five minutes, I managed to piss off the first Base Life friend I might have had.

Starting Over

After half an hour, I decide to take some of the books home with me. I can't concentrate because I feel bad for accusing Jensen. I feel bad for believing he started the rumor all this time. Just because he was popular and the rumor glorified him didn't necessarily mean he made it up. He had plenty of admirers to do that for him.

In a lovely yet guilt-ridden swirl of a moment, I realize even the most popular guy in school isn't immune to rumors. We both have our fair share.

Which makes me feel even worse.

I check the books out and head to the Mustang. Dad let me borrow it since the library was on the other side of town.

I stack the books on the hood and pull the keys from my pocket, spotting something light blue out of the corner of my eye. I glance over and see Jensen sitting on a bench in front of the library, one leg propped on the other, his arms outstretched on the back of the bench.

Maybe I can redeem myself.

"Still here?" I call out.

"My sister," he says, disappointment on his face. "I guess she forgot to pick me up."

I tip my head at the Mustang. "Hop in."

He leans forward, his elbows on his knees. "Is that your car?" When I nod, he jumps up and jogs over to it. "A '69 Mach 1? My dad says that's the best year. I've never ridden in one before."

"Now's your chance." I climb in and lean over to pop the lock on the passenger door.

He slides in with a goofy grin. "Did your parents buy it for you?"

"Ha, no. It's my dad's, but I helped him restore it, so he lets me drive it."

His eyes widen. "Wow. You really are a fix-it whiz."

"Fix-it Freak, you mean?" I toss the books in the back seat and buckle my lap belt.

"Fix-it Freaking Awesome, maybe."

I start the engine and put her into gear, smiling to myself. Jensen never did call me names. At least, not to my face.

We take off, windows down, and cruise through town. One of Jensen's favorite songs comes on the radio, and I can tell he's totally in his element. He drums his fingers to the beat. His head bobs. He grins from ear to ear. Especially when I plow the Mustang into third and bury the car behind me in exhaust.

We pass a group of guys from Jensen's basketball team on the sidewalk. I totally expect Jensen to sink down in his seat and hide his face. Instead, he waves an arm out the window and calls out to them. They wave and shout back, noticing the Mustang. They're jealous at first, calling Jensen names, which I guess are meant to be endearing in Guy Speak, but then their mouths drop when they see who's driving. They gape at us as we drive on, their stares burning into the rearview mirror. Jensen settles back in his seat, happy as a clam, totally oblivious of the social atrocity he just committed. To be seen with Wayspaz? That'll be the talk of the school on Monday.

But Jensen doesn't seem to mind.

The boy must be oblivious.

I slam the car into third again, my favorite gear change, and our hearts are pinned to the back of our seats. By the time I pull down his street and into his driveway, he's in danger of having his face permanently frozen in that silly grin.

He climbs out somewhat reluctantly, then leans down with one arm draped on the door. "Can we go again sometime?"

"Sure. As long as you forgive me for that whole rumor thing." I push my glasses up.

His smile morphs into something more sincere than silly. "Already forgiven." He closes the door and drums on the hood as I back down the driveway. He lifts a hand and waves, walking backwards.

I pause before I back out, waiting for traffic to clear. When I do, I see Tabitha jog across the street to Jensen in running shorts and a jacket. I can't hear what she's saying to him, but she's waving her arms in my direction and doesn't look happy. Jensen throws his arms in the air like he's fed up and clasps his hands behind his head. He trudges toward the front door of his huge brick house, his back to her, and Tabitha follows at his heels, still rattling on animatedly.

If he didn't know about his social atrocity earlier, he sure knows about it now.

CHAPTER 20

Linear

The next morning, I get a text from Porter telling me he left me something on the front porch. I find it tucked in a corner under the porch swing – a small, unassuming box with a digital watch inside. It's set to satellite time so we'll be in sync for our next mission. For some reason, he wants me to leave at an exact time.

I go about my day as usual, like I'm just a normal kid and not a time-traveling Descender. I finish my homework, rake the yard, put the finishing touches on Craig's DVD player project, help Dad with dinner, then hang out with the fam for movie night. We all sink into Mega Couch and watch The Maltese Falcon for what seems like the hundredth time. We devour half a dozen bowls of popcorn. Gran swoons over Humphrey Bogart. Claire sticks her cold feet under my legs for warmth. All the while I keep Porter's watch in the front pocket of my hoodie, where it's secret and safe.

Sunday morning is church, where I get a smile and a wave from Jensen both before and after service, which makes me feel pretty damn good. Normal. The whole family has lunch at Audrey's favorite restaurant in the historic district, an Irish pub called Gallagher's, and she orders the same thing as always: corned beef and cabbage. Pops orders a pint and tells us stories about his dad, who grew up in Scotland. Claire laughs at the foam clinging to Pops' mustache.

Later that afternoon, I climb the stairs to my room, sit cross-legged in the center of my oval rope rug, set my glasses beside me, and close my eyes. I straighten my back and hold the Polygon stone in my lap. I take a deep breath. All is silent except the distant sound of Gran whisking eggs in the kitchen. After a few minutes, the watch goes off at precisely 3.13. I run my fingers over the letters carved into the stone, I see the little boy, déjà vu grips me, and I ascend to meet Porter in my garden.

"Why do we have to do this at an exact time?" I ask, walking toward him through my soulmarks. "You know it won't be the same time in Missouri, right? I mean, it's November, so no Daylight Savings, but I read that the time zones were a bit iffy back then."

He's standing next to one of my soulmarks, his arms crossed. I guess to me, I'll always perceive him wearing that silly orange Orioles cap, black polo, jeans, and boat shoes. "Yes, smarty pants," he says. "But you're not going back to an exact time. You're going back to an exact age."

I crease my brow at him, so he explains.

"No time passes in Base Life when you ascend to Limbo, remember? For all intents and purposes, we'll just say time stops. It waits patiently for us to return, then picks up where it left off. Of course, the real reason is much more scientific than that – it has to do with the fact that time doesn't exist in Limbo because time is a man-made measurement – but I can explain all that to you later. All you need to know now is this: while you can travel to any past life you want, you can't travel to any time you want like other Descenders can. You can only travel linearly. It's one of your defects. Whatever age you are when you leave Base Life, that's the age you travel to in your host body. Not one minute before, not one minute later."

I really hate it when he says I have defects. It reminds me of an article I read that said leukemia is caused by a defect in a person's bone marrow production. Which makes it sound like Audrey is defective. Like she should be sent back to the factory and scrapped for parts.

My sister is not defective.

And neither am I.

But that's an argument for another day.

"So," I ask, trying to piece together the logic of it all in my mind, "is that why I was three years old in my first vision? And seven in my second? Because that was my age when I descended?"

Porter nods. "And that's why you could go back and redo your time in 1927. Because you were still in Limbo, you hadn't aged at all in Base Life. You were still the same age. Theoretically, you could spend decades in Limbo and never age a day in Base Life. You could gain all the knowledge you wanted, all the secrets of the world, then descend back to Base Life having never aged a second."

"Freaky."

"Quite."

"So then in 1927 and 1961, I was seventeen years old?"

"Correct. And," he says, "when you were seventeen years, two months, fifteen hours, and sixteen minutes old in 1876, you were on a train bound for Kansas City, Missouri. The very train robbed by the Carter Gang."

"Wait," I say, holding up a hand. "I'm going to be on the train during the robbery?"

Porter tips his head at the soulmark swaying gently beside him. "Why don't you go find out?"

I am. I'm going to be on the train. With a band of gangsters.

I bite the inside of my lip and slowly reach for my soulmark. I ready myself for the pull, the seizing connection, but hesitate before I grab hold. "Will it be dangerous?"

The laugh lines around Porter's eyes deepen. "Nothing your host body can't handle."

I guess that's all the answer I'm getting.

"Do you remember all the names?" he asks.

I nod. "There are four in the gang: Cask, Judd, William, and Yates. All of them Carters except Yates. My name is Cora Delaney, and if anyone asks where I'm headed, I tell them I'm on my way to meet my beau."

Porter gives me that proud look again. Like at any moment he might break down and give me a bear hug. As I reach for the soulmark, he says, "Have fun."

Mission Number Two

When the black faded to light, I was just where Porter said I would be.

I sat on an unforgiving wooden bench in a train car full of bobbing hats and bonnets. The rumble of iron wheels on iron tracks numbed the bottom of my feet and reverberated in my legs. Carpet bags and suitcases with leather straps and brass buckles were stacked on luggage racks above the train car windows. A plump, round woman sat beside me on my right, her perfume overpowering and making my nose itch, her dress a blanket of lavender satin and cream lace. Several strings of pearls poured over her enormous chest like rivulets of spilled milk. Two violet feathers from her wide-brimmed hat brushed against my cheek. They stuck to my eyelashes. I swept them aside and scooted away from her. I pressed myself against the window.

My reflection greeted me in the panes of glass. It hovered like a ghost before a blurred backdrop of cold, naked forest outside. I was surprised to see that, for once, my hair was the same dusky blonde as in Base Life. It was parted down the middle and pulled back in a tight bun. A dainty yellow hat with a red poppy in the center perched at the very top of my head like a cake topper. A yellow ribbon snaked down either side of my face and knotted under my chin. My dress wasn't as fancy as the woman's beside me. It was plain fabric, somewhat soft, with a stiff collar that nearly grazed my jawline. It was the color of fresh butter with a pattern of tiny red flowers. There was a long, pale green velvet coat folded on my lap. My hands were snug in creamy white gloves, my feet suffocating within the tight laces of ankle boots.

My nose was slightly different, more sleek than button-like, and my eyes were a striking shade of jade green rather than blue-gray, but everything else about my appearance was the same. I was even the same size – not tiny, not athletic, but not unhealthy either.

I hadn't realized how much I preferred my Base Life looks until that very moment. There were times in the past I thought I needed to look more like Tabitha to get Jensen's attention, or any boy's for that matter. Chuck the glasses, do something with my hair besides pulling it back in a ponytail, wear skimpier clothes, lose two sizes, have killer legs. But seeing more of myself in my 1876 body than the others filled me with relief. Thankfulness. Confidence in my own skin. It was a confidence that had always been there, but it was buried deep. Now I recognized it. I smelled its distinct presence beneath loam and moss and leaf mold. It must have been why I was so uncomfortable in my 1961 Marilyn Monroe body. I could never enjoy being a Barbie girl like Tabitha that men gawked at. I liked being me. I liked being invisible. Nerd glasses and all.

"Don't you think so, dear?"

I jumped at the sound of the round woman's wooly voice so close to my right ear. She was looking at me expectantly, her thick, gray eyebrows arched. Even the hairs rooted in the mole on her chin stood in suspense of my answer. But I didn't have the slightest clue what she had been talking about before I descended.

"What?" I blurted, then immediately wished I hadn't. I forgot I wasn't supposed to engage in conversation with the locals.

"The robberies," she said, her voice rough and raw, like she was a smoker. I couldn't smell any smoke on her, though, just her reeking perfume. "I can't get enough of the stories in the papers. My son was robbed on his way to St Louis. Not by a notable gang, mind you, but he said it was excitin' nonetheless. Wouldn't it be excitin' if our train were robbed by bandits?" She bounced slightly in our seat. It creaked.

I had no idea what to say to that. Did people really want to be robbed back then? "They'll take your pearls," I said, nodding at them.

Her thick fingers grazed the opalescent strands at her chest. "D'you really think so? That's why I wore these in particular." She bounced again, grinning.

I couldn't help but make a face. She'd get her wish when the Carter Gang arrived, and her stupid pearls would attract attention our way.

But... maybe that would be a good thing. So far, my quickly laid plan was to sneak off the train after the robbery and follow the Carters to their hiding spot. How I managed to accomplish that, especially if they were on horseback, was a whole different story. At least if they surrounded the lady and took her pearls, I'd get a good look at them.

Not that I wouldn't recognize them. I had stared at their sepia-stained photos for three days. Their faces were burned on the backs of my eyelids.

I turned back to the smudge of November forest gliding past outside and wondered when the Carters would stop the train. How long would I have to wait? The agony of anticipation pricked me so I couldn't sit still. My torso became hot and sweaty. The round woman's perfume nestled in my head and made everything thick and hazy. I shivered and shifted and rubbed my nose.

And waited.

It wasn't until the train took a corner a bit too fast that I noticed something heavy resting on my lap. Under my pale green coat, a small draw-string purse lay hidden on top of my skirt. It shifted when the train heaved to the side, rounding the corner. I pulled the drawstrings loose and peeked inside, careful not to let Perfume Lady see over my shoulder.

My breath caught in my chest. A rock tumbled to the pit of my stomach. Dreary afternoon light settled on the cool, polished nickel of a short-barreled pistol.

I cinched the drawstrings tight, sending the gun back to its hiding place. I pressed my coat down on it, smothering it, not letting it escape.

I'd never used a gun before in my life, let alone had one in my possession. Though it did make things a bit easier. If I planned to follow a train-robbing gang into the forests of Missouri, a gun might come in handy.

The question was, did I know how to use it?

Now that I knew it was there, I couldn't help but feel its weight on my lap. I became hyper-aware of it. I swore I could feel the cool steel on my thigh through my skirt and petticoat.

The train whistle bellowed, deep and throaty, and Perfume Lady jumped when I did. Another bellow came shortly after, followed by the squeal of brakes. Every bonnet and hat in the train car jerked forward as we slowed down. Perfume Lady covered her ears with her hands. I saw the glint of sparks out the window. An angry cloud of thick white steam rolled from the front of the train all the way past my window.

The train came to a stop. The steam settled around us like a deep fog high in the mountains. All I saw was white. As thick as cotton. As thin as mist. Everyone stared transfixed out their windows. There was a collective hush. A snag of breath. Perfume Lady had eyes like a cornered mouse. I could hear her heart beating louder than my own.

She didn't look so excited now.

I turned my attention back out my window. My breath fogged the glass. When I went to wipe it away, a dark figure emerged from the curtain of white steam. Black coattails billowed behind him in the winterish wind; the brim of a black hat cast a shadow over his bandana-covered face. A revolver rested casually in his black-gloved hand.

Cask Carter.

I knew him instantly.

He gazed up at the train as four more figures emerged from behind him. Arms raised, they aimed their guns at the sky. Shots rang out like bottle rockets. Plumes of smoke discharged from their revolvers.

My right hand slid into my purse and closed around the grip of my pistol. I rested my thumb on the hammer and my forefinger on the trigger. I watched as the Carter Gang boarded the train a few cars ahead.

When they entered my car, I'd be ready for them.

In Which Things Get a Little Complicated

There were gun shots. Heavy boot steps. Screams. Thuds.
Something that sounded like broken glass. All eyes were
fixed on the door at the front of the train car, waiting for
our turn with the Carters.

It didn't take long.

The door burst open, but it wasn't Cask who elbowed
his way through, revolver held high, bandana snug on
his nose. It was Judd – I could tell by the size of his ears.

Judd was Cask's brother, older by three years. He was
tall and gangly, with a high forehead, a narrow face, and
muddy brown eyes. His ears were large enough to see
light shining through them from behind. His nose was
long and thin, like an arrow pointing straight down,
and his hair was jet black and wavy under his hat. In his
outlaw photos, Judd never looked as menacing as Cask,
but there was a cool anger in his eyes that made the hair
on the back of my arms stand on end.

It didn't feel any different seeing him in person.

He aimed his gun at the ceiling and pulled the trigger.
Pop! Everyone jumped, including me. A shower of dust
dropped from the ceiling's new hole. He strode down the
aisle, boots scuffing, spurs jingling. The mouth of his gun
still smiled at the ceiling, licking its chops. Judd's eyes
slid over each person as he passed, but nothing seemed
to suit him.

Until he laid eyes on the waterfall of pearls next to me.

A low whistle seeped from his lips. He planted his
boots firmly and glared down at Perfume Lady. "What
have we here?"

I didn't know if I should look away or keep staring, but I couldn't seem to tear my eyes from his. There was a pull about him, almost like the magnetic pull of a soulmark in Limbo. It was like I knew him, and not just from staring at his photographs in Base Life. There was something about him, something beneath the surface, that was as familiar to me as my own breath.

"Are you goin' to hand those over nicely?" Judd asked Perfume Lady, gesturing his revolver at her pearls.

She sat up straighter and her fingertips rested on the strands. "Well, now, I don't know. Who do you work for? Someone notable? I don't want my pearls goin' to just any old group a' bandits."

Judd's eyes narrowed ever so slightly. The mouth of his gun smiled up at the woman's face. "Rest assured, ma'am. You can tell all your friends you were robbed by the Carter Gang. That should be worth somethin' in your circle of society."

"The Carter Gang?" she said, her nose wrinkled. "I took this train in particular, hopin' for James and Younger. If you aren't with James and Younger, then I think I'll try my luck on the next train. If you don't mind." She shifted in her seat and stared straight ahead, chin up. Like the matter was closed.

But Judd did mind. I saw a cloud of anger build on his brow. He raised his gun and pulled back the hammer with a click, his jaw set. Perfume Lady flinched.

"You'll hand 'em over, or I'll pull 'em off your dead body," he said, his voice low, his eyes black and cold. "It's up to you."

My body shivered all over. At first I thought I was just scared, but then I recognized the same yearning, the same itch, I felt in Chicago when I ran from the bakery or when I fought the Cafferelli thugs. I decided to give in to it, just like I had in 1961 when I found out I could drive the Corvette without thinking.

The moment I let go and gave in to the instincts of my host body, the shivering ceased. My boots felt heavy and rooted. My grip on my pistol was strong and sure.

I knew what I had to do. I wasn't going to let that woman die over a few strands of pearls. I'd read enough about train robberies to know that people often died for much less.

I rose to my feet, my coat and purse tumbling to the floor. I expected surprise, but Judd didn't even glance my way. Not even when I lifted my pistol, my finger still glued to the trigger. Not even when I cocked it.

Not even when I pressed the muzzle firmly against Perfume Lady's cheek.

It bit into her skin. She sucked in a breath, shocked.

"I told you," I heard myself say. "They'll take your pearls."

And a grin spread across my face.

CHAPTER 21

The Famous Shooter Delaney

The moment I realized what I'd done, I dropped the gun from Perfume Lady's cheek, even though my host body put up some resistance. I uncocked the pistol, shaking, scared to death that I'd aimed it at another human being, ready to fire.

Aimed it at her head.

And liked it.

What the hell was going on? Was this what Porter meant when he said my host body could handle danger? Did he mean I was a gun-wielding train robber in 1876?

Perfume Lady's hat dropped to the floor as she yanked the strands of pearls over her head. They clacked together as she piled them in Judd's hands.

"She can be a mite convincin', can't she?" Judd said to her, a smile at the corner of his eyes. I could only assume he was referring to me. I was the gun-wielding convincer. He stuffed the pearls into a sack tied at his belt. Only then did he finally turn his attention my way. "Who's next?"

"Pardon?" My voice was small inside my mouth. Small and weightless.

"Who's next?" His muddy eyes were expectant. But I didn't have a clue what he meant.

Stall, Alex, I told myself. Stall.

"Um…"

That was all I could come up with in the stalling arena. Thankfully, Perfume Lady came to my rescue just as Judd's smile morphed into a scowl.

"Wait," she said, staring up at me, her eyes wide. "You're Shooter Delaney aren't you? The Shooter Delaney."

"What's it to ya?" The words tumbled out of my mouth involuntarily. My voice was no longer soft and scared. It was sassy. Unrepentant. Prideful. My host body glared down at her, matching the heat of Judd's scowl dagger for dagger.

"I can't believe it," she said. "I've been sitting next to Shooter Delaney this whole time." She looked around at everyone in the car, pointing up at me. "It's Shooter Delaney!" She beamed, her chin hair bristled with excitement. "I sure hope you wear my pearls, Miss Delaney. That'd be something to brag about, that's for sure."

I felt my chest puff up, all that pride and sass inside my 1876 self uncurling like a flag in a gust of wind. Either this host body was particularly strong-willed, or I was losing my edge. There's no way Alex Wayfare would be proud of sticking a gun against a woman's face, then stealing her pearls. I had to get a grip.

I squared my shoulders and asked, "What do you know about Shooter Delaney?" There was still a bite lingering in my tone, but at least I had asked the question, not my host body.

"Same as everyone else, I guess. Sharpest shooter this side of the Mississippi, as far as females go. Your daddy's a lawman in Texas. Had a gun in your hand since you could walk, and robbed your first stagecoach when you were ten, just to see if you could do it. I bet your daddy's itchin' to give you a good whippin'," she added with a grin.

"Good Lord," Judd said, seizing my upper arm with an iron grip. "I thought you didn't want anyone to know you were on this train. Now everyone's gonna know." He yanked me out into the aisle and pushed me to the back of the car. "What's gotten into you?"

I didn't really know how to answer that, but I did know I was getting tired of descending back in time only to have some man push me around and ask what's gotten into me. First it was Ear Nibbler, now it was Judd.

"I don't know what's gotten into me," I said, jerking my arm from his grasp, "but the next time you yank on me like that, you're gettin' a bullet to the groin, ya hear, Judd Carter?" My accent rang clear the moment I relinquished the feeble hold I had on this host body and gave in to my anger.

His hands shot up in surrender before I even finished my sentence. "I know, I know, but good grief, woman," he pleaded, his voice a harsh whisper. "Why can't you ever just stick to the plan? I put my neck on the line and vouched for you with Cask. The least you could do is pretend to pay me a bit a' respect in front of everyone else. Don't I deserve that much?" He looked like a wounded puppy. In two seconds, Judd Carter went from dangerous outlaw to complete putty in my hands.

And I kind of liked him for it.

I could tell my host body did too, because I simpered (actually simpered) and touched his nose teasingly with a fingertip. "You're right. I'll stick to the plan from here on out."

Oh. My. God. Was I flirting with Judd Carter?

I watched, horrified, unable to stop myself, as my finger trailed across his cheekbone and curled behind his ear. He had a pink scar at the corner of his left eyelid. It made him squint a bit with that eye. I stretched up on my tiptoes. I was going to kiss him.

I so did not want to kiss him.

I wrestled to regain control within, but it was harder than I thought. This host body was so much more difficult to control than the others.

Forget muscle memory. This body felt like it had a mind of its own.

In the end, just as I snagged the top edge of Judd's bandana and pulled it down to reveal his lips, I resorted to physically grabbing my wrist with my other hand and forcing it down against my side.

Judd watched me struggle with my own arm, one eyebrow raised. I could tell he wanted to ask what had gotten into me again, but thought better of it this time.

The door on the other end of the car swung open with a bang. Cask Carter stepped through, followed by two others, whom I guessed were William, with his sandy hair and towering frame, and Yates, with his salt-and-pepper handlebar mustache and slight limp. Judd pushed me away awkwardly, like our parents just got caught us doing something we shouldn't.

"Don't let me interrupt," Cask said, striding toward us, his boots clomping on the floor. His footsteps shook the entire train car. He was a shadow even then, tall and black, moving confidently, dispersing the cool, muted afternoon light filtering in through the windows. He had a young, rugged face, handsome in a way. His brow was so heavy, it cast a permanent shadow over his eyes so you never could quite tell what he was really thinking. All you could see was a glint or two above his bandana.

All you could do was guess.

"Where's the good loot, Shooter?" he said, stopping in front of Judd and I, hooking his thumb on his belt loop. His black, shiny revolver hung loose from the forefinger of his other hand.

All four of the men stared at me. Judd looked hopeful, like he'd vouched for me for good reason, but the longer I stood there, silent, the more worried his expression became.

Cask sighed and scratched his eyebrow with the muzzle of his gun. "The loot?"

I opened my mouth and tried to let my host body take over, hoping I'd have the right answer for him, but nothing came out.

Cask turned his impatience upon Judd. "Get her off this train. I want her packed up and gone by sundown."

He marched off, and Judd jogged after him on his long legs. "Now, hold on, Cask. She's just not herself today, that's all. That fall from the horse yesterday; I'm sure that had somethin' to do with it."

Cask rounded on his older brother, glowering, the butt of his gun raised like he was about to strike him in the face. Everyone in the train car stared, wide-eyed and silent. "This was your idea. You said to bring a female along. You said she'd scout out the passengers so we'd know who to stick up. But look at her. She's just as useless as I said she'd be. Jesse James'd never work with a woman."

"Actually," I said, lifting a know-it-all finger, just like I would in Mr Lipscomb's class. Cask and Judd turned to look at me. Cask glared. Judd winced. "Jesse would work with a woman. And has. Many times." I knew it was true from all the books I'd read on the subject. There were quite a few female outlaws in history, and Jesse James wasn't above working with who he needed to to get a job done. "Now if you hound dogs are done howlin' over pearls and watches and pocket money, maybe you'll bend an ear long enough to hear about somethin' that'll make us all rich."

Thank God, my host body finally came through and took over. I didn't know how long I could get by with Porter's don't talk to the locals advice, especially since I was part of the gang.

Cask smiled at me, but it didn't reach his eyes. "I'm waiting."

"Turn your attention to the safe in the last car," I said, flicking my gun behind me. "There should be a chest in there with enough gold coins for all of us to retire. Not that I'd want to," I said, pulling the ribbons loose from my little yellow hat. I handed it to a young girl seated just up the aisle who couldn't tear her frightened eyes away from Cask and Judd. She seemed to calm down when I helped her situate it on top of her caramel-colored hair. "I'm quite in my element being a bandit," I told her. "Wouldn't you agree?"

She nodded, smiling.

I took Cask and Judd by the arm and ushered them toward the back door of the train car. As I passed Perfume Lady again, she tried to hand me my coat and purse. I thanked her but let her keep them.

"Shooter Delaney," I heard her say. Her voice was round with awe. "The famous Shooter Delaney."

Soup. It's What's for Dinner

I kept Cask Carter and the chest of coins in my sights all afternoon.

It was a small wooden chest, small enough to balance in one hand and stuff inside a saddle bag. When he'd knifed it open on the train, the shine of the coins lit up each of our faces. I knew from my research there were at least four priceless coins in that chest. I wasn't about to let Gesh get his hands on them.

After we left the train behind and melted into the deepening shadows of the woods, we came across five horses tied to trees. I stopped, too timid to go any closer, even though I could sense which horse was mine.

She was a black mare, strong and sleek, with a white patch on each of her flanks. Her saddle was padded and made of supple leather. She snorted at me, but I didn't step up to her.

I'd never been on a horse before.

But it would be just like driving the Corvette, right? I'd just let my host body do its thing and everything would be fine.

"Still scared of that filly?" Judd asked me. He hefted himself on top of his charcoal-colored stallion.

"Still?"

"We told you she didn't like women." Judd grinned, showing his teeth for the first time that day. His bandana was now nestled around his neck. One of his front teeth overlapped the other. "But you insisted on takin' her anyway. You never listen, do ya?" He laughed and turned his horse around, ready to ride off.

Cask, William, and Yates had all mounted their horses too. And they didn't look like the types to wait for me to get my bearings.

Taking a deep breath and flexing my hands, I untied my horse and pulled myself up into her saddle. I wedged my feet into the stirrups. The ground rocked beneath me. It was so far down. Remembering that Judd said I'd fallen off her the day before didn't help matters. I vowed to keep my chin up and eyes on the horizon, otherwise I was sure the forest floor would pull me down to meet it in a wave of dizziness.

I struggled with my skirt until I could straddle the horse properly, then nudged her in the belly with my heels. She took off after the others at a jolting trot. I closed my eyes and held on. Thankfully, we didn't ride for long.

The moment we approached our campsite, my horse decided our ride was over. She dug her hooves in the dirt and almost bucked me over her head. I climbed down, taking the hint, happy to be rid of her too. I hoped I could ascend back to Limbo before I had to ride her again. The insides of my thighs and my tailbone felt battered and bruised. Part of me thought she rode roughly just to spite me.

The campsite was deep in a wooded valley, shrouded by thick evergreens, twisting vines and brambles. It was actually a great hiding spot. No one could see the fire that crackled at the center if they happened by, but they'd be able to smell the food cooking a mile away. I hoped the Carters knew what they were doing, cooking out in the bare woods. If it were up to me, it would be jerky, bread and apples for the entire trip. Not even a fire to warm the bones. It was just common sense. But maybe this was how they'd all get caught or killed in the next few months. Stupidity.

There were three small canvas tents set up around the fire. An iron kettle hung over its lapping flames. Soup bubbled inside, offering curls of steam up into the cold November sky. A fifth man I hadn't met yet knelt at the kettle, head down under a wide-billed hat, stirring the soup. Cask, William, and Yates migrated toward the kettle, rubbing their cold hands together and commenting on how good it smelled.

Cask dropped his saddlebags against a fallen log near the fire. My eyes were stitched to its seams. The chest of coins was still inside.

"I guess you'll be wantin' to get out of that getup," Judd said, walking past me. His eyes were fixed on his hat in his hands, dusting leaves and dirt from the rim.

"Um, I guess." I looked down at my dress, not really sure what he meant. Did he mean I would want to put on a different dress? Or was that some kind of veiled suggestion to get naked?

I hated not knowing what people meant when I descended.

When I didn't budge, he looked up, his eyebrows raised, then shot a quick glance at the canvas tent to his right. That tiny glance let me know which tent was mine. I strode toward it, head held high, like I wasn't confused at all.

Inside, I found a bedroll spread out on the ground with a few blankets and pillows. A leather sack sat at its foot. I rummaged through the sack and found a pair of dark pants and a cream-colored long-sleeved shirt that looked to be my size.

So that's what Judd meant. I guessed Shooter Delaney didn't like to wear dresses. I smiled to myself as I unbuttoned my dress and peeled it from my shoulders. There were a few things I liked about my 1876 self so far. I was independent, strong, wore whatever clothes I liked, didn't get bossed around by the likes of the Carters.

Shooter Delaney was shaping up to be my kind of gal.

Sort of.

If only I knew more about her. Me. Why did I decide to become an outlaw? Just to hack off my Texas lawman father? Had I ever shot anyone? Killed anyone? Did I have blood on my 1876 hands?

I let my hair down from its tight bun and wriggled out of my corset and petticoat. I stretched my arms over my head. I hadn't realized how confining all that underwear was until my body could breathe again. How did women wear all that stuff back then?

While I was in mid-stretch, I heard a whistle from outside, followed by a few muffled chuckles. My head whipped over my shoulder. The flaps at the front of the tent were closed and no one was peeking in, but dammit. The light from the fire on one side of my tent cast my shadow in perfect precision on the other. The Carter Gang was enjoying their own private shadow peep show, courtesy of Alex Wayfare, time traveler extraordinaire.

I flopped down onto the bedroll and wrestled into my pants and shirt. My body burned red hot, through and through. At least one good thing would come from something so mortifying – sleeping out in the November cold would be a cinch.

After I pulled on a pair of worn-in cowboy boots, I sat in my tent, arms and legs crossed, face red, refusing to emerge. I couldn't face them. I couldn't walk out there and feel their eyes on me. Their teasing, hungry eyes, scraping and grating over my body.

They shouldn't have watched. Gentlemen wouldn't have watched.

I snorted a laugh.

I wasn't dealing with gentlemen. I was dealing with outlaws. Of course they'd watch. Of course they'd steal a glance and not think twice. Of course they'd stare and ogle and take what wasn't theirs. Of course.

"Dammit," I swore aloud. In all my embarrassment, I'd forgotten to keep an eye on the coin chest.

I crawled to the tent flaps and peeked outside. A deep-blue sky peeked through a canopy of naked treetops, but dark, black night had settled on the forest floor. Wind rustled in the evergreens and swayed bare branches. The four members of the Carter Gang were seated around the fire, spooning soup into their mouths from shallow tin bowls. The light of the fire licked the leather of Cask's saddlebags at his feet. The chest must still be inside. Why else would he keep the bags so close?

The fifth guy, the one I hadn't met yet, sat with his back to me beside Judd. I watched as my horse, a wisp of black movement amid the black night, stepped up to the fifth guy and nudged him with her nose. She nickered low and soft. He stroked her forehead, then handed her a carrot from his pocket. She devoured it in less than a second, then snuffled his coat pockets for more. He laughed and pushed her head away, telling her to "get."

Note to self: If you have to ride that horse again, make sure you have carrots. And lots of them.

I took a deep breath and left the safety of my tent, pulling a thick wool coat over my arms. Not only did I want the extra bulk around my body, but I wasn't as immune to the cold weather as I thought I'd be. (I would've given anything for a pair of warm sweats and a stocking cap.) I'd also found a holster in my sack and fastened it around my hips. I figured the Carters would know I'd keep my pistol close, but I didn't want to flaunt it. It made me feel safe to have my gun snug against my hip, hidden.

I wrapped the coat tight around me, shivering, and strolled up to the kettle. All eyes fell on me, followed by cat calls, laughter, and whistles. The red hot heat in my gut found its way to the surface of my skin again and spread out in a thin sheen of sweat. I tried to summon the sass and strength of my host body. I got the feeling Shooter Delaney wouldn't be embarrassed by anything. Not even an accidental peep show. She wouldn't have let them see her sweat.

I stuck out my chin and reached down for the lid on the kettle. The fifth guy jumped to his feet and snatched the lid off before I could. A puff of steam wafted up between us.

"Here, let me." He ladled the soup – chicken and potato – into a bowl. He handed it to me, along with a spoon, through the cloud of rising steam.

I reached out and took it from his hands. My palms grazed his knuckles. The steam swirled and lifted, then dissipated, leaving clear, cold air between us. He looked up and met my eyes, and for the first time that night, I saw his face.

I dropped my bowl into the soup with a splat.

It was Blue.

Again.

In 1876.

CHAPTER 22

What's in a Name?

"How?" I said, my hands trembling over the kettle.

Blue knitted his brow together. His hair was a lot longer this time, almost down to his jaw, and he was thinner, yet still muscular. His skin was bronzed from a life spent working outdoors, but his eyes were the same striking blue-green. Truth be told, he was even more handsome than ever before.

And it totally pissed me off.

"How?" This time I demanded an answer. But he only looked more confused.

All the other guys were sitting up and staring now. Yates twisted one end of his handlebar mustache, his eyelids making slits. There was a blob of soup on William's chin. Cask's heavy brow shadowed his eyes so darkly, it looked like he was wearing a Lone Ranger mask.

Blue grabbed a long-handled spoon and tried to fish my bowl out of the soup. I watched him, my mouth hanging open, unable to feel my body. I was numb, barely standing, shuddering from the inside with shock. How could he be here? How?

"Answer me." The words scorched my tongue.

"I'm not sure how you dropped it," he said, carefully lifting the bowl out of the hot soup with his forefinger and thumb. "You just... dropped it."

"You know that's not what I mean."

He looked up at me, no longer confused but annoyed. "You and your attitude," he said, shaking his head. He slung the excess soup off the bowl and onto the ground. Some splattered on my boots, but I barely noticed.

"I've tried to be cordial and accommodatin'," Blue said over his shoulder to Judd, "but she's just got it in for me, and that's all there is to it."

"You ain't the only one," Cask mumbled into his bowl, his mouth full.

Judd gave me a look that said be nice. Blue refilled my bowl and stuck it out to me, his eyes fixed on something – anything – off to my right. Why wouldn't he look at me?

I didn't take the soup. Instead, I half-stumbled my way over to sit on a log beside Cask, unable to fully feel or control my limbs. Cask eyed me suspiciously and pulled his saddlebags closer to his side. I dug my elbows into my knees and tried to steady my breathing. I stared at my boots. There were bits of leaves and sticks and dirt stuck to the splattered soup. I let my coat hang open like a blanket over my shoulders. The cold November air made its way inside to ruffle my shirt. It tangled in my long hair.

I was numb to the core.

If this was descending – seeing Blue each time I traveled back to the past – then I didn't want to do it anymore. It was enough to drive anyone insane. It was a knife prick to the bone. A reminder of our night together, the one that no longer existed. Would I experience the torture every time? Again and again and again? It felt like seeing a fresh bruise each morning on Audrey's pearl-white skin. Or seeing Mom's red eyes at the dinner table, knowing she'd been crying again, but never knowing why. Always wondering if it was me – if I was the cause of her misery.

I watched Blue lower himself to the ground beside Judd, his back propped against the flat side of a rock. He looked up at me, his eyes finding mine. Firelight played on his sun-dark skin. The flames flickered and flashed at the corners of his blue, narrowed eyes. He had never directed such a distasteful expression my way.

He didn't like me in this past life. In fact, I was pretty sure he hated my guts. I tried to tell myself it was Shooter Delany he didn't like, but that didn't help. Shooter Delany was me, after all.

It made me feel sick to see him look at me like that. So sincerely bothered by me. As Jack Baker, at least he was agreeable and sympathetic, even if he was a ghost sent to haunt me. Now what was he? Still a figment of my imagination? What would Porter say when I told him I saw the same Nick again? Would he tell me I was still grieving?

I placed my clammy hands on my knees to steady their trembling. I wasn't grieving for Blue anymore. No, I was past that. Now I was livid. And I wanted answers.

I deserved answers.

I dared to look at him again. He was still watching me, but his expression had changed. Instead of distaste, he looked like he was in deep, tormented thought. There was a struggle going on inside him. It bent his shoulders. It fisted his hands.

Was it Shooter Delaney who tormented him? Or Alex Wayfare? How was I going to get him alone to find out?

Judd glanced back and forth between Blue and I, his forehead puckered. Then he set his finished bowl aside and heaved himself up on his towering legs. "Mind if I have a word?" he asked me.

My legs were still wobbly, but I followed him as he strode tall into the woods toward his horse. Darkness slid over us. He rummaged in his saddlebags, then pinched a tiny, hand-rolled cigarette between his lips. He struck a match and cupped his hands around it as it lit. He pulled in a few puffs, then snuffed the match with a wave of his hand and dropped it to the ground. He took a deep drag and blew a long tunnel of smoke out the side of his mouth. "You wanna tell me what's goin' on?"

"What do you mean?"

"With Heath. Why are you givin' him such a hard time this week?"

Heath? Was that Blue's name in 1876? "I wasn't aware I was."

Judd quirked an eyebrow. He didn't believe me. And I wasn't about to argue. Keep the conversations short.

"I'm sorry. I'll lay off of him if that's what you want."

Judd blew another tunnel of smoke over my head, his lips curved into a smile. "Yes. Thank you."

"Is that all?" I glanced over my shoulder at Cask. He was laughing about something with Yates and William. His saddlebags rested against his calf. Blue watched Judd and I out of the corner of his eye.

"I guess so," said Judd. He flicked the finished nub of his cigarette to the ground and smashed it with his boot. "I'm tuckered. Headin' to bed. You comin'?"

My eyes snapped back to him. "What? With you?"

"Well, yes. Unless you want to sleep out here with the horses." He chuckled to himself.

"I..." I glanced at the tents by the fire. Only three. Of course we'd all be doubling up. How had I missed that? "I still haven't eaten. I think I'll sit up for a while yet."

"Suit yourself." He moved closer to me, and his hands found my hips. He smelled like tobacco and chicken soup. "I ain't forgotten, you know."

I tipped my chin down. I didn't want to give him any invitation to kiss me, if that was his intention, although I could tell my host body wouldn't have minded. "Forgotten what?"

"The house on the hill."

I had absolutely no idea what he was talking about. So I pretended. "Oh?"

"Cask said that chest is worth at least eight thousand dollars. Once we get our share, I'm gonna fulfill that promise I made. We'll leave all this behind. Head to California. Just you and me." He moved in closer. His breath mingled with my hair. "We'll buy a piece a' land. And men'll come from all over and pay us to pan our creeks." I could hear the smile in his voice.

It made my heart ache.

Judd would never make it to California. By this time next month, he'd be caught by the Pinkertons outside Mobile, Alabama. A few weeks after that, he would die in his jail cell, cold and alone, from pneumonia.

And I couldn't warn him of it. I couldn't say a word. I had to stand there beneath his hopeful smile and keep still.

"Well, don't stay up too late," he said, giving my hips a squeeze. "We've got a long ride tomorr–"

When he didn't finish his sentence, I looked up. His face was slack, the smile slowly dripping from his jaw. He stared over my head, his muddy eyes vacant and unblinking.

"Judd?" I tugged at his vest. "Are you all right?" Was he having a seizure?

He blinked. Twice. Then he looked down at me like he was surprised to find me standing so close. He took a step back, lifting his hands from my hips. He rubbed the scruff on his chin. "I'm sorry, what were we talking about?"

"You said you were tuckered. You were headin' to bed."

"Right. Right." He glanced around at the campsite and the horses, almost as if he didn't recognize his surroundings.

"Are you sure you're all right?" I asked.

"Course I am. Walk with me?"

He offered his arm, and I took it. We walked to my tent, though I seemed to lead him more than he led me.

"Goodnight," he said, stooping and disappearing through the tent flaps.

"Good… night."

When I turned around, the guys around the fire were all staring at me. Especially Cask and Blue.

"I don't think he feels too well," I said, returning to my seat beside Cask.

"Must've been the soup," Cask said, aiming a grin at Blue. Blue kicked a shower of dirt at Cask, and Cask threw his spoon at him.

"My soup ain't the only thing around here that can sour a stomach," Blue said, tossing a glare at me. Cask's booming laugh echoed throughout the rocky valley.

I rolled my eyes and stared at the fire. I had to try to keep my mind on my mission. I could deal with the Blue Situation later.

"Well, I think I'll go for a walk," Cask said, standing and stretching his back. He pulled the brim of his hat down over his already-shadowed eyes. "Don't no one go followin' after me, now." He rested a palm on the revolver slung at his side. He handed each of us a pointed look. Especially me.

We all got the hint. Except I was the only one fool enough not to take it.

He hefted his saddlebags over his shoulder and started off into the night. He melted away, silent as a shadow, leaving me alone with Blue, William, and Yates, who all continued to stare at me. I had to move fast, or I'd lose sight of the chest for good.

"I think I'll go stretch my legs, too."

I made a show of heading the opposite way toward the horses, where I'd had my conversation with Judd, and then, when I knew they couldn't see me anymore, I backtracked to follow Cask. I couldn't see him, but I could hear his footfalls. He wasn't exactly trying to be quiet, and I figured he didn't have to be. No one in his gang would dare follow him, unless they wanted tonight to be their last. Or they were out of their right mind.

I guess both of those applied to me.

I fingered the cool steel of the pistol at my hip. It held a full round; I checked before I holstered it. Not that I planned on shooting Cask. I only wanted to see where he hid the chest. I wasn't even going to move it like I moved the Raphael. If the chest had never been found in Base Life, then it was most likely still resting in the same hiding place. All I had to do was tell Porter where to find it. My gun was only a backup – in case I wasn't very good at trailing someone silently in the dark.

Thankfully, the moon gave off enough light for me to pick my way through the trees. I stepped gingerly over fallen limbs and gnarled roots, taking care to avoid loose rocks and sticks that might snap. I thought I was doing well, but after a few minutes, Cask's footsteps stopped. I froze in my tracks, then slowly dissolved into the shadow of a tree to my left.

I waited. And listened.

I heard faint rustling, as though Cask were rummaging through his bags. Then came the squeak of a hinge. The strike of a match.

Fire.

The spark caught my attention out of the corner of my left eye. Cask was over a hundred feet away, hunched down, half his face lit by the tiny matchstick flame. He lifted a lantern out of his bag and fed the wick inside, snuffing the match afterward. The lantern bathed him in a sphere of amber light. He repositioned the saddlebags over his shoulder and resumed his walk, the lantern held out in front of him.

I let the distance between Cask and I lengthen. Now that I had something to follow besides footsteps – that lantern light would pierce through the trees for miles – I could let in some space between us. Enough for a decent sound buffer.

As I watched Cask's lantern bob hypnotically up ahead, my mind found its way back to Blue. I turned the events of the night over and over in my hands, examining each facet. What was his problem with Shooter Delaney? With me? He was infuriating as Heath, this guy who glared at me and jabbed me with his words. He was infuriating as Jack Baker, being kind and helpful, then driving off into the horizon like he didn't care about me at all. Like our friendship never existed.

Which was the truth. I'd erased it all.

Was that why he didn't remember me? Had I erased it from his memory? Or was it because we were in 1876, and our meeting in 1927 hadn't happened yet? But then, wouldn't he have recognized me in 1961?

None of it made sense.

I clenched my teeth and fists. I couldn't wrap my head around it all. I wasn't used to not having an answer. Normally, no matter what the problem, I could find a fix. I'd have all the right tools to choose from. But in this situation, I had nothing. All I knew was that he couldn't be the same person from Chicago. He couldn't look exactly like the same person. It was impossible. Insanely and undeniably impossible.

And yet... here I was. Living. Breathing. Possible. A time-traveling, pistol-wielding, Corvette-driving, gang-fighting, outlaw from the future.

That proved anything was possible, didn't it?

A twig snapped somewhere off to my right. I went rigid, my muscles seized, my breath clutched tightly in a ball. I slowly, slowly, turned my head to the side. I squinted at the black forest shapes all around me for what felt like forever, scanning left to right. My breath was the color of moonlight.

Another twig snapped. Behind me this time. My heartbeat moved to my ears. My breath came in quick, shallow bursts.

Someone followed me.

With a dart of my eye, I glanced back at Cask's lantern. It still bobbed up ahead, but it grew steadily smaller as the distance between us stretched further. I had to keep moving or else I'd lose sight of him, but before I started again, I chanced another look over my shoulder.

At first, I saw nothing, just more dark forest. Then there was a faint shift of shadow out of the corner of my eye. I turned to run but it was too swift for me. A hand, deft and quick, reached out of the darkness and clamped over my mouth. Two strong arms wrapped around me. A rock solid body pressed against mine. I struggled and bucked, one hand beating at whoever had hold of me, the other hand grasping for my gun.

"Stop it, will ya? Shooter, stop it now, it's just me." Blue's harsh whisper filled my ear with hot breath. The moment I stopped struggling, he let me go.

"What the hell has gotten into you?" I hissed, driving my palms into his chest to shove him away. "Why did you follow me?" I slammed another fist into his chest for good measure. He'd scared me absolutely silly.

"I needed to talk to you."

"Now? You couldn't wait for morning?"

"I needed to talk to you alone." He looked apologetic and confused, and more like my Blue from Chicago than ever before.

I hated to send him back to camp, but I had to finish my mission. Alone. And quietly. "I can't talk now. I'm busy. Go back to camp."

I turned around to locate Cask's lantern, but it had disappeared. Vanished. I searched frantically for any sign of it, but there was nothing. Just black. And Blue. And me.

"Dammit," I said, rounding on Blue. "Look what you made me do."

"What?"

Cask had heard us and snuffed his lamp. I was sure of it. Now I'd never be able to find him in the dark. I groaned and pinched the bridge of my nose. Everything was ruined. I'd have to go back and do the entire mission over again.

Blue took a step toward me, his head cocked to the side. "Were you followin' Cask?"

I shook my head. It was all over. Time to head back to Limbo and face Porter. Tell him I failed. Tell him I'd have to go back. Ask him why I saw Nick again. See what kind of lie he handed me this time.

"I'm sorry," I said. "I have to go."

"Go where?"

I marched back the way I came, prepared to ascend the moment the campsite came into view. But I only took a few steps before I heard Blue say something that made me stop dead in my tracks. My blood frosted in my veins. My tongue fused to the roof of my mouth; my feet threaded roots in the ground.

He called out my name. Only he didn't say Shooter. Or Cora. Or Delaney.

He said Alex.

CHAPTER 23

Blue and Sousa

"What did you say?" I turned around slowly, carefully, as though Blue – the real Blue – might bolt if I made any sudden movements.

He still looked confused. "I said your name."

"Which name?"

"Shooter."

"No," I said, shaking my head, "no, you said Alex. I heard you."

"Why would I say Alex?"

I opened my mouth to reply, to say it was because he remembered me, but I couldn't. It didn't make sense for him to remember me. How could he have memories of something that hadn't happened yet?

When I didn't answer, he heaved a frustrated sigh and adjusted his hat. "Look, I just came out here to ask you to stop doin' what it is you're doin'."

"What am I doing?"

"Whatever it is that's makin' my head so foggy."

"I'm not doing anything to your head."

"Yes you are. Ever since you came back tonight, I've had thoughts I can't get outta my mind. Thoughts I didn't think up on my own." He stepped up to me, his body a solid, warm silhouette in the moonlight.

"I can't put thoughts in your head," I said. "I'm not a witch."

"But you are. You must be." He stepped closer, so close the brim of his hat cast a shadow over my face. "You bewitched me. You must've. There's no other explanation. Cuz no matter how much I try, I can't stop thinkin' about you." His eyes fell to my lips. His fingertips grazed my chin. "About kissin' you."

I sucked in a breath and pressed my lips together. He remembered me. There was no doubt.

"How else could I have thoughts like that?" His breath brushed my skin. His thumb swept across the hollow of my throat. "It ain't makin' sense. Just this morning, you and I were as sick a' each other as we've been for the past three weeks. And Judd's my cousin. So explain to me why I'm contemplatin' stealing away with his girl all of a sudden."

I bit my lip, feeling sorry for him. He truly didn't understand. And leave it to Blue to want to do right by his cousin.

He was still so good.

"I can't explain it," I said. "At least, not in a way you'd understand."

His thumb moved across my collar bone, making me shiver. "Try."

What did I have to lose? I had to redo the mission anyway. I could make all the impact on him I wanted. It wouldn't change anything.

I took a deep breath, then came right out and said it. "This morning I was Shooter. Now I'm Alex. The same Alex you met in Chicago outside Sloan's Bakery. The same Alex you stopped to help on the side of the road in Ohio."

His eyes searched my face, his brow pulled down. "I ain't never been to Chicago."

"Maybe not. But you will one day. Fifty years from now, you will. Your name will be Nick Piasecki, and you'll be a deli delivery boy."

I expected him to shake his head, to look at me like I was crazy and tell me I was talking nonsense. But he didn't.

"You remember me," I said, placing my palm on his chest. "I don't know how you do, but you do. You remember Chicago. 1927. Blue and Sousa. We kissed by the fountain. You played Stardust on the piano. You held my hand in yours, skin to skin." I entwined our fingers together, and he looked down at our hands. Couldn't he feel it? We were the same people. We had the same hands. The same lips.

The same souls.

He swallowed. His thoughts were far off, treading the horizon. Our hands were warm. "I don't know how to play the piano," he said.

I tipped his chin up to look at me. "You do. You play beautifully." I found myself caught in his eyes, unable to look away. My breath came quicker. His face was so very beautiful. His blue-green eyes, the dark stubble on his jawline, his perfectly shaped mouth. What I wouldn't give to see his teasing smile again. To see him laugh. Call me up onto the roof. Hear him call me Sousa.

Taste his lips again.

"After that night," I said, "after our night in Chicago, I went home and found Stardust on one of my grandparents' old records. I listened to it over and over, just lying there on the hardwood floor. I thought you died because of me." My throat was thick, turning my words to whispers. I pulled myself against him and spoke into his shirt. "I need you to remember. I need you to tell me you're real. That you're alive. However impossible it may be."

I needed to know his life didn't end in that delivery truck on Christmas Eve. That erasing our time together hadn't ruined his life.

He was still for a long moment, his pulse matching mine. Then he dropped his hand from mine, and I thought he was going to push me away. Tell me we couldn't do this to Judd. I thought I'd lost him – lost my chance.

But he didn't push me away.

Instead, he slipped both his arms around me, slid his hands up my back beneath my coat, and gathered me gingerly against his chest. He rested his forehead against mine under the brim of his hat. Our breath mingled in the thin space between us.

"You had brown eyes," he said.

And that was all it took to convince me. Heath, Jack, Nick, whatever his name was, it didn't matter. He was Blue. My Blue from Chicago.

I couldn't resist any longer. I reached up, sliding my hands to the back of his neck. My fingers tangled in his hair. My nose brushed his. I parted my lips, inviting him to kiss me.

A pause settled between us then, heavy and anxious. There was a reservation, a hesitation, a battle beneath his skin. I could feel it. I held my breath, waiting and hoping, eyes closed.

It didn't take him long to decide what he wanted. He clasped my shirt in his fists and pressed his lips to mine. He kissed me thoroughly, his hands hungry and searching the curves of my body underneath my coat. The small of my back, my waist, my hips. He kissed me until he'd stolen all my breath and pulled every last ounce of November chill from my body. And I would've kept kissing him, kept letting him touch me, until the sun came up, if fate would've given us half a chance.

Turns out, it didn't.

As we kissed, a sphere of amber light fell upon our shoulders. It slid across our closed eyelids, and the hair on the back of my neck bristled.

Cask was behind us.

What happened next was completely out of my control. My host body reacted before I could. In one swift, deadly motion, I yanked Blue's revolver from his holster and drove the grip into the tender spot right behind his ear. His body went limp, and he collapsed in my arms, his lips ripping softly from mine.

I had him on the ground, slumped against a tree, before I fully understood what I'd done. I'd knocked him out cold with one blow. I went to reach for him, to check his pulse and see if he was all right, but my host body wouldn't budge. Instead, I spun on my heel and faced Cask dead on. A waterfall of lies spilled from my mouth with dramatic flair.

"He went after you, Cask. He wanted to see where you were hidin' the chest. Said he didn't trust you to divvy up our shares. I confronted him, and he attacked me. Forced himself right onto me." I pretended to be out of breath and pressed the back of my hand to my forehead.

Cask stared at me. His coal black eyes glinted in the lantern light. Trying to read Cask Carter was like trying to read a book in the dark. You could see the print, but you couldn't make out the words.

Fear clawed inside me, and I tried not to let it show. He was the only Carter I was truly afraid of. I feigned a sigh and pretended to care about the state of my hair. "Judd will have to hear of this. Can you help me carry Heath back to camp?"

"Naw," said Cask. He spat at the ground. "We'll leave him here for a while."

"But it's so cold out."

"We'll only be gone a few minutes."

"We?"

He nodded. "You're comin' with me. I need your help."

I drew in a deep, shaky breath and forced a smile. "All right."

There was nothing else I could do. Cask took Blue's gun from my hand and tucked it between his back and his belt. Then I followed him the way he headed originally, before I lost his trail. I decided I would go with him as far as it took to discover if he still had the chest in his saddlebags. If he didn't, I would ascend and do the mission over. If he did, then maybe the mission hadn't been ruined after all. And maybe "Heath" wouldn't remember a thing.

Another kiss lost from his memory.

But fused forever in mine.

Stardust

I walked along beside Cask, rubbing my arms, my teeth chattering. I was frigid now without Blue there to warm me, without his hands on my waist. And the cold wasn't the only thing making me shiver. I had no idea what Cask wanted my help with, and honestly, I was petrified it was some kind of guise to get me alone.

So he could plant me in the ground.

"Do you love my brother?" he asked out of the blue. He didn't look at me. His eyes were fixed ahead.

"Excuse me?"

"Judd. Do you love 'im?" This time he stopped and faced me. He held the lantern up so he could see my face.

I relinquished control and let Shooter speak for herself. "Yes."

Cask stared at me for a long moment, trying to decide if he believed me. In the end, he started walking again, shaking his head. "No woman's ever loved Judd. Especially no woman as pretty as you. So you wanna tell me what you want from him?"

"Want from him?"

"There must be somethin' you want. Somethin' I ain't got. Cuz you see, women, they don't look at Judd." His lips broke into a handsome, arrogant smile. "They look at me."

"Well, aren't you stuck up."

"It's the truth, is all." He stepped over a gnarled root. "So tell me. What is it?"

"I dunno." I shrugged. "He's sweet. He's the only man who doesn't boss me around. And he wants what I want."

"What's that?"

"The house on the hill." I stepped up on a fallen log and hopped down to the other side. When Cask dropped down next to me, I reached out and laid a hand on his forearm. "Cask, after you give us our share of the loot, Judd and I are goin' to California. We're gonna start a life out there. No more lawbreakin'."

He sighed and adjusted his hat. "Yeah, I figured. He's been talkin' about that for a while now."

We resumed our walk down a sloping hollow carpeted with leaves, winding through mossy boulders, until we came to a ragged bluff towering over us, as tall as a tree. It looked like thin stone slabs stacked to the sky, with ledges and overhangs covered with a mantle of slippery green moss. Somewhere nearby, there was a trickle of water.

"Up there," Cask said, lifting his lantern high. "See that hole halfway up? The one that sapling's stickin' out of?"

I saw it. It looked like something a family of bats would enjoy.

"I can't get up there on my own with the chest," Cask said. "I need you to climb up and I'll pass it to you." He set the lantern down at the base of the bluff and pulled the chest of coins from his bag. I stared at it like I expected a rainbow to come shining down.

I hadn't missed my chance.

"Why do you trust me all a' sudden?" I asked.

Cask's face was emotionless. "Because I ain't got nothin' to lose." He rested his hand on his revolver. "You do."

I nodded once. There wasn't much else I could add to that.

I stepped up to the bluff and began to climb. It was difficult at first, because some of the ledges above me stuck out farther than the ones at my feet, and half the time, when my boot found a toehold, it slipped on the moss. I could see why Cask had trouble climbing up while balancing the chest in one hand. Or his saddlebags for that matter. But as luck would have it, Shooter Delaney was a sprightly climber. Maybe Cask already knew that.

Halfway between Cask and the hole, there was a decent ledge to balance on. I knelt down and reached for the chest. Cask stood up on his toes, pushing the chest up on the tips of his fingers. My nails scraped the top. I stretched further, my muscles burning, until I snagged one of the leather strap handles on the side.

"Got it." I heaved it up onto my ledge.

"Now reach your arm in that hole. See if there's any obstruction."

"Um. I think not." I snapped the sapling growing out of the hole in half, then used it to poke around inside, covering my face with my other arm in case I disturbed a few bats. After a few jabs, it seemed empty to me. I tossed the sapling aside, which almost hit Cask on its way down, and shoved the chest into the hole.

It was the perfect hiding spot. Now I just had to figure out how to explain its location to Porter. Maybe I could carve a symbol into the rock...

"Did you hear that?" Cask said, his voice low.

I froze and listened. "No..."

"Shhh."

I looked out past our little sphere of lantern light but couldn't see anything but black. Cask pressed a finger to his lips, then he slowly seeped into the wood, signaling for me to wait where I was.

"Cask," I whispered. "You gotta help me down."

But he was already gone, leaving me all alone in the cold, on a narrow stage awash with flickering amber light. It was too far to jump, and if I was going to climb down, I wanted him below me in case I slipped. I rubbed my arms, my back pressed against the striated rock behind me. My teeth chattered again. How long was he going to leave me up here?

I was right in the middle of deciding whether or not to ascend back to Limbo and let Shooter figure out how to get down on her own when I heard voices. Harsh voices, somewhere out in the darkness. It was Cask and another guy, I could tell, but I couldn't make out what they were saying. Was it Blue? Had he come to and followed us?

I strained to listen, reaching, stretching, trying to make sense of the angry tones, but they were too muddled. Too entwined. Was Cask mad at Blue for following him? Did he believe my story about Blue wanting the loot for himself?

The arguing stopped and the struggling began. I heard the scuff of boots against leaves and dirt. Grunts. The thwack of fists.

My eyes darted to the ledge at my feet, searching for the best way down. I had to get to Blue before Cask did something drastic. I was on my knees with my back to the dark forest, gripping the edge of the ledge and ready to reach my toe down into thin air, when I heard the fierce blast of a gun.

My God.

Had someone been shot? Who pulled the trigger? I hauled myself back onto the ledge, my heart in my throat, and scanned the darkness for any sign of movement. The shot still echoed through the hollow, spreading out and rolling into the distance like thunder.

The moment silence fell again, I heard two things. First, footsteps. Heading my way through the carpet of leaves. Whoever it was could probably see me by now. Lit up like a display at the bottom of the hollow.

Then came the whistling. Clear as day, piercing through the night. And it only took a second for me to figure out the tune.

Stardust.

The song Blue played for me on the piano in Chicago. Our song.

I let out a sigh. It was Blue coming for me. He must have come to and followed us like I thought. And he was whistling Stardust to let me know he still remembered. But where was Cask? And who fired the gun?

I watched, breath held, as a figure emerged from the trees, swaggering and whistling. But it wasn't Blue who stepped into the sphere of amber light directly beneath me. And it wasn't Blue who whistled Stardust so sweetly and perfectly – a tune that wouldn't be composed for another fifty years.

It was Judd.

CHAPTER 24

Soul Blocking

The jagged bluff dug into my shoulder blades. My whole world tilted to the left. The lantern light cast a wicked shadow across Judd's face. A strange sort of grin hooked at his lips.

"Where's Cask?" My voice floated down to him like a fallen leaf. A crow cawed somewhere above us.

"He ain't dead, if that's what you're askin'." He twirled his warm gun on his finger. "But he won't be botherin' us for a while."

Dear God. Did he leave him out in the cold to bleed to death?

"How do you know that song?" I said.

"Haven't you figured it out yet, Shooter my gal?" he said, with a snarly grin, "or are you still con-fused?"

My skin pricked and tingled. A black thought, sleek, round and venomous, sat on my tongue in the form of one seemingly harmless word. Gooseflesh spread out across my arms as I spoke it silently.

Descender.

Was it Gesh himself? Or had he sent someone in his place?

"Oh, hell," he said, scratching the stubble on his jaw. "I tried, but I can't keep this hick accent up. I sound like a jackass." His accent vanished, replaced with something more flat and distinctively modern. "And what about these ears?" He flicked his left one. "This guy's uglier than Dumbo's ass. Am I right?"

I reached for my gun. I had it cocked and sighted right between his eyes before he finished his sentence. The steel was cold and familiar. Comforting in my hands. My finger kissed the trigger. "Who are you? Who sent you?"

"You don't know?" A dry laugh tore from his throat. "Wow, you're even more stupid than I thought. Gesh was afraid you'd outsmarted him. He'll be happy to hear that's not the case." He laughed again.

I glared at him. I straightened my back and re-sighted. This time right at his heart.

Judd shook his head, staring up at the barrel of my gun. He clucked his tongue. "Descending rule number one: Thou shalt not kill. Remember?"

Every muscle quivered beneath my skin. I thought about putting a bullet in his chest just to shut him up. Just for coming after me and shooting Cask. Just for violating Judd's body the way he was. Judd may have been a criminal, but he was a decent man. He deserved better.

The Descender sighed like he was bored. He lifted his revolver and aimed it at me in a careless sort of way. He was tired of talking. "Why don't you just give me what I came for? Then I can be on my way."

"You want the chest? You can have it." I was going to redo the mission anyway. Erase everything. Who cared if he knew where it was hidden now? I'd just move it to another hiding place on the next go around.

"The chest?" he said. "Gesh couldn't care less about the chest. You'd know that if you had half a brain."

He couldn't? "Then what does he want?"

That same cold grin hooked his lips again. It knotted my stomach. When he spoke, his voice was golden and sweet. "There isn't a treasure on Earth worth more to him than a Descender gone rogue. And now that he knows you're traveling again? He wants you. He wants your name."

I gripped my gun with both hands. "You know my name. It's Shooter Delaney."

His grin pulled tighter across his teeth. "Come on now. Don't play games."

"Is that one no good? Try Susan Summers."

"I'm warning you." I heard the click as he cocked the hammer. He adjusted the gun in his grip as he took actual aim.

I didn't catch my name in 1927, or else I'd have given him that one too. Instead I said, "Kiss my ass."

It was too much.

He scowled at me and squeezed the trigger.

You know how heroes are always dodging bullets at the last second in films? Yeah. That's pretty much impossible. Because as soon as I heard the blast, the bullet slammed into the bluff right next to my ear. The bluff exploded, showering me in gray dust and jagged bits of rock. I dropped to my knees, shielding my head, a good two seconds too late. My only saving grace was his poor aim.

"You can't take a life," I shouted, peeking out at him from between my arms.

"Tell me your na-ame." He said it in a singsong voice, like a bully taunting someone on the playground. Again, the hammer clicked into place.

I gritted my teeth. Like hell I was going to tell him my name.

I whipped my pistol over my head and took a shot. Two blasts. My bullet knocked the hat right off his head. His sliced a chunk out of the ledge beneath my feet.

I leapt up and pressed my back against the bluff. My chest pumped in and out. My mind raced. How many rounds did he have left? Had he reloaded sometime between the train robbery and now?

Whatever the count, I realized it didn't matter. His aim would only improve each time he took a shot. But then again, so would mine.

"Your name, Sweet Stuff."

I cocked and aimed.

I fired.

But so did he.

This time, white hot pain smacked into my right hand. My gun plummeted to the ground. I never saw where my bullet went. I didn't care. All I could think about was the searing hole ripped through the meaty part of my thumb. The broken bones. The hot blood streaming down my forearm to my elbow; the hot tears streaming down each side of my face, meeting under my chin.

"Aw. That didn't have to happen," he said. I could barely hear him over the ringing in my ears.

My breathing came in short, uncontrollable bursts. High-pitched. Panicked. I knew his plan. He didn't care if he took a life. He knew I would go back and redo the mission. He was counting on it. He could rip a dozen bullets through my flesh and it wouldn't matter. He could torture me and make me bleed all night long.

Until I gave in.

But I'd had enough.

I closed my eyes and reached for Limbo. I felt my soul arch and lift, felt the pain in my hand fade, but I couldn't break free. Something blocked my path. Something dense. Impenetrable. Suffocating. I fought against it, but it was like trying to push a door open against a wall of water.

My soul collapsed back into Shooter's body, exhausted from the attempt. When I opened my eyes, Judd's unflinching grin and the torment of my mangled hand greeted me. My boots glistened with blood.

"You like that?" he said. "It's called soul blocking. Pretty handy, right? Rule number two: Don't ascend while someone's talking to you. It's rude."

I sucked in a seething breath through my teeth, trying not to think about the pain, and attempted the only feasible means of escape I had left: continue to scale the bluff. If I could just make it to the top and get off that stupid ledge, I could find somewhere to hide.

I snatched a ledge above my head with my left hand. I pushed up with my right foot. I cradled my bloody right hand at my chest, and used my elbow to balance while I reached for another ledge. I was as slow as molasses, my entire body shivering, but I could make it. I knew I could. I just had to concentrate.

And pray he ran out of bullets before another one made contact.

"I'm going to try to get you at the back of your knee this time," he called out. "Your left one. It'll probably shatter the kneecap. OK?"

I scrambled higher. I tried not to zero my attention on the back of my knee, but it was hopeless. It was all I could think about. That shot. That violent blast of bone and tendon and muscle. That pain.

I gave up trying to protect my hand – I used it, seizing ledge after ledge, the rock biting into the wound, the pain blinding me, the smear of my blood painting patterns on the bluff.

He cocked his gun. "All right. You want me to count it down?"

Just a few more ledges. Just a few more feet. I could see the top. It was right there.

Pop!

He took the shot.

And it hit exactly where he said it would.

The pain. You wouldn't even comprehend the pain. It was so intense I couldn't even summon a scream. I saw sparks. White, silver, red.

Fire.

My boots slipped from their toeholds. I dangled for a short moment before my arms gave out. Down the face of the bluff I went, my chin and nose grazing a few ledges on the way down. The Descender dove beneath me, catching hold of me at the last minute to break my fall. We both smacked into the ground, my body limp on top of his.

He pushed me off and scrambled to his feet, his gun cocked and ready. I rolled over onto my back with a groan. My body felt red. Blazing. Churning. Like lava.

"Tell me your name and I'll let you go. No more pain."

I sputtered a laugh. It caught in my throat and gurgled there. I felt hysterical. "I'm a reincarnated Transcender," I said, dragging in a shuddering breath. "My pain follows me to Base Life. You'd know that if you had half a brain."

I bit my bottom lip, trying to wriggle out of my coat. Everything from the thigh down felt like a boiling mess. I tried really hard not to picture what it might look like. I stuffed my coat under my knee to help stop the bleeding – not that it would do much good – and a wave of dizziness washed through me. More sparks. More pain.

"Oh, I know all about reincarnated Transcenders. I've known my fair share."

I winced, my head spinning, and spoke through held breath and rigid muscles. "I'm the only one, idiot." Exhale. Short inhale. Exhale. "So you don't know shit."

"Wow," he said, shaking his head. "Who handed you that load of bull? Was it Levi? Are you still working with him?"

Levi? Did he mean Porter? I winced again. "It's not a load of bull." I was the only one. Porter told me so. Unless Gesh reincarnated someone else.

Something in Judd's muddy eyes flickered. The corner of his mouth twitched into a smile. "I guess you're the idiot, Princess."

I narrowed my eyes at him. I wanted to claw the smirk off his face. "Yeah? Well you're a dick."

His nostrils flared. He bent down and pressed the muzzle of his gun to my temple. "Tell. Me. Your. Name."

"What are you going to do? Shoot my ears? My toes? My elbows?" A chill spasmed through me. The ground was so cold. I thought of Audrey's favorite movie, The Princess Bride. "To the pain." That was the line I remembered.

To the pain means the first thing you will lose will be your feet below the ankles. Then your hands at the wrists. Next your nose.

I laughed at myself, a gurgling little giggle.

The pain made me delirious.

He pressed the gun harder, pinning my head to the ground. "I'll make this easy on you. Just your last name. I already know your first." I must have made a face because he added, "It's not like I didn't overhear you and Lover Boy back there. How else do you think I knew your favorite tune?" He dug the sight at the end of the barrel into my temple until it broke the skin. Blood pooled around it. "I thought the whistling was a nice touch. Added some flair. Some suspense. Don't you think, Alex?"

I squeezed my eyes shut. Yellow spots danced before my eyelids and swirled with the red. "Alex was my name in one of my other lives," I said, which wasn't exactly a lie.

"See? Now you're just pissing me off." He knelt down and the muzzle lifted from my skin. I heard him de-cock the hammer. "There are other ways of making you talk. More painful ways that have nothing to do with flesh and blood." He leaned closer, his breath on my cheek. "Remember, it didn't have to come to this."

I braced myself for something to happen, something horrible, but he didn't make a move. The wind gusted in the bare branches above us. The crow cawed again, angry that we were keeping him awake. My blood seeped into the soil.

After a while, I noticed my pain subsiding. I felt my soul rise from my host body as the black enveloped me. Limbo tugged at my edges, calling me home. I scrambled for the black, desperate for it, so ready to be done with the mission. So ready to leave all that pain behind, collapse in Limbo, and let myself recover.

I should've known he wouldn't let that happen.

The Battle in Eremus

The moment I land in Eremus – the black, nothingness wasteland outside Polestar – the Descender's soul slams into mine like a wrecking ball. I fly through the air (or what I perceive as air) and smack hard into rocky ground. The wind bursts from my lungs.

Why didn't Porter tell me souls could battle in Limbo?

I push myself up on shaking limbs and lift my head to see my opponent. Like a flash, he disappears in the distance and reappears beside me, the perception of his soul looking like a plume of nasty gray smoke. When he moves, he sounds like a flag rippling in the wind. I briefly wonder if this is what all souls look like in Limbo, or if this is just how I perceive him because I don't know what he looks like in Base Life. But then, wouldn't I perceive him looking like Judd?

The smoke slides under my torso and lifts me into the air. It coils around my chest like a snake, steadily squeezing, crushing my ribcage inward like an iron clamp. I grasp at it, smack at it, but there's nothing to grab hold of. I end up beating at my own chest.

It coils around my neck.

Squeezing.

It stuffs into my mouth.

Suffocating.

Any minute now, my ribs will snap and puncture my organs. I can feel them start to crack and splinter. I try to tell myself there is no air. I have no lungs. No ribs. But it doesn't do any good. I'm too panicked.

"Your name." His voice hisses inside my head. It scrapes against my skull.

I struggle against his hold. I claw at my own neck. I beat at my own face. There is nothing I can do. I have no idea how to defend myself. Porter never taught me.

I'm going to die. He's going to kill my soul.

Without a soul to sustain it, will my Base Life body die too? Will Gran find me lying on my oval rope rug when she comes to tidy my room? Or will Afton find me first? Will he curl up next to me to keep me warm? Will anyone at school even notice I'm gone? Will any of them come to my funeral?

Will Porter? Will he reincarnate me?

Throughout all those thoughts, one overshadows them all: I can't let my parents lose another child. I can't be the reason for more pain and suffering in their lives. I can't leave Audrey even more alone in this world than she already is.

I can't let Gesh win.

My mind races. How can this lower level Descender have the knowhow to beat me? I'm a Transcender. Porter said I was more powerful than all the Descenders combined.

Then it hits me. I do know how to defend myself. Porter had taught me after all.

I may not remember how to battle, but that doesn't mean my soul forgot. If I learned anything from Shooter Delaney's stubborn host body, it's how to let go and give in to my past instincts. My soul can't be any different. The first time I traveled to Limbo, Porter said I'd get used to it eventually, that soon I'd be bounding around like a young colt.

Just like I used to.

The knowledge is inside me. I just have to let go and give in to the motions. Like riding a bike.

The moment I stop struggling, I drop straight through the plume of smoke to the ground. Sharp pains shoot up through my heels to my thighs, and I falter forward to my hands and knees. I try to suppress the pain. It's not real. It's just my perception of pain. What I expect to happen. Just like my need for air. I suppress my impulse to cough and gasp for breath. Instead, I use what strength I have left to push myself to my feet, my back straight, chin lifted. I let go and let all my instincts take over.

My soul expands. My body thickens from the inside out, growing stronger. There's a buzzing sound in my ears. The smoke plume slithers around me again, circling, but it can't make purchase. The black of Limbo arcs toward me, bending like a black sail caught in a gust. All the soulmarks swaying gently at Polestar bend in my direction. I can feel their energy roll out like a rug toward me as my soul tugs at them from across Eremus. Their energy pours inside me, healing me, making me stronger. Bigger. Powerful. The plume can't touch me now.

But I can touch him.

With fingers outstretched, I reach into the darkest part of the smoke and summon his soul into my hand. I pull on his energy. I inhale it into my skin. He shouts and struggles, but I bear down on him, draining his energy with all my might. The smoke dissipates, and the plume grows smaller and smaller until it condenses into a small, swirling ball of dark fog, hovering just above my open palm.

I let out a puff of breath. The buzzing in my ears stops. Limbo gives one last stretch toward me, then sighs and settles back into place. I let the Descender's soul hover above my hand, small and defenseless, while I wonder what I should do with him.

I never get the chance to decide.

Over a dozen more plumes of fierce gray smoke suddenly materialize and surround me. There are so many that the thunderous sound of rippling flags is deafening. Like a freak tornado, they force themselves upon me, swirling, pressing, squeezing the energy out of me, disorienting me until I lose my grip on the little ball of fog in my hand. My hair whips at my face. It tangles around my neck and stings my skin, blinding me. I try to scream, but the savage gray wind sucks the sound from my throat like a vacuum.

Then, in the midst of the cyclone, Porter appears at my side, orange cap and all. He seizes my wrist. We vanish from Eremus.

CHAPTER 25

Truth

We land face down in my garden. Porter's hand still clutches my wrist. The fountain he built me gurgles in the background. I don't even realize I'm crying until he gathers me up into his arms, his weathered hands smoothing my hair from my forehead.

"I'm sorry, Alex," he says, rocking me. Sincere guilt coats his words. They tremble on his cigar breath. "I am so sorry. I had no idea Gesh would retaliate so soon. I knew he would send a Descender to derail us at some point, but not this soon. Not after only one mission."

I breathe in the faint cigar smoke on his collar, and it calms me. I'm safe now, in my garden, hidden away where the other Descenders can't find me. Why hadn't I thought to leave Eremus and step below? What if Porter hadn't been there?

He keeps rocking me. I cling to him like a child.

When I've calmed down enough to form words, I ask, "Why did their souls look like smoke?"

He rests his cheek against my forehead. His stubble stings my skin. "Souls can take on many forms in Limbo. They can trick you into perceiving them as all sorts of things. The smoke is just one of a Descender's more formidable forms. Very difficult to fight against smoke. But you did so well. I felt the surge of energy across Limbo and knew right away what happened. I'm sorry I left you alone. I should've been with you, protecting you."

He holds me there, our breathing in unison.

"It doesn't make sense," he says after a while, mostly to himself. "It should've taken several missions for Gesh to figure out you were traveling again." He pauses, his eyes squinting at some unseen thing in the horizonless, black distance. "He can't have known we were behind the Raphael discovery. He would've suspected, yes, but he would've waited until he saw a pattern. Until he had proof. He wouldn't have sent a Descender after the first time. He wouldn't have burned up a soulmark on a hunch. Not unless..."

There's a sharp inhale of breath through his nose, and I feel his shoulders stiffen.

I lift my chin to look at him. "What?"

His eyes flick to mine. "Not unless someone told him you were traveling."

"But no one else knows. You and I are the only ones who..." The words crumble to dust in my mouth. All the breath seeps from my body, leaving my gut feeling like a yawning, sickening pit.

Blue.

Blue knew I was near the Raphael in 1961. Blue knew I was with the Carters in 1876.

"My God," I say, pushing away from Porter's arms. "It's Nick. Jack. Heath. Whatever his name is. He's a reincarnated Transcender like me, isn't he?"

Porter's lips part. Fear slants across his brow. "You saw him again?"

"Answer my question."

He rubs his pinky knuckle with his thumb. "Alex, listen to me. He wasn't supposed to be there. In all my research, not one record says he went with the Carters that night–"

I scramble to my feet. "You son of a bitch," I say, shaking my head, glowering at him. Porter winces, the words piercing his chest like bullets. "How could you not tell me?"

He pushes himself up, his hands palm-out like he's trying to calm an unruly colt. "There are several reasons why I kept it from you. Several very worthy reasons–"

"You told me I was the only one. The only soul Flemming reincarnated. Why would you lie about that?" My voice skips a few octaves. "You said you weren't a liar."

"I didn't think you would run into him. At least not–"

"How many are there?" I demand. "How many souls did Flemming reincarnate?"

"Only two." When I scowl at him again, he quickly adds, "It's the truth. When Flemming intercepted your soul in Polestar, he intercepted this other one as well. Your soulmarks were born at the same time. Flemming set you up as a team. He placed your Newlives in the same eras, the same vicinities. He wove your timelines together." Porter sighs and drops his hands. "You used to be partners at AIDA. You worked on the same missions."

My brow is drawn down tight. "Is that why it felt like I knew him when we first met in Chicago? When I sat with him in the alley, and it felt like I recognized him? I knew his face. His eyes. I had the same feeling when I first saw you in the cafe."

"Yes, most likely. But there's more." Porter frowns, looking apologetic. "Your connection to him is stronger than your connection to me. When Flemming reincarnated you at the same time, it fused your souls together. I can't explain why or how, but when you descend, he descends, and vice versa. It's why your travels have always seemed so random in the past. At times, you were descending because you experienced déjà vu. The cat. The Ferris wheel. What you didn't realize was that you were also pulling him along with you. You just didn't see him. You didn't know he was there. The other times you descended, when there seemed to be no explanation at all, those were times when he experienced déjà vu. He took you with him to the ship crossing the Atlantic. To Jamestown. Your souls are universally linked across time. When you die, he dies. When he is reborn, you are reborn. He is your soul mate in the very literal sense of the word. That is why you felt so connected to him in 1927, and that is why I tried to keep you from meeting him."

Angry tears form in my eyes as I try to make sense of it all. Why would Porter betray me like this? "Why didn't you tell me this when I came back from Chicago?"

"I didn't know the boy you met was him."

"But you saw him. You were inside my head. You saw what he looked like."

"Alex, you have to understand. When I knew him at AIDA, he looked very different. As far as I was concerned, the boy you met in 1927 could have been any boy. I sent you back to erase your impact on that random boy's life. Had I known that boy was your partner, a Transcender from Base Life, I wouldn't have bothered. Your impact on him wouldn't have mattered. Had I known it was him, I wouldn't have made you redo it. I wouldn't have put you through all that pain."

"But you knew it was him when I came back from 1961," I say. "You knew then. You told me it was just my imagination. That I was grieving. You made me feel like I was going crazy."

"I didn't want you to get too attached. Don't you see? By that time it was too late. You'd already formed an attachment to him. I had to make you believe 'Nick' from 1927 was just a regular boy from the past. That he was gone. That way you wouldn't be obsessed with finding him each time you descended. You would focus on your missions. You wouldn't be distracted."

"But I was distracted." This time I scream the words. Full volume. There isn't an echo. "By not telling me, it made me even more distracted."

"You wouldn't have been if things had gone my way. You weren't supposed to break down on that road in 1961. He wasn't supposed to be with the Carters during that robbery. I picked those missions specifically. I didn't want you running into him again."

I let out a short, dry laugh. "Well, you didn't do a very good job, did you?"

He wipes the corners of his mouth with shaking fingers. "No, I didn't. I underestimated Gesh."

I cross my arms over my chest. "What do you mean?"

He sighs. He looks haggard. "Your partner has defects, just like you. When you descend into a host body, you can only remember your Base Life and your mission, right? You retain some residuals and muscle memory, but you can't remember the particulars of that past life. You can't remember your parents, your friends, your likes, dislikes. Your partner is the exact opposite. When he descends, he can't remember his Base Life. He can't remember his mission. He can only remember his past life. Which made him even less valuable to Gesh than you were. What good is a Descender who can't remember his mission?"

"But he remembered me," I say. "He said my name. He remembered I had brown eyes in 1927."

"Exactly. Which is why I underestimated Gesh." Porter pauses. He looks like all the hope in the world is lost. "Nick's name was Tre back then, when we all worked together at AIDA. It means three in Danish. Gesh is number one, Flemming is two, Tre is three, and you are four. We called you Ivy, which was literally your name in Roman numerals. I-V. Number Four."

"That's why IV is carved on my Polygon stone?"

Porter nods. "I worked in the division dedicated to repairing your defects. We tried everything. Operations, hypnosis, mind control, subliminal messages. Nothing worked. But Gesh must have figured out how to restore

Tre's memories – the new Tre, the one born in your current Base Life. If Tre is remembering while he's in a host body, then he no longer suffers from his defect. And that means all of this is over. We can't win. If Tre is working for Gesh now, then you can't descend anymore. It's too dangerous. If you descend, you'll bring Tre's soul with you. He'll always be there, somewhere. No matter how far his host body is from yours, he'll find you. Because now he remembers his mission. And his mission is you."

A cold chill slides over my skin. It grips my wrists like dead fingers.

All this time.

All this freaking time?

Pretending like he didn't remember me on the side of the road. Slow dancing with me at Peg Leg. Kissing me beside the fountain. Following me out into the dark when I was tracking Cask. Sneaking up on me and grabbing me from behind. Scaring the crap out of me. I was so relieved when he said my name. Remembered me. I felt warm and safe in his arms. I thought he cared about me.

Did he tell the other Descender where to find me? Had he known the asshole would torture me? Rip a bullet through me twice? Try to kill me? Had he been OK with that? Had they sent the other Descender to do the dirty work so Blue wouldn't be the bad guy? So he could continue to distract me and deceive me on my next mission?

I shake my head, tears stinging my eyes. Blue is Cary Grant in Charade, and I'm Audrey Hepburn, the doe-eyed fool who fell for all his lies.

The traitor.

The poison-lipped traitor.

The tendons stretch over my knuckles, turning them white. I swipe at tears with fists. He won't get away with it. I won't let him play me like that. I'm not that girl.

My blood pumps hot through my veins. I want revenge. I crave it. Shooter Delaney style.

"What do we do now?" I ask. "How do we stop him?"

"Didn't you hear what I said? It's over. We don't do anything now."

"But–"

"No, Alex, listen to me." Porter steps up and squares my shoulders to his. "You can't descend anymore. I only let you before because I didn't think Tre was a threat. Now that I know he is..." Porter makes me look him in the eyes. "It's over."

"But I have to go back. I have to redo my time in 1876. I can't let it play out the way it did, with Shooter waking up and finding herself lying there, bleeding to death."

Porter swallows. His Adam's apple rises and falls. He presses his lips together. "You're right. You can go back, but only for a touchdown. That means you land on the train, then you come right back. That will erase the timeline you created."

I nod, but he makes me look him in the eyes again. "You land and you come straight back. Do you understand me? Don't make me rip you out of the past. It hurts like hell and you'll come back with some nasty, half-baked residuals." I give him a questioning look, but he just says, "Trust me."

I don't take a deep breath this time. I don't hesitate. I reach for my 1876 soulmark and dive in.

Touchdown

When I landed, the perfume hit me like a brick wall. I sputtered and coughed. I swatted Perfume Lady's hat feather out of my face.

"Don't you think so, dear?" The hairs in her chin mole stood at attention again.

"Yes," I said. "It would be so very excitin' if we got robbed. Did you wear those pearls for just that occasion?"

She bounced. "I did! How did you know?"

"Lucky guess," I said, turning to the window. The gray November forest swept past. Dark, sodden tree trunks blended into one continuous black brush stroke. My pistol weighed heavy on my lap.

OK. That's enough. Come back now.

Porter's voice dipped inside my head gently this time. Timid. Like a tiptoe. But I didn't listen. I wasn't ready to go back. Not yet. I needed a few more minutes.

The rumble of the train and Blue's treachery numbed me from within. An angry tear slipped down my cheek. I pressed my forehead to the ice-cold glass. I pressed my eyelids shut.

I could feel him. His hands on my face, cupping my cheeks. His hands on my back, fisting my shirt. His lips on mine. The look in his eyes.

God. I thought I was falling for him.

Alex. Don't do this.

I wanted to see him. I wanted to look him in the eye one last time. His soul was here in 1876 now. If Porter was right, then I brought him along with me when I descended. I tore him from his Base Life, wherever that was, and brought him back to the past. All I needed was one good look in his eyes to let him know that I knew. To see his reaction. To ask him why.

Don't you dare.

I wouldn't stay long. I wouldn't even throw my bowl of soup in his face. Just one look. That's all I needed.

What if they soul block you again? Then what?

My eyelids peeled open. They were sore and puffy. I hadn't thought of the soul blocking. Of course they'd block me again. God, what if they already had?

They have to be near you to block you. Come back now. While it's still safe.

More tears slipped down my cheeks. I sat up and looked around the train car, taking in all the hats and bonnets and dresses and crazy mustaches, trying to commit it all to memory. The coil of smoke lifting from pipes. The murmur of conversation. The sound of the steam. The smell of the coal.

I sniffed and wiped my nose with the back of my gloved hand. If it was all over like Porter said, then I would never get to experience anything like this ever again. I would never see Martin Luther King's speech or walk the Underground Railroad. I'd never find out what my life was like in the Roanoke Colony. Or in 1927.

This was my last descent.

"Are you all right, dear?" Perfume Lady asked, waking me from my thoughts. She smiled at me with kind concern.

She was sweet. Daft, but sweet. I hoped Shooter wore her pearls at least once after the robbery. It would've given Perfume Lady one heck of a story to tell.

I returned her smile, sad and true, then ascended back to Limbo. Still numb. Still cold. Still clutching my shock and fury and disbelief in my fists.

Game Over

Porter tells me it's not my fault. That I couldn't have known. He tells me he's sorry over and over. But I can't deal with him right now. I can't deal with more explanations, more talk. So he lets me go home to rest. He says to call him whenever I'm ready to talk again.

Right now, that seems like the very distant future.

When I land back in my room, I don't even open my eyes. I can still hear Gran whisking eggs in the kitchen below. I hear Audrey call out for Afton, then the tinkle of the tiny bell on his new collar. Pops sneezes.

I can't deal with any of that either. Not yet.

I fumble for my glasses on the floor next to me, then toss them on the nightstand as I crawl into bed, so very exhausted. I pull my quilt over my head, trying to shut everything out. I rub my thumb over my right palm and my left knee, making sure they're intact. No blood. I can still remember the pain, but it feels far away. Like a dream of a dream.

Why didn't I bring those wounds back with me? Maybe because of the touchdown. I'd erased the gunfight. It never happened.

I nestle into my pillow and feel its cool softness against my cheek. It smells like my apricot shampoo. Like comfort and home. So far removed from my other life. My secret life, tainted with bullets and blood, lies and more lies, and wayfaring souls. I squeeze my eyes tighter and see flashes of the timeline I erased – the timeline that exists only in my memory. Perfume Lady's excitement when she finds out she's sitting next to Shooter Delaney. Cask's shadowed eyes and barking laugh. Judd's sweet smile when he talks about the house on the hill. He didn't deserve to die like he did – cold and alone in prison. It isn't fair.

None of it is.

My thoughts eventually drift to Blue, as they always do. If Porter's right, his soul is back in Base Life now, somewhere. My Base Life. It should make me happy to know he's alive. Tangible. Real. That he didn't really die in 1927. But it doesn't. I'd feel better if he didn't exist. If I'd never met him. I guess Porter knew that all along. I guess Porter was trying to protect me. But protecting me by omitting the truth only made me weak. I wasn't prepared to defend myself against Blue, and that's Porter's fault, through and through.

One question keeps plaguing me. I keep going over it again and again, like a sore in my mouth. How can someone as good as Blue work for someone as evil as Gesh? How can he be OK with leading Gesh straight to me? Has he even considered that I might have a family I need to protect? Like he protected Frank and Helena?

The only thing I can think of is that he must believe he's doing the right thing. That he's on the right side.

He must believe I'm the enemy.

Does he know I figured it out? That I know the truth about him now? Does he even care that he took everything from me? That it's all over? If I can't descend anymore, how am I supposed to stop Gesh from hunting me down? Finding me and hurting my family? How am I supposed to go on living, acting like I don't know one man possesses all the wealth and power in the entire world and has the government folded neatly in his breast pocket? How am I supposed to trust anything, anyone, ever again?

Somewhere between cursing Blue and praying for God to erase the past month from my memory, I fall asleep. If Mom calls me down for dinner, I don't notice. I sleep straight through until morning, dreaming of a poisoned kiss, moonlit breath, dark muddy eyes, and a bloodstained bluff.

CHAPTER 26

Residuals

The next morning, Mom wakes me with a gentle nudge. She's sitting on my bed, a steaming mug of coffee in her hands. Her satin chestnut hair is down, every strand straight and perfect, blanketing her shoulders.

"Still not feeling well?" she asks.

I rub my eyes. They're raw and swollen. My body feels broken, crushed from the inside out. Pain radiates from the center of my chest – from my heart. I know if I tell Mom I'm sick, she'll let me stay home from school again, but staying home with nothing to do but think about Blue won't solve anything. What I need is a distraction, and the endless drama at school is a major one.

"I'm fine. Just tired." I manage a weak smile. She kisses me on the forehead, tells me breakfast is almost ready, and heads back downstairs. It isn't until I reach for my glasses that I realize something's very wrong.

I can see perfectly and clearly.

And my glasses are still on the nightstand.

I bolt upright and look around my room. Everything – every poster, every tool, every spare part, every spool of wire – I can see it all crisp and clear. I saw every strand of Mom's hair in perfect precision. Her tired eyes. The steam rising from her mug. It should've all been a blurred mess of colored blobs. I should've had to drag my glasses on before any of my surroundings made sense.

I grab my glasses and slide them on. Everything shifts out of focus. I take them off and my world sharpens. I scowl down at my frames like they've betrayed me somehow. Then I fumble for my cell phone and dial Porter's number.

"Alex?"

"You have to do something," I say, panicked. "I woke up and now I'm Peter freaking Parker."

"Peter who?"

"I can see. Like 20/20. I don't need my glasses anymore."

"Oh. Well, that must be a residual from Shooter Delaney. She was a sharp shooter, you know."

"Is that all you have to say?"

"What do you want me to say?"

"I want you to tell me how to reverse it."

There's a pause on the other end of the phone. "You want... your bad vision back?"

"Yes."

"...Why?"

"Because my other option is explaining to my parents how I have perfect vision all of a sudden. I'm pretty sure they won't buy the whole 'bitten by a radioactive spider' thing."

Another pause. This one longer. Then he says, "You're right. Can you stall for a day or two while I figure out a solution?"

"How do I do that?"

"Pretend. Act like nothing's changed. I'll get back to you as soon as I can."

There's silence on the other end, then a beep in my ear signaling the end of the call. I toss my phone aside and glare down at my glasses.

Traitors.

I'm surrounded by traitors.

The First Straw

I throw on a pair of faded jeans, my black sneakers, and my favorite striped sweater. I wear my shaggy hair down for once so I can hide behind it during class. I force myself to keep my glasses on all through breakfast, which results in a stubbed toe on my way down the stairs, a swear word I almost say out loud in front of Gran, and half a carton of milk poured on the table instead of in my cereal bowl.

"Wayspaz," Claire says, disguised as a cough.

I shoot a glare in the general direction of her tiny, blurry figure while I sop up the mess. At this rate, she'll make a great replacement for Tabitha at South View High one day.

On the way out the door, I snag a finger on Claire's backpack so she can guide me down the porch steps to the Mustang. She gives me a look, like I've suddenly sprouted elf ears, but lets me tag along behind her anyway.

The moment Dad pulls up to the curb at the high school, I jump out, toss a wave behind me, and hurry inside, stuffing my glasses in my backpack once the double doors clang shut. It's instant visual relief, but the makings of a wicked migraine are already in place.

At least now I have that distraction I wanted.

As I make my way down the unnaturally bright hallways to my locker to drop off my parka, it doesn't take long to notice all the staring. Freshmen, sophomores, even seniors are craning their necks to watch me walk by. I check my shoes for toilet paper and swipe at my nose with my sleeve in case something's hanging out, but there's nothing.

They can't all be staring because I'm not wearing my glasses, can they? Kids get contacts all the time. It's not that big of a deal. I barely notice what the other kids at school wear, let alone whether or not they wear glasses. Why should they care what I'm doing?

I skip my locker and go straight to the drafting lab for first period so I can hide behind a computer for an hour. Maybe after that, everything will go back to normal and I can be invisible again.

A few kids glance up and whisper when I make my way to my computer. I drop my backpack and parka at my feet and sink into my chair. I hide behind my monitor. The fluorescent lights buzz overhead.

Thankfully, when Mr Pence, our Advanced CADD teacher, starts class, everyone snaps their attention to his glistening bald head. Mr Pence is one of the few teachers I actually like at SVH. He's huge, like a professional football player, built like a tank with biceps bigger than my head, and yet he's total Computer Geek to the core. We understand each other. We speak the same language. I try to show him some respect and pay attention while he marks the steps for this week's AutoCAD project on the whiteboard at the front of the room, but when his dry erase marker squeaks out a number four in Roman numerals, my mind wanders.

IV.

The letters on my Polygon stone. My name from my most recent past life. When I worked with Blue. When we were partners.

I pull the stone from my pocket and run my fingers over the letters again. The little boy in the wire-rimmed glasses is Blue. He must be. No one else could make me feel such strong déjà vu, the kind that pulls me into Limbo so easily. Porter said something about Blue looking very different at AIDA. Maybe that's why I remember him having blond hair and dark eyes. Not dark hair and blue-green eyes.

What did he look like now in Base Life? Like the Blue from Chicago? Or like the Blue from AIDA? Either way, that little boy who played Polygon with me at AIDA, who watched as Gesh hit me, was no longer my friend.

I had to remember that.

I trace the L, V, and I on the other side of the Polygon stone. Fifty-six in Roman numerals. The exact number of soulmarks I had hidden in my garden in Limbo. Fifty-six lives lived. Is that why that number was carved into my stone? Or did it represent a name, like *IV* did?

That train of thought leads me back to 1876. The Descender asked me a question as I lay covered in my own blood.

Who handed you that load of bull? Was it Levi? Are you still working with him?

LVI. Levi. That must've been Porter's name before he changed it and went into hiding.

I push the stone back in my pocket. I dig my cell phone from my backpack and hide it in my lap while Mr Pence explains the steps of our project one-by-one. He wants us to draw a 2D model of a bicycle wheel using the Array command we learned last week, which sounds simple enough. I pull up Porter's number and shoot him a text: Who's Levi?

A few minutes later, my phone lights up. Where did you hear that name?

So I was right. The letters did represent a name.

I wait for Mr Pence to·turn back to the whiteboard before I type out my response. The Descender asked if I was working with "Levi." He meant you, didn't he? That was your name at AIDA.

It makes sense. Porter was the one who taught me how to play Polygon. He probably taught Blue too. Maybe Blue has his own stone, a black one, with *III* carved on one side and *LVI* on the other. Fifty-six. Porter's number at AIDA.

It takes a while for Porter to respond this time, like he's hesitating. The class is almost ready to start working with the dimensions Mr Pence wrote on the board. If Porter doesn't write back soon, I won't be able to check my messages until the end of class.

Mr Pence makes his way around the room to check on our progress. I keep my phone on my lap, glancing down every two seconds while I fire up AutoCAD and start my project. My knee bounces. I chew on my thumbnail. Mr Pence nears my station.

My phone lights up.

We'll talk about this later.

My knee stops bouncing. I drop my hand in my lap. Of course we'll talk later. That's what people say when they're avoiding something. It took over six months for Mom and Dad to finally tell me what was going on with Audrey. And those were some of the worst months of my life. All that waiting. All that heavy unknown.

I fist the phone in my hand, so tired of Porter always choosing what I should and shouldn't know. He wasn't protecting me by leaving me in the dark. When would he understand that? Besides, what was so dangerous about knowing his real name? It's not like I would tell anyone.

"Cell phones away, Miss Wayfare," Mr Pence says, patting me on the shoulder as he walks by. "Let's get to work."

I drop my phone in my bag, my cheeks tinged red.

The first straw lands softly on the camel's back.

Straw Number Two

When I head to second period French, everyone still stares at me. Some swap whispers behind cupped hands. I duck into a restroom just to make sure I don't have something stuck to my forehead.

I run a hand through my hair, wondering what the heck everyone's problem is. I guess I do look a little strange without glasses – I've worn them since first grade – but I don't look hideous. I actually think I look pretty good. My hair's doing this layered thing that frames my face and makes my eyes pop. They look more blue than gray today.

I actually look normal for once. More like them.

So what's the problem?

It isn't until I grab my seat in French class that I figure it out. Two freshmen behind me whisper a little too loudly behind their textbooks.

"I heard she was with him all Friday night."

"Stacy said Tabitha caught them together."

All at once, everything clicks together. Friday night. When I gave Jensen a ride home from the library.

Oh.

My.

God.

Are they talking about me and Jensen, and the social atrocity he committed last Friday? It completely slipped my mind after traveling back in time, robbing a train, and, you know, getting shot.

Twice.

I glance at the door. I can make a run for it before Madame Cavanaugh comes in if I bolt now, but I'm not fast enough. Madame Cavanaugh swoops in wearing one of her usual flowered dresses, her arms outstretched, and gives the class a jubilant, "Bonjour!" Her dark hair is permed in a perfect helmet shape around her head. Her pink sneakers squeak on the floor.

I sink lower in my chair and ride out the rest of class as quietly as I can. I should've stayed home sick.

Straw Number Three

My next period is gym with Tabitha and her friends. I'm fairly sure life can't get much crueler than that.

I contemplate ditching school all together, but something inside me refuses. Call it Shooter Delaney's stubbornness. If I can hold my own against five gun-wielding outlaws like the Carters, I should be able to stand up against five of the most popular girls in school.

Theoretically speaking.

When I enter the locker room, there's already a crowd of girls gathered around Tabitha like a support group. They all turn to look at me, eyes wide. I make my way to my locker, ignoring them, hoping they'll leave me be, but they follow me like a gaggle of ducklings. They stand behind me, a united front of school colors, blue and gold gym shorts and white shirts. Arms crossed over sports bras.

"Tell them all you did was give him a ride home," Tabitha says, standing at the front of the group. I can feel her glare on my back. Like the point of a blade right between the shoulder blades.

I don't turn around. I stuff my backpack and parka into my tiny gym locker and parrot what she says. "All I did was give him a ride home."

"But she doesn't drive," one of the other girls blurts out. I think her name is Sally. She's standing off to the side, trembling like she might burst from all the gossip she has stored inside.

"Yeah," someone else says. "I thought people who had seizures weren't allowed to drive."

"It was a rumor," Tabitha says. "She doesn't have seizures. And she can drive. Isn't that right, Wayspaz?"

I close my locker, my gym clothes in hand. "She's right. I can drive. And I don't have seizures. Now can I get dressed in private? Or are you all going to stand there and watch?"

I get a few dirty looks, but they all eventually back off and go about their business as usual. Tabitha, however, doesn't move one perfectly toned muscle.

"He's just being nice to you because he feels bad," she says.

My gut clenches. I turn on my heel and head for one of the bathroom stalls to change. She follows, stuck to my side, hissing in my ear.

"He told me you thought he started that rumor. He feels really bad about it. You know Jensen. He hates to have anyone thinking badly of him. That's why he's being nice to you. He wants to win you over. Like he wins everybody over. Why else would he want to hang out with you?"

I slip into the bathroom stall and slam the door, shutting her out.

"And now what?" she says through the door. "You think one car ride with Jensen Peters is going to make you popular? You think you can just get contacts and wear your hair down and people will think you're normal? You think that'll make them like you?"

I stand in the stall, frozen, waiting for her to leave. If I had been in Shooter's body, I probably would've had her hair in my fists by now.

"Get a clue, Freak," she says. "No one likes you. Especially Jensen. And if you tell anyone you did more with him than give him a ride home, I'll make you wish you'd never been born. Got it?"

Her sneakers finally march off, and I yank my sweater over my head so hard it tears at one of the seams. I'm not pissed because Tabitha is a bitch. I'm used to shielding myself from her barbed tongue. I'm pissed because part of what she said is true. Jensen is the kind of person who needs people to like him. He needs an audience, friends, people around to smile and joke with. He's totally the type to want to "make it up to me" if he thinks I'm mad at him. Not because we're friends, but because he feels guilty.

I slump against the stall door and slam my head back, once, twice. How could I be so stupid? I'd thought Blue was my friend, too. How could I be so wrong about Blue and Jensen at the same time?

A Whole Freaking Pile of Straws

I drag my gym clothes on and make my way out to join the class. I don't even bother putting my hair in a ponytail so it doesn't get sweaty. I just don't give a damn about anything anymore.

Everyone's outside at the track, freezing their butts off. Coach Graves, our gym teacher who's straight out of college, thinks it's the best use of our time to run a mile every day. Even in November. And if we happen to have time left over after the last person wheezes off the track? Then it's dodgeball for the rest of the period inside while she sits on the sidelines and flirts with the guys' gym coach, Mr Caswell.

Even though I've been running better times ever since I got back from 1927, without one asthma attack, I decide to take it slow this time. I've got nothing to prove, and I'd rather be at the back of the pack, alone, where I used to be, than up front by the good runners like Tabitha. But once I set off, feet meeting the pavement, I change my mind. My Shooter Delaney stubbornness kicks in. I zero in on Tabitha's golden, bouncing ponytail and make it my mission to take her down.

I spend the first lap keeping pace. By the second lap, I'm right behind her. By the third, I'm squeezing past. And when I turn the corner on the fourth and final lap, I fly past like she stopped to tie her shoe. It's not the best time in the class – not by a long shot – but it's worth it just to see her expression. The flared nostrils and the icy glare, It's the best thing to happen to me all day.

While half the class sits on the bleachers on the sidelines to cool down, the other half walks around the track. A few stragglers are still finishing their mile. Tabitha sits on the bleachers, so I choose to walk the track.

It's a mistake.

Halfway through my lap, hands on my hips, elbows out, three guys from Coach Caswell's class catch up to me. Robbie Duncan, Jake Horner, and Philip Rice. All three saw me give Jensen a ride home.

"Hey, Wayfare," Robbie says, falling in step at my side. He's the type of guy who's always getting in the middle of things. If there's a pot to stir, he's the first to volunteer. It's like he carries around his own special spoon. "Lotta crap goin' around about you and Jensen today."

I don't respond. I keep my eyes straight ahead. I watch the traffic going by on Sixth Avenue, out past the school parking lot. A silver Corvette glints by. I daydream about jumping inside and getting as far away from Annapolis as possible.

"What did you guys do Friday night?" Robbie asks. His glossy gym shorts graze the backs of his knees. His legs are covered in fuzz and freckles. He's a big dude, but he's still got quite a bit of baby fat. "Must've been real important if he blew off our pickup game."

I risk a tiny smile at the edge of my mouth. So Jensen blew off his teammates to go to the library. To check out Pride and Prejudice. I remember how embarrassed he was when I discovered his secret.

"I just gave him a ride," I say with a shrug. "That's all."

The other two guys burst out laughing. I can tell Robbie wants to laugh too, but he tries to keep a straight face. His dimpled chin quivers. "Well we heard he gave you a ride."

It takes a second before I get what he means. My jaw drops. I stop walking and spin on my heel to face them. "Excuse me?"

"Must've been one hell of a booty call," Jake says.

"I know, right?" says Robbie. He makes circles with his fingers around his eyes like he's wearing glasses. "Who knew losing your virginity could fix your eyesight?"

They burst out laughing and stumble away, clutching their stomachs, leaving me standing rigid and humiliated in the middle of the track.

Robbie turns around and walks backwards, making the hand motion for me to "call him." "Seriously, Wayfare,

I'm way better than Jensen," he calls out. "One night with me and that epilepsy thing is history."

Jake punches him in the shoulder and says, "Or maybe it's better when she has a seizure. It's like your own personal vibrator."

Philip moans Oh, Robbie, oh Robbie! while he pretends to convulse.

My hands curl into fists. I clench my teeth so hard it sends a piercing pain shooting through my temples. Anger and humiliation wring and writhe inside me, and the need for revenge climbs to the surface of my skin like steam.

I force myself to make a beeline for the locker room before the Shooter in me does something drastic. Like relieve all three of them of their manhood.

CHAPTER 27

Pudding Cups, Revelations, and the Last Straw

I change into my other clothes, ripped sweater and all, and skip the rest of gym. I'd be shocked if Coach Graves even notices I'm gone. Instead of going to lunch, I head to the AV department to start my shift early. It's this small room off the main computer lab, stacked full of equipment for teachers to check out for their classrooms. There's a tall counter to sit behind, which makes it one of my favorite places to hide. Sometimes Mrs Latimer lets me have my lunch there. Mostly because she usually needs my help fixing one of the pieces of equipment.

Seriously. I've probably saved the school a fortune on equipment costs.

Today, there's a sticky note attached to one of the projectors telling me it won't power on. I turn off all the harsh overhead lights in the room and flip on a few desk lamps. The light from the computer lab filters in, giving me enough to work by, but it's dark enough to calm my nerves. I take the projector apart at the back of the room, losing myself in wires and connectors, troubleshooting whether or not it needs a new fuse or a new power switch. Soon my mind is wrapped in a protective haze. The last few hours no longer exist.

Halfway through the second lunch period, I hear someone come in. I look up and my blissful fog of solitude vanishes. It's Jensen, wearing one of his cute, lopsided smiles. My stomach twists in half like it's a balloon and I'm shaping it into a poodle or giraffe or something. I set my tools down. My hands tremble. I really don't want to talk to him right now.

"I'd like to check something out," he says as I make my way up to the counter.

"Yeah? What's that?"

"You."

I make a face at him. "Seriously? You're seriously going to take a stab at me too?"

"It's not a stab," he says, looking down, drumming his thumbs on the counter. "I was just trying to be funny." He peeks back up at me from under his honey blond hair. He quirks a tiny smile.

"It's not funny. Not after what your boys said to me on the track." I flop down at the desk behind the counter. He comes around to my side and flops down in the chair beside me.

"Ah," he says. "You heard the rumors."

"How could I not? Robbie and his asshole friends practically made a banner and slapped me in the face with it."

"They're jackasses, Wayfare. You just have to ignore them." He props his white sneakers up on one of the TV carts behind me, blocking me in with his long legs.

His Abercrombie jeans are perfectly distressed. His gray Henley clings to his chest. He looks like he belongs on a runway, and it's kind of distracting.

"Why doesn't it bother you?" I ask him.

He shrugs. "Um, because according to them, I'm a humongous man slut. Apparently I've slept with half the varsity volleyball team and most of the cheerleaders. Even the freshmen. And the girls aren't any better. Not one of them has ever said it isn't true. So... after a while it just becomes background noise. And besides, all the people who matter to me most know the truth. My parents. My teachers. My church. So who gives a flip what the kids say at school?"

I stare at him, warily, wondering why he still insists on being nice to me. Is it because he feels responsible for the new rumors now too? On top of the old ones?

"Here," he says. "I brought you something." He drops his feet with a thud and pulls a chocolate pudding cup out of his backpack. He sets it on the desk in front of me, a plastic spoon perched on top. "I noticed you weren't at lunch."

Deep, skeptical lines crease my brow. A pudding cup? Really? He's being too nice. Too thoughtful. It makes me want to crush the cup in my hand because it's all an act. He's all an act. Just like Blue.

"You don't have to do this," I say, pushing the pudding away.

"Do what?"

"Be nice to me. Act like you're my friend. You can stop now. I'm letting you off the hook."

I can tell he wasn't expecting that. He frowns. "Um... OK..."

"I don't care about the seizure stuff anymore," I say. "It was a long time ago. And I don't really care what they say about me either. I just want things to go back to the way they were. When they didn't talk to me at all. When I was invisible. If you keep being nice to me and hanging out with me, the rumors aren't going to stop. They'll get worse. And I just want to go back to being Wayspaz the loner Fix-it Freak."

All this time I thought becoming normal, more like them, would make everything better. Turns out no matter who you are – the follow-the-crowd type or the independent soul – people will always find something to harass you about. Something shiny to peck at. Something different that sets you apart. So why waste your time being someone you're not?

Jensen leans forward, his elbows on his knees. "You really think I'm pretending to be your friend?"

"I don't know." I pick at the flaking laminate edge of the desk. "Tabitha said you felt guilty about the rumor thing and that's why you've been nice to me."

He lets out a laugh and leans back in his chair. "Honestly, Wayfare. For being the topic of so many juicy rumors, you sure aren't up to speed on the rest of them, are you?"

I frown, not getting the joke.

"I broke up with her on Friday. After you dropped me off. So... she's pissed right now. She'll say anything."

He's not lying. I can tell by the look on his face. "Great," I say, tossing my hands up. "Now they're all going to think you broke up with her because of me. I already heard someone say Tabitha 'caught us together.'" I make air quotes with my fingers.

Jensen shrugs. "I mean, we're going to have to endure some rumors if we're going to be friends, right? And some of them are going to be stupid. It's just the way it goes. But I'm willing to risk it." He lifts an eyebrow. "Are you?"

I bite my bottom lip. I'm honestly not sure if I am. "Can I think about it and get back to you?"

He kicks my shoe. "No. We're friends. Deal with it."

I finally crack a smile. He smiles too.

"I'm sorry," I say. "I guess I'm just extra cynical today."

"Because of the rumors?"

"That and something else."

"What else?"

I tuck my hair behind my ear, staring down at the vacuum patterns crisscrossed in the carpet. "I found out a friend of mine wasn't who he said he was. Turns out he was a big fat liar. The biggest and the fattiest."

"This dude," Jensen says, grabbing a pencil off the desk and drumming it on his leg. "Was he your boyfriend?"

At the mere mention of the word boyfriend, I see a flash of Blue in the moonlight, his cowboy hat casting a shadow over his face. Was that what I thought he was? My boyfriend? I remember the feel of his hands tugging at my hips. His lips touching mine. I shake my head, feeling so stupid. Even after all this, I still want to kiss him again. It was good, you know? The kissing. He was good. Somewhere, deep down, I still wish he could've been mine. Even with Jensen, my lifelong crush sitting before me, suddenly free and single.

The Descender was right. I am an idiot.

"I guess he was kinda my boyfriend," I say. "But whatever he was, he's not anymore."

"Did he cheat on you?"

"No. He just... played me."

"How do you know he played you? Did you confront him about it?"

"Didn't have to. Just figured it out."

Jensen cracks another smile. "Right. Because your deductive skills have been so sharp lately."

This time I kick his shoe, and he laughs.

"All I'm saying is, you should talk to him. Find out what's really going on. Might not be what you think. It never is, you know?"

A tiny sliver of hope pricks me. It gets under my skin. Enters my bloodstream. The bell rings for the next period.

"You should talk to him," Jensen says again, standing up. He hefts his backpack over one shoulder. "You confronted me. Twice. And look what we got out of it. Pudding cups and revelations." We share another smile as he heads for the door. "Catch ya later, Wayfare."

I lift my hand in farewell, then frown down at my lonely pudding cup. What if Jensen is right? What if Blue isn't the traitor I think he is?

Oh, but he has to be. No one else knows what he knows. No one else but Porter.

I pull out my cell phone and send Porter another text. I press the keys so hard the phone creaks under the pressure. Tell me who Levi is RIGHT NOW.

He writes back right away.

No.

I squeeze the phone in my hand. I want to slam it against the wall.

It's the last straw. I'm so tired of his stupid lies and his stupid silence. Is he refusing to tell me because he still thinks he's protecting me? Or because he has something to hide? After all the lies he's already told, and all the things he's kept from me, my gut says to place a bet on the latter.

If I want answers, I'm going to have to get them myself.

My phone lights up again and I look down, hoping Porter changed his mind, but it's from a different number.

Wayfare. 4got 2 tell u. Miss ur specs. Brng em bak, yo.

A tiny fraction of my anger lifts. I smile and touch my cheekbone where my glasses would be resting if I had worn them. I'll think about it, yo. I didn't even know Jensen knew my number.

So? U talk 2 ur boy yet?

Um. It's been like 2 minutes.

Wut u w8n 4? An invite?

Finish Pride & Prejudice yet?

:-P

Jensen thinks it's simple. Just call the guy up, right? But it's not like I can call Blue or shoot him a text. I have no idea where he is, and even if I did, making contact in Base Life would be the stupidest thing I could do. If Blue's working for Gesh, then Gesh would find out who I am.

As I'm thinking of a way to reply to text back to Jensen, a brilliant idea hits me. I may not know where Blue is in Base Life, but I know he was at AIDA with me in my most recent past life. We were partners. If I descend back there, I'll bring his soul along with me. I could confront him. I could find out what Porter's hiding.

Before I talk myself out of it, I pull the Polygon stone out of my pocket, close my hands around it, and ascend to my garden. This time I'm doing it without Porter, before he puts a soul block on me and I can't descend anymore. Before I lose my last chance to confront Blue.

I know Porter will be furious, but I don't care. That's what he gets for treating me like a child. For not trusting me. For lying to me.

Let him be the one in the dark for once.

CHAPTER 28

Trial and Error

My garden feels cold and empty without Porter by my side. Darker than usual.

I wasn't expecting that.

My soulmarks sway before me, eerily and silently. They cast a blue-white glow at my feet. The only sound is my timid breath and the gurgle of the fountain.

I'm alone, and it's very unsettling.

I know I'm safe – I know there isn't anything hidden in the swaths of shadow, watching me – but I can't help but feel like there's something lying in wait, somewhere in the deep expanse of black that surrounds me.

Like savage gray plumes of smoke.

A shiver ripples through me. I start to think maybe this was a bad idea. But it's not like I can go back and tell Porter my plan and ask for his help. He'll forbid it. He'll put a soul block on me. I have to confront Blue before that happens or I'll never know the truth. I'll never have closure. I'll just go on wondering, never knowing for sure who played me, Blue or Porter.

Even if Porter's right and Blue and I are enemies, and I have to take him down along with Gesh, at least there will be closure. I'll be able to move on.

Eventually.

I make my way toward my soulmarks, dipping my hand in the lukewarm water in my fountain as I walk by. I take a deep breath. I flick the perception of water from my fingers.

How do I know which is the right soulmark? When I found the right one to take me back to Nick Piasecki in 1927, it drew me in more than the others. Maybe that will happen this time.

I move slowly through the rows of my own personal forest of lights. The blue-white glow melts across my skin. I can feel the energy radiating from each soulmark, pulling at my edges. The pull is stronger with some than others, but even after pausing beside each individual soulmark, I don't feel drawn to any one in particular. In the end, I decide to just reach out and try one. I'd do a touchdown. Land, look around, then come right back.

I start with the first soulmark in the center row. It sways gracefully before me, taunting me, tempting me to touch it with its silent siren song. It doesn't have to try hard – I am willing prey.

I dip a fingertip into its center. The light swells, then consumes me.

I landed gently, like a feather on grass. I pulled breath into my lungs, filling them with… dry, warm air? I opened my eyes. I was nowhere near the right time period.

Sprawling prairie land rolled out before me as far as I could see, dotted with strange, gnarled trees and scraggly bushes. A balmy breeze rustled the dry, golden grass. The sun shone with reckless abandon above me, but in the far distance, a dark thundercloud hovered over a mountain plateau, smudging the horizon with slanted sheets of gray rain.

I stood on a porch under a thatched roof, barefoot, watching a wagon pulled by two oxen depart down a two track road. One of my hands was raised in mid-wave, the other clutched an old stick broom. I wore a very plain dress and some sort of wide-brimmed hat. A family of giraffes grazed amid a stand of trees far off to the right.

I was in Africa, I guess? But I had no idea what year. Sometime in the 1800s?

I was tempted to stay a while longer and explore that past life – I mean, it was Africa after all – but I forced myself to ascend back to Limbo while I still had the willpower to do so.

I reach for the soulmark directly to the right of the last one before I change my mind. It pulls me in and plunges me into its depths.

In this life, I was sitting in a rocking chair, my bare toes nestled into the fibers of a thick, warm rug. A fire crackled in a hearth before of me. I was knitting something – I couldn't tell what – and rocking, listening to some kind of radio theater filtering through the speakers of an old-timey radio. The Forties? Thirties?

I ascend back to Limbo. I grab the soulmark to the left of the African one.

I landed at the top of a wintry moor, shivering in heavy, woolen clothes under a dark, cloud-covered sky. A black lace veil hid my face. Snow fell lightly on my shoulders. The flakes lighted upon on my veil, melting the moment the ice met the thread. I stared down at a freshly dug grave. A simple wooden coffin rested at the bottom covered in a thin layer of snow. A small group of people stood gathered beside me, all dressed in thick, black layers. A priest stood at the head of the grave, reciting something in an ancient-sounding language. Gaelic, maybe? There were a dozen headstones scattered across the moor, and a foreboding, fort-like castle resting in the distance.

Cold tears had left streaks on my cheeks. My veil ruffled against my nose in the bitter breeze. I looked down and saw my black, lace-gloved hands cradling my belly – my very swollen belly. My eyes widened. I stared down at my hands. Something deep inside my abdomen shifted to the left.

I ascended immediately.

The moment I return to Limbo, I stumble backwards and fall down, staring up at that soulmark. The thought never crossed my mind that I might have been pregnant in a past life. That I might have had children. If so, then my children might have had children. Which means my own descendants could be alive and well today in Base Life.

I shake my head and run a trembling hand through my hair. I can't think about that right now. And I definitely can't think about the possibility of being a descendant of myself. That's just way too weird.

I get back on my feet. I need to focus. The soulmark to the left of my African past seemed to take me further back in time, to some sort of Celtic period. The one to the right brought me closer to Base Life – the Forties? So if I keep working my way to the right...

I take a chance and head to the very last soulmark in the very last row on the right. Maybe it's number fifty-six.

I wrap my fingers around the light.

Bingo

I opened my eyes to shadow and storm. I was lying on my side on a soft mattress, my body warm and heavy beneath a down blanket. It took a moment to orient myself because everything was turned sideways. I blinked once, twice, then made out the shape of a window. A large, metal-framed pane of glass like you see in commercial buildings. Intense, heavy rain beat against it. Thunder rolled. Glittering lights from a city outside struggled to pierce through the darkness of the storm. The driving rain distorted the lights as it streaked and swirled on the glass. Beads of shadow dappled and played across my skin.

My past life body was so content that I thought about lying there for a while longer and falling asleep to the drumming rain. I hadn't realized how exhausted I was until I felt that overwhelming sense of rest and relaxation. I was in the most deliciously comfortable position – the kind that usually eludes you until five minutes before your alarm goes off in the morning. I didn't want to move. My hips were sunken perfectly into the mattress.

My head was perfectly cradled. My cheek rested on a warm, smooth surface.

A surface that rose and fell along with my own breath.

I bolted upright to find myself sharing a bed with a boy. A bare-chested boy. My bare legs were entwined with his.

I gasped and pushed away from him, only to lose my balance and fall right off the edge of the bed. I landed on a cold stone floor with a smack.

"Ivy?" the boy said, reaching for me in the dark.

I scrambled to my feet and backed away from him. I was wearing a guy's long-sleeved collar shirt – only a guy's collar shirt – which barely came down to the middle of my thighs. I tried to pull it down further to no avail.

There were only three positives I could see in my particular scenario. At least I had underwear on under the collar shirt. At least I wasn't completely naked like in 1961. And at least I landed in the right time period. The boy had called me Ivy.

I glanced around to locate a closet or wardrobe, anything that might contain clothes. It was a cold, sterile-looking room with bare walls and floors, harsh lines and corners. The bed was the only source of warmth and softness, even though the linens were hospital white. A gray steel door stood to my right, which could be a closet. Another steel door stood behind me, a sliver of fluorescent light leaking through at its base.

I took a step toward the closet but froze when I felt a draft on my head like a frosty breath. My hands flew to my scalp. My hair was buzzed so short I was practically bald. My jaw dropped as my fingers searched the top of my skull.

I remembered the day Audrey came home demanding to have her head shaved. Two weeks after she began chemo, her hair started falling out a few strands at a time. One or two would fall and tickle her nose or cheek while she'd be talking to me. She'd sweep them away with her hand or send them flying with a puff of air. It was a small inconvenience then, but soon they fell into her plate at the dinner table. She was always picking them out of her soup. Brushing them from her shoulders. Her pillow. She said she felt covered in hair when she took a shower. And one day three years ago, when she still attended school, a boy sitting at a desk behind her raised his hand and said, "Mrs Cuthbert? Audrey's shedding all over my stuff." When she looked behind her, a layer of her hair covered the boy's desk and books. All the other kids laughed. The boy sneered at her.

She demanded the clippers that very day. She didn't even want to wait for Mom and Dad to come home. Gran buzzed all her hair off, all her long, beautiful sand-colored hair, and it fell in a circle around her feet on the back porch. I remembered the look on her face when Gran handed her the mirror. She made no expression, save the tiniest quiver of her bottom lip. Then she handed the mirror back to Gran and, without a sound, went to her room to be alone. Gran saved a lock of her hair to tie with a ribbon. I swept the rest into a pile, then scooped it into the trash.

Gone forever.

"Ivy?" the boy said again, snapping me out of my thoughts. He climbed out of the bed and eyed me with suspicion.

The shadow beads danced across his pale, bare chest. Light green pajama pants, like medical scrubs, hung from his slender hips and pooled at his bare feet. His eyes were narrowed, his mouth turned down. His short hair stuck up haphazardly on top, almost as if I'd been the one who messed it up.

That thought was enough to make me forget my bald head. This guy was definitely not Blue. I couldn't see the color of his eyes or his hair in the darkness, but he didn't feel like Blue. He felt like a stranger. Blue and I were supposed to be partners in this life. Soul mates. So why was I in bed with someone else?

I took a step back, feeling dizzy and faint. I thought back to my swollen, pregnant belly. Good Lord. How many guys had I slept with throughout my past fifty-six lives? Fifty? A hundred? Five hundred? Had I loved them all? Had I been happy? Had they treated me right? I dropped my arms slowly to my sides. This was going to gnaw at me. I could feel it.

The boy studied me from my head to my toes, then back up again. His eyes tightened. "You just descended."

I blinked, not knowing how to respond. I didn't know if he meant it as a fact or a question. He had a thick accent, but I couldn't tell which one it was.

He spoke again. "You descended from the future, didn't you?"

He obviously knew Ivy was a Descender and what she was capable of. That actually made things easier. I wouldn't have to pretend this time.

"What's wrong?" he said. "Why did you travel back to this life?"

I still couldn't place his accent. German? Irish? English? It sounded like a mixture of all three. Before I answered him, I glanced down at my bare legs. "Could I... get dressed first?"

His eyes flicked to my legs too. It took a moment before understanding dawned on his face. I wasn't Ivy, the girl he'd been snuggling with. I was a stranger standing in front of another stranger, half-naked.

He whisked the closet door open, his movements agile and quick. He rummaged through it for a minute, scrutinizing several articles of clothing and tossing them over his shoulder if they weren't what he was looking for. At last, he handed me a soft gray smock, a pair of flowing black pants, black socks, and a pair of black slip-on shoes. Thunder peeled across the sky outside.

When I reached for the clothes, I made sure not to touch his hands. I didn't care that I'd known him in my past life. I didn't know him now. "Can you turn around?"

"Oh. Of course."

He went back to the closet, his back to me, and pulled a white T-shirt over his pale torso. I turned away from him and slipped into my clothes as fast as I could. I peered over my shoulder to see if he was peeking, but he wasn't. Not that he probably hadn't already seen what I was covering up.

When I sat on the concrete floor to pull my socks and shoes on, he sat on the edge of the bed in front of me, elbows on his knees. His hands were clasped, his forefingers pressed together, pointing at the floor. We watched each other.

So this guy was my boyfriend in this past life. I guess I could see why I liked him. He was cute, in a boyish, nerdy, emo sort of way. He hadn't stopped frowning since I landed, but it was an appealing frown. The brooding kind you see immortalized as "art" in hipster magazines and photographs. Unlike Ear Nibbler, whose arrogant scowl I wished I could erase from my memory, this boy's frown came straight from a sad and troubled soul.

He kind of reminded me of me.

He leaned back, his palms planted on the mattress behind him. There was an insignia on his T-shirt – a circular red logo bearing the words: AIDA Headquarters, Washington DC. In the center of the circle were three letters.

LVI.

CHAPTER 29

Shock Waves

"You're Levi?" I asked, my mouth hanging open.

His lips parted in surprise. He sat up. "You know who I am in the future?"

"I know of you."

He leaned forward. "Am I still alive?" He held me in an intense gaze, as if the whole world hinged on the answer to that question.

"I... don't know." I couldn't look at him when I said it.

He let out a breath. His shoulders fell. "Oh. So, we're not..." He glanced at the bed and the rumpled blanket and sheets.

He didn't have to finish his sentence. I knew what he meant. "No. We're not together. We've never met. I've just heard your name."

His frown deepened, as if that were possible. A thousand unspoken sentences passed between us. Finally he looked over at me, almost reluctantly. "What's your name?" His voice was soft. Restrained.

I lifted my chin. "I can't tell you." How did I know it wouldn't get back to Gesh?

"Why are you here?"

"I need to talk to Nick." I shook my head. That wasn't his name in this life. "I mean Tre."

Levi's eyes narrowed. "Why can't you talk to him in your Base Life?" When I didn't answer, he said, "You aren't partners anymore, are you?"

I didn't want to answer that. I didn't want to tell him anymore than I had to. "I just need to talk to him. Can you tell me where he is?"

"He's still in recovery. He really shouldn't have visitors. Besides, you're not scheduled to be down in the labs today. You have the day off. That's why we..." He glanced at the bed again. The rumpled blankets.

I pushed myself to my feet. "It's really important I speak to him. Just tell me where to find him. I'll go myself."

"You don't have the proper clearance."

"I'm a Transcender. Level Five. Doesn't that mean I'm ranked pretty high?"

"Yes," he said, annoyed. "But that refers to your clearance in Limbo, not the research labs. Descenders aren't allowed in the labs without a supervisor present."

"Who are the supervisors?"

"Hr Flemming or Hr Gesh."

He pronounced it "hare," making me think he was German. I took German my freshman year, and we had to address our teacher, Mr Juniper, as Herr Juniper.

"Are they the only ones with the proper clearance?" I asked.

Thunder rolled outside. Levi sighed through his nose. "No." He leaned across the bed and grabbed what looked like a key card and a pair of glasses from the window ledge. He gave me an I-hope-I-don't-regret-this look, and said, "Come on." He swung wide the heavy steel door behind me, and I followed him out into a brightly lit, empty hallway.

That's when I really saw him for the first time, bathed in that bright light.

Dark blond hair. Dark brown eyes. Wire-rimmed glasses.

Levi was the little boy from my memory at AIDA. Not Blue. Levi was the one I remembered so strongly that the mere thought of him brought on the strongest déjà vu. Levi was my ever-present link to Limbo. My key to the past.

Why hadn't Porter mentioned him? He must've meant a great deal to me in this life. More than Blue, which seemed weird. Wasn't Blue supposed to be my soul mate? But maybe Porter had meant "mate" as in friend. That our souls were companions. Maybe he hadn't meant the star-crossed fated lover definition at all.

Levi strode purposefully down the hall to an elevator at the end. I kept pace, staring at him, trying to remember more about him. Anything at all. I didn't like the idea of having lovers in other lifetimes only to forget they existed. It seemed heartless and cruel.

He swiped his card through a card reader on the wall. It beeped and a tiny green light blinked. The elevator doors slid open. We stepped inside and he used his card again to gain access to the lowest level of the building.

The doors closed. We started to descend. It was silent inside, no elevator music, no beeping to signal the passing of floors, only the rumble of the cables lowering us. We stood side-by-side. Levi kept his eyes forward, still frowning. I kept stealing glances at him.

I couldn't remember anything about him, this boy attached to my Polygon stone. We were strangers on an elevator, and I didn't want it to be that way. I didn't want to be the cause of his perpetual frown. Something told me Ivy never made him frown like that.

"Are you a Descender too?" I asked, my voice coming out louder than I anticipated in the small space. "Is that why you have a number for a name like Ivy?"

"No." His tone was flat. "I'm just a Sub."

"What's a sub?"

"A Sublunary," he said, like I was stupid for not knowing. "It means I'm earthbound. Subs are those who can't ascend to Limbo. We're foot soldiers. We do the work here in the present, while the Descenders do the work in the past."

"Is that why you have security clearance and I don't?"

"Partly. And partly because I'm Hr Flemming's medical apprentice. I help him with his experiments."

Again with the Hr Flemming thing. "Are you German?"

He wrinkled his nose at me. "Of course not."

"You sound German."

"I do not sound German. I sound Danish. And you sound American." He said American like it was a dirty word.

"Did I not sound American before?"

He returned his attention to the elevator doors ahead of him. "No. Ivy's Danish. Like me."

Danish. That must be the language I remember he and Gesh speaking in my memories. If I could understand Danish in my memories, did that mean I could speak it too? I relaxed my shoulders, gave in to my host body's instincts, and said, "Denne elevator er så langsom." This elevator is so slow.

Levi's dark brown eyes snapped to mine. "Don't do that."

"Do what?"

"Talk like Ivy. You're not Ivy."

He was angry with me all of a sudden, and I didn't understand why. Was it because I no longer knew him in the future? Was he upset that I'd come to see Blue and not him? "I didn't mean to make you mad."

"Of course you didn't," he said with a scowl. "All you meant to do was descend into my girlfriend's body, demand I risk my neck to take you into a high security area–"

"Hey." I stood up straighter. Taller. "I didn't demand anything from you. If you don't want to come along, just give me your key card. I'll go on my own."

"Right, and once you've got what you came for, you'll go back to Limbo and leave Ivy to get caught using my credentials. I think not."

He was so bitter, so mad at me. I could feel it rolling off his skin like heat. But I couldn't blame him. I recognized the look in his eyes. The frustration in his fists. It was the same frustration I felt when I saw Blue in 1961. When he didn't remember me and recoiled from my touch. The moment it dawned on me that the Blue I knew was gone. His body was still there, still standing before me, but a light switch had gone off. I was no longer a part of his life. Snap. Just like that. Everything we shared together meant nothing to him anymore.

I was a stranger to Levi. A stranger standing there in his loved one's body.

"Believe it or not," I said, "I know how you're feeling right now. I can tell you really loved Ivy, and–"

He shot a glare at me. "No, I love Ivy. Love. Present tense. She's not gone yet."

"OK. You love Ivy. I get it. But you don't have to be a jerk to me. I'm not staying long. Once I'm gone, everything can go back to the way it was."

He turned his shoulders to face me, his glare even more piercing. "Nothing can go back to the way it was. Nothing. When you leave, Ivy won't remember your descent, but I will."

I didn't know what he was getting at. "So?"

"So?" He wiped his mouth with his hand like he was about to lose all patience with me. "How many years did you travel back in time?"

I hesitated. I bit my lip. "Seventeen." Or was it eighteen? It was confusing because of those nine months Mom was pregnant with me. Did I account for those? I had no idea.

"Seventeen. Do you know what that means?"

I just stared at him. I had no idea.

"For Christ's sake, who's handling your training in your Base Life?" He scrubbed a hand over his face. "Here. Let me put it in simple terms you might actually understand."

I glared at him. My compassion for his situation had one leg out the window, disappearing fast.

"It means that any day now, any week now, Ivy's going to die. Do you understand that? Do you get it? She's going to die to make room for you. So you can be born. Someone who won't remember who I am. I can't unlearn that. I can't just act like everything's fine. And every time I look at her, I'll wonder how much longer I have until she dies and you're reborn."

It was like a punch in the gut. Like the time Claire kicked me in the stomach on accident when I wouldn't stop tickling her. That churning, sickening feeling that makes you double over. The thought of Ivy dying never crossed my mind. All this time I thought it made things easier if Levi knew who I was. I guess it only made things easier for me. My compassion fell back in through the window with a thud. The window slammed shut.

"But I do remember you," I said, clambering to fix what I'd broken, to make him feel better. "I remember some things. We played Polygon together. I remember the first time you beat me–"

"Stop." He cut me off with a raise of his hand. He clenched his jaw, like I was hurting him even more.

I tried harder. I needed to make his hurt go away. "I can make it so you don't remember any of this. I can erase this timeline and make it so I never came here. I just have to do a touchdown–"

"Don't you dare." He glowered down at me, his eyes almost black behind his wire-rimmed glasses. "Don't you dare take my memories away from me. You don't have that right. What makes you think you have that right?"

"Then what do you want me to do? Tell me, and I'll do it."

The elevator landed softly with a clunk. The doors scraped open. Levi strode out into another long hallway, this one even more brightly lit, looking like a hospital wing. I hurried after him.

"Levi?" I said, catching up.

He wouldn't look at me. "I want you to get what you came for," he said. "Then I want you to leave and never come back."

I felt wretched. I couldn't help but wonder if I'd made a horrible mistake by descending. I couldn't even remember why I'd descended in the first place. Why hadn't I just waited and talked to Porter after school? What had been my rush?

In the end it wouldn't matter what Levi said or wanted. I had to erase this timeline whether he liked it or not. I had already made too much of an impact on him. What he knew now would change the course of his life. I hated to do it to him, but I didn't have a choice.

We came to two double doors, which Levi unlocked with his key card. He nudged one of the doors open a crack and peered through. Then he motioned for me to follow him into another bare, sterile hallway. No windows. No other doors. Just white walls and a sloping concrete floor leading down to yet another hallway at the end.

How far had we gone underground?

When we came to the end of that hallway, Levi peered around the corner. I wasn't sure what he was watching out for. If someone came along, it wasn't like there was anywhere for us to hide.

He pulled on my sleeve, letting me know the coast was clear, and we continued around the corner. The hallway opened up into a large open area. Standing before us was a wide, brightly lit room with windows all the way around like the newborn nursery at a hospital. Dad took me to the nursery to look in the windows when Audrey and Claire were born. As we neared it, however, it looked nothing like a nursery inside. It looked far more foreboding than that.

It was a robotics surgical lab. I'd seen one once at the AIDA Institute when Mom brought me in for a tour of her department. A huge, spider-like machine with half a dozen robotic arms stood in the center of the room, arched and poised over an empty surgical table. It looked futuristic, even for my Base Life. There were dozens of monitors and other machines scattered around the room, and wires and hoses snaked across the floor. Large, disc-shaped surgical lights hung from the ceiling. At the back of the room, a man with short, curly, caramel-colored hair, dressed in a white lab coat and black slacks, stood with his back to us. He seemed to be laying out quite the collection of sharp, nasty-looking stainless steel tools on a prep table.

"Get down," said Levi. "It's Hr Flemming."

Levi grabbed my hand and pulled me to the floor beneath one of the windows. Our backs pressed against the outside wall of the lab. The bright blueish light from the surgical discs spilled out over our heads and onto the floor at our feet.

Flemming was in there. The man who created me. Gave me Newlife. Wove my lives throughout time.

I inched up to peek over the window ledge. I just wanted to see what he looked like – to put a face with Porter's stories – but Levi gave me a yank and my tailbone smacked down onto the floor.

I ripped my hand from his and mouthed, "Ow."

He gave me a look that said he'd skin me alive if I tried that again.

I heard the door to the lab open and close, then two male voices around the corner to my left. They spoke to each other in thick Danish. I moved to my hands and knees and crawled toward them. I was only going to peek around the corner, but Levi grabbed me by the hips and pulled me back.

"Are you crazy?" he whispered. "It's this way." He jerked his head in the opposite direction to a closed door across the hall. He stood up, bent at the waist, and quietly padded toward it. I followed after him, giving up on seeing what Flemming looked like.

When we reached the door, Levi swiped his key card through a reader on the wall. It beeped. The green light flashed. He eased it open, pulled me through, and shut it behind me, closing us in a small white room with a single hospital bed in the center. Several monitors beeped quietly beside it. A thin, frail body lay on the bed beneath a white blanket, still as a corpse. I moved slowly forward, my body growing more numb with each step.

It was Blue, but I could hardly believe it. He looked like he was hours from death. His skin was so pale I could almost see through it. His muscle mass was completely gone. His head was shaved like mine, and over a dozen wires were stuck to his skull, monitoring his brain functions. Half a dozen more were stuck to his chest and arms. A large white bandage covered the right side of his head, just above his ear.

My hand fluttered to my mouth. Nothing could have prepared me for seeing him like that. So weak and defenseless. It was no wonder Porter said he looked so different at AIDA. I wouldn't have recognized him in 1927 either.

With my free hand, I entwined my fingers with his, but his touch wasn't comforting. His skin was cold and clammy, like the formaldehyde frogs we dissected in Biology last year. "What have you done to him?" I whispered.

"He just had surgery," Levi said, his voice as cold and lifeless as Blue's skin. He pushed his wire rims up the bridge of his nose.

"What kind of surgery?"

"An experimental procedure on his right temporal lobe. Hr Gesh hopes it will help him retain more of his memory when he descends."

I slid Blue's hand from mine and moved to the head of the bed. My stomach lurched. There were pale pink sinuous scars all over his scalp. I lifted a hand to my own head and felt the same scars. The same rivulets of tissue. My fingertips traced over a recent incision, complete with stitches, above my right ear. "I've had the same surgeries."

Levi nodded, wrapping his fingers around one of the chrome bed rails. He squeezed until his knuckles went white, then let go. "Hr Gesh has demanded we repair your defects. Your linear traveling. Your memory loss."

"And you think this is right?" I looked up at Levi, angry tears stinging my eyes. "Trying to rewire a human brain like a circuit board?"

He visibly stiffened. "It doesn't matter what I think. I'm just the apprentice. Besides, you consented to the tests. It's what you want. You're defective."

I shook my head, hot fury coiling within me. "I am not defective," I said, running my hands over the scars on my arms. The burns. The bruises. "Gesh and Flemming are defective. This whole damn Institute is defective."

I glared at Levi, daring him to argue with me, but he didn't. In fact, his well-worn frown threatened to break for the first time. The ghost of a smile reached his eyes, but only for a second.

He agreed with me.

In that moment, Levi and I came to a silent understanding. A quiet moment of truce, punctuated by the rhythm of Blue's heart monitor. He didn't like the experiments any more than I did, but he went along with them because they were what Ivy wanted. What I'd wanted in this past life. And he supported Ivy's wishes because he loved her more than anything.

It was exactly how I felt about Audrey. I hated seeing how the treatments affected her. The nosebleeds. The throwing up. The bruises. But I supported her because she wanted to go through with the treatments, no matter the side effects.

"I get it," I said, giving him a single nod. I did. And I liked Levi for it. I hated that I no longer knew him in Base Life. I had a feeling we'd be friends.

There was a shuffle of feet outside the door. The snick of the card reader. The beep signaling admittance.

"It's Hr Flemming," said Levi. "Get down."

I dropped to the floor and slid under the bed between the wheeled legs. The blankets draped over Blue hid me mostly from view.

The door opened. A slice of light spread across the glossy concrete floor. Black slacks and black shoes entered the room. The door closed. The shoes took a few steps forward, then stopped short. "Levi," said Flemming. "Hvad laver du her?" What are you doing here?

Levi rattled off his answer in Danish. Something about wanting to check Tre's bandages again. He was worried he hadn't dressed the incision well enough. He spoke confidently – no sign of anxiety. Flemming clapped him on the back and kindly chided him for being too much of a perfectionist – that he couldn't have dressed the wound better himself.

While they conversed, I bent my head down to the floor so I could catch a glimpse of Flemming, but it was no good. He stood too close to the bed for me to see his face.

Then Flemming shifted on his feet. He clasped his hands before him and did something that stopped the very breath within me.

He rubbed circles around his pinky knuckle with his thumb.

CHAPTER 30

My Creator

My heart was an icy stone embedded in my chest. It grew in weight, pulling me toward the floor. My arms wavered, threatening to collapse beneath me.

Everything Porter ever said to me came billowing back, swallowing me like fog. All that stuff about how Flemming had created me. How Flemming gave me Newlife. How Flemming wove me throughout history. How Flemming met Gesh at school. How Flemming was the second founder of AIDA. He'd been talking about himself the entire time. Porter was Flemming. Porter created me and Blue. Porter started all of this. Not me.

And all this time I've felt like I was to blame. And he'd let me feel that way. Never once hinting that maybe he had a hand in it too.

My hands curled into fists, my nails biting, digging, into my palms. I believed he was on my side. That he'd never do anything to hurt me. He let me believe Gesh was the one who experimented on me, tortured me. But he'd done it too. With Levi's help.

I ran a shaking hand across my scarred scalp. How was I supposed to believe anything Porter ever said to me again?

I felt the need to confront him. I wanted to crawl out from under the bed and scream at him, just to see the look on his face. I wanted to go back to Base Life just so I could chew him out on Mrs Yoder's front porch steps. I wanted to smash his stupid cigar in his face. I wanted to knock his stupid Orioles cap off his stupid head.

But my list of retribution ended as Flemming's black shoes turned and headed toward the door with Levi at his heels. I stared out after them, my jaw dropped, as they both passed through the door. How long would Levi leave me there before he came back? If he even came back for me at all?

The door closed, and I was alone with Blue.

Fear

I waited under the bed for what felt like forever, the pulse of the heart rate monitor counting the seconds above me. It wasn't until my legs started to cramp that I finally crawled out.

Levi hadn't come back.

I folded Blue's cold hand in both of mine, hoping to provide him some warmth. "Are you there?" I whispered, leaning over him. "Did you descend with me?"

I held my breath, my eyes searching his face, his hands, for any sign of movement, any sound. But there was only the slight rise and fall of his chest. The faintest puff of air from his nose. I wouldn't get my answers from him in this state. And I wasn't going to shake him and try to wake him up. It wasn't in me to be that cruel. Even if he did snitch on me to Gesh.

This mission was over. A failure.

I trailed my fingertips down the side of his face. I pressed my lips to his ice cube skin. Then I let go of his hand and forced myself to walk away. It was time for me to go home.

I paused at the door, my hand on the lever, listening for footsteps outside. When I was sure there were none, I opened the door and peeked into the hall. I wished I could say goodbye to Levi before I ascended, tell him I was sorry, if I could find him. Sorry for everything.

The surgical lab stood empty before me. I stepped out into the hall, letting the door fall gently closed. I listened for Levi's voice, but all was quiet.

I knew I should return Ivy's body back to where I started, but without Levi's key card, I wouldn't be able to get through the locked doors. I'd have to leave her in the labs.

I was just about to ascend when I heard Flemming call out to me from my left.

"Ivy?"

I froze. My first instinct was to bolt, to ascend as fast as I could, but something stopped me. I wanted to see the face of the man who'd been lying to me these past few months. So I turned to look him in the eye.

My heart was no longer an icy stone in my chest. It now pumped with fiery heat. Porter was, without a doubt, Iver Flemming.

He looked like he was in his late forties. His short, caramel hair was wild and curly, the kind that would turn into a crazy afro if he grew it out, which was probably why he kept it so short in Base Life. He had old-school-looking sideburns that were sprinkled here and there with gray. No sign of white yet. His eyes were the same – watery, shadowed, and red around the edges. His hands were in his doctor's coat pockets. He wore a puzzled expression.

"Er du søger Levi?" he asked. Are you looking for Levi?

My eyes narrowed and my nostrils flared. I knew I should ascend. I knew I should get the hell out of there before he discovered I wasn't Ivy anymore, that I was a Descender from the future. But I couldn't leave without saying one thing to him.

And I said it with all the bite and venom I could muster. "You're a liar."

He creased his brow. "Undskyld?" Excuse me?

An office door between Flemming and I swung open. Another doctor stepped out into the hall, his attention fixed on a clipboard he held in his hand. He looked about the same age as Flemming, only he was notably better looking. The kind of look Gran would call debonair if he were an actor in one of our black and white films. His hair was light and slicked back. He had a couple days' worth of facial hair and a deeply dimpled chin. His light blue pinstripe collar shirt was rumpled under his white doctor's coat. A red tie hung loose around his neck.

Gesh. I knew it was him immediately.

He glanced up at Flemming, then back to the clipboard, then up at me. "Ah. Nummer Fire." Number Four, Ivy's official name. He pulled off the reading glasses he wore.

"What are you doing here?" He spoke in thick Danish. His voice was smooth chalk.

The moment I met his eyes, a droplet of panic slithered down my spine. It paused in the small of my back, a dimple of anxiety, then radiated out until it had cocooned my entire body in fear. It was the same fear I felt during my memories of him. The same thing I felt when I saw his portrait at AIDA Headquarters. I struggled to suppress my fear so it wouldn't show on my face as he studied me, but I don't think it worked.

He frowned at me. "Kunne jeg have et ord?" Could I have a word?

He didn't wait for my reply. He disappeared into the room he came from. Porter-Flemming gave me one last puzzled look, then turned and walked away, veering out of sight around a corner at the end of the hall, leaving me all alone with Gesh.

"Nummer Fire," Gesh barked.

I jumped and scurried to his doorway. Not because I wanted to, but because Ivy's body seemed conditioned to do whatever he said. It was a small office, no windows, just a desk that almost filled the entire room and several file cabinets along the far wall, each bursting with papers and file folders like a bomb had exploded inside each one. An archaic-looking computer sat on the desk, surrounded by stacks and stacks of papers and books and files. More books and files were stacked on the floor. Gesh sat at the desk, his back to me, entering something into his computer.

"Komme i," he said. "Luk døren." Come in. Close the door.

I did as he said, yet again. My past life's body moved

like a robot controlled by remote control. I shut the door and stood with my hands clasped before me, waiting. Sweat pooled in my palms. I knew I should ascend, but I couldn't leave Ivy alone with him. It was my fault she was in his office to begin with. My fault she'd get in trouble for being in the labs on her day off. I glanced down at the scars on my arms. If he was going to hurt me again, I couldn't leave Ivy to bear the brunt of the pain.

He hammered out a few more entries into his computer, then swiveled around in his chair to face me. He pulled his glasses off again and tossed them onto a pile of papers. He leaned back in his chair. It squeaked. He tented his fingers. "Fortæl mig, hvordan din test gik i går." Tell me how your test went yesterday.

I tried to let go and let my instincts respond, but no answer came. So I blurted out the most neutral thing I could think of. "Det kom tilbage positiv." It came back positive. When he narrowed his eyes, I panicked and quickly added, "Sir."

His eyes narrowed further.

That was it. I was dead in the water. I had no idea what I was saying. No idea if I would've addressed him as sir back then. Would I have said Hr Gesh instead?

Gesh leaned back further in his chair. It squeaked again. "Det er... godt at høre." That's... good to hear. He tapped his fingers together, staring me down.

After a few moments, his lips slowly turned up at the edges. The creases around his eyes deepened. He reached out and pressed a button on a chunky-looking desk phone, his eyes still locked on mine. "Argus, kan du komme herind, tak?" Argus, can you come in here, please? He released the button and leaned back in his chair again. The corner of his left eye twitched.

Then, as quick as a snake strikes, Gesh leapt from his chair and rounded the desk toward me. I scrambled backward as he advanced. My back hit the wall and I flattened myself against it. He leaned in close, his hands folded behind his back, staring into my eyes. Almost as if he could see straight through to the Descender inside.

I bolted.

I scrambled for the black like a swimmer thrashing toward the surface. But he caught me. His fingers twined around my ankle. He pulled me back down into the cold, shadowy depths. When I landed and opened my eyes, he was smiling. A full-on smile, baring his teeth.

"Well, now," he said, his warm coffee breath on my face. "I never suspected this." He spoke slowly and softly, still in thick Danish, drawing out each word with relish. "Not in a million years did I suspect this. That one of my own would come back to spy on me."

He gripped my chin between his forefinger and thumb, and forced my head to one side, then to the other, examining me. It made me feel like a thing, a specimen under a microscope. I hated the feeling of his fingertips on my skin.

"Fascinating," he said, still speaking in Danish. "Your pupils aren't nearly as dilated as they should be. Number Four would be far more afraid of me than you are right now. She doesn't like it when I get this close." He leaned in further so that our noses almost touched. I drew in a sharp breath and turned my face away.

Gesh smiled again.

When he smiled, he resembled his portraits at AIDA in my Base Life. The saintly man who'd saved countless lives. It was a kind, compassionate smile, and it seemed so out of place. Like a lie on his lips.

He let go of my chin, pushing my head away so hard that it smacked against the wall. I made a small whimper in the back of my throat.

"How did you know to come back here if your defects still persist?" Gesh said. "You must be working for someone. Is it Flemming?" He nodded to himself, still smiling. "Yes. It's Flemming. I did suspect that. I've noticed a change in him. I suppose one can only stay loyal for so long." The corner of his eye twitched again. "I guess you'd know all about disloyalty now, wouldn't you, Number Four? Now that you've turned against me?"

When I didn't respond, he slapped me. Just like he had in my memory. I doubled over to my side, my hands pressed to my cheek, shocked by the pain of it. Sparks of light blinded me.

"Don't get me wrong," he said, pacing, rubbing the sting from his hand. "It's fascinating that you're here. I would love to experiment further or chat about what it's like in the future, but I already know all I need to know, don't I?" He stepped up to me again, pulling me up to a standing position, pressing my shoulder blades against the wall. "All I need to know is that at some point, you're going to become an obstacle for me." His voice caressed my skin like smoke. "So I think I'll do myself a favor and get rid of that obstacle while I have the chance. Save myself the headache."

The door to the office opened and Gesh lifted a casual hand to the newcomer, like introducing a dinner guest. "This is Argus. He'll be taking over from here." Gesh rubbed his hand again, the one he used to slap me. "I don't always do the dirty work myself. Sometimes I just like to watch."

A full-body shiver rippled through me. Argus was an ox compared to Gesh. He was just as big as Mr Pence, my Advanced CADD teacher, but without an ounce of the charm or compassion. Argus' hungry, bloodshot eyes stared me down. He swiped his bottom lip with his tongue. The fluorescent overhead lights winked off his bald head.

What was Gesh's henchman going to do to me? Torture me like in 1876? Shatter my bones? Leave me lying in a pool of my own blood? I tried to channel my inner Shooter Delaney, but it was no good. I had no weapons. I was completely and utterly defenseless. And totally screwed.

They couldn't kill me, could they? That would just eject me back to Limbo, then I'd erase the timeline so it never happened. Unless Gesh knew something I didn't, which was probably the case. I still had so much to learn about Limbo. And this time I wouldn't be going up against a lower level Descender. I'd be fighting the mastermind behind it all, without Porter there to help me.

Argus didn't have to rush when he came for me. I was already a cornered rabbit. He lumbered forward, slow and steady, a meaty hand outstretched. I scrambled backward along the wall, my fingertips grazing it to steady myself, until my heels kicked into a stack of books. I lost my balance and crashed down on top of them. Argus didn't flinch or change his speed. He simply bent down, fisted the front of my smock in his thick fingers, and hauled me to my feet. He yanked me over to Gesh's desk and slammed me down on top of it, books and stacks of papers biting into my back. His iron grip clamped over my mouth, and he held me down by my head.

Gesh's face appeared above mine, upside down. He was still smiling. "Interesting. Your pupils have dilated a fraction more. Does Argus scare you more than I do?"

I couldn't respond even if I wanted to. I could barely breathe from the meaty grip Gesh's henchman had over my mouth, blocking my nose. Black spots and silver sparks danced and twirled before my eyes. I tried to struggle, kick Argus in the crotch or bite his hand, but it only made him press my skull into the desk harder. The wood creaked. It felt like my head was in a vise.

Gesh lowered his smiling mouth to my ear. "It's me you should be afraid of. Let me tell you why. Do you know what happens to a Descender who dies while under a soul block?" He moved to my other ear. "Her past life body dies. Her Base Life body dies. And her soul goes straight to Afterlife. Do not pass go. Do not collect two hundred dollars." He moved back to my first ear. "And rest assured, I will find your soulmark in Limbo, if it's the last thing I do. I will descend into your body as many times as it takes to rip your family and friends of all they hold dear."

He lowered his voice to a whisper. "I will turn you into a monster. I will dedicate my life to it." His teeth sank into my earlobe. I flinched and jerked my head to the side.

"Ah. There we go," he said, peering into my eyes. "Fully dilated." He cocked his head to the side and grinned. "It's good to know you have family and friends in your Base Life. That'll give me something to work with. And those dilated pupils tell me you care about them quite a bit, which means I'm going to have a lot of fun with them." He slid his hand down between my thighs, and I stiffened with shock, sucking in a breath. "The same kind of fun I've had with you, Number Four."

No one had ever touched me there. It was worse than Gesh slicing my wrists. Worse than Gesh pressing the ends of his cigarettes into my forearms.

My God, if he descended into my body and laid a single hand on Audrey or Claire...

Gesh's fingers groped at me, and a scream of fury ripped from my gut, muffled by Argus' sweaty palm. I whipped my head back and forth, writhing, flailing, driving my fists into Argus' biceps, trying to break free. There had to be a weak spot. A chink in Argus' armor.

Gesh stepped backward, out of reach of my flailing fists, no longer smiling. His expression was venomous. Volatile. "I've had enough fun, Argus," he said. "Brække halsen." Break her neck.

Argus grabbed my head with both hands and yanked me up to a sitting position. I sucked in a terrified scream. He flexed his arms, ready to snap my spine with one quick twist. His eyes met mine, and we stared at each other, my chest heaving.

This was the last thing I would see before I died: The face of Gesh's bald, murdering henchman. His large, dirty pores, glistening with oil. The red blood vessels spiderwebbed across the whites of his eyes. His hateful snarl.

I closed my eyes, refusing for my life to end that way. I pictured Blue's teasing smile. Felt his hand in mine. Heard Audrey's laugh. Saw her fingers turn the pages of Robert Burns. Saw Mom's chestnut hair tangle in front of her face in the wind. Dad's grin when he throws the Mustang into third. Claire snuggled next to me during movie night, tucking her ice-cold feet under my legs for warmth. Gran singing Blue Skies. Pops rocking in his chair on the back porch, smoking his pipe.

Tears streamed down my cheeks and onto Argus' hands. I'd failed them. All because I was too stubborn and too angry with Porter and Blue to think sensibly.

"Hvad venter du på, Argus?" I heard Gesh say through the rush of blood in my ears. What are you waiting for, Argus?

My eyes flew open.

Gesh's henchman was still staring at me, but something had changed in his expression. The hateful snarl was gone. Argus narrowed his eyes at me and spoke in clear English, "I told you we'd talk about Levi later. Why didn't you trust me?"

My eyes went round. So did Gesh's.

Then Argus dropped me onto the desk, spun around, and slammed a brick-like fist into Gesh's face.

Gesh collapsed into a heap on the floor.

CHAPTER 31

Will the Real Snitch Please Stand Up?

I stared at Argus' beefy frame, paralyzed with shock, my cheeks coated with tears. "Porter?"

Porter turned around in Argus' massive body and wiped the sweat from his tall, sloping forehead. "Of course it's me. You didn't think I'd let something like this happen, did you?"

"I don't know," I said, my voice nearing the screeching octaves. My nerves were completely shot. "My faith in you is a little shaky right now."

He grabbed me by the arm, pulled me out of Gesh's office, and guided me into a medical supply closet across the hall. He flicked on the light and motioned for me to lower my voice, but I ignored him.

"How could you not tell me you were Flemming?" I screeched. "How?"

He winced and rubbed his temple. It was a typical Porter move, but it looked totally out of character for Argus.

I had to get a grip. The man standing before me was Porter. He'd descended into Argus' body. But the man down the hall, the forty year-old Flemming, was also Porter.

372

Two Porters in the same building. Two gigantic liars of epic proportions.

"All this time I thought you were some kind of hero," I said, my hands shaking. "A Descender gone rogue, just like me. When all along you were the one who created me. You were the one who reincarnated me. You were the one who did all those experiments on me and Blue."

"Alex–"

"I never asked for any of this. I never asked to be reincarnated. To be a Descender. You pushed it on me. You're nothing but a liar and a manipulator. You're no better than Gesh."

"Now that is enough," Porter said, slicing the air with his hand. Anger rumbled beneath his skin. "I know I kept the truth from you. I know I forced this life on you. And I am sorry about that. A hundred times sorry. There is not a day that goes by I don't wish I'd made better choices. But you do not get to be angry with me right now. It's my turn to be angry with you. Do you have any idea the catastrophic impact you've caused? Do you even know what you've done to history?"

"I screwed up, OK? I'm sorry you're pissed because you had to come save the day. I get it. But on the 'catastrophic impact' level, I think you've done a lot more damage than I have. At least we can go back and erase the mess I made. All your messes are set in stone."

"No, Alex," he said. "We can't erase this. I think this is a fixed point in time. I think you've created a Variant." He heaved a sigh and all his anger diffused, leaving his shoulders slumped. Like a deflated balloon.

"What do you mean? What's a Variant?"

"It means all this has already happened. You changed the past. You've created an alternate timeline." His eyes met mine. "The world is the way it is in Base Life now because you came back here to see Tre."

I shook my head slowly, almost involuntarily. "I don't understand."

His frame deflated even more. He swallowed, almost as if it pained him to speak. "Have you spoken to Flemming at all since you've been here?"

"You mean have I spoken to you?" I said, glaring.

"Yes. Have you spoken to me?"

"Yes."

"What did you say?"

I hesitated, not sure if I should tell him. Something told me I wouldn't like where this was headed.

"I need to know," Porter said. "Where we go from here hinges on the exact words you spoke to me. I need to know if I'm right about this."

I chewed my bottom lip and folded my arms across my chest. I lifted my chin. "I said, 'You're a liar.'"

His eyes closed. He deflated further until he was hunched over, holding his face in his hands. Hopelessness hung from his sleeves.

This was bad. Something was very wrong. I reached out and touched his shoulder, more worried now than angry. "Porter?"

"Alex." He lifted his eyes to mine, his hands on his knees. "That's what Ivy said to me the day she left. This is the day Ivy escaped AIDA. Only it wasn't Ivy who escaped all those years ago. It was you."

A numbness rolled across my skin, leaving behind burning tracks. I shook my head again, not knowing how to respond.

"I didn't realize it was even a possibility at the time," Porter continued, standing up. "I didn't even think about it until I got to know you in Base Life. Ivy wouldn't have spoken to me like that, but you?" He let out a short, dry laugh. "It wasn't until yesterday when you confronted me about seeing Nick again that everything clicked. I knew you wouldn't be able to let it go, thinking your friend had betrayed you. I knew you'd want closure. And that made me wonder what might happen if you decided to travel back in time on your own to get it. When I refused to tell you about Levi, it simply pushed you over the edge."

The straw that broke the camel's back.

I stared at him, unable to speak. No air passed through my lungs.

"Everything is the way it is in your Base Life because of this moment," Porter said. "After this, you escape with Levi and Tre. Gesh shuts down the program. He sets fire to these labs. I track you down a few days before you die. Then I reincarnate you and spend the next seventeen years watching you grow into a young woman all over again." Porter placed both of Argus' meaty hands on my shoulders, making me look at his ugly face. "Our lives are the way they are now because of this one choice you made. And it cannot be erased. You have to go back to your Base Life without doing a touchdown. Otherwise life as you know it will end."

My body shuddered beneath his thick, sweaty palms. My knees threatened to give out as the weight of his words weighed on my shoulders. My heels sunk into the concrete.

"Don't you see, Alex?" Porter's eyes swam with pity. "Tre wasn't the snitch. He didn't tell Gesh you were traveling again. You did."

CHAPTER 32

The Ultimate Plague

My knees buckled. Porter caught me under the arms and lowered me to the cold concrete floor. If I had been in my Base Life, I would've had the mother of all asthma attacks.

I sat like a stiffened corpse against the wall of the closet, paralyzed. Porter squatted before me in Argus' behemoth body, his hands poised to catch me in case I fainted. But I was too angry to faint. In that moment, I hated myself so much, I wanted to feel every ounce of pain this realization caused. Every prick. Every cut.

Blue wasn't the traitor.

I was.

"So all of this is my fault after all," I said. The words grated on my throat. "You leaving your job. Having to give up everything and go into hiding so you could be my protector. Living all alone in that tiny apartment. I did that to you."

Porter shook Argus' huge round head. "Don't think about it that way–"

"But I'm the reason Levi has to watch Ivy die in the next few weeks. I'm the reason Gesh is looking for me in Base Life. I'm the reason my family is in danger. All because of what? Because I was pissed off at you? How psychotically psychotic is that?"

"Don't do this to yourself, Alex. There are many people to blame…"

"Tell me how to fix it," I said, grabbing his fat, sausage-like wrists. "What can I do? What if I erased it anyway? What would be the worst that would happen?"

He furrowed his brow. "You can't do that. Life would cease to exist as we know it. You would cease to exist."

"Good," I interrupted. "Maybe that's the answer. I'm the worst thing that's ever happened to the entire world. Gesh isn't the villain, I am. I'm the ultimate plague."

Something softened in Argus' face when I said the plague thing. He gave me the most sympathetic look and ran a warm, thick hand over my shaved head. "You are not a plague."

His soft, comforting touch pulled tears right out of me. I wrapped my arms around his wrist and hugged his hand to my cheek. "Why don't you hate me?"

"Hate you?" he said with a shake of his head. "How could I ever hate you?" He lifted my face to his. "You listen to me. I have my regrets. There are things I wish I'd never done. Things I wish I'd never said. But you, Alex, are the best decision I ever made. The best thing I've ever done. Do you hear me?" He wiped a tear from my cheek with his thumb. "And if anyone can fix all the damage we've done, you can. I bet my life on it."

I sucked in a shuddering breath, searching his eyes. There was nothing but sincerity there. That proud, fatherly look he'd given me many times before. I hooked my arms around his thick neck, and he folded me into a bear hug. I held onto him until my breathing steadied.

"What do I do now?" I finally said, letting him go. I wiped my nose on the sleeve of my smock.

He brushed a tear from his cheek with the back of his hand. "You have to play out the rest of this timeline. You have to follow the Variant."

"How do I know I'm doing it right?"

"You can't mess it up. Everything you do will be right, because it's already happened. We already know you did it right."

My brain felt like it pulled a muscle trying to understand that logic.

"Try not to think about it," he said. "It'll just make you nervous. All we have to do is find Levi, and the two of you have to get Tre out of here before Gesh catches up to you."

I froze. "Wait. Gesh is going to wake up?"

Porter nodded Argus' head. "Remember I told you I remember hearing gunshots? Someone has to fire the gun. And it's not going to be Flemming."

Flight

Porter's hand swallowed mine as he led me down the hall, past Gesh's office toward Blue's recovery room. "Levi should have come back to look for you by now."

We stopped outside the recovery room door and Porter knocked. After a few moments, the lock released and the door opened. Levi peered out, his eyes peeking out over the tops of his wire-rimmed glasses, his eyebrows pulled down in his signature frown. "Argus?" Porter pushed past Levi into the room, pulling me along with him. Levi closed the door. "What's going on?"

"Levi," Porter said in Argus' gruff timbre. "Det er mig, Flemming. Jeg har nedstammer fra fremtiden." It's me, Flemming. I've descended from the future.

Levi glanced at me for confirmation, and I nodded. He looked back up at Argus. "Hvad har du brug for at jeg skal gøre?" What do you need me to do?

"I need you to take Tre and Ivy to safety. You know the quick way out."

Levi gave a stiff nod. Porter turned to me and squeezed my hand. "Good luck. I'll see you soon."

He made for the door, but I tugged on his hand. "Where are you going?"

"I can't stay. When Gesh wakes up, that's the end of Argus."

I covered my mouth with my hand. "He kills him?"

"Of course. You can't expect much else after he knocked Gesh out and helped you escape. Besides, how else would I have known I could descend into his body? He'd have to be dead to have a soulmark, and he'd have to have a soulmark in order for me to use it."

I let Porter's hand slip from mine and watched him disappear through the doorway, leading Argus' body casually, knowingly, to his death.

Levi walked over to me and rested a hand at the small of my back. "Vi er nødt til at handle hurtigt." We have to move fast.

It was like a dream playing out in slow motion. I watched

Levi's deft hands skim over Blue's frail body, unhooking him from the monitors, pulling the IV from his vein, applying a bandage on the back of his hand. I stood over Blue, holding his hand, my throat constricting with guilt.

It had been so easy to believe Blue betrayed me. So very easy. It was still hard to believe it wasn't true. No matter how good he was, no matter how big his heart, it didn't make sense for him to care about me as much as he did. To agonize over remembering me and dream of kissing me. Boys didn't dream about me. They dreamed about other girls. Beautiful girls.

Not me.

When Levi was done, he slipped out of the room to retrieve a wheelchair, leaving me alone with Blue. I lifted his hand to my lips again. I pressed my mouth to his palm.

"I'm sorry," I whispered.

Levi came back in, pulling the wheelchair in behind him. He stopped short, startled to see my lips pressed to Blue's hand. Levi's eyes were wide, like a boyfriend who'd just caught me cheating. I slowly lowered Blue's hand back to the bed. I'd forgotten that it must still be hard for Levi to separate me, Alex Wayfare, from Ivy, especially while I was wearing her body. I didn't have to show my affection toward Blue in front of Levi. It was too cruel.

Levi cleared his throat. "Help me get him in the chair?"

We sat Blue up, one of us on either side, and draped his arms over our shoulders. Then we lifted his legs and hoisted him into the chair. Blue still didn't wake up. His head lolled forward.

"Let's go," Levi said.

The moment we were through the door, Levi broke into a sprint, pushing Blue in front of him. We wove through the halls, gained quick access through several sets of double doors, and rounded corners, getting lost in the maze of cold, sterile corridors. It felt like we ran a mile before we finally came to a pair of heavy glass doors, framed in thick steel. Red letters on the glass spelled out Emergency Exit in Danish. Beyond it, the hallway sloped steeply upward out of sight.

Levi came to a stop and hunched over, panting. "This is it. This is Gesh's private exit. He always has a car waiting outside, in case the labs are breeched and the government finds out what he's doing down here."

"Can you use your key card to open the door?" I asked.

"Yes, but the moment I swipe it, an alarm's going to go off. Gesh, the security guards, everyone will know we're trying to escape. You've got to catch your breath, stretch, do whatever you need to do to help me push this wheelchair up that slope as fast as you can. Got it?"

"Wait," I said grabbing his wrist. "I've got an idea."

"No ideas. Just catch your breath. We have to move."

"But I can seal the door shut behind us. I can make it so Gesh can't get through without busting it down."

"You can?" Levi said. "How?"

"For all Gesh's high tech medical gear, he's not too smart when it comes to security. Nobody is. I've been paying attention to these doors and how they lock. It's just a simple electronic strike system. You can bypass the key card stuff. All you have to do is cut power to the strike to shut it all down. Knowing Gesh, these doors are fail secure. That means if I cut the power, the door seals shut. Nothing can release the strike. No one will be able to get through these doors without coming down here and reconnecting the power. It'll buy us loads of time."

Levi stared at me like I just recited a sonnet in Mandarin.

I waved a hand in front of my face. "Never mind. Just give me your key card and tell me where I can find some wire cutters."

"Wire cutters? Are you insane? We don't have time for wire cutters."

I glared at him. "If you have the keys to this getaway car Gesh keeps hidden outside, then by all means, let's make a run for it. If not, then I'm going to have to hot-wire it. And honestly, I've only done that once so I consider myself a little rusty."

Levi's eyes went wide. "You know how to hot-wire a car?"

"Levi. Focus."

"OK, OK," he shoved the key card in my hands. "There's a medical closet by the surgical lab. I'm pretty sure there are some tools in there."

An invisible boot sank into my stomach. "The closet right across from Gesh's office?"

Levi nodded. "Still think it's a good idea?"

I fisted my hands and set my jaw. "I've got this. I'll be right back. Don't move."

I flew down the hall, rewinding my way through the empty maze of tunnels, swiping Levi's key card and slipping through the sets of double doors. Levi didn't trust my idea, but it was a heck of a lot better than his "just run as fast as

you can from a swarm of security guards" plan. I had to seal
the deal. Cut Gesh off at the knees. Not at the freaking elbow.

When the surgical lab came back in view, I slowed
down, skimming my back along the wall and peering
around corners. When I came to the hall with Gesh's office
and the medical closet, I ran on the balls of my feet, not
making a sound, and slipped inside.

My heart was in my throat. Where was Gesh? Still
in his office? Murdering Argus? Had Porter already
ascended back to Base Life?

My eyes darted around for any sign of a toolbox. I
shoved boxes of needles and rubber gloves out of the
way on the shelves, peering behind them. I tipped the lids
off plastic storage tubs and rummaged through packs of
plastic-wrapped bandages. Nothing.

I finally came to a bulky plastic grocery bag sitting on
the floor near the door. When I ripped it open, I swore
under my breath.

They kept their tools in a grocery bag? For real?

I knelt on the floor and rifled through them. They were
the bare bones basics: a hammer, a screwdriver, a little box of
nails, a plastic container of thumbtacks. Geez, who did these
tools belong to? Porter's grandmother? Levi obviously had
no idea where the maintenance workers kept the real tools.

At the very bottom of the bag, my fingers closed
around a pair of scissors. "Bingo." They would have to
do. I just had to hope and pray they'd be sharp enough to
cut through the power cord for the electric strike.

Before I left, I grabbed the screwdriver and hammer to
use when I hot-wired Gesh's car. Then I spun the scissors

around my finger like it was Shooter's pistol. I wasn't going back out into the hall without some sort of weapon in my hands. Not that a pair of scissors would do much good if Gesh really did have a gun, but it made me feel safer. Perception is everything.

I stepped out into the hall, looked both ways, and took a single step. The moment my foot met the floor, I heard the unmistakable clack! of a gunshot suppressed by a silencer. It came from behind Gesh's office door. Then I heard what sounded like a massive body slump to the floor.

Holy crap. Gesh did kill Argus.

I bolted down and around the corner, and skidded to a stop in front of the first set of double doors.

"Nummer Firrrrrrre," I heard Gesh call out. His voice tumbled and rolled through the halls. His office door closed behind him. "Hvor errrrr duuuuu?" Where arrrrre youuuuu?

I swiped my card, saw the green light flash, heard the beep, and darted through. By the time I got to the next set of doors, I heard Gesh open the set behind me. I had to move faster.

I raced through the hallways, but Gesh didn't run after me. I could hear his Oxford dress shoes clomping casually down the hall. He was taking his time. He wasn't worried about losing us.

By the time I skidded around the last corner and saw Levi and Blue, I heard Gesh's voice echo after me. "Kommer ud, kommer ud, uanset hvor du er." Come out, come out, wherever you are.

Levi's eyes were about to bug out of his head. "Travlt!" he shouted. Hurry!

"Help me up!"

I tossed him the key card, the screwdriver, and the hammer. He hoisted me up to the drop ceiling by the door, my foot in his hands, the scissors pressed between my lips. I pushed the ceiling tile aside. I seized hold of a plumbing pipe and pulled myself up higher, Levi still steadying me by my foot. All I needed was that one dark gray wire. That one beautiful, lovely wire that would save our skins.

There were three wires coming up from the emergency exit door. The thick white one had to be the swipe card wire. The red was for the alarm. And the gray.

The gray was my power.

I pulled the scissors from my mouth with one hand. I reached my arm out and snipped the closest wire, the red one, shutting off power to the alarm. Now when Levi opened the door, it wouldn't go off and alert the security guards.

"Swipe your card," I said.

He let go of my foot. My arm slipped from the pipe and I fell a few inches before I grabbed hold with my other hand, clinging for dear life, my feet dangling in midair.

Levi swiped his card through the reader. The light. The beep. He shoved Blue and his wheelchair through the doors, then he held it open with one hand. "Travlt!"

I struggled to pull myself back up onto the pipe. I reached out for the gray wire. My entire body shook as I tried to hold steady. Sweat slid into my eyes.

"Ah." Gesh's Oxfords slid to a halt at the end of the hall. "Der er du." There you are.

"Ivy!" Levi shouted.

I reached as far as I could. I strained. Stretched my arm muscles to the brink. The tips of the scissor blades brushed the wire. Hot sweat blurred my vision.

"Farvel, Nummer Fire." Goodbye, Number Four.

In the time it took him to raise his gun, I wriggled the tips of the scissor blades around that wire and clamped down hard. It sliced through with a satisfying chunk.

I let go of the pipe.

Gesh pulled the trigger.

CHAPTER 33

Will You Remember?

I dropped to the balls of my feet, crouching down to the floor to absorb the shock. The bullet missed as I fell – I don't know by how much – and bit right through the glass of one of the doors, leaving a perfect hole. Spiderweb cracks spread out from its center.

I dove for Levi.

Clack!

Another shot. This time through the open doors, but I didn't see where it hit. I was too busy trying to squeeze through and shove them shut behind me.

Gesh sprang for the doors and slammed his body into them. He snatched the back of my shirt and yanked me back. Levi let out a feral yell as he rammed the doors closed with his shoulder. They locked. I hurtled myself forward but my smock was still caught between the doors.

Gesh took a step back and aimed at me through the glass. I ducked, sawing through the fabric of my shirt with the scissors. Another bullet lodged itself in the steel frame right above my head.

Levi grabbed the fabric in his hands and, with another yell, he ripped it in two, freeing me.

We ran.

We pushed Blue's wheelchair up the steep slope, panting, sweating, sprinting for our lives. I glanced over my shoulder to see Gesh slam his shoulder into the door again, and again, unable to open it.

It worked. I'd cut him off at the knees.

But Gesh wasn't done yet. He took his stance and fired his last two bullets through the glass. One hit the floor at my feet and ricocheted, the other must have gone astray.

At the top of the slope, we burst through another door and into a dark room. When Levi hit the light switch, a single bulb flickered on above us, illuminating what looked like a parking garage built for a single car in dingy, orange light. A sleek, black Cadillac with chrome rims and heavily tinted windows rested in the sole parking spot. Luckily, it was unlocked. I dove into the driver's seat with the screwdriver and hammer while Levi helped Blue into the back seat.

The thing about hot-wiring an older car? There doesn't have to be any hot-wiring involved. If you know where to hit the ignition cap, it'll pop right off. Then you can jam a screwdriver down between the ignition housing and the steering column, breaking enough pieces so the ignition turns, bypassing a key.

Easy peasy, popcorn cheesy.

I stuck the tip of the screwdriver into the side of the ignition cap and gave it a few good whacks with the hammer. I expected it to take longer than it did, but after a few hits, it broke through and the cap shot over into the passenger seat. I jammed the screwdriver in place, then wailed on it with the hammer. Within thirty seconds, the ignition was mangled enough to turn. The car rumbled to life.

"Ha!" I said, smacking the steering wheel with my hands.

"Um, we have a problem," Levi said from the backseat.

"What is it?"

"Tre's been shot."

I whipped around. Levi lifted blood-covered hands from Blue's side. Blue was still unconscious from his anesthesia, his head lolled back against the headrest. His mouth hung open.

Oh my God. "How bad is it?"

"Bad."

"Can't you do something? Aren't you a medical apprentice?"

"I…" Levi hesitated at first, but it only took a moment for him to shake off the shock and jump into action. "OK. Hand me the scissors and screwdriver. Then drive. Whatever you do, don't stop driving. Get us as far from here as you can."

I handed over the scissors and screwdriver, closed my door, and buckled myself in. I hit a button on the visor and the dingy garage door in front of us came to life, bathing us in afternoon light. The thunderstorm that had raged earlier was over.

I eased the car out into an overgrown gravel parking lot at the edge of a train yard, splashing through deep potholes and puddles. All the high-rise buildings of DC loomed behind us.

Levi sliced open Blue's medical gown and pulled it off of him. All I saw in the rearview mirror was Blue's naked, frail body coated in red.

Everywhere, red.

Levi balled the medical gown in his fist and pressed it to Blue's side. I slammed on the gas and tore through the parking lot, kicking up mud and gravel, searching for a way out of the lot.

"How long does he have?" I said.

"I don't know. He's bleeding like mad. I need bandages. I need my tools."

"Where's the nearest hospital?"

"How should I know? I've never been outside HQ."

"What? You've never been outside?" I guess that explained why all three of us were pasty white. I came to a chain link fence and a gate with razor wire coiling along the top. The gate slid open as we approached, activated by a motion detector.

"I was born at HQ," said Levi. "We all were. We're not allowed to leave. And we can't go to the hospital or the police because we don't exist. We're not in their records. We don't have social security numbers. You want to spend the next few months explaining that to the US government?"

Once we were through the gate, I slammed the gas again and shot down a back alley toward an open road up ahead. "Maybe we should go to the police. What if that's the thing that brings Gesh down? An exposé on all the experiments he's done on two kids down in his labs?"

"Yeah, and that wouldn't make an impact on the future at all."

I squeezed the steering wheel in my hands. Levi was right, but I didn't appreciate his snide tone.

Was this even part of the Variant timeline Porter wanted me to play out? Blue getting shot? Dying in the back of a Cadillac? Bleeding to death, just like in Chicago? Did Porter know all this was going to happen? He said I couldn't mess the Variant up. But what if he was wrong?

"You need to get me to a deserted area," said Levi. "I need to lay him out flat if I'm going to try to get the bullet out."

"The bullet's still inside?"

"Gah, he just bled through the gown." Levi pulled off his T-shirt and pressed it to the wound, tossing the blood-soaked medical gown to the floorboards. The car was already full of the acrid, rusty smell of blood. I could taste it on the back of my tongue. The air was tinged pink with it.

As I sped through an industrial-looking part of DC, past power plants and factories, I heard Levi swear. I glanced at the rearview mirror and saw Blue close his mouth and wince. He let out a sluggish groan.

He was waking up.

Waking up to a bullet wound. To his body covered in blood.

All my fault.

I turned into the entrance to what I thought was a park, but I soon realized it was a cemetery. One of those beautiful, rolling hill cemeteries with century old shade trees. How morbid was that? Leading Blue to a cemetery while he bled to death? But it was the best I could do. I wound my way through the grassy knolls and tree-lined roads, until I found a secluded place to pull off. It was a small gravel parking spot behind a utility building, somewhat shielded from view.

I threw the car into park and scrambled out to give Levi a hand. We stretched Blue out on his back across the back seat, but it was too tight for Levi to work. We lifted him up and carried him into the woods. Naked and bleeding. Arms hanging limp. His blood leaving a trail. I didn't even want to think about what might have happened if someone saw us.

We rested him on the ground under the trees, and I cradled his head in my lap, in my arms. "I'm so sorry," I said to him, my forehead pressed to his. I said it over and over, but no matter how many times I said it, it wouldn't be enough. How much more pain would I cause for him? If he remembered me at all, he probably wished he'd never met me.

Levi used the scissors and screwdriver to try to retrieve the bullet. He swore under his breath a hundred times. It was too unsanitary. The tools were worthless. The bullet was too deep. There was dirt in the wound. Every time he spoke, he shot my hopes one-by-one like the dart and balloon game at the fair.

Finally he sat back on his heels and wiped the sweat from his brow with the back of his bloody hand. "I can't do it."

The last dart punctured the last balloon.

"No," I said, looking up at him. "You have to keep trying."

"I can't do it," he shouted at me, making me jump. He clutched the scissors and screwdriver in his hands so hard his knuckles turned white. Then he let out a defeated roar and chucked them into the woods. He stood up and staggered back to the car, his head in his hands.

I watched him go, my mouth hanging open. It wasn't until then that I realized it wasn't only Blue's death Levi was angry about. It was mine. Ivy's.

Your souls are universally linked across time. When you die, he dies. When he is reborn, you are reborn. He is your soul mate in the very literal sense of the word.

Blue wasn't the only one Levi wasn't able to save.

I wanted to go to Levi, explain that it wasn't his fault. It was mine. But Blue rolled his head to the side and groaned.

"Blue?" I cupped his face in my hands. He wasn't as cold as he was in the recovery room. Was that because he was waking up? Or was it because he had a fever from the bullet? "It's me. I'm here. Can you hear me?"

He winced and groaned again, this one even more pitiful than the one before. He was getting weaker. He was going to die in my arms.

I bent down and pressed my lips to his forehead. I tasted my own tears. "I'm so sorry. Oh, God, I'm so, so sorry."

I felt his eyelashes flutter on my chin. I jerked my head up to see his eyes half open. Groggy and heavy, but open. He stared at my face for a while, then his eyes opened all the way. He lifted his arm and cupped the back of my shaved head in his hand.

"Hey, Sousa." He actually managed a small, weak smile. "You're bald this time." He glanced down at his body. "And I'm naked."

I let out a laugh, choked with tears. "You remember me?"

His body shuddered with a cough, but his smile widened. "You kidding? You're the one thing I can't forget." He reached his other hand up to touch my face, but saw it was coated in blood. "Oh." He turned it from front to back. "Is this when I die?"

My smile vanished. "It's all my fault. I came back to this life just to talk to you, and look what I've caused." More tears streamed down my cheeks. They ran down my neck. Down my chest. My torn smock ruffled behind me in the breeze. "I keep doing this to you. I keep killing you."

"Hey." He made me look him in the eyes. "This is how it is. You and me, we die. It's what we do." He winced again. Coughed again.

I sniffed and wiped my nose on my sleeve. He was right, I guess. But it didn't make it hurt any less, or feel any less my fault. "I don't want to watch you die. I can't."

"Then don't," Blue said. "Go back to Base Life." He sucked in a shallow breath. "Meet me there."

"How? Where?"

He shivered all over. His teeth chattered. The ground was wet and muddy from the thunderstorm. "You know where."

"I don't. I don't know your name, or where you live, or anything about you in Base Life."

"Sousa." He closed his eyes, his teeth chattering even more. It was becoming harder for him to breathe.

"Oh God," I said, "don't go yet. Please, tell me where you are in Base Life. Tell me your name." I cupped his face in my hands again. I could barely see him through all the tears. No one had ever made me feel the way Blue did. I wanted more of him. So much more.

If I could have it.

With the tiny bit of strength he had left, he pulled my head down. I thought he was going to whisper his name in my ear, but instead, he pressed his lips to mine. He kissed me like he hadn't seen me in years. Like he needed my mouth to survive. I poured myself into him, gave him everything, our lips salty from tears, from blood. He pulled himself up and wrapped his arms around me despite his pain from the gunshot. He ran his palms across my bare back. I clung to him like he might float away.

The moment was so fleeting. Over by the time it began. He jerked his head back and went into a spasm of coughs, bringing us back to reality, and I lowered him back down onto my lap. I held him in my arms, calming him, rocking him, until his body settled down.

"Come to Buckingham Fountain," I said, squeezing his hand in mine. "New Year's Eve. I'll be there. I'll wait for you. Will you remember?"

"Our fountain," he repeated, his voice thin and strained.

"New Year's Eve. Say it."

He let out a weak sigh, the fit of coughing over for the moment. His eyes remained closed. "New Year's Eve." He said it like he was falling asleep.

"Will you remember?" What if this was my last chance? What if he didn't remember?

He squeezed my hand to let me know I was holding on too tightly. "I'll remember," he whispered. He opened his eyes for the last time. They were so blue. Even in the shade of the trees. "I'll remember you. I have to."

"You better go," Levi said, interrupting us. He was standing off to my left. I didn't know how long he'd been watching. His expression was pained. Heartbroken. "You should ascend and take him with you before he dies."

"But–"

"I'll take care of everything," Levi said. "I'll fill Ivy in. She'll understand. She'll know what to do."

I frowned up at him, feeling awful he had to see Ivy, his Ivy, kissing someone else. Awful I did all of this to him. Put him through so much pain. "Levi, I am so–"

"Go."

"Will I see you again? In Base Life?"

He shrugged, slipping his hands in the pockets of his green scrub pants. There was blood streaked across his bare chest. Across his cheek. He furrowed his brow, his eyes dark and brooding behind his glasses. "We'll see, I guess."

CHAPTER 34

The Land of Souls

I open my eyes to the darkened AV room. Jensen's pudding cup is still sitting on the desk in front of me. I look down at my hands, holding the Polygon stone. Not one speck of blood. I slip the stone into my pocket and run my hands through my shaggy hair, thinking I might shave it all off as penance for the damage I've done. I'm the one that deserves to be bald. Not Audrey.

I take a deep, shuddering breath and bury my face in my hands. I remain there, hidden away in the dark, until everything that just happened washes over me and I am finally calm.

It's over. I came face-to-face with Gesh and survived. I broke Levi's heart. Turned Porter's life upside down. Got Blue shot and killed.

Again.

At least now I know Blue remembers me. And that he's not a traitor. I just hope he remembers Buckingham Fountain on New Year's Eve.

Half an hour later, Porter and I are sitting at a table at Ristorante Cafferelli, overlooking the cold waters of the Bay. My fingers are entwined around a mug of coffee. Ever since 1961, I can't get enough of the stuff. Porter sips his cappuccino, the steam mingling in the stubble on his chin.

There are so many questions.

"Did you know he was going to die?" I ask.

Porter presses his lips together in careful thought. "It was his time, yes."

I look down at my mug. I turn it around by its handle slowly. "How long did Levi get to spend with Ivy before she died?"

"About two months. I found you both in a cabin in Canada. You were almost gone by the time I got there."

"I didn't die the same time as Tre?"

"Not that time, no. Usually you do, but I think in Ivy's case, you wanted to hang on as long as you could. You wanted that time with Levi. You wanted to wait for me. To tell me to reincarnate you."

"Why did you only protect me?" I ask, thinking about all the years Porter lived in Annapolis, watching me grow up. "Why didn't you protect Tre too?"

"I would have gladly protected you both, but when I went to intercept your soulmarks to insert you into your Newlives, only yours appeared. I couldn't find Tre's. I went ahead and reincarnated you while I had the chance. If your souls were still connected, then Tre would be reincarnated too. I just wouldn't know where he was or who he'd be in Base Life. And that was better than nothing. I honestly didn't know whether or not you were still connected until I read about your 'visions' in Dr Farrow's notes. That's when I knew you were still pulling each other along. Just like you used to."

I stir a packet of sugar into my coffee. "You don't sound Danish at all. What happened to your accent?"

"When you're on the run, the accent is the first thing to go. It's a little too memorable. Too noticeable around here."

I nod at his Orioles cap. "And the cap? The boat shoes? I was right, it is a disguise. You're just trying to look like a local."

"Works, doesn't it?"

I smile slightly, setting the spoon down. "Why did you change your name to Porter?"

He folds his hands on the table. "Porter is the nickname you gave me when you were growing up at AIDA. It comes from an old fairytale I used to read to you when you were a little girl, In the Land of Souls. It's about a man who sets out on a journey to reunite with his dead wife. He meets a gatekeeper along the way who teaches him how to shed his body and enter the Land of Souls, where his wife's soul is waiting for him." A small, wistful smile appears at the edge of Porter's mouth as he recalls the tale. "You said I was the gatekeeper because I taught you the same thing. How to shed your body and enter Limbo."

"And porter means gatekeeper," I say.

He nods. "I wrote Porter on the flyer to see if you remembered anything from your past life as Ivy. If you did, you would've known who I was right away. But you didn't."

I fold my arms on the table. I look out across the water at the boats sailing past. "Do you think Gesh is searching for Tre too?"

"I wouldn't doubt it."

"If Tre isn't working for Gesh, then why didn't that Descender in 1876 go after him too? Why just me?"

"They probably thought they wouldn't get any information out of him, if Gesh still believes Tre has his memory defects."

I sit back in my chair, hoping that's not true. If Blue still has his defects, then he might forget to meet me at Buckingham Fountain, and I'll never find him in Base Life.

Gesh might find him first.

After a while, I finally summon the courage to ask Porter what I've wanted to ask since I sat down. "Will you ever forgive me? For creating the Variant?"

His watery eyes are sympathetic. "You don't need forgiveness, Alex. In the end, the ultimate fault lies with me. You were merely playing with the hand I dealt you. You were meant to go back to AIDA, to create this Variant timeline. It was all meant to be."

I know they're supposed to, but his words don't make me feel any better. I know what he really means. What's done is done. We can't change the past. We can only change the future.

And that's exactly what I plan to do.

Once we find Blue, we'll be a force to reckon with. Me, Porter, Blue, maybe even Levi, if we can find him. Me and my boys. We'll bring Gesh down.

Hard.

"Oh, I got you something," Porter says, reaching into a shopping bag at his feet. He pulls out an eyeglasses case. "What do you think of those?"

I open the case and crack a smile. Inside is a pair of glasses with the exact same frames as mine. I slide them on and laugh. The lenses are clear plastic. Totally fake, but close enough to fool anyone.

"Thanks, Porter."

Friends

When I arrive home, the house is brimming with the scent of Gran's molasses cookies. One of her specialties. The moment I walk through the door, she tosses me an oven mitt.

"Can you watch these for me, Allie Bean? I ran out of butter. There's a few minutes left on the timer, so when it goes off, check if they're done. If not, set it for another five minutes. Don't you let my sugar babies burn." She grabs her coat and flies out the door, her purse swinging behind her.

I drop my backpack by the back door, toss the oven mitt on the counter, and make my way to the front porch, leaving the front door open so I can hear the timer. I watch Gran book it down the street to the corner store. A breeze kicks up and scatters the last few fall leaves across the yard. I sit on the porch swing, suddenly feeling very, very tired.

And very alone.

As if right on cue, a familiar face comes walking up our driveway, hands shoved in the pockets of his jeans. "Wayfare," Jensen says with a smile. "Glad you brought back the specs. Lookin' good."

When he climbs the porch steps, I notice a fresh bruise on his cheekbone under his left eye. "Whoa. What happened to you?" I scoot over so he can sit beside me. My hands are cold and fisted in the pockets of my parka.

"Heh. Well. I kinda got in a fight with Robbie after school."

"You didn't."

He nods with a guilty grin. "Totally did. I asked him what he said to you on the track." He shakes his head. "It was low. Even for him. I don't know what happened. I've never been in a real fight before. I just got really mad and the next thing I knew, I took a swing."

"You hit him?"

He lets out a laugh. "I wish. He rolled out of the way. But he got me pretty good." He rubs the side of his face, wincing a bit.

I give him a disapproving look. "I thought you said we just had to 'ignore them.'"

"Yeah, well." He kicks his long legs out and crosses his ankles. "Maybe next time I'll take my own advice."

We sit there, staring at our shoes, rocking the porch swing with our feet. Heel, toe, heel, toe.

"So," he says after a while. "Did you talk to your boyfriend?"

I smile to myself. "Yeah, actually. I did." It feels weird referring to Blue as my boyfriend. Shouldn't that title be reserved for someone you meet in the present time period? Someone you go on dates with?

"And?" Jensen says.

"And you were right. It was a big misunderstanding."

"Told ya."

"Yeah, well. Maybe next time I'll take your advice." He bumps his shoulder into mine and we laugh. "So, can you tell all the jerks at school that I have a boyfriend? And that you and I are just friends? Maybe that'll get the guys off my back and the girls won't hate me so much."

"What? They don't hate you."

"Yes they do."

"Why would they hate you?"

"Um, maybe because you and I are friends now?" I swear, he can be so oblivious sometimes.

"We've always been friends."

"OK, well, they hate me now that you've made our

friendship public."

"That's a ridiculous reason to hate someone."

"Jensen, if you haven't figured out by now that most girls are shallow, shallow creatures, then there's no hope for you. They hate other girls for far less than that. Trust me."

"That's messed up."

"Tell me about it."

We rock the swing. Stare at our shoes. I push my fake glasses up the bridge of my nose.

"So when do I get to meet this guy?" he says.

"Someday. Maybe."

"You bringing him to prom?"

I snort a laugh. I try to picture Blue and I doing something as mundane as prom. Two time traveling teens renting a limo and wearing corsages. "No. We're sort of… bigger than prom."

"Ah. College guy, eh?"

"Something like that."

The timer goes off. I leap to my feet and head for the door. "I gotta run inside. You want to come in?"

He shrugs. "Sure."

I pull the two baking sheets full of molasses cookies from the oven. They're rich, golden brown and smell amazing. I set them on the kitchen island and hand Jensen a spatula. We both start easing the cookies off the baking sheets and onto a cooling rack.

Audrey comes in carrying Afton in her arms, wearing a pair of baggy, plaid pajama pants. "I thought I smelled cookies." Her eyes are heavy, and she has that just-woken-up look. Her stocking cap is askew. One pro of being totally bald? No more bed head.

She freezes when she sees Jensen, and her heavy, tired

eyes become big and bright. I can't help but stifle a laugh. I've never invited a friend over to the house, let alone a boy. Let alone Jensen Peters.

"Jensen?" I say. "This is my sister."

"Oh, yeah," he says with a kind smile. "Audrey, right?" He sticks out his hand. She shifts Afton over to one arm and shakes his hand, looking even more meek than usual. I like it that he remembers her name.

She slides onto one of the barstools at the side of the island and cuddles Afton to her chest. She's not usually shy, but Jensen's presence makes her clam up.

"What's your cat's name?" Jensen asks her.

"Afton."

"Cool name. That's a river in Scotland, right?"

Audrey and I both look up, eyebrows raised. "How did you know that?" she asks.

"Well," he says with a shrug, easing a few more cookies onto the cooling rack, "this is going to sound stupid and totally lame, but there's this Scottish guy who wrote a poem about it. It's one of my favorites."

"It's one of mine, too," Audrey says, perking up.

"It is?" When she nods, he says, "Well, maybe it's not so lame then."

"Did Alex tell you I'm going to Scotland in the spring?"

"What? No. That's awesome." He gives me a look like he can't believe I didn't tell him.

Audrey beams. "I've been wanting to go for so long. And someone made a donation to my foundation so I can go on the trip. Isn't that cool? The whole family's going."

"Alex too?" he asks.

"Yep," she says. "There's no way I'd go without her. When we make that final descent, I want her right by my side."

Her words hit home deeper than she could have known. I walk over to her, squeeze her shoulders, and kiss the top of her stocking cap. "You know I'll be there. Every step of the way."

I may have ruined history, the entire world, and who knows how many lives with the Variant timeline I created, but at least I can be proud of what I did for Audrey.

At least I did one thing right.

When Gran gets back, she's just as startled as Audrey to see Jensen helping us with the cookies. And he's just as kind and talkative to her as he is with Audrey. By the time the whole family gets home, he's been invited to stay for dinner four times. He calls his parents and gets permission to stay.

Over dinner, he makes everyone laugh. He talks to Dad about the Mustang, to Mom about her job at AIDA, to Pops about the Orioles, to Gran about her delicious cookies, to Claire about school, and to Audrey about Scotland. He even sneaks Afton a bit of his fish stick under the table. No one asks about the shiny bruise under his eye, not even Claire, and for that I'm thankful. I'm sure they'll quiz me about it after he leaves, which I'm already dreading. They keep shooting me knowing looks across the macaroni and cheese. Pops keeps waggling his bushy gray eyebrows at me. I just try to ignore them and enjoy the show while it lasts.

Throughout it all, I can't help but think, *So this is what* it's like to have a friend in Base Life.

After dinner, I walk Jensen out onto the porch. He swings the baggie of molasses cookies Gran gave him at his side.

"Guess I better go home and explain this thing to the parents." He points at his black eye. "And I guess you better go inside and explain it to yours, too." He tosses me a grin, then jogs down the steps. "See ya tomorrow, Wayfare."

I guess he's not super oblivious all the time.

As I watch him melt into the night, past pools of light from street lamps, Mom leans against the doorframe behind me. The great shadow of disappointment is nowhere to be found tonight.

"Do you know how proud I am of you?" she says.

"For what?" I squeeze into the doorframe beside her, and she wraps an arm around my waist.

"You're making friends. Doing better in school." She smooths my hair back and gives me a peck on the forehead. "I like seeing you happy."

I rest my head under her chin. If she doesn't feel like she has to worry about me anymore, then that's one more thing I've done halfway right. I just hope I can keep it up.

And somehow talk her into a trip to Chicago over Christmas break.

CHAPTER 35

Apology

Destiny is a funny thing. It's ironically fickle, not set in stone like some might believe. Destiny isn't immune to the bends and cracks in time. One choice, one action, can change everything. Destiny is fluid. Evolving. It carves a path through life like a river carves its way through rock. When an obstacle arises, the river changes its course. There are no straight lines. Alternate timelines are created every day. Every hour. A country decides to go to war. A pregnant mother loses her child. A man is late for work and causes a pileup on the freeway. What might have been is lost forever. The new timeline begins.

That is the only rigid thing about Destiny.

It changes.

Sometimes I feel trapped by this knowledge. I lie in bed at night, wondering what life would be like if I hadn't set this new timeline in motion. Who would be alive? Who would be dead? Have I changed your life? Is it different now because of me? Are you happy with your path? Or did I screw things up for you?

It's enough to give me nightmares and send me to the edge of hysterics.

All I can say is I'm sorry. If your lot in life sucks right now, blame me.

I did it.

It would all be different if I hadn't gone back to AIDA. All I can do now is try to make our future better, to give you the chance to have it good, from here on out.

I promise I'll try. Even if it kills me.

Dying's what I do, remember? It's the least I can do.

And I'm trying. I'm learning. Getting better. It's not easy being a Descender. It's like being in a cage – the bars arc around me and I'm not strong enough to bend them or break free. Sometimes I still resent Porter. For lying to me. For creating me. For forgiving me. But then I remember I'm no longer adrift. I'm just new to the game. The visions, the traveling – Porter is teaching me to think of it as a gift. A secret power given only to me. All I have to do is learn how to harness it, and use it to repair all the damage I've done. Use it to defeat Gesh before he can defeat me.

I try to think of all the good that can come of such a gift.

I try to remember Porter's words of comfort.

And when those dark times come, when I resent this burden on my back I'm told I can never shift, I cling to the fact that there's someone out there who shares the same load. Another burdened soul, carrying the same weight.

Deep Breaths

"You ready?" Porter asks, squeezing my hand.

The taxi pulls to the curb along South Columbus Drive

in Grant Park, Chicago. The sun is just rising, glinting off Lake Michigan. Buckingham Fountain sits covered in twinkling holiday lights, like it's draped with strands of diamonds, just out the window in the distance, past a row of neatly trimmed hedges. A light layer of snow dusts the ground. The city looks totally different. All built up and shiny and new.

There are so many cars. So many people. So much noise. But the fountain looks exactly the same. Our fountain.

Porter squeezes my hand again. "Alex?"

I close my eyes. I take one good deep breath. Two. Three. I picture Blue's teasing grin as he pulls me close by the fountain. I can't wait to see him again. To have him hold my hand in Base Life. My hand. Alex Wayfare's hand.

I open my eyes. I take one more deep breath, then finally, "I'm ready."

I am so ready.

ACKNOWLEDGMENTS

So much thanks to:

Holly Root, Amanda Rutter, and all the folks at Strange Chemistry and Angry Robot, for loving this book. Thanks for taking a chance on Alex.

The YABooksCentral.com family, for cheering me on. The bloggers and authors and publicists who told me they were excited for this book. (You know who you are). That means the world to a debut author. The OneFours, Thirteeners, Lucky 13s, and Apocalypsies, for not only supporting YABooksCentral.com, but me as well. The YA community is truly the best community. I'm proud to be a part of it. The Strange Chemists, who welcomed me with open arms. The Snowflake Posse, for those hot Savannah nights. All the friends I've made on Twitter: Who said social media isn't valuable? You all mean the world to me.

Sara McClung, Bria Quinlan, Francesca Amendolia, Jen Fisher (The "Pusher" of Books), and Christina Franke, for reading and helping shape this book. I owe you dinner. Kimberly Pauley, for being there and passing the torch.

Shannon Messenger, for late night chats and Shannonigans. Kim Baccellia, for keeping me in coffee gift cards and cheering me on. Hayley Farris, for the gift of much-needed sleep during the final edit stretch. (You know what I'm talking about). Jodi Meadows, for winter writing mitts. Andrea Summer and Tye VonAllmen, for introducing me to goetta. Heather Palmquist-Lindahl, for making me your honorary sister. Matt Murrie, for the advice and support. Jon Beebe, for breakfasts and brainstorming and WoW. Leigh Kolb, for your words. All of them.

Myra McEntire and C J Redwine, for your unwavering encouragement and belief in this book (and your belief in me). Thank you for bossing me and making me HIT SEND. I shall continue to pat heads and make my own kite string daily.

Chris Howard, for being my BFF, my BFG, my beffie. You are one of my favorite authors, bud. April G Tucholke, for keeping my neuroses in check. *Deep into that darkness peering, long I stood there, wondering, fearing, doubting, dreaming dreams no mortal ever dared to dream before.* We will have France. (And Scotland. And Quebec City. And the entire world, apparently.)

Nancy Nilsson and Stefanie Lassitter, for being the best, most inspiring professors, and for giving me many an A+ all those years ago. My teachers at UHS: you all shaped this story in some form or another. Every single one of you. Who knew a small school in mid-Missouri could have some of the best teachers in the States? Joe Zickafoose, for changing my life. You said you wanted to read my book. I'm sorry I didn't finish in time.

Claire Johnson, for introducing me to *Charade* and therefore my love of classic film. Popcorn and green grapes! The bottle and the hill!

Cara Minks Rogers, for all the sleepovers fraught with storytelling and drama. You always kept me captivated. I hope this book captivates you. (As much as *The Beast's Wild Ride*.)

Abby Templer, for *The Salem Witch Trials*, *Wayne's World*, and our dress-up "improv nights" at your house (with NSFW video evidence). We were fearless. We put ourselves out there. We went for it. We still are. We still do.

Jill Van Leer, for reading on the playground, in the girl's bathroom, and on the bus. You were my first reader, and my first true friend. You liked my quirky brain, for reasons unknown, and for that I'll always love you (and your sandals).

Nicholette Tilghman, for pushing me to finish my very first novel. You helped prove I could do it. Without you, this book wouldn't exist. This career wouldn't exist.

Royace Buehrlen, for passing down the storytelling gene, and for believing I could be, and do, anything. Donna Massmann, for sharing all your favorite movies with me, for creating an artist's heart within me, and for being my Number One Fan. Don Massmann and Marty Buehrlen, for putting up with me. There is nothing so difficult to live with as a budding novelist. You have my sympathies. Scott, Sara, Nancy, and all the loved ones we've lost. You're in our hearts. You keep us going. The rest of my huge, amazing family, who loves so fiercely.

Y'all believed in me. I hope I've done you proud.

Hiccup, for putting it all in perspective. (You're crying now, and refusing to nap, so if I've forgotten anyone on this list, I'm blaming you, little one. You are the best distraction.)

And Joel, for opening this farm girl's eyes to the wide world beyond. Thank you for The Lake. For Chicago. *We owned the city. We owned the stars. It was all ours.* It still is. Let's go explore.

EXPERIMENTING WITH YOUR IMAGINATION

"Emilie is the best kind of adventurer – curious, courageous, stubborn, resourceful, and quick to make friends. I can't wait to see where she goes exploring next."
Sharon Shinn

EXPERIMENTING WITH YOUR IMAGINATION

"For the first time in what feels like forever, I find myself wanting a YA paranormal series to never end."
Emily May, The Book Geek

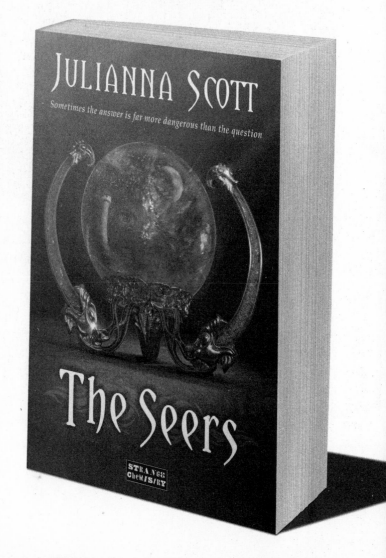